SOTOL

SAL MIRABAL

WORKBOOK PRESS LLC
187 E Warm Springs Rd,
Suite B285, Las Vegas, NV 89119, USA

Website: https://workbookpress.com/
Hotline: 1-888-818-4856
Email: admin@workbookpress.com

Ordering Information:
Quantity sales. Special discounts are available on quantity purchases by corporations, associations, and others. For details, contact the publisher at the address above.

Library of Congress Control Number: TXu 1-930-472

ISBN-13:   978-1-961845-58-9 (Paperback Version)

             978-1-961845-57-2 (Digital Version)

REV. DATE: 07/01/2023

SOTOL

SAL MIRABAL

For

Mary

and

Lorreta,

primas

with a lot

of heart.

CONTENTS

CHAPTER ONE

They shuffled through the heat like a feeble gaggle of trolls raising an imploding vortex of dust that engulfed them from head to toe. They were for the most part composed of elderly women dressed in long black dresses and head coverings. They had wept and chanted the song of death at the wake that sounded not unlike the tortured souls of an inquisitional dungeon and kept the deceased accompanied all through the night. For a fee they would even jump in the grave when the casket was implanted at the bottom of the hole; for a substantial fee, they would agree to be buried with the casket. But of course this was not true. It was the silly joking of some of the young people who giggled uncontrollably at funeral wakes— unless it was their immediate family who was in the coffin. Then they took things a little more seriously.

The air was hot and dry in the late morning. It was a dry desert heat, not a sweaty, humid, oppressive heat that drenches the garments in sweat and leaves huge discolored stains under the armpits of beefy people. The cemetery was old; some graves were only flat mounds of dirt covered with dry weeds and rusted metal crosses with cracked jars embedded in the parched earth, with dry, withered flowers flaking away in the dry summer air. Of course, if one really noticed, there was the other part of the cemetery where the people with means put in large, elaborate tombstones, which, were taken care of as if the deceased entombed demanded such care. But this burial site, let us be honest, was in the middle—not too shabby but not even near to where the elite of the town were buried. But the dead couldn't care less; it was the living who created all the fuss.

Some of the mourners had reached the gravesite. The women dried their puffy red eyes with hankies or soft tissue paper, leaving the tissue blotted with a mixture of this and that. The men, uncomfortable in their Sunday best, with their sallow faces, stiff upper lips with pencil-thin moustaches, and blood-shot eyes, seemed like they were about to puke the remnants of the sotol and Tokay wine they guzzled all night at the wake. The hole was deep and dark, a cooler place than above, where the sun was showing no mercy for anyone. The white chrysanthemums on top of the mounds of dirt played their part, struggled not to wilt, at least until the mourners were long gone. Some of the mourners were gathered close to the hole, looking in, staring toward the bottom, with perhaps a desire to jump in to escape from the burning rays of the sun. Numerous thoughts encumbered those afflicted minds: thoughts of revenge or of that illicit affair— now seen as impractical and stupid but difficult to forget—or maybe even the mountain of bills that waited back at the house. Who knew? Who cared? The coffin was approaching.

The coffin was being hand carried by six pall bearers and their alternates, all wearing black suits with white gloves, walking like intoxicated, overworked emperor penguins toiling in a tepid climate. The gloves were turning a dirty gray from all the sweat and dust, like the color of dead rats. The road from the church to the cemetery wasn't a great walking distance but just far enough to give anyone carrying the coffin a good workout and time to think, as if thinking didn't give these young bucks a headache. They didn't reflect on death or the body of the boy they were on the way to bury—a close friend to many, blood relative to others. They were certain death would never visit them; why should it? They were young and strong, built to last and conquer the world. To them life was a flip of a coin. If it didn't flip their way, well, what the hell? It was over; no reason to fret about it. Other people would do that for them. Their main concern now was to get it over with, get some food after the funeral, some strong stuff to drink, like a shot of sotol chased with a cold beer. There was always food and drink after, because death had to be celebrated in some way; this was their way. They also contemplated on that little girl with the big legs they called Pork Chop. She was a teaser, wearing those tiny shorts, showing off those legs that didn't belong to a girl of that age. They all wanted to be the first to claim the prize and bragging rights, which was what it was all about. Stuff like the imaginary bald spot on top of the head or the pimple on the tip of the nose that refused to dry up or the small amount of hair growth on the balls or to shave the lip hair or grow a mustache—things such as these, real things to them, made this death march a bitch, with the old fools carrying on about a brother they really didn't give a shit about.

Mike Montes was asked to be an alternate pall bearer. Although not an immediate member of the family, he was a close friend of Danny—well, maybe not that close. Mike was hesitant in accepting because of the emotional hardship of helping with the coffin, the nerve-wracking weeping and wailing that was going to take place, but that wasn't the real reason. He didn't like to be around funerals— or visit hospitals for that matter. He felt insignificant at those events and places. What could he contribute that would make any difference? What would change or be different if he was present or absent? He didn't get it. He didn't want to be mean or selfish, but shit, it was an inconvenience, and it bothered him to say it. He had nothing to do with Danny going with Ramon and getting killed in that crash—he had nothing to do with it—but yet here he was, putting up with the circus, pretending not to mind. But he really didn't have any real excuse not to do it. What could he say? Sorry, but I don't have anything to wear to a funeral? At least he was only an alternate; he could do that and not seem such a chicken shit, because after all, if everything went smoothly, he wouldn't have to lift a finger. Not a finger. But he was going to have to wear his new shoes; they were going to take a beating. They were his Saturday night dancing shoes. Ah, what the hell; that was small of him to even think of such insignificant shit. Get the show over with fast, get back to living, enough of this drama. He was sure Danny's relatives might get a little upset, but what could he do? He was here, and that was that.

CHAPTER TWO

ike left the funeral service as soon as he could get away. He had seen enough; he had done his duty; no one could say any different. He was going home to clean up. He had to get away from that scene; it was like a work of Goya, disturbing and melancholy. He didn't feel like hugging or shaking hands with anyone; what would be the point? He cut off the main road and made his way on a narrow path that would get him to his house faster, without having to chitchat with anyone. Mesquite shrubs hugged both sides of the path and gave the path some kind of shade. Dry dog turds and bean pods from the mesquite shrubs were scattered all over the path. The mesquite growth was like a miniature forest. The greenish and bluish veins of the long pods resembled the spider veins of old, flabby legs. The long pods hung in clusters, sparkling in the sun, waiting to be devoured by royalty. The little spiders, spinning their intricate webs in the sanctuary of the shrubs, had their own banquets to savor, all tangled up in the maze of fine silk. And the critters trapped in that fine silk gauze had given up the struggle to live, accepted their fate, and never questioned the superior will of their captors.

Mike, kept walking on the path, wanting Little John to jump out and challenge him to some kind of duel, but he was older now; that shit didn't happen anymore. Now he was a sheik, transporting harlots to his harem on a caravan of lusty camels. He almost reached the oasis of the Blue Lagoon, where he would ravish his new additions to his harem on a nightly basis, until he tasted each and every one in the tent set up by his slaves. He would twang those babies until he settled on a favorite one. Then, maybe, just maybe, he'd take her to his white castle in the City of the Cliffs. The rest of the bonbons he'd leave to his men to be indoctrinated in the subtle conformity of servitude. He made a quick right on an open space on the path, and he was on the road that led to town. To the northeast he could see the Manzano Mountains, called the Turquoise Mountains by the locals. He didn't get why they referred to them as the Turquoise Mountains. To him they resembled a giant spinosaurus dragging a huge cock, but of course he wasn't poetic enough to think of calling them the Turquoise Mountains. Even the color wasn't right. Perhaps his mind didn't visualize colors or shades of color in that way. His mind was more on the pictorial side. His images were usually heavy on the sexual context—not that he was proud of it, but that's the way it worked, and as hard as he tried to change, he knew for sure he was saddled with those twisted thoughts. They were a curse for sure or a blessing, depending on what side of the street you happened to be standing on.

He saw the first house on the right side of the street, Martinez Street, before entering the town, the town of Las Flores. He wanted to avoid that particular house, but there was no way to do that unless he became invisible to the human eye, a feature he was working on but as yet needed to master a few obstacles. He could have stayed on the path of the mesquite jungle, but that path took him straight to the irrigation canal. That was the long way around. Well, what the hell, he thought. It was too hot to run around in circles to avoid pendejos. He had to get home and take off the monkey suit.

The carport was attached to the ancient adobe house. It had never been utilized to park cars or trucks. One side was patched with worn, oil-soaked wooden planks and plywood salvaged from some forgotten construction site. On the opposite side of the carport, two large cottonwoods, dying a slow death, still provided some shade, because the limbs hugged the carport like protecting arms. The front part of the carport was open to the world a short distance from the street. Inside the carport was a cheap table with wobbly metal legs and a few chairs of different makes, all set on the hard-packed earth. On the side where the trees shaded, there was a long wooden plank set on cement-crusted bricks to work as a bench for the slackers to sit when all the chairs were busy. The carport was stacked up high on all corners with items that could be described as junk by the uninitiated. A wooden crate crowded with empty, dusty glass jars and bottles. Old car batteries arranged one on top of another like prized trophies. Jars half-filled with rusty nails and screws. A lawnmower from the turn of the century with a wheel missing and rimless tires bald as a monk's shiny head, never to test the road again. A rusted wire cage, the size of a small basket, with two plaster of paris lovebirds sitting on a termite-ravaged wooden swing, held up by peeling electrical wire. One was missing a head, the other a tail, sitting there above the rest like an intractable omen of things to come. There was also a stained shot glass resting on the decaying floor of the rustic cage, filled with a clear liquid, as if those tokens needed it to maintain their existence. A miniature box feeder, overflowing with dried sunflower seeds, was attached to the inside of the cage with a fish hook, to demonstrate, perhaps, that these replicas of nature were not altogether as perceived but a substantial abstraction comprehended by a less primitive mind, a mind not content with logical reason. A white plastic five-gallon bucket sat on top of the table, half-filled with melting ice. In the bucket, covered with the ice and water, were four or five bottles of beer.

A greeting of friendly salutations came from the carport.

Que hay? Perro flaco!

Mike turned his head, spat, wiped his mouth with the back of his hand, smiled against his will, and shot back.

Tú mama en la cama, jupando camote.

Ha. Ha. You, silly guy, said Sammy Q. Come on over, my brother, come on over—have a cold one. It's on the house; most certainly it is, for you. Sammy Q. was standing next to the wobbly table with a half-empty bottle of beer in his hand, grinning like an empty-headed fool.

Mike was too well educated to ignore him and keep on walking. He gestured with his head an OK and walked into the carport.

It's too early for me; I don't need that poison this early, man, he said.

Oh, please, spare me, spare me. We ain't strangers, brother, you and I. We've been around the block together many a time. Come on now, Sammy Q. insisted.

Left the funeral a little early, huh, Mike? Sammy asked. Too much rock and rolling for you—kind of gets into your skin, huh? In my opinion, funerals are for suckers, Sammy continued, to fill the pockets of mortuary owners, of course. They're like vultures or better yet blood suckers. They hit on people when they're most vulnerable, when they're grieving for a loved one, even if that love was just a farce. How can a husband of many years reject the most expensive casket, even though his darling wife shared her bed with many others? Or the grieving wife buy a cheaper model for a wife beater, an adulterer? Wouldn't look good, brother; people gossip. You know how it is? Anyway, I believe in the burn instead of the worm, but that's me. Look at all the expense and property used up, man; they could build a park or housing for the poor, like me, or the elderly. Que no?

Before Mike could respond, Tomasito sidled up close to him as he always did, a habit not easily broken. He seemed to appear from nowhere, silent as a shadow. And with an effeminate pat on Mike's shoulder and a shy smile, he asked him if he was going to a party or something. Before answering, Mike stepped to his right to put some distance between them, careful not to trample a sleeping dog with large patches of fur missing, exposing blotchy skin. The dog raised his head; yawned, showing slimy black and yellow teeth; and laid his head back down in the same position he was in before, more troubled with clumsy humans than with the voracious fleas that battled each other to suck his blood.

No, I'm going to the ice-skating rink to try out for the Olympics. What do think? Jesus, Mike said.

Oh! Excuse him, said Sammy, grinning. Have to excuse my friend Mike, Tomasito. He gets a little touchy when he gets close to the padre. The altar-boy gig was given to Jose Serna, a younger boy, and he still can't get over it. Am I wrong, Mike? Tell us.

Jesus, Sammy, ain't that yesterday's news? It happened so long ago, man, I forgotten about that shit. It was nothing; I just made myself a burger in the cura's kitchen. Big deal.

No, No. You were also pilfering from the alms box and drinking his Sangre de Cristo wine. I remember, my friend, yes—jumping on top of the bed, using it as your personal trampoline.

Wait a minute; we were kids, what the hell. But what about you, dick head? He kicked your smelly ass out too, remember. You remember, don't you? When the cleaning woman—what was her name? Olga, yes, Olga, caught you pissing in the gold cup, the ciborium, the wafer cup, a most sacred instrument of the, oh, then she saw you jerking off in the confessional, whispering through the little window, pretending you were a cura.

Sammy Q.! How could you? Please say you never done it. Please, I beg you, said Tomasito.

Shut up, fool. Stop crossing yourself, or I'll slap you so hard, you'll be begging Santa for new teeth come December, Sammy said to Tomasito, with his hand raised.

Look, Mike, that was all gossip, man, nothing but gossip of the worst kind. No truth in it at all; the woman had a—some kind of problem, a premenopausal, who knows. She lied, Mike. I was hurt by that shit, man, and people were saying shit behind my back, like I was some kind of heretic, shit like that and worse.

Please, come on, Sammy. Give me a break. If the truth hurt you, pinhead, you be a cripple twenty times over.

Sammy turned his head to see down the road at an approaching figure all in black and said, Look who this way comes— is it the lovesick Quasimodo or the Grand Inquisitor Torquemada?

The hatless, pietistic priest was indeed walking down the road on his way from the funeral, as if in a race with invisible phantoms. His large, rubber-soled black brogues were creating a minor dust storm under his feet. With his beaked nose and bald head, wrapped up in his black cassock, he looked like a lumbering bird of prey, the kind that fancies rotten flesh.

Mike and Sammy Q. were fighting to suppress their laughter.

Who is Quasi…Quasi…what? Tomasito asked.

Don't bust your little head over it, son, said Sammy, Mike here is the man of literature and history, quite a renaissance man. When he has a couple of years to spare, he'll fill in all the blanks for you.

You a crazy fucker, Sammy, Mike said, laughing.

Miguel, Miguel, my son. Why did you leave so soon? I wanted to exchange some words with you, my son. Father Benjamin addressed Mike, ignoring Sammy and Tomasito.

Father Benji, Father Benji, cried out Tomasito, all excited.

Excuse me! Sammy interrupted. You moron. It's "Father Benjamin." Where's your respect? What's the matter with you?

I went to confession this morning, continued Tomasito, ignoring Sammy, but the place was so empty—I mean the church—nobody there. So I came here to ask Sammy Q. where was everybody. Que no, Sammy?

The priest looked at the frail Tomasito, as if he were some wounded animal, pleading to be put out of his misery.

Sammy placed a full bottle of sotol and a shot glass on the table as soon as he saw the priest. He gave the dog a light kick to move him out of the way in case the padre joined them. Ojo Rojo, get your ass out, pinche perro. The dog continued licking his balls, ignoring him.

Come on in, Padre, said Sammy. Have one on the house. I usually give nuns and men of the cloth a discount, but since today is a special day—I don't mean special in that way, you know what I mean? A shot or two of this excellent sotol will jumpstart the rest of the day for you; that I can promise you. Please, be my guest, huh? Yes, no, maybe so?

The priest turned to look at Tomasito, then at Sammy Q. and back to Tomasito. The Priest, through his own eyes, saw a form of an alien life force, unreachable by any calculation or faith, a bacterium so malleable and adaptable that, if not exterminated soon, posed a threat to Christian civilization as he understood it.

But yet again, he could almost feel the fiery liquid burning his throat, the flame spreading to his gut, serenading his muddled mind and unruffling his feathers, until he made it home. Or even running to the plastic bucket of melting ice water, plunging his bony head in until he touched the cold bottles of beer with his feverish forehead, but he couldn't, could he? He thought, No way, impossible. It was already a sin just thinking about it. He walked off without saying a word to anyone, performing the same dust dance with his ugly shoes, a man in a hurry to get nowhere fast.

CHAPTER THREE

Mike was lying on his bed, naked except for his boxer shorts. He was gazing at a blown-up photo of a black tarantula on the wall facing his bed. His bedroom was cool, and enough sunlight was coming in from the closed curtains for him to see the imposing tarantula looking his way. He won the tarantula photo by writing one of the best Mother's Day poems in his English class when he was in the tenth grade. His English teacher, an amateur photographer, challenged the class to write a poem about mothers, and he offered as prizes his own blown-up photos of a kitten, a puppy, a polar bear, or a tarantula. Of course he was attracted to the tarantula—how could he write a poem, place in the top three, and then select a kitten or a puppy? That was pushing it. He also had an eye on the polar bear, but Beatrice Archuleta had first choice. Few could beat Beatrice at writing poems. Anyway, he was sure she picked the polar bear just to spite him, or maybe he steered her into thinking he had an interest in the polar bear. No point in thinking about it; he got what he wanted, as he usually did.

He reached down under his bed, pulled out a large plastic container, and placed it on his stomach. Inside the container was a Mexican redknee tarantula a friend had brought him from somewhere in Colima, Mexico. It was a large female with bands of orange on the joints and orange-red on the upper legs close to the body. He called her Lola the Escape Artist. Lola was out of her hiding area, a cover of leaves and twigs he had set up in a corner for her. He opened the lid, which was poked with tiny holes for air—but not too close together or too large because Lola stuck her legs through, if the holes were too large. He opened the lid and checked the soil and water dish for pieces of dead bugs. The soil was still good, no musky smell to it. He reached in, carefully picked up Lola, and placed her on his stomach.

Oh, so you're done with your molting, are you? You little bitch. You looked so ugly, Lola; that's why I put you under my bed, outta sight. But wow, look at your colors now! You the queen now, Lola. I bet your little ass is hungry; you haven't eaten in a while. I'm gonna find you a juicy cricket, sweetheart—sure I am, just wait and see. But remember, Lola, baby, whatever you do, do not escape. Don't even try it, although last time it was my fault for falling asleep. My mother —your nana—if she doesn't have a heart attack first, will pick up her broom, whack the crap outa you, and then sweep your little carcass out to the chickens; the chickens, as you know, are unpredictable. Remember, most people still believe you're poisonous to humans. I know; don't get insulted. People are stupid. I know for a fact you don't bite, but I also know you kick your hairs when pissed off. I always leave you alone when you're in that mood. I understand. I'm that way also, my friend; I don't like people to mess with me when I'm in the mood. Live and let live: that's what I say.

The tarantula moved slowly on Mike's hairy stomach toward his chest. Her body was close to four inches, her legs five or six inches, with a body weight of maybe fifteen grams. She crawled with a leisurely motion on his stomach as if she were on familiar territory. The first few times she crawled on his stomach, Mike tightened his stomach muscles, and his skin would flare with goosebumps because the image of the huge spider with orange-red bands crawling on him gave him the creeps. His skin flushed, his body temperature went up, his eyes watered, and his upper lip was beaded with sweat. He started to giggle. When she was getting close to his neck, he stopped her, telling her, OK, I'll confess to anything you desire. And he placed her gently back in her tank. With his heart beating faster than normal, he reread the magazine article on tarantulas and repeated over and over: Tarantulas are not poisonous to humans.

But now Lola crawled over his neck, face, hair, all over, like she owned him. The only time he didn't let her get her way was when she was kicking her stinging hair from her abdomen, and then he made sure she didn't get close to his face. But other than that, he let her crawl on him. He enjoyed the sensation, sometimes so much that he got a hard- on.

Mike, put Lola in her tank, secured the lid, placed the tank carefully under his bed, and closed his eyes to all physical evidence of his existence. He was exhausted over the chaotic events of the last days and only wanted to escape to the world of shadows and phantoms, the quick and the dead, the used and the useless. A world of abstractions, based on the reality of his warped mental status; a place of his own discovery and invention he never had to revisit or share but could add to its layers of absurdity when fast asleep. Dreams didn't have to turn into nightmares, grotesque and hideous all the time, like rats eating on your face and waking up screaming, all crazy with fear and sweating— no, not at all. There were always the expectations of the good and the not so good, like to kiss those lips that slipped away so many times and dissolved into nothing. What mattered if they were the lips of an angel or a she- devil; what difference did it make when you were in that stage? He was not afraid of that world of images and shadows beyond his control.

CHAPTER FOUR

It was already evening when Mike roused out of his deep sleep and reached for his dream journal and a pen, but none of the dreams came to him—nada, a blank. He threw the journal on the bed and dressed. The sun was already down but still left some crimson on the horizon for the unbelievers. His mother had left him some food on the kitchen table; he uncovered the food and ate some of it. He realized his folks were still at the home of Danny's grieving parent. His mother had sneaked out to bring him a bite to eat. Seeing he was sleeping, she hadn't bothered to wake him. What an angel, he thought. He decided to walk to the park and hang out with his friends there; nothing else to do.

The night was warm, clear, and without clouds. The sky was crowded with clusters of lit candles, set carelessly around a pagan altar used by galactic pilgrims for unrestricted homage to the infinite universe. The moon was at her best, with a courageous display of bright splendor, not at all embarrassed by the insane spectacle of all that dazzling light in that teeming sky.

They drove slow and easy in their late-model car, two in the front, two in the back. They were not looking for trouble, but if it came, they were more than ready to negotiate on any terms. They were young Tejano bucks, looking for girls in the evenings and early night. They were the folks from south Tejas who harvested the onions in the valley. They were called ceboyeros and worse. They labored in the scorching sun on their knees, freeing the onions from the vine, filling up the buckets for a quarter or more a bucket. Few natives attempted the back-breaking work, so it was up to the Tejano migrants to harvest the crops, or they would rot in the fields. Some ventured up to Washington State, with stops in Arizona, California, and Oregon. Many brought their extended family; all worked hard and true. They had to if they wanted to make any money. The young and restless, after a day of back-breaking labor in the hot sun, still had the energy to pursue the sexual thrill, the hunger that motivates the psyche to conquer and rekindle civilization. Sexual hunger turns men into savage beasts. He can rape, pillage, and even neglect death, but it can also turn him into a good husband, father, and provider, once the hunger is controlled.

The four young bucks in their smoking car with the windows rolled down and arms hanging out, cupped their cigarettes in their hands, flicking the ashes along the asphalt, as if the ashes alone eliminated all obstacles and allowed them to pursue their objective unimpeded. They drove east on Calle Catolica, passing in front of the church in hopes of seeing some skirts leaving the church. The church was dark; all activity was cancelled because of the funeral during the day. But the Tejanos were not aware of that. The car made a right and headed south on Santos Street, driving by the little tienda on the corner. Before they reached the café at the end of the street, they felt a clatter when the stones hit the back and lower side of the car. The pelting of the metal reverberated loud and clear through the quiet night, especially for the folks inside the car. They were startled shitless; their cool cruising and skirt hunting came to a paralyzing halt. But that didn't last too long. They stopped the car next to the Quiosco, and the four bolted out as if the car was on fire. Before the Tejanos jumped out of the car, some younger kids, who were congregated on benches on the north corner section of the Quiosco close to Calle Catolica, ran off laughing across the street into the dark parking lot of the church and disappeared.

The four Tejanos, led by Gorilla, rushed to the Quiosco where Mike, Sammy Q., and some other friends were hanging out. He was called Gorilla because of his muscular upper body, especially his arms. He was wearing a white tank top. His bulging, tattooed biceps glistened as the sweat beaded and slid down his huge arms and burned face. His head was shaved smooth on the top part, like it was chiseled from cast iron by a competent sculptor and finished by a drunken blacksmith with a claw hatchet. The back of the skull, connected to the massive neck, was left with ridges and open trenches of bone and muscular tissue, making him look like the bad guy in a comic strip used to give young children nightmares.

OK! Gorilla shouted out. Which one of you Kotex-wearing, cock- sucking, queer motherfuckers threw the rocks? 'Fess up before I start mopping the streets of this rat-infested town with your bloody carcasses and hang you by the balls on the flagpole—if you have any balls, that is. He was seething but still in full control because he realized these cowardly cunts were no match for him. The other three Tejanos looked small next to Gorilla, but they were game, fired up as him, especially the owner of the car.

Sammy Q. walked up to Gorilla in a friendly, nonthreatening manner.

Hey G. What up? he said. Before you start kicking our asses, you have to stop and think where the rocks came from. The rocks didn't come from us. We don't play those silly games. Look at the angle; it came from back there as your car passed la tienda. Those little kids ran off as soon as they threw the rocks. You heard them laughing as they ran, right?

Gorilla was cracking his bulky knuckles, looking down at Sammy Q., who was almost a foot shorter. The other Tejanos were egging him on.

Come on, G. let's take them down. They're a bunch of dick hounds anyway; you know most will run like scared dogs. Come on, G. Start it, man; we'll finish it.

When the kids ran off into the dark, they ran to Justo's house, behind the church, uncle to one of the kids. The kids exaggerated and flat-out lied to Justo, who was a sharpshooter army vet and hunter and not very stable. The kids, all excited and talking at the same time, told him some Tejano boyeros at the Quiosco slapped them around and threatened them with an ass kicking. Of course they neglected to tell him they pelted their car with rocks for no reason at all, besides being bored.

Justo, who was just about to take his antidepressant pills, shoved the pill bottle back into his pocket, ran to his gun rack inside the house, pulled out a Savage model 99 .30-30 carbine with a scope on it, and rushed out the door. The kids were ready to tag along all crazy with joy, but Justo turned around, stopped, raised his right hand as if he was going to give a solemn oath, and said, Stay, in a soft but firm voice.

Meanwhile, back at the Quiosco, the situation was beyond debate. Mike took off his watch slowly and slipped it into his pocket. He wanted to make sure nothing flashed in his hand in the dim light, because the Tejanos might take it for a blade. If they were packing filas, forget it—might as well pull down your pants and chonies to your ankles, bend over, and offer them your culo, because you were going to be busted up in a bad way. Cuchieros, navajeros, or fileros —depending on how far away from the border one was—was what you were known as. Some Tejanos were known for that skill and could carve up a holiday bird without breaking a sweat and perform the same trick on a vato. A stiletto switchblade was a blade of choice, but of course the roofing knife could add insult to injury. When it was pulled out of the gut, the plumbing came out with it—not a pretty sight. Some preferred the ice pick. You didn't even know you had been pierced until you collapsed because of internal bleeding. But the blade was the attention getter, the crowd pleaser, as they say. A beautiful stiletto clicks open its warning of death or maiming; a savage barbera—straight razor—in a skilled hand cuts open the shirt and shreds it to pieces and then sets up the victim for a dance of blood. A slash to the cheek, was usually to test the agility of the cutter and the courage of the poor bastard, who was many times too drunk or too full of macho bullshit to feel the blood leaking out of his severed skin and too messed up to comprehend that even with a machete; he could not hold back a true filero.

Mike stepped away from the benches; nothing worse than getting a thumping too close to benches. Not a good thing, he thought. He massaged his right wrist with his left hand. He was certain Sammy would go down with the first blow from Gorilla and stay down. And the other two, Poison and Flaco, would disappear like frightened gophers. He also knew the Gorilla would come after him next. After much consideration, he made up his mind not to run, because when you get hit on the back on the run and go down on your face, scared and exhausted, it's a done deal. Give it up. Pray, if you can think beyond fear, that the kicks are not directed at the head and face. Besides, if he ran with the others, Sammy would get all the credit for being the only one with the balls to stand alone against the Tejanos, and that wouldn't look good on his brag sheet. He looked around for a stick or rock, anything to defend against the feral ape and his chimps that were getting so close that he could smell them.

Sammy Q. managed to antagonize Gorilla even more with his defense-attorney tactics of distance, projectile, and this and that. Then Mike heard heavy boot steps rushing through the church parking lot. They slowed as they reached Calle Catolica, but they kept coming. It didn't take him long to figure out it was crazy Justo— and probably armed. He warned Sammy, without riling the ape, to step back easy away from him, but Sammy continued to incense the Tejano more. He believed his people skills could save his ass from a beating, but he usually failed. But he eventually listened to Mike, because he knew Mike had an inborn instinct for danger; besides, he was running out of options. He backpedaled easy-going still talking shit to the Tejanos, who were taking off their shirts and flexing their muscles, a little behind the ape.

A single shot echoed in the night as if a howitzer had been fired at a military target. The ape was hit. The bullet forced him back, down on his ass. It ripped a huge hole in his jeans where his leg was hit above the right knee; the dark blood gushed out in buckets. What the fuck! What the fuck! Por dios! What was that? He screamed in shock and agony. The other three Tejanos also panicked, not knowing what to do—hit the ground, run away, or what—as they clumsily bumped into each other in desperation and cursed, until Sammy told them to get Gorilla into the car to a hospital before he bled to death. They grabbed their shirts off the ground and attempted to stop the blood. Gorilla, terrified, tears washing his face, kept looking toward the church, attempting to make some sign of the cross, but he couldn't. The other three hombres finally calmed down some, and, half picking him up, carried him as gently as possible to the car. Sammy Q. approached to offer them help, but they rebuffed him, screaming at him to get the hell away. They eventually succeeded in loading the babbling, heavy, wounded package in the backseat of the car and drove off on Santos Street.

Sammy Q. was rocking up and down on his feet with his hands in his pockets, looking at the Tejanos' car speeding down the street, until it disappeared. He walked back to his friends, shaking his head and knowing deep in his heart that this was only the beginning of something ugly.

Well, well, I offered my assistance. What else could I do? Sammy said. That boy was hurt bad—very close to his chorizo, ouch. The others just kept their eyes on Sammy, not saying a word because they were already reflecting on the spirited warrior who, without their permission, clandestinely honored them by including them in an orgy of violence that with time would make them living legends, they strongly believed. Their names would be included when other heroes were mentioned, and maybe, just maybe, one day they would be given all the credit for bringing down the mighty Tejano, Gorilla, and even given the credit for firing the fatal shot, which brought down the terrible hombre. This was where their simple thinking was at, instead of being concerned about a payback or leaving the area for the summer. Mike even contemplated on some hugs and kisses, maybe more, from the grateful girls and women who would be relieved he had slain that big, bad Tejano, Gorilla; he pretended or was not really aware that those same girls and women anticipated the return of the Tejanos every summer, because they didn't mind tasting the state of Tejas while riding the powerful stallion, Gorilla. They were the same mamas who opened their legs to the traveling carnival men on the twelfth of December, during the fiesta, honoring Our Lady of

Guadalupe, the patron saint of the Eastside.

Sammy walked over to the north corner of the Quiosco, where the kids had been playing and the shot had come from. He searched the ground for a casing but no luck. A great shot, he said to himself and walked back to join the dreamers, who were now talking excitedly over each other, not listening to what the other was saying but gesturing and interrupting, talking shit, and acting bad, now that it was over.

A police cruiser came out of nowhere and stopped on the same spot where the Tejanos' car had been parked not more than five minutes before. Did you guys hear any gunshots? asked an officer through his opened car window, not bothering to get out of the car.

No, answered Sammy. We heard a cherry bomb or maybe an M80, but it came from behind the church.

OK, the officer said and drove off.

CHAPTER FIVE

The following day, after a day of labor ended for the Tejanos, six cars of different makes and models, full of Tejano boyeros, stopped in front of Sammy's house. Sammy Q. was in his usual place in the carport, sitting in an old office desk chair with his feet on the table, reading a western novel by Louis L'Amour. A tall Tejano in worn, dusty cowboy boots jumped out of the passenger side of the lead car and swaggered over to where Sammy was.

Que hay? asked Sammy, a smile on his face, pretending he didn't know.

The tall Tejano pushed his baseball cap back away from his dark shades and said, Orita nada, cabron, pero lo va ver. Tell me, who was the bastardo who shot the brother Gorilla?

Sammy Q. wasn't rattled. He remained seated with his feet on the table, smoking his Faro. Perhaps he should have been, though, because the Tejanos looked rowdy and animated, ready for anything.

Nobody knows, vato, said Sammy. Like I told the cop, the shots came from behind the church parking lot; we didn't see a damn thing, brother.

The Tejano kept pulling at his lower lip with his thumb and finger and kept studying Sammy Q. in a puzzled manner. He couldn't figure out this little mutt; he didn't seem too intimidated. He didn't like this. You're hiding the quate who shot the brother, he continued. Give up his name, and I promise not to torch your jacal and fry you and your family in it.

Let me set you straight, my amigo from Tejas, said Sammy, not bothering to put the book aside. You can burn my jacal to the ground, my family and me in it; no one will give a holy shit. No one'll raise a hand to stop you or come after you. I'm an outsider. I don't live that close to town. I'm out of the loop—you comprende, right? But if you go crazy, do the same shit in town to any house, you'll have shooters on the rooftops shooting down on your ass, shooting you down like rabid dogs. I'm serious. Most of the men here and some of the women are hunters; all have some kind of weapon, from .22s to .30-06s to .30-30s to buckshot—you name it, bow and arrows, even homemade slingshots—it'll rain down on you and yours like cinders from hell. And as soon as others from the surrounding communities, farms, and ranchos find out what's coming down, they'll join in the firefight. Then the police'll join them—lock you up, that is, if the morgue doesn't claim you first. This area is not your base. You know it. You do the same in your town in South Tejas if some pendejos attempt to harm your neighbors. Que no?

The tall Tejano wanted to grab Sammy Q. by the shirt, slap him hard across the face, and throw him into the pile of junk that seemed to be everywhere. But instead he kept his eyes on the birdcage. This little mutt seemed to be talking straight, clear shit. Doubts were entering the Tejano's mind about this crazy venture. It wasn't as simple as it looked when talked over in camp with everyone drinking and raising high fives. Shit, he wanted to leave but not look weak in front of the vatos who were waiting for the word to start with Sammy Q. and finish wherever it led. But of course they were followers; their judgment was impaired by emotion, booze, and too much mota, which tangled their thinking. He was the leader; it was his responsibility to think things through, to pay a little more attention to detail and the consequences that were sure to follow. The worst news was to return and have to retell the events to wives who were now widows and children who were now orphans or had dead brothers or cousins, left behind, buried, or in prison. One or two killed in a bad year or unlucky season was shocking, but more than two in the same rampage—that was huge, a high price to pay all the way around.

So who's this Justo we keep hearing about, asked the Tejano, as he scratched his balls with his right hand.

Well, let me see, Sammy said. There's a Justo who lives on a ranch up close to Belen. But he has eight brothers and dozens of relatives who are all hunters and of course sharpshooters. You'll be massacred before you get to the gate, if you can find the ranch. I'd never find it, but again, I'd never had any reason to look for it. I don't think that helps much, does it? Then there's Don Justo. He's ninety-eight years old, plays poker with death every day; so far he keeps winning, but you and I know his luck will change. Oh, before I forget, there's one more Justo. That's Justo Jr., who's around two years old. His father's in state prison doing time, so that leaves him out, I guess.

The Tejano rubbed his goatee as if something in there would provide him with guidance to make the right and best decision. He continued to look at the birdcage and attempted to forget the numerous confrontations with racist cops, racist landlords, waitresses, and waiters, and other racists along the road going up north to feed the same racist who harassed and humiliated them anywhere they could. But that was in the older times. He reconsidered; now they didn't turn the other cheek. Now an ass kicking would commence and blood flowed, but it wasn't usually theirs. They had an advantage over undocumented immigrants, especially over Mexicans from Mexico. As American citizens, the Tejanos understood their rights in a fundamental fashion, fought back with legal backing, if needed, and at times were successful. They knew they couldn't be deported anywhere, living in this country for so long and giving so much to the nation with so little thanks. The Mexicans from Mexico, without papers, could be leaned on hard by any racist who wanted to have a little fun. And the sad thing was that many times, they had no choice but to take it. The distinction between Mexicans from Mexico and Tejanos was slight, but for someone who hates with a passion, selecting came easy. Some racists often came after the Tejanos, and that mistake sometimes cost them a fractured skull, or worse, a one-way trip to the morgue. So "You don't mess with Tejanos" had always been the message. But now this little shit-faced border bandit was playing around with his head and pretending not to know that nobody fools with Tejanos.

The Tejano said "Ha," more to himself then anyone in particular, but looked at Sammy Q. for a few seconds and finally said, I'm leaving for now, but I'll be back. I'll find that son of a puta who shot the brother.

As you say, my friend. We'll be here, Sammy said.

On his way out, the Tejano turned and asked, What's up with the fake birds, Tonto?

Interesting you asked, responded Sammy Q. with a quick smile, but before he could explain, the Tejano turned to his car and got in, and the car started before he had shut the car door good and tight. The car cut a U-turn and left toward the same direction it had come from, away from Las Flores. The rest of the caravan followed suit, anxious to go back to the safety of their camp, where at least they felt safe from crazy shooters. They were relieved their leader decided to leave instead of heading into that hornet's nest and maybe dying or getting crippled for something they had nothing to do with. They knew venganza was OK, but sometimes the price was too costly, and to be honest, this was one of those times. So they drove on like a funeral caravan, searching in vain for their hero's gravesite, lost forever in an environment not of their choosing. Their smoking cars puttered away into the setting sun, the tires churning the gravel into dust like ancient war chariots, chasing avatars in an Old World desert dream.

Tomasito came out of the house and asked Sammy Q. if the mean-looking guys were gone.

They are gone, my friend, Sammy said. Gone and never to return. They're not mean looking; they just work hard, very hard, in the sun all day. If it wasn't for those folks, my friend, the valley would go broke and the crops would rot in the fields, because you know these lazy assholes around here ain't gonna do shit but complain. So bad times will hit the area's businesspeople, but forget them because I'm always on down time. Ain't no hit on my financial holdings, whether things go good or bad. Anyway, don't worry about it, my friend, cause it ain't worth a nightmare. If you really looking for a legitimate ass-kicking nightmare, look into your own soul. But for now, see that box over there? There's books in there. I made a trade with this guy from Albuquerque, ABQ, El Burque; you know the place? Or maybe you never been more than one hundred miles away from this cesspool, have you? They're used paper novels. A few are by my man, Louis L' Amour. I've read some of them, to be perfectly honest, but I'll probably read them again. When you free them from their box, dust them and put them up neatly on the space I cleared next to the others. OK, my friend.

I feel like doing domestic chores, declared Tomasito, perplexed by Sammy's remark.

Go for it. Start with the kitchen; we got kind of behind in there.

But not here, not in this house…it's just…

Well, what kind of domestic chores did you have in mind?

Never mind; you'd never understand.

Oh! So now I'm the idiot? I see, said Sammy, grinning.

He lit up another cigarette, a real Frajo, and put his feet, with shoes on, on top of the wobbly table and continued reading The Riders of High Rock, by Louis L' Amour.

CHAPTER SIX

As soon as Mike woke up, he grabbed for his dream journal and pen, put them down, jumped out of bed naked, ran to the bathroom to take a piss, and then ran back to his bedroom, still hard as penitentiary steel. He couldn't write down his pussy dream; he wanted to, but couldn't. The girl in the dream was Linda, but again it could have been Vivian Madrid. The dream was so vivid and juicy; he didn't want to wake up. It was one of those wet dreams best kept to yourself because the risk of telling it, even to your best friend, could label you a liar, or worse, a sex fiend. He wanted to forget it but couldn't. He put his fingers on his lips just to prove there was no blood on them. He studied his chest and legs for evidence of nail marks—nothing. He grabbed his hard boner, looking for imprints of telltale teeth—nada. He did see the stains on the white sheets already blending in, erasing all aspects of that sexual encounter that best be forgotten. He took out Lola's box from under the bed and started talking to her.

Hey, Lola, baby, you sleep well, little mama? I had a pussy dream, Lola, and you'll ask, So what else is new? But this one was a wang banger, an all-out sex feast, real as real can get. Pussy is the main thing, Lola. Sometimes it don't smell so good, but what the hell? It still sucks you in, makes you think and feel funny things. Not laughing funny things, Lola, don't get me wrong, but things that are funny in a unique way, and that unique way has pleasure written all over it. Cause, Lola, men and women have done some outlandish things for that almighty pussy, be it yesterday, be it today, and you can bet a dollar on it, even tomorrow. But who am I kidding? You know it, Lola; you were here before us. What can I tell you about pussy? We're like infants compared to your staying power. Anyway, Lola, I gotta get going. Holy shit! Look at the time. I musta overslept again. That shit two nights ago was scary, Lola; that's why I couldn't get to sleep, even last night, thinking those Tejanos were gonna pay me a visit and fuck me up. We left the Quiosco, except Sammy, after bullshitting for a while there, finally realizing the Tejanos could come back with a whole army. We went to Flaco's house and talked some more. We were all super hyper; the adrenalin was flowing like crazy. Then I began to think of all the shit that could come down if the Tejano had died. And even though we didn't fire the shot or had nothing to do with the shooting, Hector would kick me out of the program in a New York second, and my parents would be devastated—know what I mean, Lola? And that part of it got me even crazier; I ran all the way home from Flaco's house in a fighting mood. I ran straight to the heavy bag hanging from that old cedar tree and hit and kicked the bag for at least half an hour. I beat that bag like there was no tomorrow; thought the tree was gonna tumble down. Just like the old times, Lola. I even forgot to put on my gloves, Lola—look at my hands, all jacked up. But to tell you the truth, Lola, I was scared, but I wanted to take on that Tejano, just me and him, so he could pound some sense into me or me into him. He was a big, ugly, strong hombre, Lola, but I wanted to see if I could still fight the fight or give up like a pussy. And that happened two days ago, but it still drives me crazy. Wow! Look how late it is, Lola. Better get a move on; got things to do.

Mike took a cold shower, got dressed, and was eating an egg and chorizo burrito his mom left for him on the stove while reading the note she also left about his meeting at the community center with Hector el Viejo. The meeting was about the scholarship he was supposed to get to attend UNM—not for his grades, which weren't that bad, but for his leadership skills, whatever that meant. It was a program written up by Hector for young people who could be guided into college and study to become attorneys, instead of channeling their energy into criminal activity, which some might do. He had been selected along with nine others: five from the Eastside and the others from the surrounding area. He was pretty sure why Hector, the director of the community center, had selected him. He was more than sure it wasn't because of his leadership skills but because his father had been the main force in building the center, repairing and keeping up the maintenance to keep it functioning. But what the hell; that was the way things were done here and anywhere else for that matter, he thought.

He ate his burrito, drank a cup of coffee with plenty of milk and sugar, grabbed an apple, and left the house. The community center was behind the church hall a short distance from his house. All he had to do was walk up Lupe Street, and he'd be there in no time. He didn't want to drive because he didn't want the hassle of parking. There were always people at the center asking for a ride. He just didn't feel like playing taxi today; not today. He just wanted to get the meeting over with and please his parents.

As Mike arrived at the community center, Hector el Viejo was conversing with Bryan Hercules, a vato from Valencia who had also been accepted into the program and was known for his mouth. This is what he heard.

Hey, what's your dog's name, Hector? asked Bryan. Or does it have a name? Maybe it doesn't deserve a name; what do I know about dogs.

Eutropius. That's his name, Hector said.

Eutropius! What? Please don't make me laugh.

Why are you so concerned about the dog's name anyway? Hector asked.

Hey, I just saw your emaciated, worm-eaten piece of shit you call a dog always hanging around here. With a name like Eutropius, well, what can anyone think? What kind of name is Eutropius, anyway?

That's for you smart dudes to do some homework and find out.

Hey, Mike, come on in, brother. The meeting is about to start, Hector said to Mike, ignoring Bryan. And Mike, don't mention anything about what happened the other night with the Tejanos, even if they ask you. Nada. OK. You coming, Bryan? he asked without looking at him.

Hector el Viejo was called that because his son was Hector the Younger, an attorney who lived in Albuquerque and sometimes made the drive in his expensive car to do pro bono work for the pendejos who needed legal help. Hector el Viejo was a college educated veterano who had been a community organizer and teacher in many states but returned to his place of birth to retire. But he didn't retire, because they recruited him to be director of the community center, a center that attracted weak directors with programs that never got off the ground. Hector took over the center and kicked out all the useless people and set up a no-nonsense type of discipline. He didn't take shit from the young punks who hung around all day until closing. He didn't take shit from the busybodies and older folks who wanted to run the place but couldn't. And he didn't take shit from the priest, Father Benjamin, who didn't understand or pretended not to understand the separation between the church and the community center, even though the center was on church grounds. Hector el Viejo was considered a benevolent dictator, but all the programs were moving, from feeding the hungry to after-school tutoring; plus, he was a prolific grant writer—a highly successful one—and that was where he had everyone beat. You mess with Hector, the money for your pet project stopped flowing, and everyone and their mothers had a pet project at the center.

OK, guys, settle in, Hector said. Dr. Molina from the university should be here any minute. And he promised to bring along a Ms. Collins from financial aid to answer some of your most pressing questions. And please, guys, show your intelligence. Don't ask stupid questions; you were drafted into this program because of your smarts, so show these people we didn't pick losers.

I thought they selected us because we have a tendency to be aggressive? asked Bryan.

Hector ignored him and continued. And watch your language. No disrespectful language, OK? These people are here to help you have a bright future, so let's all make it easy for them to see you are serious about this. It's not every day that a top university extends its hand out to help young people with no or little athletic ability, weak GPAs, no musical ability, and zero volunteer experience, and plus you been out of school for a year now, doing nothing but—OK, I'll stop. You get my drift. OK. Is everyone here?

Everyone except Lorenzo, and of course Jr. and Javier are always late, answered Mike. But that dickhead Lencho won't leave his sheep and goats alone, even for a couple of hours.

You won't say that to his face, Mike, blurted out Bryan, because you know Lencho will kick your skinny, insignificant butt all the way to the border.

Mike, amused, smiled. You, standing on top of Lencho, will suck my dick, 'cause that's all you can do, both of you sheep lovers.

Well, I heard the other night you were shitting bricks, whimpering like a little bitch. Sammy Q. had to do all the talking to save your arrogant ass from a beating. If crazy Justo wouldn't have shot Gorilla, he would have mutilated your ass, and the mortuary be carving up another coffin.

What the fuck you know? You weren't there. You and Lencho were probably playing stick-your-finger-up-your-ass with each other that night.

I do know this, shit face: Lencho is the only one around these parts who went mano a mano with Gorilla and walked away from the brawl on his own two feet. So watch what you say about Lencho, Mike, 'cause down deep in your balls, you're aware having Lencho as your enemy can be a ball breaker. So call the shots, big man; let them land where they will. See if I care.

You always talk this big shit, Bryan, but you still don't get it; that's all it is. Mierda. You bob and weave when you talk about Lencho; you build him up too big for his own shoes, but to me he ain't shit, and I'll tell it to his ugly face, if it comes to that. We kicked Lencho's ass last month at Lena's party. When he hit the dirt, he howled like a stray and hungry dog.

OK! Basta! interrupted Hector. You two mutts want to piss on each other, go ahead, but I want to see blood on the floor. The one that goes down, stays down. But let me tell you, Mike, before the ganging up on Lencho goes to your puffy head—Lencho has been riding the horse for months now. Of course he's not the same Lencho, and he's skin and bones, weak, asking anyone to kick his ass—a certain death wish, on his part. The pain with in him is smoldering in his heart without relief. Only the soothing escapism of chiva seems to work for him. The loss of his mother at that young age devastates anyone. His father was a cold and an indifferent man after that. He was raised by his brothers and sisters, him being the youngest. I believe they did a decent job, but still, the loss of a mother, at any age, is a hurtful event.

Let me tell you guys why I selected Lencho to participate in this program, continued Hector. Lencho had the potential to be an all-star athlete. He was big and strong, as many are, but what separated him from the herd was that he was gifted. He could throw the football, hit a running end at eighty-five yards in his second year of high school, and he could pitch a hardball so fast some kids were afraid to bat against him. He was already a star baseball player with impressive statistics, and he was sure to make varsity quarterback in the fall. But let me just finish. One day the fat-ass assistant coach started yelling at him for some small shit; Lencho wasn't used to anyone yelling at him, except for his older brother, Chopo. So he ignored the screaming asshole and ran some laps around the field, giving the coach time to cool off. The fat slob didn't cool off and yelled even louder, obscenities that had no place in a sports program, all the time following Lencho onto the field. Lencho stopped jogging. Before another word escaped the coach's filthy mouth, Lencho threw a lightning-fast left hook to the side of his fat face and crossed with a powerful right. The fat man flew backward and down, rolling over on his huge stomach, holding his face with both hands, crying like a baby, unable to do anything else. Lencho continued to run his laps as the other players looked at the coach in shock, stretched out in the grassy playing field like a gutted heifer, bleeding from the nose and mouth.

Well, of course Lencho was expelled from the district, continued Hector. The police were called, and he was arrested. But the sheriff happened to be married to his cousin Sara; he took Lencho to his home. The assistant coach resigned or retired; no one knew, or they weren't telling. But they say that when he went back to school to collect his things, he didn't say a word to anyone. They weren't sure if it was because of the humiliation or his jaw wired up like a chicken coop. So when I heard the story from my connections in Valencia, I drove up there to check it out. I visited the school, talked to his teachers;

they all had nothing but good things to say about Lencho. The boy was solid in academics and behavior, and his test scores gravitated toward the gifted, so I wasn't going to allow that racist tub of lard ruin his life. So I searched for him, not giving up until I found him in a grease joint in Belen, halfway drunk but working to get there. I convinced him after a couple of hours to drive back with me to Las Flores and stay with me. I helped him get cleaned up, and he worked around the center doing odd jobs. As soon as he was sober and rational, I got him into an alternative school not far from his home and home schooling. He completed all his credits for his high school diploma; I got him in the program, as I promised him I would.

There was a long and uneasy silence in the group. Hector studied his charges and wanted to believe that he had not made a big mistake on selecting this group of animated peacocks. He knew he had lost Lencho; that broke his heart. He was too much of a realist to believe all of them would become attorneys, but he was more than certain that once in the system, they would end up educated and in a stable career.

The boys broke the silence and started asking Hector questions all at the same time. Hector ignored the questions until the boys settled down, which was what always happened.

Then Bryan turned to Mike and asked, Don't you feel like shit now, Mike? For what you did to Lencho?

Mike, wounded, answered, Yeah, I feel like, man, you don't even want to, but we didn't know. I promise we didn't know. He was acting the fool. We—well, we—you know. He turned to Hector. C'mon, Hector, why didn't you tell us? Goddamn you.

Tell you, tell you, tell you what? I'm stuck here running this busy center twenty-four seven, while you're out there pulling on each other's dicks. You should have known and told me. When I found out, he was already a stoned junky. Tell me, how can you help a junky hooked on a drug that's gonna kill him? Because that's what he wants—to die.

You can still bring him to the center and help him, dry him out, snapped one of the other boys.

We don't have the facilities to do detox here, Hector said. We do some basic prevention, but that's it. But I'll tell you what, if you can find him and bring him to me here at the center, I'll do everything in my power to get him into a detox center in Albuquerque. I don't have the time to go looking for him all over the place. I like to, but I just don't have that kind of time. I know I did it once, but this is a different ballgame.

So you just cold kicked him out of the program? asked Kiko the Pico, irritated.

Yes, I presented his case to the board yesterday. As you all know, it's in your contract: there is zero tolerance for drug use. So any one of you pinheads could be out on your ass for drug use. We have three alternates waiting on the wings to take the vacant chair.

I read the proposal, Hector, Mike said. It says, as far as I can understand, the full board has to vote on the alternates before they can be accepted into the program.

I'm relieved you read something besides porn, Mike. But if you had read the stipulation at the end, it is specifically written that I as the director have full authority to contract the alternates into the program without the consent of the board, and once in the program, the board can add their signatures anytime later. Do you think the university is going to wait for anyone if they start in the fall? Hold up everything 'cause some hicks in some hole-in-the-wall place are having a discussion about potential students getting on board? Get real, my friend; you might have read the proposal, but I wrote that puppy.

So when were you going to tell us about Lencho being out, next year? asked Bryan.

As a matter of fact, I was going to tell you after the meeting.

At that exact moment, Connie, Hector's secretary, walked into the meeting room without knocking. She walked in with a note in her hand, wearing tight jeans and with high heels amplifying her tight ass, not giving a shit what was going on in the meeting. The boys turned lively, all smiles, and "Hi, Connie" was all that was heard. They were all giddy as if a porn queen had walked in and offered them a free blowjob. Connie handed the note to Hector, all smiles as she returned the helloes on her way out of the room, knowing down deep in her heart that most if not all of these clowns would end up in dingy prison cells, sucking shit-smudged cock and being nailed in the ass by diseased, half-witted lifers. She was already taking college classes at night, and she swore on a stack of Bibles she would never marry a man without a degree. She didn't want to bust anyone's wild dreams, but she knew these apes wouldn't amount to, well, anything much. Besides, Hector was almost laughed out of town when he proposed the ridiculous proposal to the board of directors to get these losers into university.

Connie. Hector called her before she exited the room. Next time, knock. And then he added an uneasy Please.

Connie, amused, turned and said, Sure thing Boss. She walked back to her desk with an elated grin on her sculptured mouth. She knew the old dog would vehemently apologize later and beg her not to leave as she threatened numerous times in the past. She was fully aware Hector didn't want to hire on a semiliterate, garlic-smelling, boob-sagging, fat-legged, poor excuse of a secretary who couldn't even spell "back off." Besides she wouldn't leave until, with his connections, she also got a full scholarship at the university like those bozos he was grooming in the conference room, instead of the crappy classes she was taking at the off-campus circus in Las Flores.

Hector read the note Connie delivered. His face turned livid, obviously annoyed.
Sonovobitch! he yelled and tore up the note into little pieces and flung them to the ceiling.

You said we're not supposed to cuss, cackled one of the boys like a wounded hen.

Hector ignored the comment and paced the room in a fuming intensity. He stopped, stared at the boys while squeezing his hands, and told them what the note said.

The sonovobitch cancelled. He won't show until next week, he said, working to gain his self-control. Goddamn that puny little shit. It's not the first time. There's not a goddamn thing I can do about it; one outburst from me, and he can cancel the program, and all the hard work down the gutter. So I have to eat it, boys, suck his cock till you sewer rats are in the program solid, attending full-time classes, living in the dorms, maybe with a small stipend to buy your condoms or whatever you purchase with small change. You don't mind me calling you names, do you boys? You know I love you all, know in my heart you're college material, even if the other morons don't. I've got the tests to prove it. All of you scored high on the IQ and college- bound exams I gave you. Of course, Lencho scored higher, but he was special—what a waste of talent. I've done this before. Don't think it's a lamebrain idea I concocted while having an orgasm in some whorehouse. I have a solid track record of working attorneys all over the country, my son included; I know what I'm doing here. I won't let you down, guys—I promise. You just do your part, do your best, just give it your best shot, your best shot; you'll never regret it. There's always some crap at the inception, but let me take care of that end. The fuddle duddles will always be around. They made it; they have to show off they did; that's fine; screw them. I'll let you know when the next meeting will be held. Thanks for coming in, guys; you guys are the best. Never forget it.

Hey, Hector, do you have any vouchers you can spare? asked Bryan. We're hungry. We wanted to go to the Azteca and get some real food.

No sir, Hector said, the vouchers are for emergencies only, for people who are really hungry and needy. Go check with Concha in the kitchen; there might be some leftovers.

I don't want any institutionalized food, I told you.

Well, then eat shit. See if I care.

Hey, Hector, did you know that Santos is gonna open another restaurant in the Westside? asked Mike.

Who gives a shit about Santos? interjected Bryan, pissed. Santos is a Tejano, always talking shit about what he's about to do, but he never does anything.

Hey, watch your mouth, son. Don't be bad-mouthing Santos; he sends a lot of food to the center. When you can do the same, then talk. Besides, Santos will never go back to Tejas. He's one of us, a primo. Never doubt that.

CHAPTER SEVEN

While all of that was happening at the community center, Javier and Jr., who belonged to that same group, were late to the meeting as usual. Apparently their car ran out of gas a short distance from the center. They decided to walk and leave the car until later. They walked in a slow, patient pace, lacking interest in anything or anybody but their own debased conversation.

Javier gave Jr. a scornful look and then turned away with a disgusted look on his face. Then out of the blue, he blurted out, You looking more and more like a faggot. Why doncha do something about it. Your pants are eating your ass; you walk like a puto. I ain't trying to put you down, brother, but it's becoming to be obvious. It's gonna take a lot of cunning to get over, if you know what I mean. The populace round here are still skittish. I don't wanna use "homophobic," 'cause I refuse to judge 'em, one way or another. So if I was you—thank God I ain't, but if I was—I'd tighten myself up and put in a little down time on that walk of yours.

Faggot! Whatcha mean, said Jr. I don't getchu, man. Why you coming off with this shit? If I'm a faggot, you a faggot too, shithead. 'Cause we hang together night and day. So if you're concerned about who's sucking who, you got your own little problem, carnal. If I embarrass you in any way, shit, I'm the one should be embarrassed to be seen with you. I just loaned you twenty-five dollars yesterday. You didn't have the good sense to put gas in that piece of shit you call a car. You shiftless, homeless, beggar; you sure got the balls, doncha? And by the way, needle dick, these are old jeans, the only ones I could find that were washed.

At least we ain't walking, said Javier, grinning.

We walking now, ain't we, replied Jr.

And I ain't homeless; I stay with my mom, if you want to know.

Well, shit, you're always crashing at my pad or sleeping in your trashy car. Whatcha call that? asked Jr.

And the conversation shifted like a harmless breeze, cooling the evening for a night of hugs and kisses. They could do that forever and still remain friends; that was friendship to the bone.

Hey, Javier, you think Hector is gonna get mad at us 'cause we late? asked Jr.

I think Hector can go dick himself if he even brings up the topic. And talking about Hector, what is this CBY bullshit? asked Javier.

That stands for College-Bound Youth, which happens to be the same program we're in, bonehead.

Yeah, I know what it stands for. I just don't get it why the cocksucker chose such a lame name. Every college uses that logo. I'm just saying, couldn't he been more original? Anyway, I can hardly wait to get there and stay in those dorms; it'll be like a hotel, 'cept we don't have to pay the bill when we check out, ha fucking ha. And we get to eat all the food we want in the cafeteria and sneak some out for a midnight snack. But the best part will be screwing all the white chicks and laying our hands on some valuables, not necessarily in that order.

You know, Javier, I want to do me a black chick. Just to get into that blackness so deep it'll set me in a merry-go-round of pure pleasure that leads to real love, without restraints of any kind. Don't you think so?

You're crazy, mutton head. Just get a real dark Latina with spongy hair; you'll keep your sanity, what's left of it.

Hey, you think Hector can still take a punch? asked Jr.

You know some old dudes can take a punch, answered Javier. Some can't. Remember my cousin Rudy?

The boxer?

Yeah, Rudy. We wanted to enter this bar in Barelas; there was an old bouncer at the door. The place was a dump; I have no idea why they even bothered with a bouncer. Anyway, this old guy refused Rudy entrance 'cause he bloodied a fool in the dive and was banned.

Rudy attempted to explain to the old guy we were only there to pick up some chonas that were waiting for us inside, and we were gonna leave. The old thug started to mouth off, getting nervous like he was getting in the mood to break some bones. He told us right to our face, You hoodlums ain't from round here, so why doncha go back to where ever the fuck you came from? He kept slapping his hand with his little club like a Keystone cop. He came up to Rudy real close and said, That boy you beat up and bloodied last month was my nephew. How you like it if I push this club up your stinking ass? I'm sure I wouldn't like it, answered Rudy, unless you do it gently. Smart ass, said the old dog. He pushed Rudy, and I said, holy shit, the wolves eat us alive here tonight. Rudy hit him so hard and quick on the kidneys with a solid left hook that the old fool went down. Rudy didn't have to bother with a right cross or double hook. The old mutt went down hard on his ass, cracked his head against the wall of the building, and started bleeding from the mouth. It all happened so fast. One minute the clown was playing bad with a club in his hand, convinced he was gonna put the hurt on Rudy. The next second he's on the ground bleeding, with his head crunched up against the rigid wall. Man, we were in Barelas in a tight-ass joint, where only guys like Rudy can survive.

Did you guys leave the place pronto? asked Jr.

Yeah, hell yeah, like you leave a restaurant when you don't pay.

Anyway, whatever happened to Rudy?

He moved to Eh-Ley to pursue his boxing. He claimed he couldn't get any real competitors round here, but I believe he just wanted to get away 'cause the place just bored him to death; he felt confined. He got to Eh-Ley and was staying with his uncle Tomas and tia—I forgot her name. Anyway, he landed a job in a factory and was boxing after work in a gym close by. He soon realized those vatos wanted it for real, not just as a side event to impress people at parties. He lost his first two pro fights by knockouts, one in the second round, the other in the fifth. He took a severe beating in both fights and discovered his face was too pretty to let it get ruined by too many chingazos. Anyway, after that, he decided he was gonna be a gambler and quit his job at the factory, but I heard they fired his ass after breaking the foreman's nose for bossing him around. He was kind of touchy on people telling him what to do. He played the ponies at Santa Anita and visited the card clubs on Normandie and Vermont Avenue. He wasn't good at either; he was constantly on a losing streak. It was easy to get loans at high risk and high interest with no collateral. The first time he was late on paying it back, he was given a verbal warning but didn't seem to take it seriously. The second time they broke the bones in the fingers of his right hand. He was given twenty-four hours to come up with all the money plus interest, or his life and those of his uncle and aunt would be cancelled. My uncle and aunt here and all the rest of the family scrambled to come up with the money. They sent him the money with a warning: this was the first and last time they send him any money for anything. Last we heard, he was in Frisco with his girlfriend.

Wow—sure fucked up, didn't he? asked Jr.

Yeah, big time. Hey, look—Hector's dog, Tupi, said Javier.

They walked up to the door of the community center and stopped in front of the dog. They patted the dog on the head, giving him a little scratch behind the ears.

Good dog. You a good dog, Tupi, they repeated several times. The dog made a gurgling sound of approval, shaking his snarly tail. He liked these two guys; they were always nice to him. He wanted to lick their shoes to show his appreciation but was afraid they might kick him. Why spoil a good thing? he thought.

Javier and Jr. walked into the community center as the others were leaving.

Meeting cancelled, they said, on their way out.

Hector looked their way and ignored them as he walked into his office and shut the door without saying a word.

They walked to Connie's desk, all smiles. Connie got up without moving her lips, went into Hector's office, and shut the door before they could utter a word.

What the hell. Let's try the kitchen, said Jr.

They walked into the kitchen. Concha was putting away the leftover food. Concha was a big woman, happy, comfortable in a place where food was abundant, and she was in control of it, all of it. Her heart swelled with pride as she scooped some leftover tuna casserole into plastic containers. She was agile as her thick hands gingerly scooped the tuna with a large wooden spoon into plastic containers without dropping a morsel outside the containers. Before Hector became director, she remembered so well that the kitchen was always a mess, with different women cooking whatever their favorite happened to be and people wandering in and out with plates in their hands, food falling off their plates to the floor. But when Hector became director of the center, he put her in charge of the kitchen and food distribution. She hired a cook to help her and a dishwasher and kept everyone else out of the kitchen and in the dining room. The servers, all volunteers, would take the food to a long table in the dining area and serve the food. They could get all they wanted, but had to eat all they got. That cut down on waste. One woman cleaned up any food that hit the floor as soon as possible before it was stepped on. There were no more elderly people shuffling back and forth trying to make up their feeble minds on what to eat. A menu was posted in Spanish and English on Monday; that was the ticket for the week. No more potlucks brought by certain people for certain people; if they refused to send it to the kitchen, they had to take it back home or shove it up their asses. And after they finished eating, they had to vacate the table for someone else instead of nursing a cup of coffee and lollygagging with neighbors the rest of the day. The hours for lunch were posted in several places, and if they were late, they were out of luck. Food was served Monday through Friday, twelve to one; the kitchen was locked on weekends, except if Hector had a special meeting on those days. Concha made some coffee served with pie or cookies or maybe cheese enchiladas with beans and rice, but that was rare because Hector didn't have many friends, and he was frugal. She was expected to keep the books in order, and her daughter, Francisca helped her keep the food purchased with vouchers on the books and donated foods off the books. Every receipt was kept, dated, and recorded for Hector and the federal auditor who showed up on certain dates. The health inspector was happy because the kitchen was immaculate. The throwaway food was placed in a large garbage can and hauled away every day by Mr. Martinez for his hogs, and the can returned smelling of soap. The kitchen could now be locked when not in use; only she and Hector had the key, although that little bitch Connie was always pestering Hector for her own key. The snacks for the students were ready at four after tutoring, and again everything was simple and brought out to them: a peanut butter sandwich with jelly, milk, or water; a slice of cheese on a corn tortilla, grilled until melted; an apple or pear in season or dry fruit out of season. Some of the students complained about the snacks and brought in their parents. She reminded them it was free food, and, if they were unhappy, they could bring their own. Or on occasions she repeated Hector's famous saying: "Eat shit, and see if I care." By four thirty, the kitchen was cleaned and locked up for the day. So she was humming, content she was being paid—although not much—for a job she loved, plus she could take leftovers to her gluttonous husband and children and not have to slave in front of a hot stove cooking dinner every night.

She turned her head and saw Jr., her nephew, and his friend Javier standing close to her. A huge, sincere smile dominated her entire face. Her eyes almost closed as the flesh on her cheeks pushed upward as soon as she saw them.

Mijo! Let's have a hug you, handsome man. She was a big-time hugger. She enclosed her pulpy arms around Jr. and almost lifted him off the floor. Jr. couldn't do anything with his arms; it was like hugging a side of beef. When he was on solid ground again, he pointed to Javier and introduced him as his friend. Javier put out his hand, but Concha put her arms around him too, even though she had met him on several occasions, but Javier was taller and beefier than Jr., so his feet didn't leave the floor as easily.

You guys are going to college; aren't you excited? You have made us all so proud, Jr., I tell you. Your mom is happy—so happy that you wouldn't believe it. But you guys don't forget to thank Hector; he put a lot of hard work to get the program off the ground. Are you hungry? Let me fix you a tuna or chicken salad sandwich, OK, mijo? What do you want?

Is the tuna fishy, Tia? asked Jr.

No, Lord, no. I put in lots of pepper, onions, lots of mayo, and for you, my darling boy, a little relish. Do you want toast or plain bread?

Make it on toast, Tia, but not too toasted.

Done, sir. To drink, milk or chocolate milk?

Chocolate milk from the bottle, not that instant stuff you mix.

No, of course not, my dear; I'll cut the crust from around the bread, OK?

Javier looked at Jr. in disbelief and felt like slapping him for being such a pussy.

And what about you, Javier? What'll you have?

Oh, just a chicken salad on plain bread and a glass of milk, please. You don't have to cut off the crust. I like crust.

Sure thing—anything for the attorneys of the future. It's my pleasure, said Concha, still smiling. You guys can sit on that table in the corner; I'll prepare your food in no time at all.

As the boys ate in the kitchen and Tia Concha continued mothering Jr., strong words were heard coming from the reception room.

I tell you, someone stole my fucking pen. I want my pen back; the sonovobitch took my favorite pen better give it back right now. I can't write with any other pen. I want my own pen back. I catch the asshole stole my pen, I'm gonna wrap my fist around his stinky mouth. Everybody knows I can't write anything worth a shit without my special pen. That pen was a goddamn gift from general of the army, Ike Eisenhower. If I call him up, he bring the whole army in here to look for my pen and kick some ass while doing it. Goddamn! What shit is this? Can't turn away for a second, for some asshole take your shit.

Connie attempted to calm the old man. She offered him another pen, pleading for the old guy to take it, but the old man wouldn't hear of it.

Finally, Hector charged out of his office like a man unhinged while Connie disappeared, not wanting any part of it.

What the hell is going on? What is all this profanity about I've been hearing? What?

Look, Hector, my pen, boss, my pen—gone.

Shut up, you old goat. Use another pen, or get the hell out. We are fed up with your senile, profanity-laced gutter language, so use another pen. Sign the goddamn papers if you want any help from us, and get the hell out. Or I'll call the police, have you dragged out, and I'll ban your bony ass from the center for the remaining days of your miserable life. Do I make myself clear?

Yes, boss, but—

Don't say a goddamn thing; just sign the papers where Connie tells you. Period. Basta. And he walked back to his office and slammed the door shut.

CHAPTER EIGHT

s Mike was leaving the community center, Bryan tapped him on the shoulder and said, Hey, Mike, your pal Ramon wants to see you.

Mike, taken by surprise, said, I thought he was in serious condition.

Naw, I saw him yesterday while I was checking in on my grandma. He's all right—a little beat up, but he'll live. He started crying like a baby and said it was urgent he talk to you. I told him I be more than happy to pass along the message, but he got pissed and said no. I said, Well, OK, then; have it your way, I'll tell him when I see him. He must be feeling pretty bad for what happened to Danny. I'm sure he's aware, especially if he was driving, 'cause he knows damn well he has no business behind the wheel with his seizures and all.

Listen, Bryan, Mike said, let the cops do their work. I'm sure they don't need any input from you. If Ramon was driving, let them make the case, que no?

No, I'm just saying he was crying—maybe, just maybe, he felt guilty about Danny. I mean, wrapping a car around a utility pole and walking away with a mild concussion, while Danny checks out on a one-way ticket? I guess I be crying too, and the reason would be obvious, que no?

Well, whatever, Bryan. I gotta go.

Mike walked back home at a fast pace. He needed to get his car and drive out to the hospital to visit Ramon. He first noticed Ramon in junior high school. There was a circle of boys laughing at someone on the ground in the PE field. He ran up, thinking it was a fight. It was Ramon on the ground twitching and convulsing, with his eyes rolling up into his sockets and white stuff drooling from his mouth. He was having an epileptic seizure, and the boys were laughing and pointing at him as if he was some carnival freak that fell off the truck.

He was about to laugh also, but he recalled Margret, this girl he met at a Saturday night dance a couple of months before. He had danced with her and kissed her all through the dance. On Monday, she was on the ground, on this same field, having severe convulsions, and he and his friends laughed at her instead of helping her out. They got a good talking-to by the teacher, but she also told them about epilepsy. He was glad his parents never found out about his behavior at the PE field with Margret. They would have been so disappointed and sad at his barbaric behavior.

This time with Ramon, he ran and brought back the PE teacher, who yelled at the boys to back off, reached into Ramon's pocket, and pulled out what resembled a popsicle stick but a little thicker, and placed it horizontally in Ramon's mouth. It was to protect the tongue, which suffers bruising by the strong jaw contractions, was his explanation. He gently rolled Ramon over onto one side and placed a windbreaker under his head. He let Ramon relax in that position until the contractions and convulsions stopped. Ramon had suffered a grand mal seizure, as the school nurse educated Mike later, known in the medical world as a tonic-clonic seizure because it hits in two phases. The tonic phase, where the victim falls down and loses consciousness, lasts from ten to twenty seconds. Then the clonic phase kicks in, and the muscles go into contractions and convulsions, lasting usually for less than two minutes. Mike walked Ramon to the bathroom after the seizure and helped him clean up. Ramon, with his gray eyes and pale skin, obviously sleepy, attempted a weak smile, not remembering what occurred but knowing there had been an incident and that he had been the main attraction. He was embarrassed, of course, as he touched his crotch to check if there was an involuntary leakage, which sometimes happened; it was dry. But he was equally satisfied that he couldn't recall any part of it, besides the beginning and the end. But Mike soon realized that Ramon had become his responsibility and would have to shadow him for many years. The countless bloody lips and black eyes attested for the price he had paid to protect Ramon from the bullies who cared nothing for his disability and wanted to pound him only because somebody had to be pounded on. Ramon was an easy victim, and was never given a dime's worth of consideration because he didn't back down from a confrontation and had a mouth that wouldn't quit insulting your mother, even though your fists were all over his face. And now, Ramon, who couldn't be watched every minute of the day and night because he wasn't a child, was in the hospital and could be in a whole lot of trouble, serious trouble, for the first time in his life. And Mike had to go visit him and assure him that he was going to help him in any way he possibly could, but the hospital was one place he didn't feel at all comfortable.

Mike was driving his old Chevy, an older model that needed work. He put in leather seats, but the inside top was never done, so he ripped out the old, dry cloth material, which was tattered, hanging like sheets on an outside clothesline. He spray painted the smooth inside top with white paint to match the white leather upholstery. He did it at the end of summer, in the winter, when the weather turned frigid; it was like riding inside a metal bucket—especially at night, when his lady friends complained about freezing their asses on the cold leather seats. He knew and with plenty of reason that he was in need of a newer car, a more comfortable fit suited to his lifestyle. He also understood money was tight; he didn't want to ask his father for any cash because his father would make him work construction. He didn't like to spend too much time in the sun; the heat could be unbearable, and the cold could bite. He wanted to work but not in construction. He wanted a job with no responsibilities and high pay, the kind of job where you didn't have to sell yourself to be popular or raise worthy. He wanted a job where he could go and come as he wished, without explanations to anyone. He was picky and not easily employed. He questioned authority—an unreasonable quality to many—but he was always superfriendly to women of all ages. He took a job once in a restaurant as a pearl diver, working the swing shift, but the mountains of dirty dishes, pots, and pans discouraged him, and his nightlife suffered. He couldn't score with the corpulent waitress, so he had no choice but to tend his resignation, but not before he recommended a more compatible employee, positive that his mother would understand his dilemma and back him up, in case his father misunderstood his reasons to quit.

He wanted to be a good son because he had wonderful parents, but he couldn't be like his father, and he didn't even try. His father was a saint, and everyone who knew him was aware of it. He was a true communist but was never called that, because some people freaked out, especially the ones who still believed the world was flat. He had his own construction company, a one-truck, mom- and-pop operation, and hired people when he needed them. He did a lot of patch work, but his specialty was leaking roofs. He was one of a few in the Eastside barrio who could put a pitched roof on a flat adobe. The old way was a torta, a layer of mud over the old dried mud. His father refused to do tortas because they didn't work. The water came through eventually, and he hated to take hard-earned money away from people he had known all his life. When he put up a pitch on a house, the homeowners never had to worry about leaks anymore. At times he even helped with the financing, and they would pay him with venison, hog, goat meat, and other produce and fruit, either harvested or stolen, most of which he gave to people in need. He never made any real money, but he was happy and content, knowing he was doing his best to help others without any sanctimonious pretentions. His maturity was on a level few men reached; he subdued petty desires and passions and kept them from tempting him and causing pain to his family.

Mike drove west on Chavez Street for about half a mile. Chavez took him past the railroad tracks, leaving the shabby Eastside barrio behind as he drove into the more glamorous Westside. He noticed the difference right away. The houses were bigger and the streets less congested, with uniformed lawns that had never known neglect. Many of the cars were newer and more expensive, and even the streets were better kept, a sign of political muscle. To Mike it was a trip because in the old times, the housing in the Westside was off limits to Pisanos, and that in itself seemed incomprehensible. How could a few bigots prevent people of color from living in the

Westside, if they wanted to live there and had the means to live in the Westside? Who was going to stop them?

But Mike was too young or too naïve or both to comprehend that in the early times, the Westside was populated by many—not all, but many—who moved in from areas that accepted segregation and saw it as the natural order of things. There were laws in the books that favored certain people. And naturally, these people took advantage of their favored status and formulated barriers to keep people of color from buying property in their precious Westside. And the most numerous people of color happened to be Pisanos. Native Americans and blacks were easy to keep out because of their numbers; they were on the fringes, with no political base. The Pisanos, native New Mexicans, believed in the American dream as much or more than anybody else. Many returned from both wars, determined to live where they could afford to live and fight for that right, even if they had to resort to violence. They were numerous, with high expectations, and some were ready to leave the seedy Eastside and move into more expensive housing, seen by them as an investment first and a home second—quite a cultural shift from their parents' and grandparents' affection for their humble adobes. Some were college-educated professionals who took advantage of the GI Bill, and others were businesspeople who became successful at an alarming rate and expanded to the Westside. Some bigots left; what else could they do? They saw the future and didn't like what they saw, so they left, searching for more favorable hunting grounds.

Mike chuckled as he made a right on Armijo heading north to Alameda Street. Now the Westside was full of Pisanos and other people of color, and all the fuss was over nothing—a few antiquated words on some outdated municipal code, utilized by some real estate flunkies to steer prospective Pisano homebuyers away from the Westside housing market, racist laws that could have been turned into mush by any second-year law student. But now the growth was to the east, toward the mountains, and he knew he had to get his hands on some of that land while it was still cheap. The city was expanding, and it was expanding east. A new hospital and new schools were being discussed for that wilderness area. Million- dollar homes on up to ten acres of land was the buzz in private gatherings, and speculators were getting hard and salivating at the mouth just thinking about payday.

Once he reached Alameda, he made a left, driving west to the hospital. The Las Flores General Hospital was in between Alameda and Sierra Streets. The traffic was heavier on Alameda; many businesses were located on this busy street. He noticed construction being started on the new Azteca Mexican restaurant on Alameda, not too far from the hospital. Santos must have taken in many inches of dick to get a good price on this piece of property, he thought. It was close to the hospital and not far from the off-campus college on Sierra Street. With a bunch of hungry people always looking for good food, it would be a gold mine for Santos. His food was the best, but if he watered down the green and red chili, as others did, then it would be crap, and he would eventually lose money. But Santos was a clever businessman and a great cook and knew how much he could push the button on people's taste buds.

Mike parked his car in the hospital parking lot and walked to the main entrance. More people were leaving than arriving; he wondered if visiting hours were over. His watch wasn't that dependable anymore. A few feet from the main entrance, he recognized Manny, a character from the barrio, walking out. Manny worked at the hospital, helped the nurses clean up, and was always smiling and talking to anyone who listened. Manny's face lit up when he saw Mike.

Hey, Mike! Long time no see, brother. How you doing? Hey, Manny. I came to visit Ramon; have you seen him?

Yeah, I passed by his room and said hi, but the cat turned his face and ignored me. I was hurt by the snob, man, but hey, you can't win them all. Chale, but Mike, Manny continued, changing the subject. Remember that chick you told me about? Remember? C'mon, you remember, you said she had big tits and a tight ass. Was a dynamite lay, you said.

Mike noticed people turning to look at them and walking away fast, especially when the word "lay" came out of Manny's loud mouth.

Yeah, Mike, remember? You told me how you put her legs over your shoulders and—

Listen, Manny. Mike had to break in. Sometimes people exaggerate. I was probably bombed or joking. Forget it, man, OK?

Anyway, Manny continued, gesturing with his hands as if directing traffic, anxious to tell his story. I saw that little bitch at the Red Rooster Saturday night. It was her, I tell you. She was sitting at the bar, sucking on a drink next to a couple of pinche apes. I walked over to her in hopes of making a sale, maybe scoring on a little flatbread. The apes were too close to her, so I said, Hey, you remember Mike Montes? She looked at me as if I slapped her on the mouth with a dirty dick. I asked her again, thinking she didn't hear me the first time. This time she looked at me as if I was some kind of vermin asking for permission to crawl on her skin. What of it? She finally answered, twisting her mouth and starring me down. Then I didn't know what the hell to say. They were all looking at me, expecting I don't know what. I wasn't sure if the two baboons were narcs or what. So I said, Oh, he joined the army; they sent his ass overseas. Then one of the brutes blurted out, Why doncha join him, like now. I wanted to come back with something smart and sassy, but I didn't. I walked away— shit, what else could I do, Mike? I ain't suicidal, chale.

You did the right thing, Manny. Listen, don't throw my name around like that anymore, OK? It's not healthy for any of us, know what I mean?

Sure, Mike, sure; don't get mad, ese. And he pulled on his upper lip with the index finger and the thumb of his right hand, but not for long. He did a little dance with his feet, and then he said, Romero the Giant is in town, Mike. You know Romero? He's a collector—a fixer, I guess you can call him. He's connected to the big boys in El Burque.

Mike, losing his patience, said, Look, Manny, I don't give a rats' ass if he collects rents or fixes cars or broken hearts. I don't know him. I don't want to know him, I don't owe him any money, and he doesn't owe me any money, so I don't give a fat fuck who this clown is, goddamn it, or if he is here or not. Get it?

OK, Mike. Got it, man. Simon, ese. He made a gesture with his right hand as if he grabbed some invisible something and put it in his pocket. He continued, still sidestepping with his feet, unable to stand still. Listen, Mike; you need something to make your days lighter, your nights more tolerable, and your dreams a heavenly paradise? Or a little something to caress your imagination and jumpstart that little something deep in you that you never knew existed? How about it, my friend? Or I got performance enhancers will help you get in touch with the real you, man. I call it semen of the sun; others call it jaguar's nectar, but after you take it, you can call it anything you want. You've earned that right, brother. But I tell you right now, it's the best yaje I ever had, 'cause I got more juice than a Mazatec shaman. But if you prefer chemicals, well, that bodega is also open. Just say the word, Mike.

No, Manny, thanks but no thanks. I'm good. I really have to go see Ramon.

Guys like Manny could sure screw up your day, he thought, as he entered the hospital with its clean, scrubbed floors and walls, a sterilized atmosphere where white-uniformed employees tried to present an aura of importance, while sick people patiently waited for attention, suffering in silence. He walked to the receptionist's desk and asked for Ramon's room. He was directed to the second floor. When he was almost at Ramon's room, he kept his fingers crossed that Ramon wouldn't be in one of his incredible moods. Ramon had the tendency to go off road—and Mike wasn't referring to his seizures, because that reference could take hours—but to the everyday obstacles he created to impede the facility to climb out of chaos. Ramon had to be talked out of a suicide mission because no girl or guy invited him to the high school senior prom; as if it was mandatory someone had to ask him, as if he couldn't take the initiative and ask someone himself. That was an issue that lasted several months and drove him to an iffy scenario. There was another time he claimed he was the father of a child by a girl he never had sex with, another delicate situation that had to be put to rest before the boyfriend and the brothers of the girl took matters into their own hands. Mike was concerned where this more serious episode could land his friend Ramon.

He went into Ramon's room, which was shared with an elderly woman who had dislocated a hip taking tango lessons. A white plastic curtain separated the two beds. The elderly woman pointed to the other side of the curtain in a manner that indicated she had given up on anyone paying her a visit, not even the dance instructor, who probably promised her that the young studs would be attracted to her because of her dance skills. Mike smiled at her, not really warm, but a polite excuse-me type of smile, the type that doesn't encourage conversation.

Mike walked around the curtain to see Ramon. Ramon was staring toward the window, not exactly out the window but at the glass or curtains at an invisible something only he could see and would refuse to share with anyone. It wasn't a sad face or a face in pain; no, it was a face of unquestionable defiance, like, OK, asshole, you took my best, but you can't have the worst. The worst is the real me; the best is only shit I pile on to get through.

Ramon. Ramon, Mike called softly, attempting to bring him back easy, because sometimes Ramon refused to leave his soft spot and ignored all calls to the here and now. Like the time he didn't eat or talk for a week because he believed Mr. Parker, his history teacher, was tailgating his mother, but it was never clarified if it was his own mother he was concerned about or Mr. Parkers.

Hey, Ramon, hey, buddy. Look at you, man. If I didn't know better, I would swear you were in a car crash. Oops!

Ramon turned his head and smiled or tried to smile, but it hurt. He knew it was his amigo Mike; no one else would start a conversation like that—not with him, anyway.

Hey, Mike. He talked as if he was coming out of a heavy sedation and he was just learning how to speak fluently in a language someone had made up on a night of heavy drinking. I'm in pain, brother, but it's in my heart. I'm positive they don't have any painkillers for that sort of pain. I know; I've asked. They talk shrinks or a pastor. That's the answer they give me.

Now, Ramon, let's stay focused. OK. What happened? Do you know? Tell me—if you care to, that is. All kinds of stories are leaking out, man. You were driving drunk; Danny was drunk, letting you drive; Danny was driving, you pulled on the wheel 'cause he didn't stop for a burger. What the hell, Ramon. This is serious shit. Danny died, dude.

Ramon studied Mike as a lizard studies a precocious child who hesitates at first, not sure if it's OK, but then grabs for it, spoiling the lizard's time enjoying the rays of the sun. He felt like the scampering lizard run out of the sun, interrupted. But he had to talk to Mike, and as he talked, the bandage on his forehead shifted down toward his eyes, as if the crusty bandage, when it covered his eyes, would close out all the ugliness in his sorry life. But Mike was here to keep that bandage in its place and remind him of the deep shit he was in. The crazy thing about it was that he invited him, because only Mike could break any bad news in a way he wouldn't feel offended—his friend, his best friend, his only friend.

Look, Mike. Ramon's voice was apologetic, like when you try to explain to your old man you wrecked his car. I was, uh…I was, it was Danny, man. He was drunk. He couldn't drive. He was throwing up all over the car; he drove off the road and stopped the car. He said I had to drive, had to, no matter what. We were about ten miles from Las Flores, on the old Albuquerque road. It was getting late. I wanted to get home as bad as Danny; we been out driving around all day. I sure the fuck wasn't gonna walk or put my thumb out in the middle of that wilderness that late at night. So I drove the damn car. I can drive, you know. I got behind the wheel, drove slow but Danny kept pushing me to drive faster, pushing me, messing with me. He was sick from all the booze he sucked up and needed to get home to Mommy. I drove faster to get him off my back. The last thing I remembered was a huge rock, a giant boulder, crashing, slamming into the car, and the car spinning out of control. I wake up here; cops are asking me all kinds of stupid questions. Don't worry, Mike; I didn't say a thing. Nada.

Mike studied Ramon, thinking of something to say. Except for the bandage on his head and forehead and a few scratches on his face and arms, he seemed to be in one piece. But Ramon was difficult to help; he always did the opposite of the reasonable approach. Mike knew he had no choice. Ramon was a true friend. He'd never run out on him, even when the odds were against them. Ramon would get his ass kicked two times before he'd abandon Mike. And besides, Ramon had alienated most of the little family he had with his erratic behavior. His mother was his only back-up, and she was in no condition, physically or financially, to help Ramon much, although she did her best.

Listen, Ramon, you did the right thing by not saying anything to the cops. But let me ask you: right before the accident, did you sense a warning sign, an—

Stop it, Mike, Ramon interrupted, a little ticked off. The answer is no. I shouldn't of never told you about the aura. Some people never get it or get it too late. You always want to know about the aura. Just forget about it, OK.

Sorry, Ramon. Anyway, the best thing to do right now is get you an attorney. We'll get Pa Hanks. I know he's old, but he is still the best and reasonable. I'm sure by now they know how much alcohol was in your blood, if any. They'll probably try to dick you for driving under the influence, then the more serious charges. Even if the DUI doesn't stick, they want to make a case because of your disability. That's why you need Pa Hanks. That new district attorney is a real ball cruncher—wants to be governor, I hear. So remember, Ramon, don't say anything to anyone. If they insist, tell them to fuck off, and ask for your mouthpiece.

OK, Mike. I promise. I promise to do everything you say, Mike. I don't want to do time. I can't do time. It'll kill me…you know, you know.

A chubby nurse waddled in humming, wearing the traditional white uniform, walking on soft, blue-rag slippers. She was carrying a metal tray in her fleshy arms, checking on her patients, and dispensing their nighttime medication. When she saw Mike, she sang out, Visiting hours are long over, sweetie. Unless you want to spend the night here with me, you best run on home, OK.

I was just leaving, ma'am.

I'll take good care of this sweet child; don't you worry about him, she said, cracking a friendly smile, exposing tobacco-stained teeth. You go on now.

Does he sleep OK? Mike asked over the loud snoring of the elderly woman.

Ramon gave Mike a hostile look, like saying, How dare you ask that skank about me? I told you all there was to tell.

This one fidgets and talks all night about God knows what, answered the nurse, while handing Ramon a pill and a paper cup with water. But he's such a cute little darling. I just leave him be.

Ramon snatched the pill and water from the nurse, annoyed with the liberty with which they were discussing his nighttime routine. Mike didn't want Ramon to get crazy, so he said good night, unsure of what to do—hug him, shake his hand, or what. So he just walked out, more than glad to get the hell out and breathe some fresh air.

CHAPTER NINE

A man and a woman were sitting on the sidewalk outside of the community center, close to the front door, waiting for lunch to be served. On the marquee above their heads, the block letters encased behind yellow plastic read in English and Spanish, Welcome All Visitors and Partake of All the Services and Amenities Available in the Las Flores Community Center. The man was dressed in a black smock that covered his bony knees. The smock was held at the waist—if his waist could hold anything—by a strip of wire rope, twisted in front by so many knots as not to become undone by any sudden frivolous movements. His hair fell to his shoulders in a tangled disorder of gray and filth, and his beard had the inexact measurements of being cut with a broken piece of jagged glass. His eyes were large, as black as a night with a missing moon and stars, and they gazed into a world he longed to be in. He was the kind of fellow who probably do poorly in a job interview.

The woman with him was also dressed in black, a long dress that covered her bare feet. Her hair was covered with a black shawl, but her eyes were alive, and a smile never left her unwrinkled face. She was animated and talked to strangers as if they were neighbors. Her favorite topic, which happened to be her only topic, was about her wingless angel, the man she had seen fly, and how she had become attached to this man. Santiago, as he had been christened. But she called him her angel without wings—a more appropriate name, in her estimation. She told the story to anyone who cared to listen of how she had followed him from that day on and had never left his side since.

They walked into the community center when lunch was announced, hand in hand, like a concerned, loving mother holding her child by the hand, a man-child who never developed to his expected expectations but nevertheless attracted curious attention from both friends and strangers. His feet were shoeless and crusted with a thick cake of dark, dried mud, but the feet were leathery, keeping the crust intact. His toenails were splintered and cracked, damaged to the point of not existing.

They sat very close together, and she spoon fed him because he refused to eat anything with his own hands. He chewed his food slowly, contemplating whether he was indeed a real angel or only a mirage in the creative imagination of the woman who kept telling him so. A mother with a baby girl on her hip was talking to a friend, and the child, with her thumb in her mouth, was facing the Flying Man. Her baby eyes were fixated on the Flying Man as if for the first time in her baby life, she had seen a distortion of such magnitude that she would age a year or have a disproportionate number of grisly nightmares in the coming years. The Flying Man locked his ink-black eyes on the eyes of the child, and his heart pulsated with the memory of a vanishing dream. He picked up a cookie from his plate and gestured to the child to take it. The baby girl freaked out and let out a horrifying scream as if being pricked by a needle. The mother instantly turned the child away and stared at the Flying Man as if he were a leper on the last stages of the disease. The Flying Man dropped the cookie to the floor and stepped on it, crushing and crumbling it to dust with his armor-covered foot. He pulled on his fishhook earring with the same fingers he had held the cookie, making it bleed some. His heart stopped fluttering, and he returned to his own world of falling stars in an upside-down universe.

The woman in black sitting close to him ignored the frightened, crying child and the mother with her hateful stare. She held the scabrous hand of her man and assured him everything was good, to continue to ponder the world as he saw it. And then, with her infectious smile on her smooth face, she asked the woman and her teenage daughter sitting next to her if they wanted to hear the story of how she met the Flying Man. The young daughter wholeheartedly agreed, and another pair of teenagers also moved close to hear the tale of the Flying Man and all the intrigue that such a tale might conjure.

She motioned with her opened arms to other women and men to also join them and listen to the strange story and perhaps learn the mysteries of life. Few accepted her invitation, having heard her silly story many times before. One woman made the sign of the cross and left; another placed some coins in her extended hand and patted her gently on the head; a third woman walked out the door disgusted, sickened by the fact that this Jezebel, this wanton, shameless, libertine, could abandon her family and her household responsibilities and run away with a man she had never seen before in her life and tell the whole world, without a hint of regret, that he had fallen out of the sky to save her from damnation. How could people be so gullible? she wondered. Why didn't they see her for what she was: a woman with a craving for the flesh, a woman wanting to be free of society's restrictions and showing everyone how easily it could be accomplished? She, on the other hand, had to run home and cater to a jobless, demanding husband, active children, and the grind of cooking and cleaning, and for what? she asked herself. So her neighbors could say she was a good wife and mother? Shit, life is so unfair, she mumbled, as she stormed away from the community center.

Please sit; all is peace. I beg you, sit, the woman insisted. Call me Shonofa, please. That is the name this dear man gave me. It means "teller of truth" in our language. I will confess the source of my contentment, this rapture, far greater than any other. I was outside hanging clothes on the clothesline next to an empty field where the children play ball and fly kites on the evenings when it gets cooler. I was humming the Lord's Prayer, when I looked to the heavens to admire the bright-blue sky. I saw, and God is my witness, a man flying—awkwardly, but still flying, moving his arms as if he was in a liquid sky, looking down at the ground, searching for a chosen one to witness his miracle of miracles. I dropped the wet clothes and pins and stared ecstatically at the flying man, who by now had landed, not on his feet, but as he touched the ground, he tucked his head to his chest, rolled in, and landed softly on his back like an experienced acrobat. I jumped on one foot, then the other with joy and ran to the field, not knowing whether to call the priest or a newspaper. I was beside myself with excitement. A joy never before known streamed through my body from head to toe, like a bolt of electricity. I extended my hand to help him up, and the touch of his skin on mine punctured my soul. I melted in heavenly delight. I saw in his dark eyes my old life flash by and a new life beginning. I asked myself, Mother of Christ, am I worthy?

I came to my senses, and I helped him up without saying a word. We walked hand in hand, silent as the stones in the desert. We walked and walked, without effort, without direction or discussion, wherever our hearts would lead us. We didn't eat or sleep those first few days and nights. Our journey was endless, without thinking or caring where fate would lead us. Our energy was inexhaustible but serene, a time to reflect on faith and love; it felt so good. For the first time in our lives, we knew we had to share this feeling with others less fortunate. And now, here you find us among good people with a vast thirst for faith, a faith in yourselves to do the impossible.

The Flying Man pulled on his fishhook earring, but this time there was no blood, only flakes of dried blood mixed with earwax from the infection around the fishhook earring. It flew and fell on his shoulder like miniature dead leaves tumbling from a tree during an autumn breeze. The woman, Shonofa, didn't say another word about their life together, but she was still smiling, preparing herself mentally for questions that never failed to come and would have to be answered gently, as not to offend a sentimentality that had been structured in an upside down world. She would never hurt any one's feelings, and if she did, she apologized and still felt terrible for a long time after.

The woman next to her was in tears. Her teenage daughter had her two hands over her heart, whispering to no one in particular, Why doesn't anything like that ever happen to me? One of the two teenagers, the one with the pleasant smile, asked the woman in black, Shonofa, in a nervous giggle, if she missed her children. All eyes but the eyes of the timid were on the woman in black, Shonofa.

The smile was still on her face; she didn't move a muscle

when she absorbed the weighty question. She was confident that her answers came from her heart, and her heart was one with the Flying Man, in that his goodness was also hers. And she treasured that honest goodness enough to open her heart and let people have a taste of it, if they wished to.

As a mother, let me be honest. She cleared her throat and looked straight into their eyes. There are few things that are worse to do, if you do what I did, but my destiny was not to be compromised by a situation that was not difficult to remedy. I miss my old life, but what I live now not only has more meaning, but it has the tranquility that settles the mind. So I see my other life and my children as I see a shooting star in the night: I admire it, and I am awestruck by it, but when it vanishes, I don't give it much thought. And that doesn't mean I'm thoughtless, because I'm not—it just means that the distance between me and my past is the distance the shooting star has traveled to delight our senses.

The little group stared at Shonofa with uncertainty, not sure in what category to place her. To the nervous teenager with the pleasant smile who asked the question or to the older woman with the teenage daughter sitting next to her, Shonofa's answer was profound but interpreted in different modes. The teenager, nervous and insecure, was impressed with the articulate words and riddles used to recite an orgy of nonstop sex. To the woman sitting next to Shonofa, Shonofa was a woman full of love and tenderness, a woman to be admired, because she had the courage to be different and live a distinct life. But she was also worried that a story such as this could perhaps encourage her daughter to be more aggressive and engage more readily in animal behavior with the opposite sex, wanting to make that wet dream that they think is so great become real.

The other teenager with the full lips, encouraged by her friend, asked Shonofa if the Flying Man was ready to fly again any time soon. Again, all eyes were on Shonofa, even the eyes of the timid, for they had lost their shyness as they heard the flowing, soothing words of Shonofa, the woman in black.

Shonofa was beaming as if she had just received news that she had won the lottery. Her skin had a perfect tan, and her teeth were still in good condition, considering the punishment they had taken.

She studied the group and was positive all other questions would be simple. But she still had to be careful as not to offend, because a misquoted phrase could be taken out of context and exploited in order to put her and her man in the defensive and make them reclusive and live a hermitic existence. And she was not going to allow anyone to put them in a situation that contradicted their way of life.

My flying man, Santiago, will fly again, but only time will tell when, she said. He has to be inspired by a higher order, a higher order that does not consult as to when it is time. It is a calling that is felt in the heart and soul and moves them with so much benevolence that the physical body acts, at times against its nature. So the question cannot be honestly answered at this time; it is an event that can only be substantiated by a superior force.

The Flying Man started twitching his head and scratching his infected ear, like a cat trying to scratch out worms embedded deep in its ear using its razor-sharp claws. Shonofa stopped talking; she knew it was time to leave. She began placing the leftover food in a little soiled cloth bag she had taken out from the folds of her smock. Santiago, the Flying Man, had never gotten used to being around people. He tired easily of people who attempted to interrogate him as if he were a criminal. He didn't like the way people stared at him as if they wished him locked up in a cage and used for experiments. When he had enough of the talking, he did his ear number, and that meant it was time to split, baby.

During the time that Shonofa and the Flying Man were entertaining guests in the main dining room of the community center, Hector was doing his own entertaining in his office, although not as grandiose. But let's get real now—who could outperform the Flying Man and his sidekick, the woman Shonofa? Hector was on a one-on- one with the priest Father Benjamin. Father Benjamin was on the warpath, so the entertaining was not the usual "have a bizcocho and a sip of cognac" type of visit, no sir, not today. On this visit, the priest, the proud Father Benjamin, Spanish born but of poor parents, insisted that Hector go along with his proposition to open space in the center for high-stakes bingo. And even though they had bingo at the dance hall practically every night of the week, the priest wanted to set up tables in the center for high rollers, create a Las Vegas– type atmosphere, bus in people for bingo specials, and generate a stronger cash flow for the church fund. Hector responded by saying that the regular bingo already brought in plenty of cash, and there was no need for high-stakes bingo because it would split the bingo crowd into the haves and have-nots and breed resentment among a community on the verge of exploding at any hint of insult, at any given moment. Father Benjamin threatened to take the issue to the full board of directors and go over his head and get what he wanted. But Hector knew the proud priest would never go there, because if he could get his way with the board, why waste time with him?

As the priest opened the door to leave Hector's office, he saw the Flying Man being led out of the center by the hand like a monkey by the woman in black, Shonofa. He made a face, turned to Hector, and said in a venomous intonation, See, those are the kind of people who shouldn't be allowed in the center for anything.

They are the poor and the hungry, Hector responded. Wasn't that what Jesus Christ was all about? Helping the poor? Well, that's what we do here; that's what the center is about, not high-stakes bingo.

They should have never appointed someone—and he pointed his long, bony index finger at Hector—who has so little faith in God as director of the center.

Our perception of God, Hector countered, may differ, but he is the same God, and deep in your heart, you know it, Father Benjamin.

Spare me your atheist lecture. I know it by heart. And father Benjamin walked out of the office and out of the center in a huff, without saying another word. He refused to get into a serious discussion with Hector, especially about religion, a topic very personal to him in more ways than were obvious.

CHAPTER TEN

The sun was already way ahead of Mike, claiming its day, and no fluffy clouds were going to interfere, because it was going to be toasty, no doubt about it. Mike woke up late, as he usually did during the summer. He showered and, while drying his thick, black hair, he examined his pimple-free, handsome face, t h i n k i n g how good looking he was. He had never known a moment when he considered himself ugly—maybe in deeds but never in looks, because he knew that could be bad news for anyone. Shit, his skin was perfect, he thought, not too dark and not too light; olive, yes, that was it. His lips were full but not excessive; his teeth were white and straight and had never needed braces, thank God. His nose was good—never been broken, knock on wood—and was free of blackheads. His eyes were light brown and turned hazel in the bright sun. So why was he still unhappy? He didn't know; he couldn't figure it out, and that concerned him even more.

Miguel! He heard his mother call from the kitchen, where he knew she was fixing him his late breakfast. Sometimes he felt bad because she did so much for him, but he loved it anyway. He never had to do dishes or clean the house, except his room, because of Lola, but that was nothing. He always had clean clothes and food on the table; it was like having a maid around but not having to lay out any cash to keep her. His father sometimes tried to make him feel guilty about doing nothing to help, but she defended him, saying that they had only one child and that it wasn't that difficult to do, what she loved to do.

He entered the large kitchen wearing a white T-shirt with cut-off sleeves made into a tank top, showing off his tight biceps. He gave his mother a hug and a kiss on each cheek. He checked out the eggs scrambled with fresh green chili and onions and a side of refried beans. The spicy scent set his stomach to roaring, and he wanted to chow down.

Mamasita! That looks delicioso. He beamed, sat down like a king, and sipped his café con leche, made Mexican-style, just for him.

Man, this is the best coffee ever. You make it perfect, Mamasita, bonita. I was at that Café on San Pedro Street, Mi Casita—you know the one, right? Anyway, I ordered a café con leche, and the waitress brought me a cup of black coffee with a little pitcher of milk. I asked her, What's this? She said, You ordered café con leche; well, there it is. No, sister, I insisted, this ain't café con leche; that's not the way my mama makes it. And she answered, a little ticked off, I'm not your sister. If that's not the way you like it, go drink it at your mama's house. We all started laughing; she laughed along with us. You, can't make those girls mad at you 'cause they'll spit on your food or worse.

Miguel, café con leche Mexican-style is the way they make it in Mejico. They boil the coffee and then add milk, sugar, and some canela; it's almost like a light chocolate. That's why you like it. They're not going to fix it like that at the restaurant. Too much work.

Francisco Montes walked in from the patio with a cup of coffee in his right hand and the Las Flores Sun tucked under his left elbow. Morning, Mike, or is it afternoon? He sat at the table across from Mike.

Morning, Pops. It's not twelve yet, so I guess it's still morning. Francisco smiled, wanting to give Mike a slap on the face to bring him down to earth, but he knew he would never lay a hand on his only son, never had, but he still thought about it. Hey, Mike, did you see Ramon? The paper claims he was the driver, according to the police report, and if he was, he could be in serious trouble.

Mike was forking up the eggs and green chili when his mother dropped a spoonful of refried beans on his plate, fried in lard, as were the eggs and green chili. Before he could answer, his mother brought him a couple of hot handmade flour tortillas in a cloth napkin.

Wow! This is a feast, Mamasita, Mike said, while chewing. Thanks. I love this.

Who wouldn't? added Francisco, his full-brush black-and-gray moustache hiding his smile.

Mike, wolfing up the food, didn't catch it. The green chili was roasted on an outside grill Francisco had converted to natural gas to avoid the hassle of wood or charcoal. The chili had a bite, and when the lid of the grill was opened, the roasting chili made the eyes smart when some of the smoke sneaked into the house and also gave the neighborhood that delightful odor. Francisco had turned the grill off because of the heat, but the rich odor lingered in the still air for the rest of the day. Alma, Mike's mother, brought in some of the green off the hot grill, let it cool a bit, and then peeled it. She cut off the heads of the roasted chili, placed the long, savory pods on a wooden slab, and cut them into smaller pieces using an empty tin can. She used the open end of the can, with the label removed, to crush the chili into manageable pieces. She added a pinch of garlic, salt, pepper, and a few cubes of vine tomatoes and threw it in with the frying eggs. Her chili and the vine tomatoes were from her own garden, her pride and joy. Even the eggs were from chickens she raised.

Mike was still chewing, looking at his father, wanting to answer him, but he didn't want to stop and let the flavor get away from him.

He took a sip of coffee, and, with beads of perspiration over his upper lip, he said, Wow, this chili is kicking—but he didn't finish the thought; he never cursed when he was talking to his parents. I saw Ramon yesterday. He seemed confused, but I'm sure he'll survive. He'll need a lawyer, that's for sure. I'm gonna talk to Pa Hanks; he'll tell us if Ramon needs legal help or not.

Well, Pa Hanks sure got you out of some tight spots, Francisco said, but that's neither here nor there. If Pa Hanks takes the case, I'll pitch in with some money to help out; maybe we can start a collection with some of the folks. I don't want you to get in debt, OK? Maybe we can have a carne asada cookout. That always brings in some coin. What do you think, Alma?

You have to consider the other side of the coin, Francisco, Alma said. Delfina Madrid will not be too happy when she finds out we are raising money for Ramon's attorney. As you remember, after the funeral, when we were at her house, she was very upset with Ramon, and she wasn't hiding it. Poor woman; the loss of a son or daughter that young can darken your life forever.

Francisco and Mike were silent, sipping their coffees. Alma's wisdom could not be denied. Francisco had nothing but respect and love for his wife. He knew that grief was not unfamiliar to her, having lost three children during birth in a culture where big families were a status or a necessity, where his own relatives had advised him to leave her and find a more fertile woman to give him heirs so that the Montes name could continue as it had for generations. And during that sad and difficult time, Delfina Madrid had always defended her and encouraged her to pray, because only almighty God knew his plan for her. When Mike was born, a healthy and beautiful child, the black clouds disappeared from Alma's life, and she embraced her new happiness, forgave all those who gossiped about her infertility, and loved and admired her husband even more for being a man and supporting her through thick and thin. But she also loved her friend, the widow, Delfina Madrid, a proud woman who accepted Alma for what she was, not for what she had or didn't have.

I know, Alma. Francisco broke the silence. But Ramon is still alive and in serious trouble. That boy will never survive prison or even the local jail. And his mother is ill; you saw her at the funeral. She was hurting. She will need money for an attorney, and we have to help her. Delfina Madrid, as you know, has been bitter for many years. I offered more than once to help fix her old house, but she was offended. She told me she didn't accept charity. I understand she's your good friend, Alma, but what else can we do? Tell us, please.

You do what you have to, Francisco, said Alma, but all I'm asking is that one of you should go and explain to her what your plan is; that's all. At least she'll have an idea of what is going on. She wants Ramon locked up. She blames him for her Danny's death. But maybe, Miguel, if you go talk to her and her daughter, Vivian, maybe Vivian will help you make her at least look at the alternatives. Que no?

Mike bit his lower lip and looked out the kitchen window at the golden sunflowers touching the window pane, as if they were listening in on their conversation. He didn't want to see Delfina Madrid. He still recalled her scene at the funeral, and it was still scary. Vivian Madrid was a fox and conceited. He didn't mind talking to her, but she was close to Danny, her brother, and she had been difficult before Danny's death. Now she might be impossible. And, she was always playing with Ramon's head, promising him things she would never give him, and the fool was madly in love with her, believing that she was going to keep her word, as other fools had.

OK, Mike consented. I'll go talk to her. Maybe you're right, Mother; maybe she'll listen and accept what has to be done, and Vivian might help me convince her it's the right thing to do. But Pops is also right: she's a proud widow, upset with Ramon and anyone who wants to help him.

They all sat quiet around the kitchen table, sipping coffee and eating pan dulce. Mike dipped the sweet bread into the coffee cup, soaked it, and then ate it, mushy and savory. The house was still cool because of its double adobe walls and high ceilings. His father put a huge swamp cooler on the roof of the house with ducts in every room. He used cedar shavings in the pads and, when it was turned on, the smell of fresh cedar saturated the chilled air, which felt damper because of the dry heat outside. Besides, it used less energy and chemicals than the regular AC. It was turned on if the heat became unbearable. His mother did much of the cooking outside on the grill, which was in the shaded patio. Old cotton, pear, and peach trees encircled the perimeter of the house and added needed shade during the hot days of summer. There were even some mora trees, but those were kept further away because when the berries ripened and dropped, they made a purple mess. "High maintenance" was the word his father used when they discussed the moras. His father had to practically rebuild the old house that belonged to his grandfather and his father, because it was built on sand and dirt without a proper foundation, as most of the old houses were built in the early days. With time, these homes built without a solid foundation would start to cave, and as they sunk little by little, the adobe would lose the stucco, dip, and crumble. Francisco Montes was more practical than nostalgic; he didn't want to tear down his grandparents' and parents' home, a home they had struggled to build from scratch. But he wanted to build a more comfortable place for his beautiful wife and future children. Besides, the adobe could be baked and utilized again, saving big time on resources and cash. With his father's permission and help, he rebuilt the old adobe into a larger, modern, comfortable structure, solidly built to last for years.

Mike studied his father's face. It was sunburnt but had few wrinkles; his hair, graying on the temples, was still thick; but what distinguished him was his thick mustache covering his upper lip, giving him a Zapata look. It was unreal, he thought, how this man could build a home from the ground up, including the plumbing and electrical, do the payroll for his men, and a variety of other things, and he didn't have a high school education. He was proud of his dad more and more every day that he paid attention to his accomplishments. He was also a great auto mechanic; he rebuilt car engines and transmissions as if he was putting together a toaster. The saying was that if you could overhaul a car or truck engine with a wire clothes hanger, you were bad; his father was close to that. But Mike loved his father because of the kind of man he was, not because of the things he could do. First of all, he wasn't a boozer, loud, a bragger, or mean, but best of all, he loved and treated his wife, Alma, Mike's mom, as the queen she was, and to Mike, that was gold—that was solid gold. Wow, he thought, if he turned out half the man his father was, he would be happy, maybe.

Alma broke the silence. Well, Miguel, what did you decide? Shall I call Delfina?

Oh, sure, Mamasita. I'll talk to her, but try to talk to Vivian also. She might influence her mother, and even a little would help. Who knows. She might agree to see me.

Good, Miguel. I think it's better this way. I'll go into our bedroom and use the phone there.

As Alma closed the door to her bedroom, which was in the back of the house, Mike's grandfather, Francisco's father, Arturo

Montes Sr., walked in the kitchen with his arms out, ready to hug Mike. Mike stood up and hugged his gran dfather in a tight embrace.

Que hay? Mikey!

You got it, Gramps, he answered. Sit; un café?

Porque no? Then he turned to Francisco. Hey, you old dog, que pasa?

Francisco smiled that smiled of his but said nothing.

Arturo Sr. was the patriarch of the Montes clan. He was retired and lived in Albuquerque with his oldest son, Arturo Jr., but stayed on and off during the cold winter months with his youngest son, Francisco, or with his other children scattered around the country. He always dressed up, wearing black dress pants, expensive shoes, and white polo shirts during the summer. His prescription sunglasses and white Panama hat of the finest palma always made him stand out in Las Flores. He gave the house to Francisco, as his father had given it to him, but not because Francisco was the youngest, but because Francisco was the only one that liked Las Flores enough to stay and not sell the house. His advice to anyone who listened was if you own property, don't sell it; if you don't own any, buy some. He was a self-made man; he took his boys out at an early age, as his father did, to work and learn a skill, any skill. His eldest son, Arturo Jr., took to the plumbing business in a big way. Arturo Jr. knew early on, he had to leave Las Flores if he was going to ever see any real money. And he did. The city was growing at a rapid pace, and he organized a skilled crew that was hired anywhere there was work. Arturo Jr.'s big payday came when he started working on government contracts, state and federal, and not only as a subcontractor but as the real vato. He worked up to twelve, fourteen hours a day; he worked hard, but he partied harder, paying for pussy in the cat houses of Ciudad Juarez and anywhere he could find it. His wife finally left him with six kids, but that didn't stop him. He married his Canadian housekeeper after a messy divorce. She worked as his house cleaner and caretaker of his two-thousand-acre ranch he had purchased in Montana; they fell in love and married. She gave him three more children but spent most of her time at the ranch in Montana. He used the ranch as a hunting lodge to impress his gringo contacts—men with the power to award contracts—wine and dine them, get them some girls, and he was in the running, ahead of the pack, always ahead.

How did you get here, Gramps? Mike asked.

Oh, your uncle Turi—as Arturo Jr. was called—dropped me off at the community center, and I walked here. Turi was gonna gas up; he'll be here any minute. We're on our way to Juarez to pick up some bottles of tequila and Oso Negro; my compas in El Burque love that Oso Negro. I stopped by the center to talk to that numb nuts Hector to make sure he got you in that program. Because I told him, Cabron, you better include Mikey; after all my, father helped build the church, I helped with the dance hall, and Francisco practically built the community center. I reminded him we built his parents' house for almost nothing and that I still had some influence with the board, so he better do the right thing. I also wanted Ramonsito in the program, but Hector gave me some mierda about this and that, but maybe the second group, he promised. I heard about the car crash; that breaks my heart. So young to die, that Danny boy. I don't recall him so well, but of all your friends, I liked Ramonsito the best. He was always so quiet and respectful, a perfect gentleman, rare to find these days. Is he OK, Mikey?

Oh, yeah. He'll make it, if we can keep him out of jail.

You talk to Pa Hanks yet?

That's where we're going next.

See that you do, and I'll send you a check when I get back to Albuquerque. If Pa Hanks can't do it for any reason, I'll bring in Hector's son; he owes me, but let's try to keep it local, if we can.

At this time, Alma walked into the kitchen. Arturo Sr. stood up to meet her. Mira nomas, la bella de las bellas, he announced and gave her a hug.

Alma was all smiles. Sit, sit, please. Coffee, eggs, and beans? Pan dulce?

No gracias, querida. You sit. We should be serving you, not you us. How has my boy Francisco been treating you? Tell me; he's not that big I can't take him out to the woodshed.

They all laughed, except Francisco, who only smiled. Alma loved her father-in-law and had forgiven him many years ago for the hard times between them when he had advised Francisco to leave her because of her inability to have children. Although he lived with them on and off, she never tired of his energy and know-it-all attitude. She missed him when he left, because he brought a certain joy into their lives with his funny jokes and stories of times past, and Mike seemed to listen to him and take his advice, especially during his difficult time, a time that still gave her nightmares.

Who brought you? Alma asked. What a surprise.

Turi; he dropped me off at the center. He's gassing up right now, and I hope it's the car he's gassing.

How is Turi? she asked, before he elaborated.

Working, you know, always working. He has to; he has six kids here and three in Montana with his Canadian wife, who still refuses to live in Albuquerque. He lives in the Northeast Heights, not in the South Valley, for Christ's sake. And Daniel, he's still in Okinawa with the navy, a lifer for sure. Otilia, she's in San Francisco with the post office. Not married yet; maybe she likes girls. Who knows. Ruth, she's still married to that idiot Pete. They run two muffler shops in Denver. Can you imagine? A muffler shop—it's just like running a doughnut shop, verda? Just open a garage and repair the whole car or truck. A muffler shop, que honda? And he allows her to manage one of them, por favor; she should manage both of them. And Ernest, Neto, he sticks with Turi; he has his own crew, but he lives in Santa Fe. They got a big contract at Holloman Air Base in Alamogordo, there's plenty of work, Mikey, if you care to get your hands dirty. He didn't even look at Francisco. But before Mike could answer, Arturo said, No, Mikey, you don't want to go out there in the desert; it's too hot. You stick with your plan. College is the best place for you. Que no?

They heard the heavy Cadillac on the driveway, and Arturo Sr. stood up, gave Alma a hug, and said good-bye to his son Francisco on his way out the door. Mike walked out with him to greet his uncle Turi. As they were walking out to the waiting car, Gramps slipped some money into Mike's pocket and placed his finger on his lips. Mike kept silent.

Remember, Mikey, he said as they approached the black Caddy, a kick to the balls, left hook to the head, a right cross, if needed. The bum'll go down and out, unless he has balls of steel. Few have. They will never mess with you again, believe me. That's the kind of pain a fellow never forgets. A black eye or busted lip, that's nothing, but a hard kick to the balls, which stays with you for a long time, a long time, Mikey.

OK, Gramps, gotcha, and thanks for the…for the advice. He gave his gramps a strong hug and then walked around to the driver's side to say hello to his uncle Arturo Jr.

Hey, Tio, how are you?

Arturo Jr. extended his large brown hand and grasped Mike's in a tight grip. I'm doing good, how are you, mijo? Hey, your cousins are waiting for you in Albuquerque; they can hardly wait for you to go to UNM this fall. Jr. already completed his first year, so he'll teach you the ropes. Remember, you can always stay at the house during the weekends or live with us if you find the dorms boring, OK? Give my regards to your mom and dad. Tell them I didn't go in 'cause we're short on time. Next time. Gotta go. See you soon. And they were off. Mike waved as the big shiny car glided into the morning sun, effortless and powerful, a gem of efficient technology, a status symbol of economic vigor.

Back in the kitchen, Alma studied her husband, who still sat in the chair with that look of a man who had drifted into the past or somewhere while he remained anchored to the present. Alma didn't say a word because it wouldn't have made any difference. She knew her husband as she knew herself, and when he had that abstruse, pensive look that seemed to reduce him to a lifeless statue, she knew he needed some space; she excused herself and went outside to water her garden.

Francisco never understood why, but every time his father and older brother were together, the memory of his mother pulled at him, and he relived those sad times. He recalled with exact certitude all the grief and suffering his father had inflicted on his sweet, frail mother for so many years, until he depleted her of the little vigor she possessed. Like the many times he disappeared Friday night after work and didn't return until Monday morning, smelling of alcohol and cheap perfume. He walked into the house in a rush, changed into his work clothes, picked up his metal lunch pail and coffee jug, dropped some bills on the kitchen table, and walked out again without saying a word to anyone. He went to work with the energy of a raging bull, and if you worked for him, you had to show the same energy or run the risk of losing your job. He pushed Arturo Jr. as the oldest, most of all; if he assigned him a job, he expected perfection. If Arturo Jr. fucked up, he had to redo the job and take the loss out of his own pocket. That molded Arturo Jr. into a fanatic, a perfectionist without a soul. He even took his two daughters to the worksites and worked them like men. His rationale was that if they stayed home and didn't lift a finger to help their mother around the house, then they were going to go work with him and earn their keep. He pushed them like he did the rest of his crew but paid them an honest wage when he felt they had earned it. They in turn hardened and changed and became scornful of men, sarcastic, and vengeful. They worked next to them, saw how weak and insecure they were, how full of shit and bravado they all were, except for their father and Arturo Jr. They respected those two, with their balls of steel, giving orders and demanding respect, taking chances few would take, and kicking ass when all else failed. Their father was their new God; they had a love- hate relationship with him that would last for the rest of their lives. Their mother they loved and respected in a detached way, because their father demanded it; if not for that, they had no emotional need of her enfeebled existence.

Francisco still remembered vividly when his father encouraged him to drop out of high school and join his crew. He was in his senior year, and, although his grades weren't great, he was still passing every class. His mother, who surprised him, objected but of course was overruled. She wanted him to be prepared to enter the seminary, something his father would never allow. He insisted on grandsons, not priests; his clan had to expand, not diminish. He forcefully argued that there were plenty of families that would be more than happy to donate their boys to the priesthood and their daughters to nunneries. He was not against religion; he considered himself a devote Catholic and even escorted his wife and children to church when he wasn't on one of his binges. But he always had an excuse to leave during the Mass. He walked around the outside of the buildings, looking for areas that needed repairs, smoking his long, thin cigars, and striking up a conversation with anyone who stopped and listen to him. He would be the first to admit that he never could comprehend what the priest was saying or trying to say; he didn't get it, so he left it alone. After Mass, he would be outside the church door thanking people for attending, shaking hands with the men, and checking out the women, always soliciting for work, always hustling for something.

When Francisco left school to join his father's crew full time, he was impressed with the knowhow and knowledge base his father had to work with. Before he had worked for his father only during the summer, a couple of hours here and there; all he did was dig trenches for pipe and load and unload the trucks. But now that he was full time, he saw that his father and older brother Arturo Jr. could read blueprints, do electrical work, do most things to put a building together, and patch things up pretty good. He also understood his father as an astute politician who worked the people and delivered the Eastside vote when called for. He was encouraged to run for the Eastside council seat but was too clever to even consider it; he knew that if he ran and lost, he'd have numerous enemies at city hall, and he needed those pinheads on his side when the contract bids went out for extended city water and natural gas for the areas of the Eastside and Chiva Town that still didn't have those services. He was pushing for Arturo Jr. to get the contracts. That would give him the experience and contacts to get more lucrative state and federal contracts, eventually. That's exactly what happened. He approached the homeowners who were on the list to get city water and gas to allow him to clean and cap their old septic tanks. He convinced them that he could empty the old, stinky tanks, fill them with sand and gravel, cap them with a concrete cap, and fill the cap with dirt so that they could even plant a garden on top. He also reminded them that if the city sent a letter mandating that it be done, they had to pay the city, and he could do it for half of what the city charged them. So he paid his cousin on the side, who worked for the city, to bring in a city truck during his lunch hour, suck up the piss and shit, and no one knew the difference. Then he sent Francisco and a couple of men to fill up the truck with sand and gravel from the huge arroyo that was a couple of miles southeast of Las Flores and do a couple of tanks a week.

Francisco understood now his father's insistence that his two daughters join his crew. It wasn't that he wanted them out of the house for wasting their time, as he told it to others. No, it was to shame the men on his crew to work harder and not be left in the dust by a couple of females. This was made clearer to him when one of the men asked him on a hot day while he was cutting pipe, Whatsa matter, brother, can't keep up with your sisters? And he answered with a smile, You keep up with them; they're Amazons. Another reason he wanted his children on the crew was to keep expenses low. Francisco was sure his father didn't pay them what he paid the other workers. But his men loved him; on Fridays after work, he invited them all to the local cantina and got them liquored up at his expense. He had a tab and wouldn't allow anyone to spend their own money on anything. They drank, sang, and danced until the cantina closed, and some would go home, but others kept on going until Monday morning, broke and hungover but ready to work. One fuck- up and they were let go. Francisco went home on Friday, like the other days of the week, and handed over his pay to his mother. She was always embarrassed to take his money, so she always gave him half back, knowing he wasn't going to throw it away on drink, for he had his cars and his savings to take care of. The girls would rush in, clean up, give their mother a kiss on the cheek, and rush out again. They didn't ask permission or say where they were going; they didn't have to. They knew their daddy wasn't gonna be home to pull the reins. So they left, searching for dances, as far away from their brothers as they could possibly get, knowing that the guys would never invite them to dance or even talk. If they knew Arturo Jr. and his crazy friends were around, only the very drunk and the very ugly asked them to dance, not knowing any better.

All that was in the past, history by now, but Francisco still couldn't shake it loose—but only when he saw his father and older brother together. Other than that, he was fine. They had their life, and he had his, but he had to get out of this mood and pronto. Alma would get worried, and Mike would want to know what was happening, and he didn't want to go into it; it wasn't worth it. So when Alma and Mike entered the kitchen, he switched gears.

Hey, Mike, what time did you get in last night? he asked in a conciliatory tone.

It was a little before midnight. I was at Linda's house. They were having a dinner for her brother; he enlisted in the marine corps. When I left the hospital, I remembered that she had mentioned the dinner and wanted me to join them. It was only family.

Oh, Linda called for you, Alma interrupted, excited that Mike was still seeing her. She called early, but you had just left. She is so nice, Miguel; she is the right one for you. Please don't break her heart. Don't hurt her. She will make some lucky man a perfect wife. I pray every night that lucky man is you; I just like her so much, Miguel. Please forgive me if I sound anxious.

No, no, there's nothing to forgive, Mother, but what if she breaks my heart? What if she hurts me?

I don't think so. She's not that kind of girl, and what do you think, Francisco?
I don't know, Alma, Francisco said. Remember, Mike is still kind of young to get too serious about...you know.

There you go, Mamasita, Father knows best. I better get going. See Vivian's mom and get that over with. I'm gonna hook up with Linda later on. Maybe I'll bring her over, and we could have dinner. How's that?

Oh, that would be wonderful, Miguel; wouldn't that be wonderful, Francisco? The four of us?

Well, don't go out of your way. Linda might have some other plans, but I'll call you. He gave Alma a kiss on the cheek and squeezed his father's shoulder and walked out the door.

CHAPTER ELEVEN

orenzo, Lencho Reyes, pulled up on his old pickup and parked in front of Sammy Q.'s junk-infested carport. He sat in the truck for a minute or two, holding the steering wheel with both hands, arms straight and stiff. He finally killed the engine and pulled a soiled handkerchief from somewhere and wiped away the sweat from his face. He climbed down from the pickup and walked toward Sammy Q., who was sitting in his old chair with his feet on a couple of used tires. He had seen Lencho sitting in the truck but didn't say a word, giving Lencho time to compose himself. Lencho approached Sammy Q. like a man who was behind two months in his rent and had come to ask, to beg, his landlord for more time to raise some cash, before he was put out on the street. He had been sleeping in his truck and had the look and smell of the unwashed. He was wearing a greasy Levi jacket and a long-sleeved work shirt under that, even though it was a hot day.

But Sammy Q. seemed happy to see him and welcomed him with a sincere gesture. He held out his hand, embraced the much taller Lencho, invited him to sit down, poured him a shot of sotol, and gave him a cold beer to chase it down with.

Lencho was embarrassed, but he shot down the fiery sotol with one gulp and hit the cold beer with the same determination. Sammy hit him again with another shot; it was a small shot glass, and he wanted his friend Lencho to relax and take a load off.

Thanks, Sammy, but I don't have any bread to lay on you, man, but...

Lencho, Lencho, my friend, Sammy said, que te pasa, amigo? Don't even go there, please. Don't insult me; no need to talk about that. Just enjoy it. Relax. It's a beautiful day, que no?

Lencho picked up the cold bottle of beer with a trembling hand, placed it on his cheek, and closed his eyes, allowing the cold glass to lower his temperature, if only for a brief moment. He opened his bloodshot eyes again, blushed, attempted a garbled apology, and put the bottle of beer back on the table. He excused himself, walked to his truck, placed his index finger on the side of one nostril, and blew out the other. He repeated the same procedure with his other finger, blowing the snot on the truck's tire. He pulled out his soiled hanky from his back pocket and wiped the leftover snot from his nose and hands. He walked back to his old sitting place, apologized again to Sammy, and took a hit from the bottle of beer. Lencho looked at Sammy, and Sammy looked at Lencho, like two men playing chess, but their hearts were in different places.

Finally, Lencho burped and then asked Sammy Q., I hear you wanted to talk to me, Sammy, dime. What's up?

Sammy hesitated; he had never seen Lencho so bad off. He reminded him of a tall pine tree, devastated by bark beetles, his sap sucked dry by the parasites. What was left was a dry profile of the tree, ready to tumble with the first breeze. But Sammy decided to go ahead with his plan; what else could he do? If it worked, it could help him and benefit Lencho—for a while, anyway.

Listen, Lencho. He poured him another shot of sotol. I need your help, brother. That's why I wanted to talk to you. I think we can work together in this thing.

Lencho shot down the sotol with a slam dunk, made a face, shook his head, and yelled out, Hot damn! Then he giggled, as if he just heard a silly joke.

You want me to sell junk for you, Sammy? Lencho asked, looking straight at Sammy. Get serious, my friend. Look at me brother, look at me. I rather ride the horse than eat. You think you can trust me—ha! Look at me, and look at you. You trying to set me up? Is that it? Shit, I'll do it. Anything to get some caballo blanco, anything. I'm hurting, brother. And he placed his hands on his face and rocked back and forth, moaning.

Sammy placed a small packet in Lencho's pocket and told him to go to the backyard and take his medicine. Lencho shuffled to the backyard with tears in his eyes and his nose running again.

Sammy picked up the novel he had been reading when Lencho drove up. It was The Tall Stranger, by Louis L'Amour, his favorite author. He wanted to find out if Rock Bannon was going to kill Zapata before Lencho returned from his little odyssey. But as he was in the middle of the messy fight, Lencho returned, in a better mood.

Thanks, Sammy. I appreciate what you've done for me. I feel much better now; thanks again. If there's anything I can do for you, just let me know, carnal.

Sammy placed a bookmark in the novel and scratched his head. He closed the book and carefully put it away. He looked at Lencho and said, in a deliberate manner, You know, there is something you can help me out with. He sat closer to Lencho and looked around to make sure they were alone. He lowered his voice, but not too low, because he didn't want to repeat what he was going to say, unless it was absolutely necessary. Lencho, he continued, it's very important that what I tell you is not—never—repeated to others, no one. I trust you to the max; that's why I'm sharing this story with you and no one else. If you agree to help me, and if we are successful, there will be a good reward for you. It will be worth your time.

And if we fail? asked Lencho.

Well, that's not even a given, said Sammy, sure of himself. Hear me out. There was a drop made in the desert, not too far away from here, about two weeks ago. It was a special gift for the big boys in Albuquerque and Denver. It was ten pounds of almost pure chiva. It was dropped at around three or four in the morning from a low-flying aircraft that disappeared beyond the border as quickly as it appeared. I was given the exact location of the drop area. I failed to find anything. I visited the area several times and returned empty handed. The big people in Albuquerque insist I find it, or else. I'd never try to rip those people off. If you enjoy living, you don't do dumb shit like that—only in the movies do you pull off shit like that. You know what I mean, right? Now, this shit is so pure that the people are concerned some jackass might have accidently picked it up and is selling it straight out, without working it. It will send a lot of junkies to hell and create a public outcry—bad for business, as you know. Now, I'm gonna ask you this first. Lencho, have you heard of any bragging by any thick-skulled fuckwit that he can produce top-of- the-line product?

No, man, nothing that good, ese, said Lencho, scratching his stubbled chin.

OK, Lencho, so here's where you can help yourself and help me in a big way. I want you to go back up there—I know you know the area. It's east of town, off the old Albuquerque road, but don't get too close to the mountains. You'll be off, way off.

Is it close to Snake Town?

It's between the old Albuquerque road and Snake Town but not close to Snake Town; stay away from Snake Town. Pretend you're hunting rabbits or looking for rocks in case you run into somebody. I doubt you will; you might. And don't forget to take some water 'cause you'll be doing a lot of scouting on foot through the dry scrub. There is a bag wrapped in heavy plastic and bound with tape. Do not—and I repeat, Lencho, do not open the bag, if you find it. Bring it to me. If I'm not here, wait till I return. I will reward you with cash, booze, or product, whatever you want. And Lencho, please don't share this information with anyone; it wouldn't be healthy for any of us. Comprende, amigo?

Lencho was on the nod while Sammy talked, but he digested most of the info, and he said he'd give it a try. He stood up and was scratching the back of his neck when Sammy asked him where he was going.

I'm going to find the stuff for you, brother. I like the desert. I like to walk out there alone. I like to get high in the desert and see the awesome colors when the sun sets. People call me a loser, Sammy; they say I had everything going for me. Even Hector kicked me out of the program, you know, the college program.

Hector! That sonovobitch. How could he?

No, man, Hector's cool; he saved me once, and I signed the contract, man, no drugs. Not his fault if I like to get high, escape from shit. I trip out in the desert, man. No big deal. People don't know me. I gave up what I never had; that's why it was so easy. I was never happy, Sammy, except when I was high. I couldn't keep up with all the demanding rules, man. I wanted to be free and run naked in the desert, but I couldn't do it because it wasn't kosher, but if I was high on drugs, then it was OK; it was expected. I could do whatever the fuck I felt like doing, as long as I was on drugs. So I did drugs. People left me alone, ignored me. And here I am, a free spirit— messed up but free. I have this itch, Sammy. When I scratch, it gets worse instead of better. So I scratch till my nails rip through the skin and draw blood. Then I need relief. You know the rest, Sammy Boy. Sometimes you're the relief and sometimes the curse. But I ain't blaming you, brother. I had a huge hole in my heart, and I believed I could fill it by being the best. And it was flattering for a while, but the hole kept growing, and I kept shrinking. I was missing her so much, Sammy—my mother. I couldn't stand it any longer. The smack brought me closer to her till I couldn't leave her anymore, and I won't, ever.

Sammy saw the tears running into Lencho's mouth and the despair that Lencho was struggling with. He felt bad for this talented young man who was so full of potential but was on a downward spiral toward self-destruction. He wanted to put his arms around him and console him, but he wasn't sure how Lencho would react. He wasn't even sure how he'd react, having no experience with this type of heavy emotional display. He was thinking that maybe, just maybe, there was a slight possibility that he was to blame for Lencho's fall. No, he in all honesty couldn't accept blame for Lencho's fall; sure, he took liberties when selling Lencho product, but Lencho was already an invalid when he first came to him. He was a broken spirit with a childhood desire to recreate his past, change his fate—something that was impossible to do, with or without drugs. If Lencho was a victim of things gone wrong, then where did it leave him, with baggage worse than Lencho's? He should be a basket case, and maybe he was to many, but he was far from reaching the bottom of the well, in his opinion.

Sammy stepped up closer to Lencho's right elbow, and then as Lencho lowered his right hand, Sammy put a small packet and some crumpled bills into his hand.

That's for gas money, Lencho, and the other—well, you know, to be taken as needed. Remember, if you find the bundle, don't open it. It has to be intact; that's vital. Bring them here as fast as you can get here, but be careful; don't drive too fast. We want to avoid problems, not create any. You gonna be OK, my man? By the way, I feel your pain, brother. One day I'll share my pain with you, but not today. Today is your day, and I respect that. So tell me, you gonna be OK? Yeah, I gotta be OK, Sammy, answered Lencho, rubbing his eyes with the inside of his hands, 'cause I want to find that chiva for you. I won't let you down. If it's out there, I'll find it. You've treated me like a real bro, Sammy. Thanks for your kindness. Most people stay away from me, but you, man, you're one of a kind. Thanks for being my friend, Sammy. I mean it.

Lencho walked to his pickup like a man in a dream, wondering when he was going to wake up but not really wanting to. He finally started the old pickup, and he sputtered away, leaving a cloud of black smoke behind to dissipate in the clear air of a warm day.

Sammy, vigilant as ever, watched as Lencho, in his old pickup, disappeared in the horizon, driving away from Las Flores into the vast, mostly empty area of jackrabbits and dry scrub, dirt roads, arroyos, abandoned mines, and skeletons of things that once were. It was a place of deep beauty for the creative mind and a desolate environment for others, but a real estate bonanza for the speculative souls who had the vision and the money to act on the future. But Sammy Q. didn't fit in any of those categories. He was just Sammy. He lived a day at a time, with no inclination to worry about the past or the future. As long as he had his friends around buying his stuff, he was happy. He never made any money—just enough to keep up his inventory and sell a little bit of this and a little bit of that. He understood his limits and refused to set himself up for disappointment, so he stuck to his area of expertise and left it to others to change the world. His only concerns for now were that he wasn't setting up poor Lencho and that the big boys in El Burque and Denver wouldn't somehow connect Lencho to the missing product. That was a major concern because he knew this was a special prize. A little over 5 keys of special shit would send anyone into a tailspin and bring the dogs of war on his ass. For that much clean product, the big boys would sell their mothers down the river with no qualms. He was sure that they were smart enough to know he couldn't push that much product around Las Flores. And if he had it and made a run with it to Los Angeles or Chicago, the word would get back to them before it hit the streets. What a tangle, he said to himself and walked into the house to give his Granny a bite to eat before his friends arrived—some to drink, others to talk, but most of them to hang out with the affable Sammy Q.

CHAPTER TWELVE

The circle was in order, and the people sitting in the circle were patiently waiting for Hector to arrive and get the damn show on the road. It was a support group for men and women who had been hurt in romantic relationships, like a painful divorce where perhaps there was still a semblance of love and respect, a lover who had been rejected and told to go to hell, or any other occasion where pain was involved—lots of pain and grief—and someone had the misfortune to absorb the majority of the suffering.

It was a small group, never more than ten people, just perfect for the painful heartaches the group could exorcise from their troubled souls, if they were honest and didn't attempt to play games. Most in the group were older than thirty, but one or two were younger and had already experienced, with disastrous results, the doings of Cupid. Everyone had a story to tell, and Hector did his best to draw it out, little by little, if possible. The group had become acquainted, a cohesive unit that functioned at times in dynamic fashion. Hector was fascinated with the moral lapses these people had tumbled into, and all for the temptation of feeling the strong, emotional, and physical pull that demanded more than an individual could many times give or wanted to give.

Hector, when first approached with the plan, dismissed it as not practical. But when the off-college campus offered it at the center, he jumped on it. Although Hector never completed his psychology degree, he had enough practical experience to make a professor proud. He had led many types of groups throughout his career in the many cities he had worked. He always considered himself a counselor first. He loved to disentangle the human heart and expose it to alternative visions, and although this time it wasn't about substance abuse or at-risk youth, it was fundamentally the same: emotional scars that widened if not stabilized. He followed the premise that talking about your emotional baggage could never hurt, and it might even help, in some cases.

The session was held once a week on a Saturday morning at eleven sharp in the dining room at the community center. The tables were moved out of the way, and the chairs were placed in a circle, and on occasion, Hector asked Concha to lay out some coffee and snacks for the group. Eventually they brought their own treats and laid them potluck-style on the table. Although Hector frowned on the practice—he didn't want it to become that kind of group—he never mentioned it or denied them the sharing experience. During that hour or longer, depending on the intensity of the discussion, the center was closed, and no one was allowed to enter. It was a private and sensitive session that could be easily sabotaged by intruders. Flyers were posted outside and inside the center weeks ahead, announcing the times and dates that the center was going to be closed, for how long, and why. The flyers also stated what kind of class it was and the deadlines for enrollment. After that particular date, no newcomers would be admitted, and the reasons were obvious.

Hector at first pretended, for no apparent reason, to dislike the group. The diversity of personalities, he thought, would be difficult or even too boring to stay engaged. But after the first meeting, he loved it. This was the kind of action he had always enjoyed, and even though they weren't the younger, low-life druggies he had worked with in the past, there was a lot of heat and passion in the group. And as with the phony toughness of those insecure and suicidal drug addicts, who refused to admit it but welcomed the attention, of a group who listened, and showed concern. That was the magic moment that melted the animosity and they were hooked in talking about their lives, then there was little difference in the dynamics of the groups. Hector understood that. He had seen it work again and again and never tired of being part of it.

The group sat in silence, waiting for Hector. Three members had dropped out, and three new members had joined. Today was the last day for new members, and the others felt uncomfortable because they had not been introduced to the new group. They were suspicious of a young man in work clothes, a local, who didn't remove his dark shades, didn't smile, and scuffed the floor with his black steel-toed work boots. Hector walked in with a mug of coffee in his hands and closed the double doors of the dining room. He had been in his office all the time working on some papers. He set his mug of coffee on a table and joined the group.

Good morning to you all. As you know, this is the last day to join the group, he said. Now, people may drop out but won't be able to join, so the group will be solid. My name is Hector, as you all know; I'm the director of the center. We added three members, and they completed the group. I will go over the rules again and explain the sessions for the benefit of our new members. Then they will introduce themselves, and we can start. This class is six weeks, and I will issue certificates of completion to the brave ones who complete the course. We decided to convene on a Saturday morning in case you work during the week and have other things to do weeknights. They have advised me that the completion certificates can be utilized to satisfy some court-mandated hours for anger management, some cases of domestic violence, and other minor offenses. I can't advise you on those issues; I'll send the paperwork to the off-college campus, and you can take it from there. The rules are simple: when a person is talking, they get complete attention with no interruption whatsoever. When they are done, they can answer questions, if they so desire. Go to the bathroom before we start so the person talking does not have to alter the flow or change mood as you leave and return. If you have to miss a session, it has to be an emergency, and you have to give me at least a twenty-four-hour notice. More than one absence, and you will be dropped. Be on time, because the doors are locked, and no one will be admitted in after we start. If you have any questions, see me at the end of the session.

The last person to introduce himself was the young man with the dark shades. He removed the shades and attempted a shy smile. He had two missing front teeth, and his upper lip sucked in at the empty space when he talked. Now everyone relaxed because they could see why he didn't smile much. My name is Leo Lemon, he said. I'm from the Eastside barrio; I have to report to work after class. I work at the glass warehouse on Sierra, next to the hospital. I drive a forklift and sometimes make a delivery; that's why I'm dressed as I am.

Only Leo Lemon was in fact from the Eastside; all the other nine were from the Westside or areas outside of Las Flores. The folks from the Eastside barrio didn't believe in sharing their lives with strangers; that just wasn't their thing. They could do it drunk at a bar or a party, maybe in a confessional with a priest, but never in a setting where they could perhaps get some benefit out of the exchange. But Hector could relate to this; he hadn't expected anyone from the barrio to sign up for the group. That was the reason he never proposed any groups such as this, because he knew they would stay away and look down at the few who might risk it and make an effort to attend—and not only attend but participate in the give and take.

Well, well, and welcome all. Hector beamed, scratching his salt-and-pepper beard, which he had neglected for months. I'm elated you are here on this beautiful morning. I will go first. I know I already did on the first meeting, but it will break the ice for the new members. I will talk about a different episode of my life, one not very pleasant that left me if not devastated then close to it. And I'll remind you all again that whatever we discuss here is confidential, so please respect that, and I guarantee you the group will be a success. So let's get started.

I fell in love with my first cousin at a young age when visiting my grandmother, Hector said. She was left to live with my grandmother by her mother, my aunt, for an unknown reason. I wanted to confess to her that I loved her after seeing her on several occasions, but was intimidated by her beauty and sophistication. She was a couple of years older than I was; at that age it was difficult to approach a female and admit you were crazy about her and even more difficult if she happens to be your first cousin. I saw her grow up with relationship problems and the pain they can cost. She eventually got married, but after two children and a messy divorce, she ended up living alone in a house not too far from here. One way or another, some years later, I landed on her front step on a hot July night with a cold six of brew. It wasn't if we were strangers, but she had dismissed me once with a get-lost look from her divine face, which hurt me more than I would ever admit. But this was now a different time and a different person. She was soft and needy, willing to give, if the giving was mutual. She was still firm and young looking, a delicate maturity, common only to a selected few. After going through many of life's tribulations, she remained sensual and easy to love, regardless of the blood that ran through our veins. My love for her that night brought back the passion of my youth, when my heart was attached to that love, to her.

Hector fell silent, his eyes on the group in an attempt to gauge their emotion, to see if they were with him, feeling the forbidden love he had kept secret for so many years. And they all were. There was not a sound from them but a heavy beating of the hearts, longing to be in his place and taste the pleasure of that unforgettable hot night. It was an event that, although never tasted by them, was still theirs, if only through the words of another, and they wanted more from Hector—they wanted his soul on a silver platter. They wanted his heart exposed to the limit to deliver the real man behind the mask, a naked man who is not afraid to be touched by demons in the night. And Hector was more than ready to give them the works. He was like a man on a mission, a mission to purge his soul and release a river to saturate a parched land.

He cleared his throat and sipped coffee from his mug. As I was telling you, he continued. That hot summer night, on that indistinguishable step, my life changed. My life changed, and I had no idea it could happen so fast and so deep. I felt the heat of her voice, the tenderness in her heart, and the simple desire to never look back. I felt it was time to go beyond conversation and explore the possibility that our time to love each other had arrived, and nothing or no one could stop us. Falling in love, my friends, deeply in love, can be a serious proposition. Falling in love with your first cousin can impose all kinds of sanctions and taboos. The gossip of family and friends in their most insulting manner, as you can imagine, had to be set aside and ignored, because I had opened my heart, like a flower breathing fresh air. I was still in love with the woman. The girl who had turned my life upside down during my youth was now so close, I could touch her marvelous skin, and nothing was going to keep me away from the woman I loved, from the woman of my dreams. Hector paused for a few seconds.

I picked her up in my arms, Hector continued, scratching his beard but still at a steady pace and low voice, but clear and strong, as if he were on the stage. And in a way, he was. I picked her up in my arms and walked with her through the front door, all the way to her bedroom, and placed her gently on the bed. I was already kissing her wildly on the lips and face. We made love the entire night, as if we were long-time lovers separated for years, but our love for each other had never been forgotten. It was that tender and passionate. We talked in low voices, almost whispering, as if afraid our inflections would wake us from our enchanted dream. We talked about the numerous divorces and drugs that had invaded the community like a plague and had brought down so many of our friends and relatives.

And at this time, my friends, she told me about her loveless marriage, her ugly divorce, and giving up her two small children to her husband. It was a decision that crushed her heart, because she couldn't fight him anymore. She was exhausted, and by then, she only desired her freedom: freedom away from him, freedom to choose her own destiny. And in every word she expressed, there was a sense of loss, a sadness that cloaked her in a dark cloud. And I promised that with my love for her, I would help her forget most if not all of the pain in her life, because I loved her with a passion I had never experienced before and would never experience again, I was so sure of that. We were brought together by an unexplainable force that made every minute spent with her an occasion of jubilant success. We made love as if it was going to be the last time, never knowing what kind of action the family was going to implement to separate us. It was if the closeness of the blood made the intimacy more intense, more pleasurable, and I wanted it all the time. I was having infrequent sex with my girlfriend, and the reason was obvious, of course; there was plenty of apprehension, but I denied every word of gossip about my cousin until another cousin walked into the bedroom unannounced and found us naked in bed.

Well, what can I tell you, my friends, Hector continued, but this time staring at the floor, as if the floor could provide him with a quick end to his intimate confession. I thought I was willing to sacrifice and live with the heavy burden that was for sure coming, all for that love, that love that made my life livable. But when she confided in me she wanted to have my baby and move away with me to start a new life, my heart stopped, and my flesh felt like a raging wildfire that couldn't make up its mind where to go. Sure, I was flattered, as any man would be, but the idea of me being a father seemed to me huge and somehow strange. I was young and ambitious and had a whole life ahead of me to start fathering, especially when I still needed a father myself—see my point? If our love had been dismissed by some relatives as a fad or an immature infatuation, fathering a child with my first cousin would for sure have alienated those folks who had given us some support. So I did what I believed was the best thing for all of us. I ran like a criminal in the night.

I left town alone with a broken heart and left the love of my life behind, a decision that haunted me for years, a decision that had a major impact on my relationship with women for many years after.

Hector, with his head down, sighed like a condemned man whose execution had been delayed for twenty-four hours. All eyes were on him, each deciding what action they would have taken: run away like a coward, alone? Run away with the delicious prize? Or stay, marry, and face the consequences that would eventually inflict some pain in the relationship? Hector had tasted the forbidden fruit and left it in the garden to spoil. How many of them had not fantasized about having sex with a close relative? And here was Hector, exposing their dirty little secrets and making them resurface in their sick minds, but he at least had the balls to talk about his, air it out, as they twisted in convoluted spasms of regret, because they hadn't taken any action. And if they had, it wasn't beautiful love like Hector's, but hideous and sinister, an ulcer of recrimination and self- loathing that usually ended with some type of abuse.

Leo Lemon was the only one in the group from the Eastside barrio. He didn't know Hector that well, but he knew who Hector was. Leo must have been very young when Hector left Las Flores, but he remembered his older siblings mentioning Hector on his rare visits to his parents' house. He really didn't pay attention until Hector returned to live in Las Flores and accepted the job as director of the Eastside Community Center. He couldn't believe this was the same vato who at times ignored you, even though you were standing right in front of him. The same pendejo who people said had so many degrees he could fill a sack of mole with them. Leo was wondering which cousin Hector had screwed; Hector had a few, but Leo was confident his older sisters or brothers would know. He was dying to tell them what had come out of the mouth of Hector el Viejo and wondered if Hector Jr. was a product of this mischief between cousins.

Hector raised his eyes and scrutinized the group. He searched for that quick reference, that body language that would tell him if his admission was a success or a futile exercise in lip aerobics, a K-5 through a desert of dead people, a left hook to the liver that was all but useless. He knew they were mature adults with enough baggage to sink a battleship. Except for Leo Lemon, who was young and stupid, these vatos could provide him with a wealth of personal tragedies. He wanted to help them, but they had to help themselves. This was a sure way, but that didn't mean he couldn't enjoy their bouts with reality, their battles with windmills, and the barking at trees that was now accepted as part of their personalities. He wasn't going to attempt to publish any of this crazy shit; it was just for him to reflect on while sipping a cup of tea on quiet evenings.

Hector scratched his beard and said in the same low voice he had utilized all day, I have disclosed deeds that I'm not particularly proud of—things not even a priest has heard, no offense to the religious. But sometimes you have to drag the past out of yourself, even if it's intimate and painful, and expose it to the light of day. And if it's the present that harbors this nausea, by all means, let's see if we can stop this hemorrhage of, you know, delusions, but don't allow me to put words in your mouth or in your mind. That would be counterproductive, as you all know. Now, we must have someone else share, share whatever they feel comfortable sharing. Please, anyone.

The group waited in silence, waiting for the next volunteer to open that secret chamber that allowed only a few to peep in and see the landscape of jumbled journeys and hijacked dreams. They all wanted to talk, but their mouths were filled with gravel. Only the mind screamed and tore itself to pieces in a desperate attempt to flush out the angry vipers that showed no compassion for the owners of the house. Finally, a mature man volunteered, a high school teacher who had married one of his female students. She later ran away with a football player after three months of marriage, but not before convincing him to cash out his retirement fund, leaving him with nothing but memories of a young fox and longer years of service in the public schools. Not a pretty story, but one that made some rethink their priorities.

My name is Pete Rios. I teach auto mechanics at the high school. In love and sex, he continued with a strong voice, a little on the angry side, you can have sex till your nuts turn blue, but it ends. When it's over, it's over. You don't need a special telegram to let you know. If you do, you're in a hell of a fix. When you're not wanted anymore, and the reasons are too complicated to bother explaining them to you, your mind takes a hit; your self-esteem bleeds. You cannot convince yourself you failed in your effort to give it your all, to be sexy, a good lover, or a better husband, and the hurt eats you up alive. You have no references to fight this level of grief, because it's so dark and deep that your life becomes a shadow the sunshine cannot easily penetrate. The anger and the frustration are so compelling that I not only wanted to hurt myself but others, and I considered myself a pacifist, a man of peace. The humiliation was another kick in the balls I had to live with. I had to face my family and colleagues and humbly listen to their sanctimonious sermons and their pretentious advice every time they had a chance to dish it out. My career was on the line, but thank God, the girl was eighteen when we married. That is what love can do and does, as we speak. It destroys trust and tramples it on the dust. For no instrument to inflict pain has ever been devised to lacerate the human heart in such a forceful way.

And the man, Pete Rios—Mr. Pete, as he was called by the most disrespectful students—placed both hands on his face and closed his eyes in an effort to erase the image of that young woman, that young woman who had been like a thorn in his ass for the last few years. His life had been wrecked, his life savings depleted, and there was still no relief, no escape from that demon Madonna, who awakened his desires along with his sorrow. The sensation of skin touching skin in a naked race to satisfy and be satisfied was new to him, and the consequences were never considered because his heart was engulfed in a flame he thought could only spread. The sucking of one firm, young breast after the other was to him compensation for a long road traveled. The hot lips and tongue, the succulent nectar that the hummingbirds know so well, was his; his confidence extended beyond all horizons, and he believed he had reached the pinnacles of heaven. But it was an illusion, an illusion that only pent-up lust can create, and instead of holding onto it like a hard-won trophy, he wanted to expel it from his soul. It was a difficult task, even to the most disciplined disciples.

Mr. Pete removed his hands from his war-torn face, red and wrinkled from the pressure placed on it from his large, strong, hands, and attempted to compose himself, because he still had something more to add to his sad journey. And was it worth it, he exclaimed in a voice too loud, even to his liking. I mean, look at us, he continued, more self-contained. Look at us: all men, all wounded, with bullets in the heart, looking for a lonely den to crawl in like a wounded wolf, knowing he's useless to the pack. And for what? A piece of ass, a promised love that never materialized. Was it worth it? Of course not, and you all know it. And if you say it was, you are deluding yourselves in a big way. What happened to the three women who were in the group? They dropped out, as you all know, and three men joined the group—all hurt, I presume, by the opposite sex. They dropped out, in my opinion, because they didn't want us to learn their secret on how they hurt men and hurt them deep. Don't misunderstand me; I don't hate women or have turned into a misogynist. No, not at all. It's just that…they…they…I have nothing else to say. And he stopped talking suddenly as if something deep inside him had advised him to stop the nonsense and instead reflect on his mother and the other women in his life who had made the rough sailing in his life a little smoother.

Well, well, Hector interjected, attempting to up the tempo before everyone was swallowed up in the depressive mood that Pete had introduced. We have to understand, he continued, that the women that were in the group had their reasons for dropping out. We must respect those reasons, whatever they happen to be. We can't force anyone to stay in the group; as you all know, it's up to the individual. What more can I say? Does anyone have any questions for Mr. Rios?

Leo Lemon was dying to ask that old fool Pete how he ever made himself believe he could hold onto that young pussy. And if Lencho Reyes was the boy she ran off with. But since it was his first time, he wasn't sure if it was appropriate.

OK, then, Hector continued. If there are no questions for Mr. Pete, we have time for one more participant to share. Anyone?
They kept quiet, hesitant to participate, not wanting to look foolish as Pete Rios always did when he discussed his young chick. They looked at each other like sheep waiting for the sheepdog to bite them on the ass and direct them to their next destination.

Leo Lemon said to himself, Hell with it. He raised his hand, forgetting he wasn't in the classroom but in a therapy session, where raising your hand didn't get you any brownie points. Hector, I like to try it, man. I mean, I know this is my first time, but if you all don't mind, I got a little something to say about a real good friend of mine, a real vato.

By all means, Leo. You're part of the group, my friend. You don't have to ask; just jump in when you feel you're ready, as long as no one else is talking. The floor is yours, brother.

Thanks, Hector. Well, like I started to say, this happened not too long ago. I was at my friend's apartment. He'll remain nameless, to protect his privacy, you know.

Leo looked at Hector, then at the others, with the assurance of a district attorney who had an airtight case against an unlucky sucker. His upper lip sucked in between the gaps where his front teeth used to be, but he didn't seem to mind. He just pushed his upper lip back out with his tongue and kept on going, looking a little like a flathead catfish sucking up crap at the bottom of the lake. But he was articulate enough to make everyone keep his eyes on him and take in every filthy word he uttered.

Anyway, he continued, the vato was taking the cheese out of his toenails using a little pointed stick, the kind the professionals use, when the chicks we were waiting for walked in the front door and made themselves comfortable. My friend continued to dig for the cheese and wiped it off on a tissue resting on his lap. The girls, sitting on a sofa opposite from him, pretended that what they were witnessing was too nasty to be happening. They averted their eyes as much as they physically could, not wanting to attract unnecessary attention to themselves.

Then the puto—my friend, but not that kind of puto—got off his ass, pitching the tissue on the floor, close to the girls' shoes. They wanted to kick at the tissue but thought it rude. He walked into a closet and returned with a can of air freshener. He sprayed the two-bedroom apartment with about half the can. It was as if he was spray painting his placa on a public wall.

Leo Lemon paused and gazed at the strangers in the group with his large eyes and fish mouth as if he was in an aquarium, and the strangers were peering back at him in silence. He enjoyed this: no obscene jokes, no interruptions, and no lewd gestures directed at him. He had a captive audience for the first time in his life, and they were listening to him, every word. He only wished his secret hero was here, Mike Montes. He always wanted to be like Mike: smart, a fast talker, a good-looking ladies' man, and he could throw blows, as many assholes had discovered when they were picked up from the dirt with busted lips and blood-spattered faces. Mike wasn't a cookie cutter, and he had proved it. But Mike would rather hang with that weasel Ramon than him; that was irritating, he concluded. Leo Lemon was satisfied, for the time being, that he had joined the group, trying to remember if had to go to work, as he told the group, or go back home and wash the dishes his mother had asked him to do. What the hell? he thought. It didn't matter.

Then my pendejo friend, Leo continued, after the spray adventure, which seemed to give him much pleasure, started flossing his teeth and flinging the used floss, loaded with product, into the kitchen sink. He had no relationship with the fact I was gonna prepare dinner in less than an hour. That's what I promised the girls if they visited us at the apartment, and they seemed to be projecting a bit of an appetite. Then my friend looked straight into my eyes and asked me, with a concerned look, if everything was all right. I didn't answer him because I didn't get the question; I wasn't sure what he wanted to hear. But I comprehended my friend; he still had implanted in his confused head a rigorous mental image of times past when being busted with a joint in your possession could get you hard-core time in a prison in Tejas. And that could ruin your career, if you were fortunate enough to have one. He smoked pot in Tejas during that time and never considered the consequences until he got busted. After that, he was a changed man. He smelled the police everywhere, and when he smoked, he couldn't sleep thinking of different places where they were going to raid his apartment. He decided to move, leave Tejas, and relocate to Frisco, where he was sure he could find a more tolerant system. And he did move, and he smoked weed anytime he wanted and even kept a whole baggie instead of a couple of jays at a time—can you imagine that? But then the weed affected him different; the quality was better, or the quantity was excessive because he got nervous and edgy. The high was creating another side in him that was sometimes dark and the other times harsh, nothing in between. He wasn't enjoying what he once thought was gonna be a wonderful experience, and since my friend, my main friend, is smart, he stopped smoking. The trip wasn't worth it anymore, so he gave it up, cold turkey, can you believe that? But the transition to booze wasn't as profitable as he once believed it would be.

I'm afraid it wasn't, Leo continued, because he started hitting the bottle more and more. The alcohol became a daily doings, 'cause he didn't get paranoid while getting drunk, but it altered his personality somewhat. He thought himself a badass, a guy who thinks he can kick ass. The only problem being was he didn't have the experience to back up his lip. When drunk, his personality shifted. He became overly aggressive and even physical at a drop of a hat. Let me give you an example, OK? He came upon a fellow in a bar that was pulling a girl's hair in a not-too-tender manner. My amigo rushed over to save the poor girl from further humiliation and pain. It turned out the girl was the guy's younger sister, and he was reminding her, as gentle as he could in public, not to repeat going to the bar without his consent. But my vato was already in too deep to change the conversation. The assassin couldn't really punish his sister in public, although he wanted to, because he was worried it get back to his parole officer, who would never understand the cultural nuance—although they had the same beliefs in many other things. But here was a chance to release his hostility and stay on the good side of those who hate men who beat women. My friend said the pinto was shaved bald and heavily tattooed on the neck and head. There was one on his neck that particular screamed out, done with India ink and a sewing needle—a favorite of prison inmates—in large block letters. It spelled out "KILL." He was wearing a tank top, and his bulging biceps and forearms were also covered with tattoos of the most dangerous predators in the animal kingdom.

Leo paused, but only for a second or two, maybe longer. He didn't want to lose his flow. He wanted to tell his story; he needed to tell his story, even if he had to embellish some of it, and why not here? So the pinto asked my friend, Leo continued, he asked my friend a very simple question, if he—meaning my friend—had the dangerous habit of meddling in other people's private conversations, but before my friend could answer, the brute shoved him with both hands so viciously my friend almost flipped over. He came crashing to the floor, sliding on his back until a table leg stopped him a distance from the bar. His head hit the metal table leg so hard that he suffered a concussion and was hospitalized for a couple of days. The ape and his sister left the bar, hand in hand, conversing as if nothing out of the ordinary had happened.

Another time, my buddy got into it with a cop who was going to arrest a drunk who urinated on the door of the patrol car. My friend protested to the officer he couldn't take him in for such an insignificant act and that the car door, in any way, seemed not to be bothered by it. The officer turned to my friend and advised him not to get involved, that interfering with an officer of the law, while that officer was performing his duty, could get him arrested and worse. My friend inched up too close to the cop and started an argument. He must have known there was no way he could win. When the officer got fed up with my friend's insults, he forgot about the other drunk and clubbed my friend to the ground with his club, cuffed his ass, threw him in the back of his patrol car, and booked him in the drunk tank of the city jail, charged with public intoxication, assault on a police officer, and resisting arrest.

After that last incident, my friend said, No More Frisco, and he ended up here. The booze was killing him, and here he has been sober for a time now, although he takes a little toot now and then. But when he does, he still gets nervous and can't relax until he sprays, barricades the doors and windows, and makes sure everything is in order. But other than that, the dude's cool. He can hang through the tough times; God knows all the experience he can provide when the chingazos are flying everywhere, and you're going nowhere but down. You need a guy like that to help you escape some ridiculous set-up and save your ass from an embarrassing ass kicking from some punk-ass pussy who wants to enhance his reputation or some pendejitos who want to make their bones and attack like a pack of hungry wolves, and you go down, if they are determined and are led by an alpha nutcase who doesn't take no for an answer. Or they'll run away if you hit hard and kick harder and beg for help from their big brothers, but that's another story.

No, my friend has this natural gift of perceiving an area with bad karma where the shit is gonna explode, and you don't have any business being there, see what I mean? So you take care and avoid the area where your ass is not wanted, for whatever reason. He also gives helpful advice on what not to take when you cross the border: mota and guns. He is full of wisdom and dispenses it kindly, not in an exaggerated way, not in a way to offend your masculinity and leave you groping for answers in an empty closet. No, man, he's not that bitter. He's not gonna challenge your fundamental foundation of who you are and make you look into yourself with the mask off. He would never do that; no way, ese.

Hector kept looking at his watch, trying not to be too obvious that he was concerned with the time. This shit face Leo Lemon was a motor mouth, something he never expected. He thought Leo would give a short bitch about his penis being too small or how he had dreams or nightmares of doing his grandmother, but no, the weirdo went off on a tangent about his friend, and if that friend was for real, then he should be in the group, and if the friend wasn't real, then Leo Lemon had some real problems with dual personality issues and should be seeking real help, not pulling his dick for attention in front of these nutty but honest people. He looked at his watch again; this time he lifted his arm to make it obvious that time was up. He had a ton of paperwork, and the auditor was coming on Monday to go over his books. He had to make sure every goddamn receipt was in its proper place, all money accounted for to the last penny, because that was federal and state money. Those dimwits could waste millions in useless shit, he thought, but when it came to feeding and assisting the have-nots, watch out. Less is more; spend what is allocated and not a penny more.

Hector cleared his throat. Well done, Leo, Mr. Lemon, he said. Well done. Where has the time gone? Any questions for Leo before we break it up?

The men in the group stood up, looking at Leo with mixed reactions, some with admiration for a gutsy performance, others seeing "crazy" written all over him. Then Pete Rios asked, before the group broke up—although some were out the door, running to salvage the rest of their Saturday—What did you fix the girls for dinner? Pete found food much easier to manage than women.

Oh, shit! Hector said to himself. Don't get Leo started again, Pete, for Christ's sake. Leo should have his own talk show, and Pete, you could be his lap dog and converse for eternity—but not here, not now, please. Hector couldn't leave until the group had exited the building. Then and only then could he engage in something else.

Kind of you to ask, Leo perked up, smiling, exposing his toothless, purple gums where his two front teeth were missing. I fixed them shrimp enchiladas with cheese and no onions: New Mex– style stacked enchiladas chatas—you know what I mean, doncha, Pete? I bought the shrimp and red chili at Santos's. I cut the heads and tails off the shrimp—a small amount; that's all I could afford— and washed them good. Then instead of boiling them, I fried them in lard for a few minutes, for better taste. The corn tortillas, with plenty of red chili, were stacked on plates in the oven after swimming in hot lard for a few minutes; then I added yellow American shredded cheese on top and in between, then the shrimp on top, and let them sizzle until the cheese bubbled, took them out, added a pinch of garlic salt and pepper, served them with cold Mexican beer, and you got yourself a feast, brother. Oh! And a small side of Spanish rice, dry, and refried beans. You don't want to eat too many beans, sabes? You might get some action with the ladies after, but one of the girls was my cousin, and the other I wanted to fix up with my friend, but he was still going through serious divorce withdrawal.

And for dessert, Leo? asked Pete.

Ah, for dessert, I served them glazed apricots.

Oh! How did you do the apricots? asked Pete, all excited, frothing at the mouth.

Hector was glancing at his watch, thinking that those two comadres should be in the kitchen with Concha.

Well, answered Leo, knowing what he was doing to the hungry Pete. I put half a cup of water, half a cup of honey, and half of sugar in a large olla and stirred and stirred until all that was mixed in good. Then I added the apricots and cooked them until the apricots were tender. I kept on stirring on and off for about twenty minutes or so. Then I let the apricots cool in the syrup for about a couple of hours. I did all that at my mom's house; of course she helped out. Don't think it was all me. Then to finish, my friend rewarded us with a bottle of vanilla cognac, muy rica, Pete.

Where did you learn to cook such good stuff, Leo? asked Pete, sincerely interested.

Oh, I was a pearl diver at the Azteca.

Pearl diver? asked Pete, a little confused.

A dishwasher, Pete, lava truchas, you know. I got to know the chef, became friends, and he taught me a lot of stuff. Santos didn't mind 'cause I could help out during rush hours. He even offered me a job as a cook, but I said naw.

Hey, Leo, Pete said, I'm going to the Azteca right now. You care to join me?

Thanks but no thanks, Pete. I need to talk to Hector.

As Pete left, Leo turned to Hector. I need to talk to you, Hector. It's urgent.

Hector thought to himself, You've talked enough, pinhead; what else can you say?

OK, Leo, but I have a lot of work to do, so say what you have to say.

Well, it's kind of touchy, Leo said, but if you don't mind others getting into your business, well, that's up to you.

Hector looked at Leo with murder in his eyes, all the time thinking, This little turd face is pushing—what the hell can be so touchy as needing a private audience?

Hector conceded and walked toward his office. Leo followed as people entered the center. Once in Hector's office, Leo advised Hector to close the door. The less interruptions, the better. Hector shut the door after hanging a sign on the doorknob that stated, Meeting in Progress. You happy now, Leo?

You better sit down, Hector, Leo suggested, as he sat in a chair in front of Hector's desk. I have a message for you, he continued. And remember, I'm only the messenger. I hold no grudge or loyalty to either party, but as I speak, you're a dead man, Hector. Concha's husband, Tito—I'm sure you know him—is aware you are boning his wife. Now, Tito is losing his patience—not because you're doing Concha; he gives a shit about that. It's a matter of a bruised ego because his friends are making jokes about it. You know how that goes, Hector. Now, Tito, as you know, can be pretty unpredictable. When he gets drunk, which is often, he can be dangerous, not only to himself but to others. He will put a bullet in your back when you're not expecting it or throw a brick through your window in the middle of the night when you're lost in sleep. And you know what that can do to your nerves, Hector. He is already a pinto, so he knows he'll return a hero, and the county will take care of Concha and the kids. So you can't scare him about doing time, Hector; he's unemployed and has been for a while, so in his twisted mind, he ain't got nothing to lose, but you do, and you know it, brother.

Hector looked at Leo Lemon in contained shock. He attempted a futile smile, but it didn't work; nothing worked to calm his screaming mind. He wanted to jump over his desk and grab Leo by the throat and make him retract his words, and even though they were true, he wasn't used to the idea of being rebuked by young pendejos.

Leo Lemon continued, and although he was a little uncomfortable at addressing Hector like this, he got a little buzz out of pushing the old dog into a corner. See, Hector, you're probably used to the big city where you could take a married woman and bone her in a motel or in your office and get away with it, but this is Las Flores we're talking about, a small hick town. You don't have a married woman who you see every day at work, have her clean your house, and then let her hang around for dessert. Of course people are gonna talk shit; that's big news, Hector. People make a career out of that kind of gossip. You can get away with it, as many do, but you have to know who's on the screw list before you compromise yourself and others. As far as I know—and of course, I'm not familiar with the complete list, because I don't do married woman yet—but as far as I know, Concha was not on the list. Maybe when Tito was doing time, but when he's out, watch out.

OK, Leo. Hector was finally able to put words together. You've made your point. I got the message loud and clear. If that's all, I've got work to do.

No, Hector, that's all. I just wanted, you know, to warn you, man. It's just that I know Tito. Anyone else, I say ignore them, but Tito, you never know. But anyway, Hector, I'll leave you; I know you have a ton of work, and I have to go to work myself. He held out his hand to Hector but brought it down to his side, seeing that Hector was in no mood to shake hands.

Leo Lemon shut the door to Hector's office as he left. He was certain Hector was going to need some time alone to get his head together.

As soon as Leo shut the door, Hector, still sitting behind his desk, placed his hands on his face and repeated many times, Stupid, stupid. How could I be so stupid? And fat Concha, of all people, goddamn her to hell. Now he had to watch his back every minute of the day and night because that drunken fool could hit him anytime, anywhere, and there was nothing he could do about it. How could he go to the cops and tell them he was going to be shot by a crazy man because he had sex with his wife? They'd probably shoot his ass first.

Concha kept looking at Hector's office from the kitchen of the center. She had seen Leo Lemon walk out, but he closed the door behind him and had a silly grin on his fish face. She knew Leo because she had seen him boozing with her lazy husband, Tito, in the garage behind their house. She could hear the loud laughter as they probably exchanged dirty jokes. The office door was still shut, and the stupid sign was still hanging on the doorknob. It wasn't like Hector to keep the door shut for so long, especially on a day like today; by now he'd be all over the coffee pot and helping himself to the pound cake Concha had laid out on a tray next to the pot. Hector had asked Concha to come in and help out with the books and get everything ready for the federal auditor, Mercedes Sosa, coming in on Monday. Even Connie was asked to come in, which was rare, because Connie, the party girl, didn't do Saturdays unless asked by Hector. Concha invited her comadre Rosa and her daughter, Francisca, to help her out—Rosa with the carne adoboda, Hector's favorite, and Francisca with the kitchen receipts. The carne adoboda was for lunch. Rosa always prepared it the best because she used the best cuts of pork and red chili from the Hatch Valley, Hatch Valley red, as some people called it.

The women were having a lively conversation about corpulence and health, mostly Connie and Francisca, as the older women listened. Connie, who was thin and fit, was attempting to convince the other women, who were stout—except Francisca, Concha's daughter, who was going to be eventually because of her genes and large bones— that too much fat was not good. But she had to do it in a diplomatic way, as not to offend, because after all, she worked with Concha and was a friend of Francisca. But when obesity is discussed, even among friends, it tends to become a hot topic, and even the best intentions are not always tolerated.

You shouldn't use the word "fat" like that, Francisca said, raising her voice, going to bat for her mother, Concha, and Rosa. It's not looked down on in our culture.

It doesn't make any difference what word I use; it means the same thing, responded Connie, hungover and tired of being nice. It's still fat and it's unhealthy; what more can I say? I don't mean no disrespect.

Maybe unhealthy in your mind, said Francisca, but to normal people, it's the norm.

The norm is not to have a heart attack at age forty and cancer of the colon ten years down the road—or am I missing something here?

You say and think "fat" with a disdain, and that face, Connie—my god, that face, twisted as if you had tasted manure. You have circled the wagons around this frame of mind and nothing short of ah, of ah, oh, I don't know, will ever change it; that's my guess.

Concha and Rosa were uncomfortable as the two girls talked about something they knew nothing about. Let them walk in her shoes for a day, and then they could talk, she thought. She kept looking for Hector to come out of his office so the girls would shut up. But knowing Connie and knowing her daughter, the two would continue to talk nonsense all morning.

Please, Francisca, don't go there. You always try to tie in the facial features with the person's viewpoint; it don't work with me, honey, so don't try it. All I'm saying is that too much weight is unhealthy, and a chubby baby is going to be a chubby adult because we feed them tortillas and atole until they explode. They all started laughing except Rosa, who had no idea what was so funny about feeding a baby good food like atole and tortillas.

Hector was still in his office, and Concha was still worried. They had work to do, and she had no plans to stay at the center the whole day. Mercedes Sosa was all business, not like the health inspector, who would accept a cup of coffee and a couple of doughnuts, talk about his grandchildren for an hour, sign off on the paperwork, and leave. Not Sosa; she expected accountability for every penny spent as if it came out of her own pocket. Concha finally said, The hell with Hector. She asked her comadre Rosa to start the carne and took the girls to a table in the dining room along with a box full of papers and receipts and put them to work.

CHAPTER THIRTEEN

encho Reyes was sitting on a broken-down chair in a broken-down shack, and he was deteriorating at a fast rate. He couldn't remember how long he had been in the withering shack. He didn't leave the depressing shack because he couldn't find the keys to the truck, and he wasn't sure if he had it in him to navigate on foot through the difficult landscape back to town. He was tied down by the relentless force of his own inertia and remained immobile for all purposes, other than taking a piss. The shack was a one-room pile of crap that had been utilized by miners who had worked the mines years ago. The shack remained as the miners departed and since then had been host to many visitors, all with diverse itineraries.

Lencho's mouth was dry; he didn't have any drinking water, and his vision was blurry, but the memory of his mother was as clear as was the day outside the miserable shack. And he hung on to that memory, that image of that beautiful, kind, and loving woman he had only known for a few short years. Her absence after her passing left him with a yearning he was never able to satisfy, although he tried. His blurry eyes were focused on the door, the only door, as if expecting a visitor, someone with a human form, not the visitors he'd seen in his spaced-up dreams.

Lencho was out of buzz; he was dry and had nothing to sustain him. The keys to the truck were somewhere; he didn't know exactly where, but he did know he didn't want to spend another night in this shithole. But he had to admit he did get a lot of privacy, a luxury some people didn't care for, and the john could be anywhere. The bed was a rancid, shredded mattress on the worm-eaten floor, but he had slept in worse. The view wasn't bad from the top of the mound a little way behind the shack, but one had to be careful because there was an open mine shaft, covered by a flimsy piece of aluminum, on the side of the mound, not far from the front door.

Lencho was sitting on his ass, like the rent collector waiting for his rent, studying an empty can of sardines, his only food while in the stifling shack. The can had been mutilated when opened, and the evidence was clear. Lencho could see, when his vision cleared, through the jagged top, tiny puddles of fish oil, flakes of skin, and white bony spines in a corner of the can. He was positive the morsels in the can provided food for the critters of the night. He could still see and smell, so that meant he was still alive and breathing in the world of humans and not in the world of ghosts. He looked down at his vomit bucket, an old, rusted bucket that had been utilized for countless things throughout the years and was put upon again to hold his puke. The bucket was not full, as he expected, but there was such an assortment of waste in the rusty pail that he averted his eyes to keep from getting sick.

Regrets entered Lencho's thinking, and he felt too ill to fight them off. He regretted he had never fallen in love and felt the sensation of loving deeply. He always wanted to share that feeling with some girl and be taken on the rollercoaster of thundering hearts. Girls had been in love with him, but it was always a one-way adventure, although he tried and faked emotions that didn't belong to him. He regretted never knowing the sensation of making love to a woman all night and going to sleep with the feeling that perhaps he had touched paradise or that paradise had touch him. He regretted not dancing with a girl he really loved, especially the slow dances, holding her tight and letting the music cement that love even more. He longed for that love, even when he had been introduced to that other woman, a dark and mysterious woman who satisfied all his other cravings—a true love, demanding, but in a different aspect. He, at the end, became devoted to her, but the price was high, the dance was limited, and he didn't have the resources to support her. He wanted a separation, but it wasn't that simple anymore. But maybe, he wondered, that was the price one paid for devoting all his love and energy to the real woman who sacrificed her world and everything in it to let him live and get to know her in all her gentleness and goodness, if only for a short time.

Lencho was feeling sorry for Lencho, something he had never indulged in before, not like this. But it didn't matter anymore; nothing did. He had dumped the bottle of rubbing alcohol he was drinking when he finished the last of the bottle of cheap sotol he had brought along. He couldn't drink it anymore, and he didn't need it. He didn't bother looking for the keys to his truck because he didn't give a shit about anything, except the memory of his sweet mother. He knew what he was doing when he arrived at this nameless tomb in an unknown cemetery. He tried to find the chiva for Sammy, a real brother, but he failed, and he was sick of failure. He searched on foot until his boots almost fell apart and the heat did a number on his head. He got back in his truck and ended up here—a good place, he thought—to fight off the demons that never left him in peace. Here, he let the demons take their victory because he was too weak to fight anymore. Maybe now he could be with his mother, out there in the spirit world; that was all he cared for. Not even an offer of a fix would make him change his mind. Not now.

While Lencho was contemplating the perfect solution to his dilemma, Romero and Sammy Q. drove up in Romero's big truck, as if they were real estate brokers reviewing a hot property. That's Lencho's truck, said Sammy, happy that he might see Lencho again.

Romero gave him an angry look and said, I'm gonna check out his truck and around the back. When I go inside this shit can, your friend better have the right answers for me, or somebody is gonna be hurting, and it sure the hell ain't gonna be me, you get me, Sammy Boy?

Take it easy, Romero. Lencho might be sick.

I don't give a fat fuck if he's on his deathbed. The boy is gonna tell me what he did with my chiva. Now you go in there and talk to him while I look around out here. You got five minutes, Sammy Boy, so get to it.

Sammy walked into the dilapidated shack and shut the door behind him. He couldn't believe his eyes when he saw Lencho slouching in an old wooden chair too small for him. His hair was grimy and greasy, plastered to his head. His face was black with dirt and dried sweat. His eye sockets were like empty black holes, and his lips were dried and cracked, with a white crust on them that resembled week-old, rancid buttermilk.

When Lencho saw Sammy, he attempted a weak smile, but his lips were so crusted they ripped, and blood seeped out, forming tiny red pools in the white crust. Lencho gave it his best effort and said in a voice that would rather not say anything, I tried, Sammy, but the shit just ain't out there, man.

That's fine, Lencho. I believe you, brother. Let's get you to a doctor. C'mon, Lencho. It's not too late.

No, Sammy…no doctor. I don't feel pain anymore, I—

Before Lencho completed his words, Romero bust in like a wild man and yelled out, Where's my shit, motherfucker? I know you found it, I know you have it, and I know you're using. Look at you, you filthy piece of shit. And Romero started tearing through the shack, looking for the invisible chiva. He stood in front of Lencho again and grabbed the table and threw it against the wall.

He didn't find it, Sammy said, trying to reason with Romero.

And you believe this scumbag, Sammy Boy? Look at him—just look at the son of a bitch. Getting high with my shit, getting high at my expense, and you don't see it?

Lencho's sick, Romero. He needs a doctor.

A doctor! I'll doctor him. You better step outside, Sammy. You don't have the guts to get at the truth. Step outside; wait in the truck. I'll be out in a minute. Close the door on your way out.

I'm gonna ask you one more time, shit bag: where is my chiva? Just tell me where you stashed it. Give it up, and I'll leave you a fix or take you with us back to town. Whadda you say, cowboy? Romero's temperature lowered a bit.

I didn't find anything, Lencho said, almost in a whisper, coughing all the time. I didn't find nothing.

Romero looked around the disheveled shack. He moved around the small space, kicking objects as if they were footballs. He found pieces of rusty wire and fastened them together to resemble a crude rope. He tied Lencho's hands behind his back and brought the wire around his waist, wound it around his legs, and wrapped it around a leg of the chair.

Lencho attempted a weak grin. I ain't gonna fight you, big boy, and I ain't gonna run, so save yourself the trouble, he said.

Romero struck Lencho with an open hand across the face, an explosive slap that snapped Lencho's head to the side and made his nose bleed. Romero didn't want to use his fists because he could crack Lencho's skull and put his lights out; he needed him conscious for a little longer.

See what you get for being a smartass? You think this is a fucking game, right? I'm gonna show you what kind of a game this ain't.

Romero moved junk around until he found what he was looking for. It was a thin metal rod about a foot long with a broken, jagged point. He took out his Zippo lighter and put the flame on the tip of the rod, which he held in his right hand, holding the lighter with his left.

Lencho observed what Romero was doing and closed his eyes. He knew what was coming but didn't know where it was going. He smiled to show the brute he had no fear of anything or anyone.

Romero kept his eyes on Lencho the whole time, holding the crude branding iron, making it hotter, so Lencho could see it. But when Lencho closed his eyes, Romero raged even more. Then, without saying a word, he thrust the red-hot rod into Lencho's left cheek, singeing the skin but not pushed in too deep—he didn't want to kill him—but deep enough to wake up the dead.

To Lencho, the pain was beyond pain. It raced from his face all the way to his toes and back again, and it gripped him like a steel bear trap, and he couldn't set himself free. But he didn't flinch or made a sound, although he was dying with pain. He recalled when his older brother Chopo, was teaching him how to box. He hit him hard on the face and said, Don't cry; don't show pain. Boom—hit him harder. Don't show weakness. Boom. Take it like a man, or don't talk to me anymore. He took it and was still taking it, but this time, he didn't understand why. He never in his life hurt anyone, not even when playing football or boxing. Jesus, he said to himself, set me free.

Romero pulled out the metal rod from Lencho's cheek, burned flesh hanging on at the tip, and flung it on top of the junk scattered all over the floor. When he saw that Lencho was in a lot of pain but holding it in, he said, Shit. This son of a bitch ain't human. He kicked away junk until he cleared a space to the door. He grabbed Lencho around the waist from behind and dragged the bleeding Lencho on the decaying chair toward the door. He struggled to get through the desiccated doorframe, and that pissed him off even more. He didn't realize until now that Lencho was a tall boy, almost his height. He had lost a lot of weight but was still heavy to budge. He finally pulled him through the doorframe, leaving splinters embedded in Lencho's clothes and skin. Romero pulled and jerked until he got Lencho to the open mine shaft and placed him right in front of the open pit, facing him. By now Lencho was either dead or unconscious, but Romero didn't give a shit. He removed the corroded aluminum cover, placed his huge boot on Lencho's knees, and kicked him into the pit. Lencho and chair tumbled in backward and, with his weight, probably flipped over going down, but it didn't matter. Romero heard a splash, and Lencho was history. Romero picked up several large rocks and tossed them into the pit, just in case, he thought. He placed the cover back on the opening of the pit and walked fast back to the truck, still angry because he had worked up a sweat, and now he was going to have the beefy-guy odor until he took a shower.

Romero got in the truck, started it, put it in reverse, and stepped on the gas pedal, spinning the tires, backing away from Lencho's truck and the shack. He braked, got off the truck, jerked back a canvas tarp in the back, and hauled out a five-gallon can of gasoline. He walked back to the shack, entered, and sprinkled gas all over the interior. He did the same to Lencho's truck, picked up a piece of old newspaper, lit it with his Zippo lighter, and flung it inside the cabin, which was like dry tinder and set ablaze easy. He did the same to Lencho's truck and then ran to his own truck and told Sammy, Don't say a word. Not a word. Sammy, scared half to death, stayed mum. Romero drove off like a man late to his next appointment.

Unknown to Romero and Sammy Q., they were being observed from a low mesa not more than half a mile away by a man with high-powered binoculars. Although the man couldn't see the doings inside the shack, he witnessed everything else.

CHAPTER FOURTEEN

Mike, on his way to the house of Delfina Madrid, drove east on Calle de las Golondrinas and passed Santos Street. On the corner of Santos, across from the Quiosco, was Mi Casita Café, and Mike could see the café was doing brisk business with the menudo crowd. The menudo, with good hot chili and plenty of pansa, was a Saturday and Sunday ritual and believed by many to be a cure-all for everything from a hangover to impotency. Mike wanted to stop and say hi to his friends but decided against it because he knew one thing would lead to another, and he would never get to Delfina's house.

When Mike passed Mi Casita with a longing to stop, he came to San Albino and cut a left, heading north at a leisurely pace, not anxious to arrive at his destination. His thoughts were on what his mother had said about his girlfriend, Linda. He liked Linda a lot but didn't love her enough to want to marry her. He had already been down that love road and was ambushed and demolished by an emotion he couldn't control. He had been in the ninth or tenth grade when it hit him, and it tore him up from the ground up. It mangled him so bad that he was even afraid to say the word. It was like a desert storm he could never forget, even if he wanted to. Thank God she married and left Las Flores, because he knew he would go after her, married or not. No thanks, baby, he said to himself, I want out of here—taste a bit of the world and then settle down and raise a family, maybe. A big maybe.

Mike kept on driving at low speed on San Albino. He didn't want to hit a dog, as they sometimes chased cars as if they owned the street. He stayed on San Albino, which was mostly residential, with newer and older houses clustered together; some newer with pitch roofs, built with bricks, and others older, built with adobe and flat roofs. Most were painted in a variety of colors. Most of the homes had a little garden in the front yard or a larger one in the back. Some gardens were utilized to grow food, the home owners not wanting to waste precious water on flowers, which, although nice, had no practical use, except to place on graves. But others grew only flowers for that exact purpose. Many still had chickens and pigeons. Although the city was cracking down, the people resisted. They knew of nothing better than pigeon soup to cure that cold that persisted and made life more miserable than it had to be. The same with the dogs; they kept as many as they wanted and, when tired of them, took them on a one-way ride far from the house and gave it a kick out the car door. But soon they would adopt another mutt and treat it the same way. Others took them out to the arroyo, tied them to a rock, and shot them in the head or placed the puppies, as soon as they were born, in a burlap sack and smashed them with a shovel. What the hell; they loved their animals. They never called animal control because the dog catcher asked silly questions, and besides, the dogs would be gassed and clubbed at the pound anyway.

Mike continued driving north on San Albino. When he reached Esperanza Street, he cut into a dirt road lined on both sides with cotton trees but kept going north, away from Esperanza and off San Albino. He drove for a short distance on a rutted dirt road until he reached Delfina's old adobe house. The house was situated in the middle of a jungle of trees and vines. Alamo, cedros, peach, and apricot trees closed in on the house, as if protecting it from an encroaching alien world, recognized only by Delfina Madrid. He parked and sidestepped rotten fruit on the ground, which was scattered throughout the property all the way to the sagging portal. There was a yellow, ragged dog that crawled over to smell him, but seeing he wasn't his beloved master, the dog ignored him and crawled back to his shallow hole under a tree.

Mike knocked several times on the screen door, hoping someone would hear the knock. Finally the wooden door opened, and he stepped inside the house, which was dark, with a heavy smell of candle wax invading his nostrils. He squinted to adjust to the dim light. All the windows were covered with black cloth, but he did see Danny's guitar hanging on the wall. A musical instrument enjoyed by many under Danny's talented hands was now a silent sanctuary for little spiders.

The door was closed as soon as Mike stepped into the house, as if something indispensable was going to escape. Vivian, in a black dress a bit too long for her, moved across the room without saying a word. Her pale, fair, delicate face made everything else, seem even darker. Her green eyes studied Mike, but her full lips didn't move. She held a large, black rosary in her manicured hands. Her auburn hair, brushed back away from her face, cascaded almost to her waist.

Vivian was catered to from a young age by her godfather, Juan Jose, who had baptized her in the holy church. In high school, she was taken and picked up by her godfather in a brand-new Buick. The boys never approached her; they knew she was too beautiful, and she might reject them in front of their peers. The girls avoided her also. They couldn't believe she could be a true friend and was too good looking to trust their boyfriends around her. So Vivian became a legend and was well aware of it. She gave up on making friends and stayed close to her brother, Danny, who was a couple of years older and had many of the same interests. Sometimes a boy proved to be persistent and followed her to the waiting car, where her godfather, Juan Jose, was always waiting. The stubborn boy continued to have a one-way conversation right up to the car. Juan Jose, with his military buzzed hair, eyes behind aviator sunglasses, and his drill-sergeant attitude, urged the boy politely to get lost. Vivian Madrid was born beautiful, and that beauty never abandoned her. She was aware of her beauty and also of the pain it could cost if not handled right.

Mike was impressed with the dramatic look; that was what Vivian was famous for. He wondered if Delfina would outdo Vivian, not only in dress but in theatrics. He waited for Delfina to enter. She wouldn't let Vivian steal the performance. Vivian was the warm-up act, nothing else; the show opener, never to be confused with the main attraction.

Mike was getting anxious. The candlelight; the waxy odor; the silent Vivian, pretending to be an apparition in a haunted house— that was over the top, he thought. He could understand grieving for a loved one, the hurt and all, but this was a little much. He decided to break the silence; this could go on for God knew how long. He didn't know how to approach Vivian. He had stayed away from her, which wasn't cool, but she was difficult. So he said hell with it. He was going to say what he came here to say.

Vivian, he said and walked over and gave her a hug. Her hands as well as her body remained limp, like a rag doll that you hug when in pain and expect something back. He moved back, not surprised. He knew her. He said, I'm sorry about Danny, Vivian, I really am. I know you were close to him and how you blame Ramon, but I'm here to—

Before Mike completed his words, Vivian came alive and hissed his name. Ramon? Ramon? That little shit, that worm of a boy, is he capable of understanding what he has done? Are any of you? Danny was my only brother, she said, with tears in her eyes, the love of my life, my window to the outside world, and he's gone—gone, doncha see? And she stared at him with such intensity in her eyes that it seemed to Mike she was going to float up into the air and come down on him, crashing down on him, and then strangle him with the large rosary, like in a B horror movie.

Mike, not knowing how to respond, asked, Is your mother home, Vivian? I wanted to, ah, talk to her. Is that OK?

Vivian, with that frigid look, said, My mother is ill in bed. She refuses to see or talk to anyone. Not anyone.

Well, I'm sorry to hear that, Vivian, Mike said, but my mother thought it a good idea if I told your mother that…uh, we are gonna hire an attorney for Ramon, if he needs one, that is.

Vivian's face changed from glacial to a smirk. You are going to do what? Ramon deserves to rot in prison and be abused night and day by filthy convicts. Not even then will he ever pay for the harm he's done to us.

I understand you're hurt, Vivian. And Mike attempted to put his arm around her shoulder, but she inched back. But you, he continued, you always messed with his head. You let him fall in love with you when you knew there was no chance for Ramon to get close to you. That's why he wanted to hang around with Danny—to get close to you. Don't tell me this is something you knew nothing about; you were well aware of it. C'mon, please.

Listen, Mike, and listen good, she said, lifting her chin, trying to look taller. We, Danny, let him hang around. Ramon was always bragging about how he was going to score some money for our trip to California. Of course we had to take him along; that was the deal. So I talked to him in a nice way to find out how much money he could get and from who or where, but I never promised him a thing. That Rat Boy was nothing to me, nothing, nothing but trouble. You should know; you and him were—anyhow, don't bother wasting money on an attorney. The Rat Boy flew the coop. He left the hospital in the middle of the night, like a thief, and no one has seen him since.

Mike bit his tongue hard to control the harsh words that almost came out of his mouth. He looked at Vivian with a desire to kiss her fleshy mouth and force her to the floor, strip her naked, and do her. He had seen her in short shorts, and she had the best-shaped legs of any girl anywhere, creamy silk, and a flat tummy, with large breasts, damn her. But he knew it was crazy even to think about it. Vivian could be his, but it would take too much time to cultivate her, to bring her around to his kind of thinking, and he didn't have that kind of time to spare. Not now, not tomorrow, not ever.

He calmed down, released the grip on his tongue, and said, Are you sure, Vivian? I visited Ramon two nights ago. He was cool and said he'd wait for a formal discharge. I was gonna pick him up and drive him home. How did you find out? I mean—

I know what you mean, Mike, said Vivian. We might be isolated out here, but people in town keep us in the know-how of things that happen. So now you know the little shit can't keep his word, but please, don't tell me that is news to you?

Mike was upset with Ramon but wanted to act cool around Vivian. Maybe it wasn't even true what Vivian said about his friend Ramon, he thought. Maybe she just wanted to play with him, but he knew Ramon and wouldn't put it past him. Ramon was capable of anything.

So what are your plans now? Vivian asked Mike, sort of smiling, content she held on to her surprise just when Mike was getting comfortable and cocky, as he always did.

I'm gonna look for him, Vivian, Mike said. If Ramon left the hospital, there must have been a reason for him leaving. And until I get his side of the story, I still plan to help him. That's what I promised, and that's what I'll do. And now I have to get going, so give my regards to your mother. I'll stay in touch.

And you to yours, and do that, she said, with the graciousness of a southern belle who was saying farewell to a dear, dear friend.

Mike left Delfina's house with a hard-on for Vivian while trying to figure out why Ramon left the hospital when he was about to be discharged. He was going to call the hospital to confirm what Vivian claimed. If it was true, he would go visit Ramon's mother to see if she knew anything about it. He had to be sure; Vivian could be playing him for a fool—a cruel game but a game nevertheless.

After calling the hospital and confirming that Ramon had indeed checked himself out without a doctor's release, Mike stopped at Ramon's mother's house to see if he was home with her. The poor woman was saddened with the news and reduced to more crying and apprehension. She had thought all along that her son, Ramon, was with Mike. Ramon was her one and only, a son who had introduced more problems than happiness into her despairing life. Ramon had few friends, so Mike didn't even bother going there. He was not on speaking terms with most of his relatives, so that was out. Mike had a hunch Ramon might be in their old hideout in Snake Town. He didn't feel like driving out there, but something told him he'd better.

Mike kept east on Esperanza Street until Esperanza ended at the edge of town. He passed the Old Albuquerque Road, which ran north and south. He kept driving east on a dirt road called by many El Camino de Lagrimas, the Road of Tears. He loved that name; he didn't know why, but he just did. The road was rutted like an old washboard in areas, with loose sand and gravel in other areas; it was the kind of road best avoided with a cherry lowrider. A flash flood could wipe out sections in seconds, but the road seemed to have a life of its own and persisted on maintaining its status as a road, defying nature at will. It was also a lonely road, with nothing human seen on it for miles. And although it was less than five miles from town, it seemed like a hundred. The dry chamizo dressed the ground close to the road but was denser away from the dirt road, and the cholla was more dominant as the dirt road curved northeast and the landscape elevated toward the rugged hills. The terrain now was rocky, and the majestic yucca could be seen in the distance with their stiff, sword-shaped leaves and white flowers that added color and perspective to the otherwise barren hills. The road was solid now, and Mike could drive a little faster, but it didn't make any difference because he had arrived at the old, abandoned village of San Lorenzo, called Snake Town. The village was built on a slope close to the hills, and the hills behind it gave it the illusion it angled higher than it actually did. There was an ascent, but it was minor. The adobe and few stone houses were on solid ground, and most were gutted, and graffiti from many creative minds was carved or painted all over the place. The building that the Baptists took over when the Catholics abandoned it was still standing but with most of the roof caved in and the doors missing.

Mike left his car outside the village. The streets were littered with useless junk. Rusted hulls of old cars and trucks rested under piles of stones and dirt. Broken-down, antiquated refrigerators and stoves had been looted years ago of anything valuable. Mike made his way to the old Baptist church, because if Ramon was here, he'd be in their old hiding place in the basement of the church. And knowing Ramon, Mike thought, he had bet money that Mike would show up sooner or later.

Snake Town had been a mecca for the flower children who sought love and drugs and an escape from the mechanized society of their middle-class parents. They searched for a new God and a simpler way of life with mother earth in the lonely deserts and mountain valleys of the vast continent. They came like the plague and inhabited the run-down, abandoned dwellings of Snake Town. They believed they had found Eden and a communal brotherhood that would see them through the new millennium. They worshipped the sun during the day and the moon at night. But the sun they worshipped burned fiercely and without pity during the long summer months. It roasted their measly gardens and fogged minds, while the crows and the insects finished off the rest, leaving them scratching like fleas for water. Then the sharks from Las Flores entered the picture, dealing them another blow. They burned them on drug deals, selling them shit instead of drugs, screwing the better-looking chicks and roughing up anyone who protested. Snake Town became a circus of despair as rape and venereal disease became rampant. The authorities finally decided to act, but a freak blizzard beat them to it. No visible evidence was left behind to show that those dreamers had once existed in Snake Town. The dreams they brought with them, most of them solid and full of hope, melted like icicles in the hot sun, when they vacated Snake Town.

Mike entered the building, which had been used as a dance hall by the Catholics before the Baptist took it over. The center of the huge, decaying building was stacked with falling rubble from the ceiling. He walked on the edges toward the back of the building where the door to the basement was located. The door was open, and Ramon was sitting on top of an empty wooden box, studying a pair of brass knuckles. The brass knuckles were rudimentary, to say the least: nothing but a U-shaped piece of metal, half an inch thick and about two inches wide, heavily taped on the inside. What made them look wicked and dangerous were four pointed, rusted screws riveted on the face of the metal about a half inch apart. The screws weren't large; they were small but big enough to rip through skin and bone, if put to the test.

Mike walked carefully on the termite-infested ramp that led down to the dim, foul-smelling basement. The light came in through the open door. Ramon was sitting in the faded light, contemplating the brass knuckles.

Hey, Ramon. Gonna use those on me? Mike asked.

Hey, Mike, Ramon answered. What took you so long? Remember these? Remember that smartass used to butt vatos on the face in a fight? That puto had a bone-crushing forehead, put suckers down, bleeding. Remember—tried that shit on you? You had these babies on; he tried to butt you; you put out a straight right; his forehead collided with the brass babies. The dirt bag carried that signature on his forehead for a long time.

Alex, Alex Padilla, was his name, said Mike. He wanted to break my nose. He'd done it to others—the Nose Breaker, what some called him. What else you find down here?

Ramon pitched the knuckles on a heap of junk and picked up a couple of rough-crafted arrows. I also found these, he said. Remember Juan Jose taught us to make arrowheads with old teaspoons we found among the junk? He said to hammer the heads on a rock till they got sharp and pointed, cut a slit at the end of the shaft, and slide in the stem of the spoon, leaving the flattened head out, and tie the baby tight with string. These were mine, not as straight as yours; the branches I collected were never straight. You found a tablespoon and made a spear with it. That baby saved our ass a couple of times.

It sure did. And Mike couldn't help it but smile. Juan Jose owned a fifty-five pound, draw weight double-recurved, Turkish-style bow. It had layers of wood laminated into the bow and a strip of fiberglass on either side of it; who could top that? He could hit a moving target a hundred or more yards away. Sure hate for him to be after my ass. And they both laughed. He also told us we could dip the points in shit to make them more lethal. He used rattlesnake poison and coyotillo, that thorny, poisonous plant found around here. I always said, Don't fuck around with Juan Jose, and not many did.

Where did Juan Jose learn all that stuff he talked to us about? asked Ramon, poking at the wooden box with the point of the arrow.

I heard rumors he was in a special unit of the military—US Navy SEALs or did some secret shit for the CIA—but who knows?

I do know he coordinates the firing range for the state police and sheriff's department, so he knows his way around firearms. I also heard Juan Jose owns Snake Town—bought it with cold cash.

Yeah, right, responded Ramon, half smiling. Juan Jose needs Snake Town like a deer needs a hunter.

They remained silent, looking at the dusty junk scattered all over the gloomy cellar, thinking of the excitement first felt as they made their way into the cellar. The cellar became their designated hideout. They cleaned up a space, supplied it with candles and water, and set up shop. They made a secret compartment for their weapons and even invited girls for a little action. That was during the day; at night, it was scary to come out here. The place was a little too spooky for comfort.

So, Ramon, why did you leave the hospital? asked Mike. I mean, couldn't you've waited for a proper release? Why give the cops more ammo?

Ramon poked the arrowhead so hard into the wood box that the shaft splintered. He hurled what was left onto a pile of junk. They weren't doing shit for me they hadn't done already, he said, a little pissed off by the question.

C'mon, Ramon. I'm trying to help you. What's really going on? Your mother is worried sick about you when you pull your stunts. At least think, man, think about the hurt you put on your poor mother— that asking for too much?

Ramon kept his eyes away from Mike, saying nothing. He blew it, as he always did, and he knew it. But then he had a change of heart and realized he had to come clean. He looked at Mike and said, Mike, I'm gonna tell the truth, man. I can't keep it inside me any longer...if I...if I don't tell you, who else can I tell? This is what happened, Mike, a la brava, bro.

Danny and I were rabbit hunting not too far from here. Danny parked the car off a dirt road; we walked to a small hill a short distance from the car. The hill, not even a hill, had clusters of sotol we liked to shoot at. As we walked to the sotol, we shot at beer cans, bottles, bones, anything but rabbits. Danny with his .22 repeating rifle used a lot of ammo; my single shot, well, you know. Anyway, before we reached the cluster of sotol, we saw a bundle wrapped in heavy plastic. Danny handed me his .22 and fell on his knees, as if he was in church. He cleaned away some loose dirt off the bundle and started laughing. He looked every which way for signs of cars or people. He kept asking, Do you see anyone? Keep your eyes open. I said no, several times. He bent down and picked up the bundle as if he was picking up an infant. He cradled the bundle against his chest and ran full speed back to the car. When I reached the car, carrying a gun in each hand, Danny had already secured the bundle in the trunk. He was laughing, jumping up and down, waiting for me, saying, C'mon, Ramon, c'mon, hop to it, motherfucker. You know how he liked to use that word.

So what happened next? asked Mike, biting his lower lip.

We got in the car, said Ramon, his eyes almost shut. Danny was still drinking his quart-size jug, singing, driving back to town. I asked him where he was going. He said, Home, to hide the shit. I said, Ain't that kind of stupid? Why you gonna take the heat to your pad and endanger your family, in case someone saw you when you picked up the shit? Then he turned to me, grinning like a fool, and said, Ray Ray, you a smart hombre. You know how I hate for people to call me Ray Ray? He made a U and headed back the same way we were coming from. Then he asked, Where we hide this shit, Ray Ray? I said without thinking, How about Snake Town, in our old hiding place? He said, I told you, you a smart cookie, Ray Ray. Like I'm supposed to be stupid, is what he meant.

Mike starred at Ramon and couldn't believe what was coming out of his mouth. He wanted to take off and leave Ramon there, pretend he dreamed this story and forgot to write it in his journal. What the hell; it was too late. He was already involved, like it or not.

So what happened when you got to Snake Town? asked Mike.

We checked around to see if the place was deserted, keeping an eye out for Juan Jose. He was tight with Danny. Danny didn't want to, you know, share with anyone else. When we made sure no one was around, we brought the shit down here. Danny cut the large bundle open and separated the two smaller bundles. He took out his fila, made a small opening on one bundle, stuck his index finger in the shit, and put it in his mouth. I asked him, Whatcha doing? He said, Whatsa look like I'm doing? He tasted the sugar, made a face, and said, this chiva's sweet, Ray Ray. Ain't tar. He meant it wasn't Mexican black tar. He said, It's gonna bring us some coin, Ray Ray, you can bet your boots on that. He went to a corner of the cellar and returned with a kit, spoon and all. He said, I gotta try this baby. Want some? I said, Fuck, no. I left him slamming. I went outside to get some fresh air and be his look out.

Hay! Ramon, Ramon, Mike said, running his hand through his hair, smoothing it back. Then what happened? As if he didn't know.

I came back down to the cellar, said Ramon, looking at Mike, trying to read his reaction, after about ten minutes, maybe longer; seemed like hours. Danny was sitting on the filthy floor, nodding, eyes glazed, saying, This is good shit, Ray Ray, the best I've ever had. Try some, vato. The package he took a sample out of was already fixed up as if it had never been opened. He told me to stash it in the hiding place and cover it really good, which I did. But then his mood changed. His eyes were almost closed. He said he didn't feel good and that we had to leave. It was already dark when we left Snake Town. He got sicker. He had to pull off the road 'cause he was throwing up. He told me to drive him to the hospital. I told him many times I couldn't drive. He insisted I had to and kept saying he was gonna OD, 'cause the chiva was uncut. He got out of the car, fell out, barfing all over, so I had no choice. I helped him back in the car and drove slow, but he kept saying, Faster, damn you, faster. His head was between his legs. He was on the passenger side, throwing up, telling me—begging me—to drive faster, to get him to the hospital before it was too late. Well, Mike, you know what happened after I took the wheel.

Is it still here? asked Mike, getting pissed off and nervous at the same time.

Yeah, it's still here. Who the fuck gonna take it?

Listen, Ramon, were you a little pissed off at Danny for finding and picking up the chiva? You knew if Danny sold it, he wouldn't need your money or wouldn't need you for anything. Could go to Califa without you, just him and Vivian. Still have the hots for Vivian? 'Cause if you do, you know you're wasting your time. Vivian wants to go to Hollywood big time to get into the movies or modeling or something. Why do you let her mess with your head?

No, Mike, said Ramon, with his arms crossed, hugging himself. I feel nothing for Vivian; I just—

Is that why you hung around with Danny? asked Mike, not letting him complete his thought. Don't feel bad, Ramon. You're not the only vato she played with. You saw at school she was the queen —not even the football jocks could score with her. And if you pressed her, she told her godfather and Juan Jose come down hard on your ass.

She talked to you, Mike, Ramon said, frowning. I see you talking shit to her.

Only because my mother and her mother are friends. That's the only reason. Other than that, Vivian wouldn't give me the time of day.

What about Linda, the chick you seeing now? What about her? She's as good looking as Vivian.

Please, Ramon, Mike said, trying not to smile. You know and I know that Linda, although beautiful, can't be compared to Vivian Madrid, and you know it. I still don't get why you wanted to go to California with them. Danny, if alive, was going for the drugs and girls, Vivian to be a star. What were you gonna look for, Ramon? I could see you going out there and staying with family. Weren't you born in Watts?

Compton. Sure, Mike, I can go searching for a father who abandoned us when I was born, and when I find him, if I do, tell him what? Oh, Dad—may I call you Dad? Here is the son you abandoned nineteen years ago; can you put me up? By the way, I have a condition. The meds aren't expensive, but they ain't cheap either. Fuck him, and fuck California. I ain't going nowhere. And another thing, Mike, I'm giving you the chiva; do with it as you like. If you don't want it, I'll open the bags and scatter the shit all over Snake Town.

Mike was thinking fast as Ramon walked to the place where he had stashed the sugar. Hold on, cabron, he said. Wait, Ramon. maybe we can work something out. Maybe we can sell it and get some much-needed coin.

What do you mean "we"? Ramon, with his back to Mike, was smiling. I told chu, I want no part of it. You do whatchu want with it—sell it, give it away, flush it. I give a shit. If you do make something out of it and hand over a bit, I might take it, but I ain't gonna promise.

Mike knew Ramon was playing with him. Mike also knew Ramon was no jackass when it came to dealing and wheeling. He was nervous; he didn't want to take the chiva, but he didn't want to throw it away either. There was money in it, if he could get connected to the right people. But there was also a risk, a big risk, especially if it was as good as Danny said it was.

Mike and Ramon drove away from Snake Town as fast as they could go considering the conditions of the road. He had placed the two bundles of chiva on the backseat—easier to dump, Mike figured, if they had to. He estimated the bags weighed around four or five pounds each. It could be ten pounds of joy or ten pounds of sorrow, depending on how you looked at it. Ramon had dumped the responsibility all on him, but that was Ramon's favorite game; no point in blaming him. But he was still nervous and plenty scared, moving the chiva from a safe place to another place that was not as secure perhaps. He kept looking in the rearview mirror and sideways, not wanting to see any strangers following.

They headed west on El Camino de Lagrimas toward Las Flores. The sun was going down, leaving the horizon blood purple, interspersed with streaks of red orange, giving the Road of Tears a certain beauty not appreciated during the day, when the full sun was out. It was the same road that had been used by many refugees as they departed with their broken spirits and dashed dreams to seek greener pastures. Ramon was silent as a statue, looking straight ahead, peeved with Mike because he was going to drop him off at his home where he belonged, not knowing any other place to leave him at. Mike had things to do. He was still deciding whether to keep or dump the chiva. Besides, he had a date with Linda, and he sure the hell didn't want Ramon around. He had fixed Ramon with a date many times, but it had been a disaster every time. It ended with him having to explain to the girl that Ramon wasn't gay, just difficult.

Mike had to practically walk Ramon into his own house. His mother was in tears and held on to her dear boy, thanking Mike many times and pleading with Ramon to sit and have a bite to eat. Mike said he had to run. He told Ramon and the mother he was going to contact Pa Hanks, the attorney, and get some legal advice for Ramon concerning the car accident. Mike walked out the door as Ramon's mother continued thanking him profusely, insisting he stay for dinner while holding onto Ramon. Ramon sulked but didn't say a word.

Mike drove south on Santos Street toward the church. He still had the sugar in the backseat and was still nervous. He had placed the two bundles in a burlap sack they found in the cellar. He was trying to decide what to do. If he sold it, the money would be his ticket out of Las Flores. But what if they sent out bloodhounds to find it? Then he was putting his family in danger; that really gave him the chills. He couldn't take it home; that was the first place the hounds would search. He drove slow, not wanting to see anyone, and if he did, he'd simply ignore them. Why not, he thought. From Santos he cut a right into Santa Teresa, drove a few blocks, and entered the church grounds. This was in the back of the church, and he parked close to the house where Father Benjamin lived. He walked to the fence and opened the chain-link gate, the burlap sack in his hand as if he was making a delivery, which he had done on several occasions when his mother sent Father Benjamin a sack of chili. But this time, instead of going to the main house, he went to the side of the house and entered an unlocked storage shed. Once inside, he opened an old freezer that had sat there, along with other discarded furniture, for years. He removed some odds and ends and placed the sack containing the sugar at the bottom of the freezer. He placed the other items on top, shut the lid, and walked out without seeing a soul. When he got to the gate, he yanked off a big red pomegranate from a pomegranate bush that was close to the gate. A gift for Linda, he said and smiled. He was clever, no doubt about it, he thought as he got back in his ride and left the area.

CHAPTER FIFTEEN

When Mike left the church grounds, he was going to drive home and take a shower, but he said, Better not. It'll take too much time, he thought. The sun was setting, and his mom would want to start a conversation, and he was still too shaky to converse with his astute mom. Besides, a little musk might turn Linda on, but he doubted that because Linda didn't need a match under her ass to get moving. She was hot; any hotter, she'd set herself on fire. She was in love with him, and that was a perfect excuse to turn up the burners. Their love making was intense and pleasurable to the max because there was an absence of guilt. They made love like honeymooners, no questions asked. But they both knew it: sex this ambitious had to lead to something else. And tonight was the deciding factor of that emotional truth. "If you really love me, you'll do anything to make me happy" was a line familiar to him and avoided as much as possible. "My parents want to meet and see where you stand" was another expression that made him run for the hills. Tonight was it. She was expecting an answer that would clarify everything, and it fell on him to provide it.

Mike loved his girlfriend, Linda Barela, hot as she was, with a deep passion, but she didn't do the trick for him. He was positive that Linda—and he hated thinking about it—would be, in the near future, like a used shirt, abandoned in the closet with yesterday's fashions, if they continued their heated pursuit of pleasure and married. And now that he had this other responsibility making him more nervous and paranoid than was usual, it was more difficult for him to perform at 100 percent capacity. He could get it up and in—that was the easy part—but the emotional component was difficult to fake. He loved her less than she loved him, and that made it more difficult for him to square things away. And although that soothed his ego, there would be pain on both sides at the end. Mike knew he had to tell her and tell her tonight that there weren't going to be anymore tomorrows, especially now that he could put a grab on some cold cash and make a faster escape from Las Flores than he ever anticipated. He couldn't be held back by a one-sided love affair that was doomed to fail, and nothing in heaven or earth, not even a miracle, could change his mind or his heart about it. The big problem for Mike, as for anyone, was actually telling her face to face, but that was better than other forms of communication, without a doubt. But often the speech memorized proved useless when their lips met and that familiar tongue entered his mouth with a definite purpose. And his thumbs were placed inside her mouth along with his tongue in search for more delicious pleasure, to moisten the bizcocho and make the entrance to la concha wet and slippery. Then after it was over, he ended up apologizing, making up some weak excuses, and delaying the decision until next time. Well, there ain't gonna be a next time, thought Mike, as he drove up to Linda's house, trying to decide which mask he was going to wear.

Linda was waiting for him on the front porch, sitting on a rimless car tire held up by a rope attached to the ceiling. She was in tiny shorts with a sleeveless top, and her black, wavy hair flowed behind her as if it had a mind of its own. Her long, slim, bronzed legs touched the floor until she pushed off with her sandaled feet and swung her gorgeous legs upward. She had on little makeup, but her full lips and healthy smile could make a celibate man doubtful.

She waited for Mike to get out of the car and then walked to meet him. A perfect ass, Mike thought, as she approached. A perfect, hard ass: not too small, not flat, and not a bubble butt. Perfect.

Hi, Mike! She gave him a tight squeeze and a kiss on the lips.

Hi, said Mike, not wanting to release her too quickly because her breasts felt good when she squeezed him. She had breasts that were made for sucking, not tiny and pointed, like a goat's, but round and firm. Real breasts, in his opinion. Mike was a leg man. He loved the feel of well-defined, firm legs—smooth, silky, long legs that made a statement in short shorts; he never got tired of looking and caressing legs like that. But lately, he noticed he had become a tit man or was on the way to becoming a tit man. He fully appreciated a full, scrumptious teta but with a small nipple, not a large one that resembled a penis, because when he wrapped his tongue around and sucked on it, he didn't want the image of a little chilito in his mouth. He might like it and go for the real thing; who could predict such things would never happen? And girls were proud of those mighty mountains; they had good reason to be. A good-looking girl and even an ugly girl with a pair of handsome knockers could get anything she wanted, especially if she was aware of the pitfalls of the sex game.

You wanna come in and say hi to my parents? Linda asked with a big smile on her pretty face.

No, Linda, not tonight. I'm not dressed for it. Can we just go? Next time, maybe, OK?

C'mon, babe. Just a quick hi, and we'll go. Nothing to it.

Naw, not tonight, Linda, some other time, I really don't feel…

All right, whatever, said Linda, disappointed. Let me wash my hands and get my bag. She walked into the house, and Mike was alone on the porch like a solicitor attempting to hustle a sale, but the door was shut in his face.

Shit, said Mike. He hated this. He should have gone in, he thought. He was standing alone out on the porch as if the parents didn't want him inside the house for whatever reason. The neighbors passing by would give him a sly smile, saying to themselves, You screwed up, boy, and now the parents don't want you inside their house, and we don't blame them, 'cause you have the look of a fuck- up. Why did he care? But he did, not knowing why, and he was about to go in when Linda came out.

Let's go, she said.

They drove west on Piñon Street where Linda lived toward Mora, about a mile away, and made a right, headed north on Mora, without saying a word. From Mora, Mike cut a left into Loma Street and drove west, toward the setting sun. The homes were set further apart, and the traffic was light. But Mike could see that was changing. New homes, although not many, were coming up, and the countryside wouldn't stay country for long.

The sun was going down and dispersing color in a dynamic fashion. The deep crimson and purple, mixed with gold, wrapped around the narrow clouds and created a tapestry of unequal beauty. Not only were the colors bright and intense, but the vastness, the sweep, the range of the horizon enshrouded in a translucent light and color transformed the landscape, if only for a short time, into a fairyland of splendid possibilities. Mike slowed the car because in this marvelous radiance they could see the yellow comets with their bronzy, yellow flowers as the falling sunlight made them sparkle. The thick, white stems glowed, making the comets look like candles spread out on the desert floor. Then he recognized the desert milkweed a little further up. The sunlight, what was left of it, also played with the desert milkweed. The clusters of green-white flowers seemed to light up and expose the capsules of flat seeds, making the tuft of white hairs in each seed float, as if suspended by the golden light.

What a sight, he thought. Can she see this marvel? Or am I asking for too much?

He decided to break the silence. They were acting like a married couple who had been married for years and had nothing to talk about anymore.

Hey, guapa, did I ever tell you that when I was a kid, my grandmother would take me with her in search of herbs and wildflowers. She knew the names of yerbas and wildflowers she searched for. She always sought out the ajamete along the edge of washes. I learned how to find the yellow-green ajamete with its leafless stem; it was a trip. My grandmother used the milky juice as a purgative and always had a list of people who also utilized it. She was so sweet.

So you're a botanist now? Linda said in a curt manner. I thought you wanted to be an attorney.

That hurt, but Mike stayed with it. He could throw something back, but Linda was his babe, and he didn't want to upset her any more than he had to.

She used to bake apples, he continued, topped with cinnamon or baked pumpkin fresh from the fields on those late, crisp autumn days. I could smell the apples baking in the oven of an old wood stove she had when I came home from school. I remember I was in the third grade, and my grandma always had a special treat for me. She was an angel, Linda, a real angel. Food tasted so much better when prepared on the wood-burning stove, Linda. I tell you, that's God's truth. I helped my grandma make the cheese and feed the chickens as a light snow fell, turning the world a fluffy white. But she died, Linda, and I almost died with her. I took it hard. A hard, terrible blow.

Linda looked at Mike and said nothing. Then, as if she changed her mind, she said, Why are you telling me this now, Mike? Is it because when it happened, you never really appreciated the kindness, never thanked your grandmother or gave her a kiss and hug? You just stuffed your face with the treats she worked so hard to make for you and then ran outside to play with your creepy little friends, without even saying thank you? And now, after all these years, you want to turn back the clock and do the right thing. Well, it's too late, sugar, to damn late.

Mike didn't say a thing; what could he say?

The profile of the landscape was changing as they came closer to the river, and nightfall was upon them. The dry scrubs gave way to greener, fuller vegetation. Cotton and willow trees were seen all along the river bank. Mike kept on driving and switched on the radio to a rock station.

Linda turned it off and said, Please!

They crossed the bridge, but it was too dark to see the water flowing south as it did during the summer months. Before reaching Highway 25, Mike cut a right into an unpaved road and headed north. The dirt road was dusty and narrow. It led up a small hill that was mostly barren. When they reached the top, Mike parked close to the edge and turned off the car lights. This was a lover's lane, or people called it that. Trunks of dead trees were placed at the edge to protect drunks from driving over, and it also afforded seating for the lovers to gaze at the lights of Las Flores down in the valley and the millions of stars in the sky. It was a perfect place to make love in the backseat of a car or wherever the mood presented itself. It was also a perfect place to gaze at the moon and stars and let your imagination soar. The higher elevation kept the pesky mosquitoes away, and the temperature was just right because of the low humidity. It wasn't known as a party place because of its location. The party places were next to the river, closer to town. The couples that drove out here were serious—madly in love, in most cases—and felt comfortable enough to take off their clothes and do their thing. Mike had visited this location many times with Linda and others, but with Linda it had become his favorite sex zone.

Mike opened the car door for Linda, and they sat on a tree trunk, looking at the lights of the valley below and at the lights in the sky above. Mike turned to Linda and said, You are the essence of beauty, equal to the stars up above, and I mean it, Linda, with all my heart. And he put her soft hand in his.

Linda pulled her hand away but did it gently, as not to offend him. Why did you bring me out here? she asked, as if she didn't know, but in a tone that was still civil.

We have to talk, baby, but give me a kiss first. I can get the sheets from the car, and—

No! Wait. She separated from Mike, stood up, put her hands on her waist, and looked at him like a schoolteacher ready to scold a rowdy student. You wanted to talk about us, so talk.

Linda, Mike said, choosing his words carefully, You know I'll be leaving to UNM soon. I don't want you to wait for me, if you feel the need not to—

To what! Linda jumped in, forgetting her civility. To what, Mike, to screw around, like you want to do up there? Say it!

No, Linda. Mike was pleading. Wait—what I mean is, you know, might get lonely, and—

And what, Mike! You talk as if you're moving to another planet. Jesus, Albuquerque isn't that far. You could be here every weekend, or I could drive over, no big deal, unless you have other plans, that is.

No, listen, Linda, listen to me, I beg you.

I'm listening and waiting for you to man up and tell me what you're plans are. That's what I'm waiting for.

Linda, you know I love you, Mike said, in a desperate attempt to salvage something. But it's too soon to make that kind of commitment, and what if you get pregnant? I mean, I'd have to stop studying and get a full-time job to support you and the baby.

Oh! So now you're worried about me getting pregnant, are you? You never showed any concern before. I could be pregnant right now and surprise you with a little bundle of joy down the road, while you're pretending to be a scholar at UNM.

Mike was sweating, and the night wasn't even that hot. This was, to him, the most difficult part of a relationship. Getting in was easy; getting out was serious business. He had to do it, though. He knew she was kidding about being pregnant—or was she?

I didn't worry about it, Linda, Mike said, a little worried, because I knew you were taking care of it. I knew you were up on the thing. After all, you always said you weren't ready for the huge responsibility, after seeing your cousins and friends having children at a young age. I knew you were on top of it without me asking about it.

Sure, Mike, sure. Tell me the truth, Mike. Do you really love me? I mean really, down deep in your heart, like I love you? Might as well tell me, Mike. What else do we have? Do you love me like you loved that girl Marisela, which you said was your first love?

Mike saw a break here—confessing that he loved someone else more but saying it tactfully, as not to offend or make less of the girl he was about to break up with. It was risky, but it could be done. And the best part was that Linda brought it up. It never failed, but he had to go in easy and not brag about it in a way that hurts, because he had to show that it was that pain that caused him to shy away or prevented him from loving anyone else. He had to admit it, he was good at this, but he had to watch his words; they had to be sincere because Linda was as intelligent as she was beautiful.

Linda…you know, Mike said, not rushing it. I never liked to talk about Marisela because Marisela was like a mirage that affected my life in a profound way. I fell in love with her, not believing in love. I made fun of others who were cuckoo over it, bragging I was too smart to get entangled in it to a point where it could strangle me. It happened with Marisela, and I didn't realize it until it was too late. I felt her presence all the time, and I loved to hold her hands in mine and kiss them tenderly. When I kissed her sweet lips, Linda, I was turned on to a world of beauty, and there I lived with her. I lost my desire to eat and trembled with the thought that I was going to be with her later in the evening. I was so happy to be alive that I danced to our music at midnight and sang to the moon that I was crazy in love with her. I saw her sculptured face everywhere I turned, Linda. I could not live without her love, and I will confess it to you now and forever. She was my love, Linda, my life, my dreams and happiness; what can I tell you?

Linda, tearing up because she knew she could never live up to that love, asked, So what ever happened to your precious Marisela?

Mike sensed some hurt and anger in Linda's voice and knew that now was the time to tell her about the love that was so great and caused him so much pain. He wanted Linda to open up her heart for him and feel for him something, some compassion, perhaps. He could do this, he thought, by convincing Linda that Marisela was a two-timing bitch.

This is the difficult part, Linda. That's why I never wanted to tell you about her. I was going through her purse; I can't recall why, but it doesn't matter. I saw some letters and read them. The letters were addressed to her from an ex-boyfriend. The words written in those letters presented me with a painful and frustrating dilemma. Do you see, Linda, what I was up against? Do I confront her and ask her about the letters and make myself more of a fool, or do I tear them up so she knew I read them and leave? I left, Linda, hurt like never before, and I was almost killed or seriously injured when I drove into a wall, wasted. Someone introduced her to a sailor on leave, on that same night, at that same party, and they married a few months later.

Linda was looking at Mike, barely visible in the in the dark, and thought, OK, you little cocksucker, you got some of the medicine you dish out. So what? She wanted to scratch his eyes out, but what was the point? She had been used, and there was nothing she could do about it. She had thought this was the real thing with Mike, a sure thing, until lately—the beginning of summer, really—when he seemed edgy and always making excuses to be somewhere else. Damn it, it hurt. She wanted to cry and scream, but that would be out of character. It would come later, anyway, in the privacy of her bedroom. For now she had to hold it in, all of it, because of the slight chance Mike might change his mind and stay with her. Oh! Please, let it be so, Jesus, she said to herself.

So you brought me out here, she asked, to do what? Were you expecting a farewell blowjob to put you in a better mood so you can leave satisfied you accomplished your mission successfully? Or to tell me about Marisela, the love of your life? Why, Mike, why did you wait so long to tell me? I gave up my full scholarship at Colorado State because I believed you were going to ask me to marry you.

Linda, it was your parents who refused to let you go, remember? They thought it was too far away, and you were too young to be so far away from home. I encouraged you to go for it.

No, Mike. My parents believed, as did I, you were going to ask me to marry you, and then—what a laugh—we could have gone together as a married couple.

Mike touched her bare arm, getting turned on and hard, ready to take out the sheets from the trunk and lay them in the backseat to avoid the hot, sticky leather when their bodies tangled in ecstasy.

Don't. Don't touch me, she said, obviously annoyed, and pulled her arm away.

Listen, sweetheart, I—

Don't call me that. I'm not your sweetheart, and maybe I never was.

No, listen, Linda. Hear me out, please, Mike said, attempting to stay in close, not yet ready to pull the plug. Still a slim chance for a little action, he thought. I love you, Linda, as much as I've loved anyone. Our love is special, and you know it. It's just that I'm afraid to get hurt, you know, like I was with Marisela. I'm not saying you would do the same thing, but I still have nightmares about it happening again—you know what I mean, right? It almost killed me once, Linda, but with you, I'll die for sure. I know I will.

Our sex is special, Mike, Linda said, frustrated at not getting her way. Just say it. I'm good, and you're not bad, so you call that love? To you, maybe it's love, but to me, sex is only a part of it. The emotional part, the commitment, the sharing, the planning for the future—that's what makes love, that's what gives it essence, and not sexual acrobats in the backseat of your car. Grow up and be a man Mike. Marisela was a fantasy, and you use her to skate around, to escape from your reality and not take responsibility for your actions. Jesus Christ, do I have to spell it out for you?

Mike knew this was the put-down stage, and he wasn't offended; it had to come out, and his response was crucial. Linda was hitting below the belt but not in a crude way. She had class and brains, so she used the psychological approach. She wanted to wound him but not cripple him, just in case they would get back together. He couldn't go toe to toe with her because it could get personal and ugly. He had to give her a victory, something to hold on to, something juicy she could tell her friends later when the subject came up—and it would. It always did.

Maybe you're right, Mike said, hanging his head, as if confessing to a strict mother that she was right, that he had eaten all the cookies and not his friends, as he had told her. I can't stand rejection, Linda. I'm weak in that area, and about Marisela—

Forget it, Mike. You're pathetic. Just take me home, and don't call me or go by my house anymore, get it?

Mike said, Yes! to himself. Just what he wanted to hear. Too bad he couldn't score a little piece of ass, but under the circumstances, that was to be expected. He'd have to beat his meat when he got home later, checking out the bitches in Playboy. Not that he was insensitive to Linda, hell no; he wanted to be in love and have a mate for life, like doves do, but not yet. He looked around and realized they were the only ones there in that dark, isolated place and said, Shit. It was a perfect place to be ambushed, if anyone had followed them. He had forgotten about the gold bricks he had hidden away, and this was not a good place to be, especially with a girl. They would go for Linda first, and he didn't want anything to happen to her, not on his watch. He remembered motor-mouth Manny saying something about a collector in town. Mike was certain this collector, whoever he was, wasn't collecting memories of his lost childhood. He opened the car door for Linda and drove faster than usual down the hill.

Mike drove to Linda's house without a word being spoken by either of them. Mike kept looking in the rearview mirror for any headlights getting too close to them. He looked to the sides at intersections, suspicious of every car and truck that happened to come along. Linda was even more upset because she thought Mike was in a hurry to drop her off at her house so he could go on the hunt. Mike relaxed a little more when they were approaching Linda's neighborhood. He was missing her already and wanted to hold her in his arms and make it up to her in any way she wanted. He wanted to be with her and kiss her lips, as he always did. He didn't want to be alone, not tonight. Maybe tomorrow but not tonight. He was scared and was sorry for the bullshit he had told her. He wanted to take it back, all of it. But it was too late; he had to write another chapter about his life, and this was the sad beginning or the ending—who could tell?

He parked in front of Linda's house, and she almost jumped out of the car and slammed the door shut.

Hey, babe, Mike said, as she was walking to her house, here's your pomegranate.

Shove it, she said, without even turning around.

CHAPTER SIXTEEN

Ramon sneaked out of the house as if he were a thief, and he didn't like it all. He was a man, he thought, but was still treated like a child, a child with no mind of his own. And even Mike, his best friend, didn't give him any credit for doing the right thing. Sure, he screwed up, but didn't everybody, sometimes? He hated to leave and not tell his mother he was going for a walk, but she would ask all kinds of questions and want to come along to keep an eye on him. That was too much; he couldn't handle that, no way. So he walked out the front door while his mother was occupied watching her favorite Mexican novela, something she wouldn't miss unless it was an emergency. He walked out without saying a word, closed the door behind him, grabbed his walking stick, and ventured out into the night.

Ramon walked east on Esperanza Street. It was around eight, a little after, he figured, because his mother watched her first novela at eight sharp. There was a full moon out, and the sky was full of bright, twinkling stars and clusters of stars that created a menagerie of pulsating lights for the stargazer with a resourceful imagination. When a wisp of cloud crossed in front of the full moon, an image was formed, usually black, and that image could be anything. He at times had seen a witch on a broomstick, pointed hat and all, the silhouette as real as you wanted to make it. But tonight was a perfect night for walking, he thought, a warm night, but not too hot. Traffic was light, and he kept to the right of the street as much as he could without walking on people's yards. The stick was for the dogs, the ones that were extra protective of their territories. He wasn't going to run away from any dog, not tonight, unless it was in the shape of a human and too large for his stick. Some of the dogs recognized him because this was the way to Danny's house, and the dogs had seen him walk this way night and day. Danny's house, he thought. Was he going there? Who was he trying to kid? Of course he was going there. He had to; he had to see Vivian Madrid and no one else.

Ramon wanted to turn back. He was close to San Albino Street, and he wanted to turn back, but did he? He kept walking. His legs couldn't stop, and the urge to see Vivian, to talk to her, drove him toward her house like a man starved for food, but not any commonplace food. He didn't even consider the fact she might not want to see him, that she hated his guts and always would. He kept on going, hitting the walking stick harder on the ground every time he took a step, blaming the stick for his inability to compose himself, to formulate a plan that would advance his cause. But he couldn't. His love, his obsession, his reckless desire for Vivian Madrid dominated his every thought, night and day. His attempts to forget her were numerous and unsuccessful. At times he despised her and made plans in his agitated mind to abduct her: to tie her up, take her to Snake Town, strip her naked, and sexually devour her. After he tired of her, he would shave her hair, slash her beautiful face and body with a straight razor, and sodomize her with his walking stick. Then, in his final sadistic, violent orgy, he'd put a rope around her neck and parade her naked around Las Flores. He wanted to damage her, hurt her bad; maybe then she would beg him to take her, to take her as his lover, and maybe he would, but on his conditions only. When his morbid, wicked thoughts ran their course and he was rational again, he battled severe melancholia, which left him incapacitated for at least a couple of days. And during that time, he cried, he pleaded in his mind, for her forgiveness. He whipped himself with a belt like a flagellant for even contemplating such sacrilege against the woman, the woman he loved with all his heart and soul. That was the power Vivian Madrid had over him, and he didn't know how to tame it or whether it could be tamed. He wasn't even sure if it was love. It was a pain in the ass one day and a rainbow after a summer shower the next.

Ramon arrived at the corner of Esperanza and San Albino. He stopped and looked at the streets that would take him one way or the other. If he went left on San Albino, he end up in Chiva Town, a place he avoided. If he turned right, a longer walk, he'd end up at Sammy Q.'s place; not a good idea, he thought. He crossed the street to San Albino and from there entered the dark dirt cul-de-sac off San Albino that would take him to Delfina Madrid's old house. He knew where his heart was taking him, and there was no debate about it. He had to see her; he had to talk to her, even if he got a slap on the face, which was better than nothing. He felt the need to protect her against the incursions of randy, horny guys like Mike. Mike, like others, would defile her with their tainted dicks and leave her to fend for herself. He, on the other hand, would never violate that precious body and tender heart. He loved her and respected her too much for him to indulge in that disgusting act with her. Sure, he thought about it in his crazy yearnings for her, but he had to shower with cold water several times to disinfect his mind from those vulgar thoughts. He wanted to keep her a virgin, as he was, and be able to keep each other's company without resorting to animalistic lust. Pure love, he liked to call it; it would be so much easier if she went along with it, he thought, as he made his way to the medieval house.

Ramon slowed his pace as he approached the jungle of trees and shrubs that enclosed the adobe house with its sagging front porch. The silver light of the moon disappeared as he entered the vault-like sensation felt in the claustrophobic ambience of ripened fruit and decomposing vegetation. He knew his way to the house, and even though it was pitch dark, he knew what to avoid—like the ankle-deep trench overflowing with leaves and weeds that ran along the side of the house and was always muddy. He knew exactly where the dog slept and at what time Delfina Madrid retired to her bedroom to recite her prayers with her rosary wrapped in her hands, as if holding on to a lifeline cast down from heaven, kneeling in front of a small altar she kept in her bedroom. Now and then, when Danny was alive, she used to come out and join them on the porch when Danny played his guitar and sang the favorite love ballads his father used to sing. Delfina, after listening to a few songs, returned to her bedroom with a hurt expression on her sad face. Now she had no reason to come out, Ramon thought, with her two men in their graves and a daughter who was not the best of company; who could blame her?

Ramon stopped a short distance from the house to watch and listen for any signs of people about. He whistled, quickly and low, for the dog to come to him, as he always did. Although the dog was along in years, he could still bark when he had to. The barking might not sound any alarms in the house, but he didn't want Delfina Madrid, deep in prayers, interrupted by the barking dog. They would never call the police if the dog barked; they didn't have to. They knew Juan Jose lurked around in the shadows and would take good care of any intruder insane enough to compromise his well-being. That's why Ramon stayed put, patting the dog on the head and waiting for Juan Jose to see him, if he was around, and recognize him as a friend of the family and as a visitor with good intentions. He was worried because Juan Jose had not lifted a hand against him over the death of Danny yet. Was he waiting for Ramon to fully recover, or had Juan Jose realized that Danny would do himself in, sooner or later, without any one's help? Even if Delfina or Vivian put pressure on Juan Jose to put Ramon in his place, Juan Jose would only act if he felt it was the right thing to do, and maybe, Ramon assumed, the right thing for him was to do nothing. He was positive he would never see or hear Juan Jose, but he was also positive Juan Jose had seen him come and go with Danny, night and day. But he wasn't going to take any chances. He knew Juan Jose could snap his neck like a pretzel and dump his body in a mine shaft and do it all, clean, in a matter of minutes, without him even seeing the man. And perhaps that was better, he thought, instead of going nuts over a difficult girl whose heart seemed to be embedded in an ice field.

Ramon waited patiently in the dark, scratching the dog's head, with his eyes on the house and his heart thumping with anticipation. He had been standing there with the dog for about ten minutes, he calculated. If Juan Jose was around, Ramon would be on his way home or on his way to the hospital, if he had put up any sort of argument or any bullshit about having to see Vivian. He had placed his walking stick next to a peach tree as soon as he entered the property because he didn't want Juan Jose, or anyone else, for that matter, to think it was going to be utilized as a weapon. That was hilarious, he thought, him using his walking stick to ward off an attack dog like Juan Jose; no way. Ramon decided to make his move. He couldn't wait any longer. He wasn't going to the front door to knock, which would be a wrong move. He was going to the back of the house to tap on Vivian's bedroom window. He was sure he wouldn't scare her; Vivian didn't scare easy. But if Juan Jose caught him pecking on Vivian's bedroom window at night, Juan Jose would cave in his skull with one blow from his huge hand. If Juan Jose caught him at the front door, and Vivian gave the word she didn't want to see him, he would be escorted off the property, and no one would be embarrassed—except him, maybe. But in the back of the house, next to her bedroom window, it was a killing zone, a DMZ with a survival chance of "slim." And that's why he had been so careful making sure Juan Jose was not around.

Ramon walked slow and cautious, getting closer to the house. He kept his eyes on the dim light that came from the living room. He rounded the corner of the house on the left side—that side of the house faced west—staying out of the trench that ran along close to the house but not next to the wall. He was careful not to make any unnecessary noise because Delfina's bedroom window faced that side. Her window was ink black; no light escaped, but he was sure she was in there praying. He reached the end of the wall and turned right to the back of the house where Vivian's bedroom was located. He saw some light reflected on the dark drapes, and he was positive Vivian was in her bedroom, alone. His heart raced; he couldn't contain his excitement—or was it fear? He was losing his nerve; he couldn't do it; this was insane; he was going to retrace his steps and get the hell away. But then the dog, which had followed along, bumped his shaggy head into his leg, wanting more TLC. He had probably been ignored since

Danny's death, except for a few scraps thrown out at him by Vivian, if that. Shit, it felt good to have his head scratched again, didn't matter to him, even if it was the Rat Boy, Ramon. The dog's insistence gave Ramon the courage he needed, and he decided to tap on the window as lightly as possible, considering the circumstances.

Vivian Madrid was in bed, on top of the sheets but dressed. She was wearing short shorts and one of Danny's short-sleeve shirts. The only light in her room was a small table lamp on her nightstand next to her bed. She was in tears; she had just finished rereading Emily Bronte's Wuthering Heights. She was in tears because she wanted to love and be loved like that, like in the story. She blamed herself for isolating and detaching herself from people her own age. It started in middle school, she remembered, when her body started to blossom and boys started to notice. She would ignore them or intimidate them. It was fun then, she thought, but when she got to high school, it was the real thing. She was Cinderella twenty-four seven, with no Prince Charming to call her own. She was driven and picked up from school every day by a man who looked more like a bodyguard than a chauffeur. She was well read and an A student in every class. Her teachers adored her, for obvious reasons, and her enemies list kept getting longer. None of the girls ever confronted her; they wouldn't dare because there was never any basis behind the silly gossip. She never invited any girls to her house because of her mother's eccentric behavior and Danny's reputation as a drug user. She spent many nights alone, reading novels and plays, emotionally involved in that fictional world and not in the realty of her real world, with all its struggles and pain, until now. On occasion, she'd go out with her brother, Danny, and Ramon. They would cruise down Main Street downtown and go to some parties, where the Rat Boy stayed close to her as if they were a couple. When they went to dances at the Knights of Columbus Hall, few asked her to dance, and the ones who did were usually polluted. Her brother, Danny, danced with her and sometimes Mike Montes, but he only danced the slow ones. He was touchy feely; he squeezed her tight and always wanted to stick his tongue in her ear. Ramon, the Rat Boy, didn't dance; he just stared.

Vivian wiped away the tears with her hands. She hated feeling like this. She was out of high school over a year now and still didn't hold a job, no friends, no California. Her mother refused to let her go to the University of Arizona on the full scholarship she had won. Said it was too far and that she needed her at home to help out. Now she was stuck here in this miserable town with nothing going for her. Her mother would never leave Las Flores and move to California with her. She was sure her godfather, Juan Jose, would take her, but he'd return to be close to her mother, even though her mother, at times, wouldn't even give him the time of day. She was more than sure Juan Jose gave her mother money and had offered to marry her after her father's demise. Delfina still acted like the proud widow and would never allow another man to share her bed. Vivian knew that Juan Jose had paid for Danny's car in cash and offered to buy her one also. She also knew her mother, on her measly monthly check, could never afford to pay for the costs involved in raising two kids and maintaining a household.

Vivian placed the novel between her breasts and held it tightly. She loved Emily Bronte and wondered if she could ever write a novel —not just any novel but a novel that would touch women's hearts. She strongly believed she had been born to accomplish something special, something that would endure for years after she had passed on. That was why she never minded the restrictions put on her by poverty, by the absence of a loving father, being without girlfriends her age she could talk to, and all the rest of the bullshit she had to put up with. She knew it was a trial run to build up her resiliency, her tenacity, for the future struggles in the competitive world she wanted to live in.

Vivian felt a little better now as she looked around her small bedroom. She kept it as neat as she could with the little she had. Everything was old and run down. Even the old television in the living room was broken, and her mother refused a new one from Juan Jose. She had to play her radio and record player low, so she just left them alone. It had been difficult to dress up for the part of the spoiled princess she had been cast in. Her closet was impoverished, and thank God for jeans, she always used to say. She could combine different tops with tight jeans and get away with murder. Shoes were no problem: tennis shoes and on occasion high heels, and that was that. Attending church on Sunday was another thing though. She refused to go until her mother bought her decent dresses, and she did. Other than that, she didn't need much in the way of clothes because her social life was limited, and she would rather spend any extra money her godfather gave her on books.

Vivian kept looking at her bare feet, wondering if they were too big. Shit, she said. She started thinking about going to California and staying with her aunt on her mother's side. She lived in East Los Angeles and was as rigid as her mother. Her aunt would want her to get a job as a secretary, as her daughters had. But Vivian couldn't see herself playing bump and grind at the water cooler with some jackass who thought himself clever. But her aunt really believed she would meet a decent man who would see beyond her silliness and ask her to marry him. And the responsibility of children and raising a family would be enough to settle her down and stop her dreaming of something that was beyond her reach. This was what made her angry; she had had to put up with this provincial attitude all her life, and she was sick of these witches telling her what to do with her life. She was going to be an artist, she thought, even if she had to sell her ass on the street to accomplish it.

Vivian was looking at her homemade bookshelf, built by her brother, Danny, from rough boards he had been able to gather from here and there. She studied the collection of books, mostly fiction, she had kept throughout the years. Most were tattered, used paperback copies she had bought at the farmers' market or had been given to her by her teachers. She loved her books because they had opened up many frontiers to explore and exposed her to other worlds altogether different than hers. She went through emotional highs and lows, like when she attempted to comprehend Heathcliff's tormented vengeance and enduring love for Catherine. A love created in hell, she thought, but still powerful love, in her eyes, by a man plagued by demons. She remembered when she first read the novel, as a freshman in high school, for an English class assignment that rocked her world. She was in suspended animation for at least a couple of months while the teacher and other students seemed to be oblivious to the pain and love the story evoked. She wanted to scream to her classmates, Wake up, you morons; can't you feel the power of the written word? Have your imaginations petrified; have your hearts turned to steel? But she didn't. She realized she was different; she didn't want to be, but she was and had to live with it.

Vivian was studying her small but precious library from her bed, deciding between two plays she wanted to get into. One was Montserrat, by Lillian Hellman, one of her favorite playwrights, and the other was a little-known work given to her by her godfather: Night over Taos, by Maxwell Anderson. She preferred the older works because they brought her to a time in history when people were divided by great distances but still shared the same emotional concerns, dealing with life and death, love and hate. She was just about to get up and grab both of the books when she heard a light tapping outside her window. What the hell, she thought, must be a rat. The tapping continued. This is ridiculous, she said to herself. It couldn't be. She turned the lamp off and moved the black curtain a bit to the side. Staring at her from outside, close to the window, like a ghost, was Ramon, the Rat Boy. Shit, she said and inched back the curtain. The tapping continued; she moved the curtain again, a little wider this time, and gestured to Ramon to get lost. But Ramon didn't move; he did hand signals suggesting he wanted a word with her. She said, Crap, cracked the window slightly, and said in a whispering and not-too-friendly voice, Get lost, Ramon. I don't wanna talk. Leave, now. Ramon, nervous and sweating, pleaded for five minutes of her time. Vivian conceded. Five minutes, she said. Meet me out front, and if you wake Mother, you're dead meat.

Ramon was waiting with his hand in his pockets, catching his breath but still nervous. The dog was sitting on his hind legs next to him, two travelers seeking asylum in an unfamiliar land. Vivian came out the front door onto the dark porch, moving like a cat. She walked in her flip flops, watchful not to step on the parts of the wood floor that would squeak. She kept walking to the far end of the porch, away from the front door, without saying a word and waited for Ramon with a book in her hand, in case she was forced to slam him in the head with it. She had on a black terrycloth bathrobe, and her hair was braided in a long, thick ponytail.

Ramon walked up the creaky wooden steps, avoiding the areas where the wood was weak and creaked more with his weight. He was also careful on the porch, where the dog rushed up to Vivian, who scolded him in a whisper until the dog settled down. Keep your voice down, Ramon, she said. I don't want Mother to wake up and find you here. If she does, you're gonna be sorry you ever came. You got five minutes. Say what you came here to say and leave.

Ramon walked up close to Vivian but not too close, because he was aware Vivian was uptight about anyone getting too close to her. It was dark on the porch but not so dark for him not to see her and bump into her and put his arms all over her. Vivian, he began, with a speech he had practiced ever since he had been in the hospital. Vivian, I don't have in me the words to express how bad I feel and the harm I've done you. If only I had the power to move back the clock, I—

You do what? she asked before he finished his sentence, seething. You do what, Ramon? Stay away from Danny? Stop him from taking that poison he was taking? What? Do what, Ramon? Haven't you done enough?

No, listen, Vivian, he begged. I couldn't stop Danny from doing what he wanted to do. I tried, but he called me stupid and other names, said I didn't know shit about nothing. Said taking me along to California was doing me a big favor, as long as I came up with some cash. Everybody blames me, Vivian. It wasn't my fault; he was sick, so I had to drive. He was dying, Vivian; what could I do?

Yeah, right, Vivian said in a high whisper, that's your story, Rat Boy. We'll never know the truth. You need to do time in prison, Ramon. Maybe the time spent there will clear your messed-up head, set you on a new path, who knows?

Please, Vivian, don't be so cruel. I'll kill myself if that'll make you feel better. Tell me what to do, and I'll do it for you. Anything. Just say the word.

Vivian was so angry, so upset at Ramon, she wanted to thrash him bad, but her mother would come outside to see what all the racket was, and she'd have to explain to her what Ramon was doing on their front porch at this time of night. She clenched her teeth tightly to stop the vile words that were screaming to come out of her mouth. You must go, she finally said, without raising her voice. There is nothing to talk about. There never was.

No, please, Vivian. Please listen to me. What about California?

What about it? Don't tell me you believed you were included in our plans. Ha! Danny was right; you are stupid. Who would want to take you anywhere? You fucking cripple. Go home before your mother comes looking for you.

Please, Vivian, don't hurt me like that. Ramon was almost in tears, doing his best to stay dry. I might be able to get hold of some money, and we can still go, you and me.

Stop it, you little shit. You get some money; it has to be lots. Bring it to me, all of it, and then I'll decide. For now, get off my property, and stay off. I'm going inside. If you have a seizure, it's on you; maybe the dog'll help you. She walked past him, almost pushed him out of the way, and went inside the house and turned off the light.

Ramon remained in the dark, alone. The dog attempted to follow Vivian inside the house, but she shut the door before he could get in. He decided he had enough of these crazy people, so he went back into his hole under the ancient cedar next to the house. Ramon remained on the porch with his hands in his pockets, thinking. God, it hurt him when Vivian put him down like that. It hurt so deep, beyond anything he had ever suffered. He wanted to be with her so bad. He wanted to be near her and share her pain, but she didn't want anything to do with him. She called him a cripple, and maybe he was, but it was out of love for her that he acted, at times, like one. He forgave her, he decided. She was blinded with grief, and her words were harsh. It was because of that grief, the loss of her brother, that made everything else pointless to her. He'd never abandon her, never, he thought, even if he had to lurk in the shadows as Juan Jose did, waiting for Delfina Madrid to open her heart. He'd wait for Vivian to at least forgive him, acknowledge his existence, and be on talking terms; for that alone, he could die happy, if he got only that. But wait a minute, he thought. Didn't she say to bring her the money, all of it, and she'd see? Well, now, was that a spark of hope, a lifeline to a dying man? Where there's hope, there's life, he said to himself. Did I make that up? he wondered, already feeling better, as he walked away from the spooky house with all its dark secrets.

He found his walking stick and hurried along, realizing it was still early, and he didn't want to confront Juan Jose, if he was around, and have to explain his reasons for being at the house. It was none of his business, anyway, but he still didn't want to risk it. Ramon could afford to act brave now that he was off the property on San Albino. No one could tell him shit. No one, he said, out loud. His business was with Mike Montes and no one else. He thought of going to Sammy Q.'s but changed his mind; things could get rough at Sammy's. He decided to take a bus downtown and hang at Jimmy's Pool Hall; maybe he'd see Mike there. Things are looking up, he sang, as he headed to the bus stop.

CHAPTER SEVENTEEN

he following day, Sammy Q. and Romero were in downtown Las Flores, having a green-chili cheeseburger at Fat Henry's Restaurant on Main Street. The sign at the entrance read "Fat Henry's Restaurant" and, in smaller letters underneath, "Home of the best green-chili burger in the state—if not the country." Fat Henry, the mayor of Las Flores, was sitting behind the counter where he worked the cash register. He was sitting on a large wooden spool, the kind used for heavy cable. The section in the middle was carved out, splashed with numerous coats of polyurethane, and upholstered with soft cowhide with pillows placed on the sitting section, and it made a reasonable place where Henry could sit his fat ass. He smiled at Sammy and Romero as they walked in. The fleshy slabs of fat inched up toward his green eyes, making them look slanted— thus the nickname Buddha Henry. He knew Sammy Q. didn't vote, and Romero was a stranger, but he made it a habit to greet all his paying customers with his familiar smile.

The restaurant was nothing special. It was typical, with a long counter for the coffee crowd with several booths framed in beige leather. It had large windows in front and on the side where the booths were. A view of the courthouse, city hall, and other buildings could be seen from the booth where Sammy and Romero were chowing down on their green-chili cheeseburgers and fries. Romero had smothered his fries with ketchup, attempting to cool the flame in his mouth, with beads of perspiration on his upper lip but not saying a word to Sammy because he had asked for the extra-hot green chili, Hatch Valley green, after Sammy had warned him. He refused to order another glass of ice water because the waitress had brought him the last one with a grin on her face.

Fat Henry paid his cooks decent salaries to keep them happy, and most had stayed with him for years. The many awards and trophies plastered and hanging all over the wall behind the cash register, which had been won in chili-burger cook-offs, attested to the skill of his cooks. He'd send his main man, Sabino, to the Hatch Valley to secure the best green before other buyers got in their bids. He knew many of the growers by first name; they knew him as a man who kept his word and would grant favors, if ever needed. Sabino, an expert in roasting green chili, roasted the mild to hot varieties of the chili on a large, long, boxlike metal roaster covered with a thin metal cover and fired with mesquite wood. After roasting, Sabino cut off the heads of the pods and peeled them. He put them in containers, froze half for the winter months, and used the rest for green-chili burgers, fresh and hot. There was a smaller roaster or grill also outside in the back where the burgers were done. The burger meat, bought fresh every day except Sunday, was seasoned with Sabino's secret ingredients. The buns were heated just right, and the beef patty was placed on the bun, already saturated with green chili salsa, and a square of American yellow cheese went on top of the sizzling patty. Lettuce, tomatoes, and onions were added as soon as the cheese started to melt on top of the patty. They slapped it on a plate and rushed it inside, where other condiments could be added. The Special-Special was a long, green, roasted or raw chili placed directly on top of the meat, no cheese. Fat Henry didn't allow Sabino to make many of the Specials—only for friends and relatives, many of his gringo compadres having gone native in language and eating habits. He charged the tourists extra for the Special-Special. Some had read about it in the New Mexico Magazine or heard about it from other visitors and believed they could handle it. It was usually a waste of good chili; most couldn't eat it. Sabino had at hand a container of watered-down, readymade green chili for the tourists, so as not to hurt their feelings and keep their business at Henry's.

Sammy Q. and Romero were in the booth, Romero on his second cheeseburger, hooked on the burn. Sammy had only one, eating his chunky fries one at a time, dipping them in a small bowl made of hickory wood and filled with Hatch Valley green salsa for the brave ones who dared go beyond the burn.

You OK, big boy? Sammy asked, not wanting to smile because Romero might take it the wrong way. As Sammy was finding out, Romero was unpredictable.

What you think? Romero responded, sweat on his forehead but not shying away from the burger as he sat facing the front door—a habit judiciously followed. He never sat anywhere inside a dwelling unless his back was on a wall and his eyes on the exit or entrance door. A careful fellow, one might say.

See the library over there on the corner of Main and Church? Sammy asked Romero.

Yeah, what about it, Romero answered, sucking on some ice to quiet down the burning in his mouth.

That library is named after Elfego Baca. You know about the man, right?

Romero said, Yeah, wasn't he an outlaw or something?

In some people's minds, but he was a lawman, and in 1884, at age nineteen, he appointed himself deputy sheriff of Socorro County, to the south from here. He was a brave hombre, wasn't afraid to tangle with the crazy gringo cowboys who got drunk and raised hell. When the library was being built, there was a debate on what to call it. Of course, to the primos, Elfego Baca was a perfect name, although some didn't know who Elfego Baca was. They knew he had to be a badass though, because not only was he born in Socorro, he was also Hispano. But there was an element in the Westside, crackers, who wanted to name the library the John Robert Baylor Library. Baylor was commander of the 258th Texas Calvary who in 1861 occupied Fort Bliss and raised the Confederate flag in Old Mesilla—what balls, huh? Anyway, there was another group in the Westside and hereabout with deeper roots in their Southern heritage who said, Fuck Baylor; he didn't do shit. They wanted the new library to be named after a deserter from the Northern army, Major Henry H. Sibley, who took Albuquerque and Santa Fe for the Confederate cause. Now there's a man we should honor, a real American hero, not a greaser bandit like Elfego Baca, whoever he was, was their reasoning.

Sammy smiled and paused. He knew Romero was a dickhead, dumb as dirt, when it came to history. He took out a pack of Faros and placed them on the table, looking for a light.

Put that shit away, Sammy. Jesus, I just ate, Romero said, wrinkling his forehead in disgust. He was jealous that Sammy knew stuff; guys like Sammy, in his opinion, were supposed to be stupid, ignorant, not informed about anything beyond the confines of their hick surroundings.

The waitress, all smiles, approached Romero and asked him if he cared for anything else. She ignored Sammy as if he was the Invisible Man. Sammy winked at the waitress several times, a grin on his round and dark pockmarked face.

Just bring the check, Romero said in a dry, mechanical tone, not looking at her. His full attention was on the library building outside with its interesting history. The waitress, with her protruding belly and short, chubby legs, disgusted him. He was used to come-ons like that from ugly bitches; he didn't even make an effort to hide his disdain. He figured that was the kind of dog Sammy would cut off one of his balls for. The waitress, seeing Romero had no interest, turned to Sammy and gave him a dirty look before walking off to add up their tab.

So then what happened? Romero asked, glancing at his watch. It went to the city council, Sammy said, happy Romero showed some interest. But back then, the council had only four members; the mayor usually broke the deadlock. The fucking council was split, two for and two against. Buddha Henry told them from the git-go that he ain't gonna get involved, either way. You see, Buddha Henry married a woman from Chihuahua, years ago. His kids are half-Hispano, with the Catholic faith ingrained on both sides of the family. He was Irish Catholic, from New York City, and didn't want to be pegged a cracker. He refused to alienate his family, friends, and voting base. He'd gone native years before, so with the Hispano vote in his pocket and a liberal block of progressive gringos, who could touch him? He won on every election he ran for; not a thing the rednecks could do to get him out of office. But then again, Buddha Henry was also a businessman and didn't want to chase away people with money in their pockets. So it worked out better for him to stay out of it, remain neutral, which he did.

Sammy paused, chewing on a fry, dying for a smoke. So you see? he continued. The name of the library was on hold, and it was almost completed. The two council members who wanted it named after Elfego Baca insisted Elfego Baca was never convicted of any murder, was sheriff of Socorro County, a US Marshal in 1882, studied law, was admitted to the bar, and joined a Socorro law firm. What the hell did the pendejos want, Francis of Assisi? Besides, he held public offices like county clerk, mayor, and school superintendent of Socorro County and district attorney of both Socorro and Sierra Counties. Tight credentials, don't you agree, Romero? Not a mad-dog gunman, as the other side painted him, hell no. Sure, he took a nip here and there, maybe had a weakness for women, but shit, who doesn't?

OK, Sammy, get to the point, Romero said, looking at his watch again.

Sammy held a fry in his fingers that were already as greasy as the fry. So the numb nuts, he continued, were tied up, not even close to a compromise. Both sides lobbied Buddha Henry; he remained above the fray, refused to break the tie. So finally, Sammy added, sucking on his fingers, Arturo Montes Sr., Mike's grandfather—you know Mike, don't you?

Why keep asking me that? I don't know anyone except you in this town.

OK, thought you might. Anyway, Arturo Montes Sr. was the owner of a small construction company and knew all the dicks on the council. He cornered the two council members—one from the Eastside, who wanted Elfego's name on the library—and sold them on a simple plan to get what they wanted and what a lot of people wanted. He said to them, Incorporate Chiva Town into the city, and elect someone to the city council who is on your side. He also told them he could guarantee the votes 'cause he hired many of the men of voting age to work for him. As you know, Chiva Town is right next to the Eastside barrio. Some of the people there wanted their goats to run wild all over the place, like they been doing for years.

Well, Sammy said, they got enough votes to incorporate, especially after Arturo Sr. and his men went door to door and convinced many of the people they were gonna get better services from the city than they were getting from the county. They got the votes, just enough to pass and elect a new city councilman, who of course was sympathetic to their cause. The library was named the Elfego Baca Library; there she sits, in all her glory.

Why the Pueblo architecture? asked Romero.

Oh! Sammy said. After the library got its name, other pendejos came in with names of their own. Small groups with obscure names of people nobody gave a shit about. The only legitimate group was the Native Americans. They said they had naming rights 'cause the library, the whole town of Las Flores, was built on land stolen from Native Americans. Who in their right mind could argue with that, 'cept the southern migrants, who said the savages didn't have a right to protest anything—in other words, fuck 'em.

So why the Pueblo style? asked Romero again, crunching ice in his mouth.

Before that, Sammy continued, sucking the salty grease from his fingers, the Native Americans wanted the library to be named the Popé Library, after Popé, the medicine man. You heard of Popé, right?

I'm from Colorado, Romero answered, not knowing what else to say.

I'm sure history books are allowed in Colorado, said Sammy. Correct me if I'm wrong. He didn't want to sound like a smartass, but the fool left himself open for a whipping.

Anyway, Sammy continued, not wanting to antagonize Romero too much, Popé was a medicine man from San Juan. He led the native uprising against the Spaniards and their mixed-blood Mexican compadres in August of 1680. The natives killed hundreds of settlers and cleared the northern areas of the pinche Spanish. The hated Spanish and their allies fled south to San Lorenzo, near present-day El Paso, where they stayed for about thirteen years, until the reconquest by Diego de Vargas and his Indian supporters.

Romero looked at Sammy and tried not to show his dislike for him. He knew Sammy was showing off; he also knew Sammy Q. would be cut down to size anytime soon. The little mutt must pay and pay dearly for being so arrogant, he thought. Sammy was acting like a history teacher; a subject Romero had never taken to.

You're quite the historian, aren't you Sammy Boy? Romero asked, sucking on some ice. Did you learn this stuff in college?

Sammy, with a grin from ear to ear, said, Hell, no. I dropped out of high school.

So then where did you—

I pick up a lot of facts from Jiggers. He's one of my friends that stops at the house to talk. Knows his shit.

Jiggers, Jiggers, repeated Romero. What kind of name is that?

I don't know, said Sammy. That's what everybody calls him. His real name is Victor Mondragon, Dragon Slayer, but he likes Jiggers.

What does this Jiggers do?

He drinks, said Sammy.

You mean he's a wino? asked Romero, working not to smile.

I don't use that term, said Sammy. He is what he is. All I know is he knows his history, lays it out, if you show interest.

I see, said Romero. Jiggers, huh? Yep, that's right, said Sammy.

One more question before we go, Sammy Boy, said Romero, hoping to trip him up. Why were the Confederates interested in New Mex? There was nothing here.

Sammy studied Romero: his clean-shaven face; clear, light-brown eyes, set apart; a good nose, not too large, not too flat; well-shaped lips—a little feminine, perhaps, but by all means not a bunny. His forehead was high and his hair dark, thick, and brushed back, not to the side and not too short like a weenie. If he liked guys, thought Sammy, Romero would definitely be his chorizo. He was thinking whether to answer the question or not. He could play dumb, let Romero score some points, let it be the end of it. But then he thought that his friend Jiggers would be disappointed he didn't pass on info to others, especially if he had a handle on the info. Hey, he thought, the fool wants more; who am I to deprive him of knowledge?

Well, then, said Sammy, like a man not sure of what to say, running his hand through his bristly hair, cut short to the skull but not so short as to see the bone. The taking of New Mex—like you say, a barren, poor territory with Indian problems—was part of the Confederate plan to get California. You have to know a little bit of what was going on. The Confederate States needed cash to defeat the North. The gold and silver of the Southwest could buy a lot of stuff. The sea coast of Califa, of course, was perfect for this, you know, for supplies to come in from Europe and—

OK, Sammy Boy, interrupted Romero, abruptly. That's enough. We gotta go. He picked up the tab and walked to the cash register without giving Sammy an opportunity to complete his thought. Buddha Henry, the mayor of Las Flores, was still smiling behind the cash register. He was wearing an expensive white linen short- sleeved shirt with green chili peppers embroidered with silk in the front and back of the shirt. He had on a leather bolo tie around his opened shirt collar with a spiderweb turquoise clasp encrusted in old silver. It was the size of a corn tortilla, a pawn-shop piece he had picked up in Gallup. He was chowing down out of a large bowl filled with grilled chunks of beef smothered in Hatch Valley green, with a pile of homemade flour tortillas used to spoon the chile con carne to his mouth. Romero paid the tab. Buddha Henry said thanks many times, thanking Sammy for bringing in a new customer. Sammy was about to start a conversation with the mayor when he noticed that Romero hadn't left a tip. He walked back to the table and left a couple of dollars, hoping to see the chavita again, but no luck. Romero was already outside waiting for him, looking at the library.

C'mon, Sammy, let's go. Where's that place you're gonna take me to?

It's called the Swamps by the locals, said Sammy. It's next to the river. There's an event taking place today. If there's any good chiva going out, you can bet your booty we'll find it there.

Romero gave Sammy a look, like saying, Yeah, right; in other words, a perfect place for an ambush.

Main Street was getting busy. Henry's and the other business outlets on Church Street were doing brisk business. Jimmy's Pool Hall had early customers, and the Welcome Inn Bar and Grill was also getting busy. A diverse group of shoppers turned up on Saturday, along with a few tourists. The field workers, with ready cash in their pockets, were looking for bargains, and the locals came more to chitchat than to spend money. They interacted with the merchants in a friendly manner. Part of Main Street was blocked off for the farmers' market held every Saturday.

Sammy remembered he'd promised his Granny to pick up some hierbas for her. Romero, Sammy said, wait up, man. I've got to get some hierbas for my Granny. I'll be right back; won't take but a sec. He took off to the farmers' market, which was a short distant from Henry's, before Romero could say a word.

Romero said, Shit. He waited next to his truck, parked on Church Street. He was studying the Elfego Baca Library and didn't get tired of looking at it. To own a home built in the Pueblo style was his dream—a dream he had never shared with anyone, yet. He'd seen them in Santa Fe and vicinity, and his boss had one outside Taos. He wanted the real stuff on his. He wanted the flat roof with rounded contours and deep windows and door openings with arched, curved entryways, doorways, and walls. The ceilings supported by huge vigas and a curved kiva fireplace in every room, with bancos for sitting close to the fire on cold nights, that was his idea of comfort. He wanted nichos on the walls where his mother could place her Santos de Palo and feel at home. And of course he must have Saltillo and Talavera tile for his floors and Red Dragon granite countertops; a must, he insisted. And he must not forget portals in front and back of the house to sit and check out the colors of the setting sun. Yes, why not, he thought. It could happen. That's why this deal was so vital. The boss had let him put in some of his own cash to buy the smack. He put in all his savings—not much to them, but to him it was a small fortune. He was positive he could double or triple his investment. He could get a teaching credential and coach football or basketball or open up a business and go straight, make his parents proud. But he had to get his hands on the chiva, which wasn't like the chiva sold every day. Chiva was black- tar heroin, cheaply processed in dirty labs in Mexico and other places. He didn't even tell Sammy—maybe he did, it didn't matter— that this sugar was almost if not completely pure, the best of the best. He had to recover it, take it back, to cash in and have his dream house built, get out of the trade, or become a partner in the firm. He was getting tired of being the errand boy all the time. He deserved better, he thought. Going after junkies and setting them straight was a drag on him; it wasn't fun anymore. Killing poor, strung-out Lencho had been tough, but he had to show Sammy he meant business. He smiled when he saw Sammy with a paper bag in each hand containing the herbs walking toward him. Sammy lived such a simple life, he thought. Getting turned on by buying dry weeds for his Granny from an old witch at a farmers market. Jesus, give me a break, he said to himself.

Look, Sammy said, showing the paper bags to Romero, happy as a boy busting his first piñata. This woman drives all the way from Juarez to sell her hierbas. She had what my Granny wanted. In this bag we have abedul, whose sex is female, planet is Venus, and element is water. It's used for exorcisms, evil eye, and protection from lightning. In the old times, witches' brooms were made from the branches of the abedul, and cradles were made from the wood to protect babies from the evil eye and other difficulties. In this other bag we have alcaparra, also female, with Venus for its planet and water for its element. This is used to prevent masculine impotency and enhances fertility, desire, and amor. Now who doesn't want amor? Sammy said, laughing. My Granny fixes up the herbs for the women who need them. The woman from Juarez and my Granny could write an encyclopedia on herbs and their uses, let me tell you. Some people need help with fertility and impotency; if you can't get it up, you can't get it up, and of course evil eye—that's big, right, Romero?

Romero answered without even thinking about it. I don't believe in that shit.

It don't matter if we believe in it or not, said Sammy. They believe in it; that's what counts.

As Sammy opened the door to the truck, he noticed people putting out boxes of used books in front of the library.

Look, he said to Romero. They's selling books at the library. Let's go and take a look; you never know what treasures we can dig out.

No way, said Romero. I have to drive to Denver tonight. I have to report the progress of the missing chiva to my boss. I'll drop you off later. You can look all you want, OK, Sammy Boy? Romero was annoyed because Sammy turned a simple act or question into something more complex and made him feel somehow less clever, as if he existed in a cultural vacuum—and he didn't, he strongly believed.

OK, Sammy Boy, Romero said when they were both in the truck, which way?

Sammy put on his little beat-up hat and lowered the brim toward his eyes. Stay on Church till you reach Maricopa. On Maricopa, turn right and go all the way to Loma, cut a left on Loma, and Loma'll take you to the river. The traffic was lighter as they reached Maricopa and drove north toward Loma. Sammy loved to be a passenger. He didn't like to drive, and he didn't own a car or a truck. His driver's license had been suspended so many times for driving under the influence that he didn't bother to mess with it anymore. He was given a ride when he had to take his Granny to the doctor; besides, he could always take the bus. He didn't like taking the bus because of the waiting, but if he had to, he did. Groceries were delivered to his Granny once a month by a special program he had gotten her on. It was the basic stuff—beans, cheese, canned goods—but that saved him trips to get them himself. His Granny was in a wheelchair and legally blind. She got a check every month, and that paid most of the bills. He was trying to get on SSI, but he had been denied twice. His case was appealed, and he was certain he'd get it, one day. He got a small stipend from the state for taking care of his Granny, but that wasn't much and could dry up any day. The Social Security supplement was a sure thing. If he got that, he'd be on easy street, he figured. Although he never worked long on a job, he was claiming alcohol abuse and dependency, as many of his friends had, and it worked for them. He thought about getting a job at times but never convinced himself to do anything about it. No way, he thought, they owed him. He figured he was at least one-quarter Native American, but no tribe claimed him because of proper bloodlines and paperwork. Forget the paperwork, he used to say. Need paperwork for every goddamn thing. The only paper he needed was the kind to wipe his ass, and he laughed about it. So here he was, a passenger in a big Dodge Ram, with the air on, sitting high, looking at the sights, with a mad dog killer as a driver.

At the corner of Mariposa and Piñion Romero stopped at the stoplight. Sammy looked to his right and saw the Alleluia Bookstore on the corner.

Hey look, said Sammy, excited, as if he had spotted an old girlfriend. I got busted in that place some years ago.

Try to rob it? Romero asked, amused.

No, man, Sammy looked at Romero, like asking, What, me rob? I went in there looking for a book, and I was pretty wasted. I had an idea it was a Christian bookstore, but I didn't know all they sold was religious books, see what I mean? I couldn't find the book I was looking for, so I go off on the guy working there. He tried to tell me it was a religious bookstore, but I didn't listen. I started throwing books from the shelves to the floor. They called the cops, and I slept in the slammer. The owners were cool; they dropped the charges, and I was released. I apologized and donated some religious books I kept in my collection. My way of saying, Sorry, folks, I blew it. Romero looked at Sammy, at his hat. You look funny wearing that stupid hat, he said, no longer amused. I look funny without the hat, Sammy responded. So what's the big deal? You look like a pinto; I never say nothing. Oops, only kidding, brother.

Romero had suddenly stopped the truck on the curb, almost crashing into a city bus.

What did you call me? he asked, furious. You little bag of manure. Look at you, and look at me, he continued, pointing a finger at Sammy. You're dark, short, and ugly. Your face looks like dried asphalt mixed with dirt when scraped off the road. You got tattoos on your neck, all over your arms; you don't think you look like a pinto? Gimme a break. You the kind of vato makes the rest of us look bad. You the greaser dude white folks make jokes about. Now look at me, Sammy Boy. I'm college educated, fluent in English and Spanish, and don't have a single tattoo on my sculptured body. I've eaten in the most expensive restaurants in Chicago and have selected the best bottles of wine when I order for my boss; have you ever done that? I doubt it. The only reason I'm having this conversation with you now is I need to find the chiva, and you're gonna help me find it. Oh! And another thing, Sammy Boy, that hat on your fuzzy head ain't a tango. A tango is a cool hat; everybody knows that. Your hat is a piece-of-shit hat; I wouldn't even offer it to a homeless man begging in the street.

Sammy was hurt; he tried not to show it, but he was hurt. This cruel bastard can hurt people, he thought, and Lencho came to his mind. He helped murder poor Lencho, same as if he had kicked the poor boy down the mine shaft himself. He took the beast to Lencho. Lencho was cancelled out, and he didn't do shit to help him. He let his friend be tortured, murdered, and didn't lift a stick to at least attempt to put a stop to the cruel treatment of his friend Lencho. And the same monster who killed Lencho was taking liberties with his physical and social status. And although it was nothing new to him, put-downs had forced him to grow a second skin to fight off the needles and pins thrown at him since he was a youth. But this time, it hurt; it penetrated his thick skin and made him bleed. He had taken shit from racist whites and even from his own people—more of it from them because he was around them for longer periods of time. He always had a comeback, especially when he got older and his facility with language improved. But this was the second time he had to eat Romero's shit. It was leaving a bad taste in his mouth, and there was little he could about it.

Sorry, Romero, said Sammy, uneasy, if I offended you. But that was the rumor about you—that you had done time. You know when shit starts, it goes all over.

Who started that rumor about me, Sammy? Tell me. I'll put a stop to it.

A rumor is a rumor, Romero. Don't know who started it or how long it's gonna run, for that matter. It's like a tornado. No one can tell for sure which is gonna be the last house it's gonna wreck before it calms down.

Romero said nothing. He put the truck in gear and drove toward Loma. Maybe this little mutt was taking him to this place called the Swamps to get him ambushed with the help of his friends, he thought. They could shoot him in the back or run him over with a truck and finish him off with baseball bats. But he didn't believe little Sammy had the balls to go through with any rough stuff. Maybe his friends—Sammy had a lot of friends—but Sammy had to sell them on the idea, and those plans never worked exactly as expected. Romero was confident Sammy Boy was a coward, a slug who sucked the juice from the most passive plants. He could rest easy and go anywhere with Sammy Boy without a care in the world.

Romero reached Loma and cut a left, heading toward the river. There was a long silence in the truck, the silence of a young married couple's first tit tat—nothing big, but a huge disappointment on both sides because boundaries would have to be established so early in the marriage. Besides the silence and the awkwardness, the ride was pleasant enough. The day was sunny and warm but not too toasty, a perfect day to picnic along the river with family and friends. It was indeed a perfect day to take a dip in the cool waters of the river and refresh body and soul. That's what Sammy saw: families, some heading to the river; couples; and single guys, all heading to find their favorite spot along the river. Cook some food, drink a few brews, and have some fun, nothing wrong with that, he thought; he'd done it many times and planned do it many more, especially in the summer months. He was taking Romero to the Swamps a part of the river not for families with kids.

As they approached the bridge, Sammy could see the cars and trucks on the levee, driving slow, looking for the perfect spot along the picturesque riverbank. The tires crunched up the loose gravel as if it were peanut brittle, leaving a cloud of gray dust behind. The levee, on a higher elevation, was like a narrow, rutted, unbroken ribbon, racing the river south in a continual monotony. The river was flowing in the same gracious rhythm as it had for centuries. And except for a few whirlpools that spun in the brownish water, the river advanced south to collapse into the great pond that patiently waited at the end of the world.

Sammy broke the silence and said, a little dejected but fighting to leave it behind, This is the end of Loma; cross the bridge, and cut a left. Stay on the dirt road as soon as you cross the bridge; see how it goes down, away from the bridge? Stay on the dirt road until I tell you where to cut into the Swamps. It's not really a swamp. The river washes into the area when it runs high, then recedes back. There's no levee on this side, as you can see.

Why do they call this place the Swamps? Romero asked, milder now, knowing he needed Sammy to get around. The place must have a name.

Well, if it do, I sure the hell don't know it. It's been called the Swamps since I can remember; older vatos always called it the Swamps. But let me tell you, not many people venture in there alone at night, especially late at night. It's so dark and creepy, you scare yourself, and that's no joke. A couple of years ago, we were in there, six couples in two cars, all right? It wasn't even that late, about eleven or twelve. I walked off to take a piss not far from where we were parked. As I was pissing, I saw a white boy standing right next to me. I didn't see or hear him walk up, and I'm positive he wasn't there when I started pissing. Luckily my friends were right behind me, and they asked him what he wanted. He walked off into the dark without saying a word. If it had been daytime, I tell you, he'd have gotten his ass kicked. But don't you see, Romero? He could have slit my throat, cut off my dick, done anything he wanted to do to me. Man, I sobered up and headed back to the car with my friends, afraid to even glance back. They have found mutilated bodies drained of their blood in the Swamps. Not even the cops like to come out here. Shit, they come if they have to, but they don't like it.

Sammy warned Romero to watch the road that slinked suddenly into the intricate maze called the Swamps. Romero drove his truck slowly into a canopy of giant Alamo trees and shrubs with striking leaf forms. He followed the single, sandy road further in until the river disappeared and only the sloshing of water could be heard. The mangrove next to the river looked innocent enough during the day, but at dusk, the interwoven tree trunks and branches, half sunken in the sand, resembled a gnarled nightmare of tangled, bony arms and legs, grabbing for something to hold on to. There were dozens of singular, narrow paths that started or ended at the river and led to God knew where and seemed to circle this way and that.

Trucks and cars, old, new, and in between, began to appear, parked every which way. Romero began to worry again. This was a perfect place for his demise, he thought. He forgot his gun, and he couldn't turn back; it was too late for that. He couldn't show Sammy or anyone else any hesitation or any kind of fear; that wouldn't do.

We're here, Sammy said, elated. Park anywhere. And he jumped out of the truck as if he had just arrived home for the holidays.

Romero parked and followed Sammy to an open space next to a giant cotton tree. Sammy was giving hugs and high fives to people he seemed to know. The air was saturated with the odor of cooked beef. Sammy called Romero over and introduced him to the Leyva brothers. The Leyva brothers, he said, prepared the meat. They got here early in the morning or last night, butchered the calf or hog here or somewhere else, and brought it ready to cook. They added spices, wrapped it up in wet burlap, wrapped it in chicken wire to hold it together, and threw it in the hot fire hole on top of the coals. They used pitchforks to move it around or turn it and took it out when it was ready to eat. But before that, the Leyvas placed that metal lid —see it, a short distance from the tree? —on top of the hole and covered it with dirt to cut off any air from getting into the pit, or the burlap and meat would burn to a crisp. Gotta keep the fire free of oxygen. But you knew that, right, Romero? And Sammy held back a smile. The meat's ready, he continued. Here, try some. Sammy passed a paper plate with chunks of beef in it and whole pinto beans on the side. We'll have to share the plastic fork, he said, leaving Romero with the plate and fork. He returned with a paper cup of beer in each hand. He offered Romero one. The Leyvas, he said, also bring the beer. See those kegs in tubs of ice under the tree? One works for Coors, the other for Bud; they use their discounts to buy it. So when you have a free hand, throw in a couple of bucks in the donation kitty. That helps cover expenses.

What is this place, Sammy? asked Romero.

Well, said Sammy, taking a drink from his cup. It's a swap meet, yard sale, auction, and more. Difficult to explain. You can buy or sell almost anything you want or need: guns, cars, trucks, tractors, and drugs. You can buy car parts, beef, and lots of stuff. Just ask and find the seller. Most of it is hot, and it'll cross the border eventually, although some stuff is from across the border. The best part is that none of it is here. Maybe some drugs. Most of it is hidden away, waiting to be picked up. If you burn a customer, you'll be banned and punished—just don't ask how, 'cause I couldn't tell you.

Sammy left again and left Romero with the plate of beef in one hand and cup of beer in the other. He wanted to dump the beef, having just eaten at Fat Henry's, but decided against it; it wouldn't look good. He walked back to his truck and placed the plate on the tire, hoping no one would notice. He walked back to the same place he was before, with the beer cup in his hand, checking out the scene.

He saw a lot of shady characters talking and eating— conducting business, Sammy would say. Some had on well-worn cowboy hats, brims low, almost on the eyes, and dusty cowboy boots. Others had on baseball caps worn backward, with dark shades covering their eyes, wearing steel-toed work shoes and motorcycle boots. Romero was uncomfortable because he was wearing a light-blue Polo shirt, tight on the biceps and chest. Too tight, he thought. He had on some pressed khaki pants with low-cut tennis shoes. He was glad he hadn't worn shorts; then he would really look like a tourist.

A tall, lanky vato walked up to him and checked him out. He was as tall as Romero, but he was wearing boots. He had on a Levis jacket with the sleeves cut off and no shirt. His jeans were patched up with leather strips, hand stitched by him or his girl, not a designer label for sure. The baseball cap was brown and had an insignia of a rattlesnake wrapped around a rifle with the letters CTS above the snake and rifle. The point of the cap was low, over his dark shades.

Who you with, bro? He asked, lively, with a beer cup in his hand and a toothpick in his mouth.

Romero studied the vato, ready to say, It's none of your business, but decided against it. Sammy Q., he said.

Sammy Barbecue! said the other and laughed up a storm, not caring if Romero got the joke or not. He finally settled down and took a drink from his cup, still chuckling some. I guess if you come with Sammy Q., you ain't no cop, huh? Before Romero answered, he asked, You packing heat? If you is, you gotta put it in your vehicle, or we take it and return it when you leave. No one packs during the cosido, 'cept me, that is. I'm delegated to be the chota today, and I ain't giving no one a break, not today.

I ain't packing, Romero said, a little edgy.

Its good then, and he turned around, singing "I Shot the Sheriff" out of tune.

As he walked away, Romero noticed an M29 8.25-inch-long- barreled .44 Magnum S&W revolver, Dirty Harry, in a holster hanging from his waist down to his ass, making it look like he had a tail. He also noticed the same insignia stitched on the back of his Levis jacket, but larger.

What's with the beards? thought Romero. These men ever learn to shave? Everyone seemed to be sporting some kind of beard or mustache. Romero was alone again; he felt out of place but couldn't explain why. They ignored him, except for the crazy dude who approached him to ask him if he was packing. Everyone seemed to be busy about something; money exchanged hands, but it was organized, not wild. But by the looks of the characters, it seemed to him anything could happen any minute. And how the hell could they all get the hell out, if something did go down, on that narrow road? He saw Sammy talking to a big fellow sitting on the tailgate of a pickup with his huge arm around a young kid with a shaved head. He also noticed other vatos hanging around the truck with the same leather or canvas patches sown on their jeans and shirts or a patch on their brown baseball caps of a rattler wrapped around a rifle, with the letters CTS above the snake.

Sammy returned to where Romero was standing like a tree trunk, moving only his eyes. You ready for another brew, bro? You gotta circulate, man; don't just stand there. It looks like you looking for girls or something. There ain't no girls here, bro. This ain't the place for girls.

No, I'm good, said Romero, looking at his warm cup of beer, still half-full. Who's the big guy you were talking to? asked Romero keeping his eyes on the smoking hole.

Oh, that's Tiny Tim, leader of the Chiva Town Snipers, answered Sammy. The boy with him is his nephew from El Paso. Tiny's talking the boy into wearing a hat before he jumps into the hole. They all Vallesteros. The Vallesteros are a numerous clan outa Chiva Town; relatives all over.

This clown came over and asked if I was packing; what's up with that, Sammy?

Oh, that's Oso, the Bear. He got the marshal gig today. His job is to make sure no guns are brought in. If you bring 'em, you leave 'em in your ride, locked up. You fuck around with Oso and the Snipers, they cut your head off and put it in a jar with alcohol, raza pesada. Sammy pushed his little beat-up hat upward, away from his eyes. He was grinning, thinking, You believe that, fool, you believe anything.

Romero, with a fake smile, said, Yeah, right. Let me ask you, he continued. That boy over there—and he gestured with his head; he knew better than to point—is he—

Before he completed his question, Manny, the hospital worker, let out a loud, Sammy Q., my man, my main man! and gave Sammy a double hand slap. Sammy held out both hands and then repeated the double slap on Manny's hands.

You gonna bet on me, Sammy? he asked, excited. You know I'm gonna win. I can stay in the hole longer anybody; you know it, brother. I want the lid on. Go on for sixty, Sammy, fucking A, go on for sixty; ain't nobody can touch me, no sir. Manny had on an old leather aviator cap. He had removed the goggles and cut off the flaps and removed the lining from inside the cap. He was wearing the cap tight, covering his head and ears. He also wore a long- sleeved light sweater, clinging to his torso, and tight leather jeans tucked into military jungle boots.

Take it easy, Manny, Sammy said. The kid's a Vallesteros. Don't kill 'em the first time down. Give him a break.

No matter what the boy is, said Manny, almost yelling, doing his little dance, inside the black hole, the debil don't give a fuck who you relatives are, 'cause you ass belong to him and only him. Now if you got the balls to dance with the debil, he let you go; if not, you fucked—I mean fucked. And he started laughing and doing his little dance on his toes. When he stopped laughing, he dug into his pocket and pulled out a couple of pills, threw them up in the air, and maneuvered his open mouth to catch them, and he did. He walked away to another group without saying another word. He had ignored Romero all the time he had been talking to Sammy.

Romero looked down at Sammy, took a sip from his warm beer cup, and then said, Don't tell me, Sammy.

What? Sammy asked.

Don't tell me those crazy vatos gonna jump into that burning hole?

Naw, man, it's not burning anymore. It's hot but not burning. I wouldn't do it, but hey, to each its own.

Who's this character, this nut case, anyway?

Oh, that's Manny. He's a brain slut.

A what? asked Romero, uncertain.

A brain slut, you know. Manny works at the hospital, right? Somehow he met certain doctors who were looking for volunteers to test new drugs, to test them on humans before presenting them to the FDA and getting them cleared for public consumption. One step above rats and chimpanzees, you know. Anyway, Manny gets paid and manages to take samples for his own use and sells what's left. A very resourceful vato, wouldn't you say?

What sort of drugs do they try out on the monkey?

You know, the usual: antipsychotics, painkillers, hallucinogens, new shit they come out with. They got a guinea pig. Ain't gonna give him Aspirin. He signed all kinds of documents; they ain't taking any chances with Manny Boy.

So they jump into the hole and then what? Romero asked, attempting to get a grip on what the hell was going on.

No, they don't jump into the hole together, Sammy said, looking at Romero, as if asking, Don't you know, dumbass? If they go in together, and they get tangled up trying to get out, I don't have to paint a picture, OK? It's a sport, Romero, a dangerous sport, but a sport. You know, you done sports, que no? They go in one at a time; you bet on the one you think has the staying power. Simple as that.

You gonna bet on crazy Manny?

Manny was five to one when we got here; now it's about seven to three or four. I'm gonna put my money on the Vallesteros kid. Manny's unpredictable; he can see the debil, as he calls him, freak out, and pull out anytime. The kid is cool and collected. It's his first time. Needs to prove himself, you know? He's like, hypnotized, not saying a word, not scared, but silent. Don't wanna wear a hat either.

Why would anyone let him do this? He looks twelve, and his skin is so white, Romero asked.

I don't know, and I sure the hell ain't gonna ask Tiny Tim or anyone else in that gang. Maybe it's a gang thing, a point to be proved, know what I mean?

Why are you gonna bet on the kid? He looks weak. Scared, even.

No, man, look at him. He's focused; his mind is cleared, ready to go and stay in. Now look at crazy Manny. He's flying, all juiced up, but he'll freak with the smoke, the heat, and the fumes. He'll see the debil, as he calls him, and scream for help to be pulled out. See those long sticks or poles next to the tree? They use those to push out the meat when it's ready; they also use them to help the fire eaters when needed, or someone jumps in to help. Say, Romero, did you put any cash in the kitty?

I was going to, but I…

C'mon, don't be cheap, Romero, Sammy interrupted, the Leyvas need the cash to break even. They use some of their own bread to get all the stuff.

Romero pulled out a wad of cash from his pocket and peeled off a five.

Can you slip me a twenty? asked Sammy. I'll pay you back; I can make me some easy money, ese.

Romero handed Sammy the cash without saying a word.

I'm gonna bet the twenty-five on the kid, then put some in the kitty. And he took off to place the bet with the Leyva brothers, who were holding the bets.

The vatos were gathering around the hole, placing bets and laughing, enjoying the spectacle, and hoping to make a little money. There was no concern among them that someone might die or get hurt bad; what the hell. That wasn't their problem. If stupid shits wanted to jump into a fire pit, hell, who were they to talk him out of it? they reasoned.

The mouth of the hole was a circle, not a perfect circle but close. The circumference was a little over six feet, and wet burlap was placed around the top to keep the sand from falling in. The smell of burning beef was still strong, and little puffs of blackened smoke escaped from the pit, but not as often as before. The walls of the pit were lined with soot and other matter not recognizable. The center of the pit was still smoldering, covered with blue-black grease, burned scraps of burlap, and charcoal from the burned wood and coal, all blended in among the ashes, giving the floor of the pit a mosaic texture no different than the ground floor of a vulture's den.

Oso the Bear was warning the vatos to stay back and not crowd too close to the hole. He wasn't being mean about it, just doing his job; with that .44 Mag hanging on his ass, who could argue? The Leyvas continued to collect money, and the odds were getting away from Manny. Manny had to act soon, and he did.

I want the lid on, he yelled, like a crazy man. I want the fucking lid on till I say different. I'm gonna go for one twenty plus; ain't nobody gonna stop me. I'm the champ here. Get the lid ready; cover the pit when I'm in, and make it look more like hell. I jump in, I stay in; bet your money on me, cabrones. I won't let you down, I promise. He was doing his dance, jumping up and down; he couldn't stay still, and his bloodshot eyes were all over the place, except where they should have been, checking the inside of the vaporous pit.

Settle down, Manny, said one of the Leyva brothers. We all agreed no lid this time. So stop jumping around, and get ready.

I'm ready, primo, answered Manny, grinning, probably relieved the lid was staying off.

OK, the Leyva brothers said. No more bets, no more bets. Manny's ready. You need the stick to help you down, Manny?

Fuck, no! And he jumped in the hole with the same grin on his freakish face.

Sammy had told Romero that the trick to survive the pit was to walk around the edges and stay away from the middle. And not to hold your breath, as some did, because when you had to breathe again, the crap you inhaled could put you on your ass. The other thing, he said to Romero, that Manny did was count the seconds slowly as he walked around inside the pit. If he could get to sixty, still strong, he'd go for another sixty. Two minutes in a hot hole was unthinkable. Two minutes with the lid on was hara-kiri. Manny had performed the impossible numerous times, but his nerves were fracturing; that's why he needed to take more powerful meds, meds that were likely never to be approved for public consumption.

Romero wanted to get closer to the hole, but he still felt uncomfortable and out of place. One accidental shove or a boot placed in the wrong place could lead to an altercation, and he didn't like the odds. He stayed where he was, and since he was taller than most of the vatos around the hole, he could see Manny squirming around in the pit, but he couldn't see if Manny still had the same belligerent look on his ugly face. Romero thought this was the craziest event he had seen, and he had seen a lot of crazy shit in his travels in and about the darker corners of society.

Oso the Bear kept pushing vatos away from the pit. Most were counting and yelling at Manny to stay in. Stay in, bro; chingate pendejo; go Manny, go; and side bets away from the Leyvas continued. Sixty! Sixty-one; you can do it, cabron, they screamed, all excited at the prospect of winning some cash. The Leyvas had the official stopwatches, one each. They didn't take their eyes off the watches because things happened at lightning speed. They didn't start the time until Manny was inside the pit with his hands away from the walls of the pit and his feet solidly inside the pit. Seconds ticked off, but they couldn't be counted until the Leyvas felt the time was perfect to start. Vatos were pushing and laughing, wanting to be close to the pit and see Manny succeed or perish. The shorter vatos were jumping, trying to see over the heads of the taller ones who were closer to the pit. Oso the Bear finally pulled out his long- barreled .44 Mag out of his holster and pointed it up in the air. The boys pulled back a little, and then there was a loud, painful, terrified shriek coming from the noxious pit.

Hep! Hep! For the love of God, hep; the debil in here! Hep. Manny was screeching from inside the pit in a desperate attempt to get help and be pulled out.

Oso the Bear, who was closer to the edge of the pit, grabbed Manny with his free hand by his scruffy collar and jerked him out of the pit with one thrust. Manny flew out of the pit and landed on an intoxicated vato who was too slow and drunk to comprehend what was taking place and move out of the way, as the others did. With the steaming, stinking, greasy, screaming Manny on top of him, the drunk freaked out and pushed him violently off him. Manny rolled off the drunk and attempted to crawl on all fours, still screaming for help and water. Finally, with no one moving to help him, he jumped to his feet and ran at high speed toward the river. He disappeared into the dense disarray of tangled trees and shrubs that fronted the river.

Everything unfolded so rapidly; Romero kept looking for Sammy, as if he needed Sammy to validate what was happening. The drunk vato was arguing with Oso the Bear as to why he unleashed that slimy creature on his ass. Oso the Bear had holstered his .44 and was laughing at the drunk, as were many others, but at the same time was trying not to provoke him into any activity that for sure would leave the drunk bloody or worse. Romero thought if he was into making movies, this would be a good comedy to make for the more serious moviegoers.

Tiny Tim and his nephew started to walk slowly toward the pit. The crowd settled as the Leyva brothers were announcing Manny's time in the pit. Eighty-six seconds, called out the Leyva brothers in unison, as if they were calling out bingo numbers. "Aw, shit" and "Fuck you" came from many in the crowd. They believed Manny had stayed in longer, at least 120 plus, as Manny had repeated again and again.

Tiny Tim and his nephew kept coming toward the pit. Romero saw Tiny Tim up close for the first time. The vato was huge, taller than him by at least an inch, with arms that wouldn't go away. At least six-five in bare feet, Romero estimated, not over 220 pounds in weight, mean and lean cuisine, front and back. He had biceps on him that could only be defined in prison, where a routine was established early on, and survival depended on that discipline. He was wearing the same sleeveless Levis jacket and brown cap with the CTS insignia on front. His military-style fatigues looked tapered and were inserted or bound on top of his jungle boots. He had a long, black, thick, braided ponytail that almost touched his waist, with a little metal rifle replica holding the end of the ponytail together. The peak of the brown cap was low, touching his wraparound shades, so Romero couldn't see his face that well—not that he wanted to. He had seen enough.

Tiny Tim had his huge hand on his nephew's neck. He walked him to the pit, whispering encouraging words in his ear, as if he was a sacrificial lamb climbing the stairs to the bloody altar, where the temple priest waited patiently to hack out his heart with an obsidian knife.

As they approached the pit, Romero noticed that the kid was older than twelve—closer to twenty—and tall, not as tall as Tiny Tim but not as short as Sammy. No one was. He was thin, and his jeans were sagging on his skinny butt. His skin was fair, a true guero, and he was heavily tattooed on his bony arms and neck. Someone probably talked him into wearing a hat because he had on an oily, beat-up baseball cap that covered his ears on his shaved head. The young man kept his eyes on the ground and didn't show any emotion at all; that didn't mean he didn't feel anything. He just didn't show it.

The crowd settled down, moved out of the way, and kept silent. Even the drunk that was arguing with Oso the Bear made himself scarce. Tiny Tim said to Oso the Bear, not loudly but loud enough for most to hear, Anyone acts the fool, shoot the pendejo. Oso the Bear smiled, nodded, reached behind with his right hand, and pulled out the long-barrel .44. He held it up, aiming at the sky, with his left hand gripping his right wrist for support, daring anyone to pull some shit.

Tiny Tim glanced at the Leyva brothers; they nodded, gesturing that it was time to let the young man go into the pit, if he was still up to it. Tiny Tim helped him in by holding one thin arm as the vato slid in, holding to the side of the greasy pit with his other hand. Once both hands and feet were in solid, the Leyva brothers started the time. Not a word was spoken by anyone. The only sounds came from across the river, where people were frolicking in the water, having fun, while on this side of the river, the crazy kind were betting money to witness a probable suicide.

Romero wanted to inch closer, but wacky Oso the Bear, with a loaded gun in his hand, discouraged him. He saw the young dude being helped in the pit by Tiny Tim, saw him in his dirty, oversize T-shirt disappear in the pit as if the ground had swallowed him up. What Romero couldn't see was that when the vato placed both feet in the pit and was released by Tiny Tim, he crouched with his arms on top of his knees, as if he was going to take a dump. He didn't walk around the pit talking shit like Manny. He just kept his face down and waited for someone to call him from upstairs.

Ninety seconds! the Leyva brothers shouted.

Tiny Tim, kneeling on the edge of the pit, called his nephew. OK, Neto. Apparently his name was Neto. OK, Neto. You got it, little bro; you won. C'mon, now; we can go home. Neto didn't move or make a sound. C'mon, Neto, gimme your hand, insisted Tiny Tim, serious. Nothing from Neto but silence.

One hundred twenty seconds! shouted the Leyva brothers. Tiny Tim took off his Levis jacket and was ready to jump in the pit when Neto got on his feet and stretched out an arm. Tiny Tim pulled Neto out as gently as he could without separating his bony arm from his shoulder. He put his arm around Neto and walked him back toward the truck. As soon as the young man, Neto, was out of the pit, he yanked off the dirty, oversized cap and pitched it in the pit. He still didn't say a word, and the expression on his smudged face was the same. A wet towel was placed over his shoulders, and Tiny Tim wiped his sweaty, sooty face with a large, wet handkerchief. About ten Chiva Town Snipers, all in uniform, formed a wall on both sides of him and Tiny Tim.

The Leyva brothers started to distribute the winning bets after they had taken out their 6 percent. The vatos formed a line, with Oso the Bear next to them, his gun holstered, joking with the vatos as if he never had any intentions of shooting them, if he had to. Some of them gave the Leyva brothers tip money, thanking them for all their hard work, good food, and drink. They were the businessmen, the entrepreneurs who recognized the value of networking to buy and sell their products in an underground economy, an economy many times frowned upon by the mainstream establishment. This was their country club, their golf course, where deals could be cut in a social gathering, so a cash reward to the Leyva brothers was the right thing to do.

Romero still couldn't believe that the young vato didn't say a word or utter a sound. He's probably a deaf-mute, he thought, and a little slow in the head. But when he saw him back at the truck with his entourage of Chiva Town Snipers giving him high fives and gulping down cups of cold beer, he knew the vato was OK. He had a slight smile now that he was the center of attention but still didn't say a word—nothing that Romero could hear.

Sammy Q. appeared from nowhere with his beat-up hat over his eyes and baggy jeans sagging low on his hips.
Where the fuck you been? asked Romero. You missed the happening.

Here and there, Sammy answered, buzzed. I didn't miss shit; seen it all before. Deeper in the bush is where the vatos with the heavy stuff congregate. Tiny Tim don't want 'em around here; bad for business.

What is he, the king or what? asked Romero, incredulous.

You saw him; whatta you think?

Well, did you find anything worth talking about?

Nada, nothing but caca. The shit ain't here. Le's go, man. The Snipers are leaving soon, after the Leyva brothers, and I don't wanna be around when they leave. Anything can happen.

As they were walking to the truck, Romero asked Sammy, Did you collect your winnings, Sammy Boy?

Oh, yeah, Sammy said, amused. Here's your twenty, sir and I put in your five and my twenty in the kitty. You don't wanna get the reputation you cheap, Romero, not around these fellows. I won a little, paid off some debt, so I'm good for a time, thanks to your loan.

How did you know crazy Manny was gonna have a meltdown?

They were in Romero's truck heading out, and Sammy was waving adios to the vatos he knew. Manny's been on the slide for some time now, he said, still waving, so it was bound to happen sooner or later. I had a gut feeling today was Manny's day; he was acting over the top, way over.

So what happens to Manny now? He disappeared.

Oh, someone'll find his ass and take him to the hospital. He got doctor friends at the hospital. The doctors love Manny. They'll get him a private room if he needs it. They'll patch him up good. Shit, Manny tells the doctors all the crazy shit he does, everything that happens out here in the wild. The doctors get their rocks off better than doing their wives. They like to know how the better half lives.

Romero stared at Sammy and asked, Whatcha been smoking, Sammy?

Only a churro, but it wasn't that good, Sammy replied with a giggle. Let me tell you a little about Manny, he said, grinning, and settled down low in the seat, brought his hat over his eyes, and acted as if he was going to take a nap. Manny took a trip to Oaxaca not too long ago—that's in Mexico, as you know. He stayed with relatives, cousins his age, who took him to the Sierra Mazateca and introduced him to vision-inducing plants, hallucinogens. Manny's favorite was the psilocybin mushroom, or the magic mushroom, as it's commonly known. He met curanderos, shamans, and they tried to help him understand the visions and explained to him that this was serious stuff, not games. Finally they tired of him and sent him packing, labeling him a druggy pocho who lacked the discipline to respect the religious rituals and follow the path to becoming a better human being that the magic mushroom was showing him. He ran out of coin, and his parents refused to send him any. Manny eventually came back home; he had no choice, see what I mean? He started working at the hospital, talking shit he was a Mazatec shaman to anyone who listened. He also started telling people he could make yaje, which was a lie. Yaje, as you know, is ayahuasca, made from jungle plants found in Peru and Bolivia, also strong vision-inducing plants. The shamans mix it to help them crack open the sky. Manny caught the attention of some doctors at the hospital, and they in turn introduced him to others. So you see where all this was leading, right? Sammy asked, not bothering to look at Romero.

Sammy was still slouched in the seat of the truck, not giving a shit where the truck was taking him. So the doctors, Sammy continued in his sleepy voice, the doctors knew they had a good man to work with. They provided him with synthesized drugs, acid, mescaline, DMT, and others. He didn't have to go through any time- wasting religious rituals, they told him. Just take the psychedelics, and trip for the fun of it. He did and loved it; didn't wanna do any more toad licking, as he used to put it. Eventually, they used him to test other newer drugs, and they paid him decent money, but you can see the results, right? Manny babbles and jumps into fire pits, too fucked up to know what he's doing, too fucked up to care.

Romero was listening to Sammy but thinking about his girl, who wasn't really his girl, yet. Alicia Juarez was the only daughter of his capo, and he was very protective and very positive about the kind of man he wanted for his daughter. The old man was old-school, hardcore Mexican macho. And he was but another obstacle that Romero confronted. She was lovely, as lovely as he had imagined a real woman to be. She was in her last year of college and was breaking too many hearts, including his own. Her father was a tough nut but a good boss. He hadn't gotten in the position he was in by being nice. He was known to release his dogs on anyone in the business whose margins of profit came under suspicion by the authorities, and he considered himself the main authority.

But Alicia, Romero thought, was above that brutality. She was sensitive and spirited. She wanted to help humanity; she wanted to help people in need. She believed, deeply, that through education, quality education, the poor, in their most desperate situations, would rise beyond expectations. He was positive they were connecting; their eye contact was promising, and her smile was contagious— sincere perfection, he liked to call it. It was difficult to talk to her alone; the old man had her pretty well covered, in case anyone was trying to jump the gun. He had been meaning to ask the old geezer for permission to take his daughter out—maybe to a nice dinner, why not? But he knew deep in his bones it was never gonna happen; his blood was not azul enough for them. Besides, the old man wanted Alicia as far away from the business as he could get her. He knew Romero would always have a leg or an arm in the business, and that would put his daughter at risk. He also knew Romero was a coldblooded killer. Having a college degree scored him a few points but not enough to position him anywhere near her.

Romero kept driving and thinking. Sammy kept talking and talking— not that it wasn't interesting stuff; it was, but he had other priorities. He was in love with a woman, the woman of his dreams, and he hadn't even kissed her, except in his fantasies. That's why this deal was of the essence. It could get him some cash to work with and move up in the world. He needed to access some money and power to approach Alicia's father on an equal basis and put the cards on the table, once and for all. He didn't want to muscle up on the old guy because he was a good chap, in his own way. But they couldn't stop him from being with the woman he loved and making her his wife. He would show them that the blue blood that ran in their veins was not as blue as his. Maybe it was his fault for falling for her, a blue-eyed, blond Mexican woman, as Mexican in her heart as anyone from the old country. He could get the best of both worlds, he thought. He wondered if he loved her because she looked white—or did he love her because he loved her? Could he love her if she didn't look white? Could he love a woman with darker characteristics? Why was he asking himself these stupid questions? he wondered. He was influenced by Hollywood movies more than anything, and it was their fault, as far as he was concerned, for showing all that blond ass on screen.

Romero continued to think as Sammy continued to talk. He could pass for white if he wanted to, and maybe he did, he thought, but there was no effort in it. He never shied away from his Chicano background. Hell, he even embraced it, most of the time. It was just that living in both worlds got a little complicated at times. For him it did, anyway; for others, it was the most natural thing, like breathing. A cultural traitor he was not, although he had been accused of being one. His culture, his cultura, was stamped in his heart and soul, and that was the force that drove him. And he loved his culture and his people more than anything else in the world—not all his people, but many. As for being a killer, that was something he never set out to be; it came with the job. He was a collector, a big, mean hombre, but he had to be. He dealt with people from both sides of the tracks. He worked in loss control, one could say. He saved his boss money and product by eliminating the weak links who started by pinching a few to sell on the side or, worse, to use. They could take and take; the product had no end, but they had to pay for what they took. The interest could be high, and they weren't given much time to pay back what they owed. Running away was useless because someone like him would be on their asses night and day. He came to collect what didn't belong to him but was obligated by his employer to retrieve it nevertheless. He had to tell a brother he would kill him if he didn't come up with the money owed or the product used. A carnal who could be his relative he'd kill in a New York minute, if he didn't come up with the cash to pay for the product he had taken. They knew the risks of coming short and the promises of putting it back later. When it became too obvious to cover up the many fuck-ups, it was time to investigate. If the warnings didn't seem important to them until he was facing them with a gun, it was too late to negotiate about anything.

The best thing for him was to kill them fast but not to shoot them in the head, because if he missed, then things got messy. He'd fire two shots at the torso, close to the heart. But sometimes, depending on the case, he'd smash them on the mouth with his gun, knocking out the front teeth, if they still had some. That was to show them that he enjoyed doing what he was doing and also for them not to get the idea that it was going to be easy. He liked to see some teeth come out, but the blow had to be just right to the mouth. Sometimes the mouth was so infected that the teeth were already exiting. By then he was out of control, and nothing or no one could stop him. He had to set an example for the others who were contemplating a little run at the store just because their credit was no longer viable. They had to understand that taking from the man and not replacing what they took to use or sell on the sneak only led to an uncomfortable situation. This was preventive medicine, a deterrent, he liked to say, and prayed that they would see the savage violence and death as the optimum outcome of their vicious habit. He still didn't like it when they labeled him a coldblooded killer. What if Alicia Juarez, his babe- to-be, heard that shit? He didn't even want to think about it.

As Romero drove into Las Flores, he asked Sammy, who was still cannabis happy, Where do you want me to drop you off, Sammy Boy?

Sammy pushed his little hat off his eyes and said, as if awakening from a long sleep, Oh, just drop me off at Jimmy's Pool Hall. That's across from Fat Henry's on Main Street. And gathered the herb bags and hugged them to his stomach. I'm gonna ask around; see if I'll get any leads. Besides, I have to pick up some dinner for Granny. I'll get a ride home, no problem. Before Sammy got out of Romero's truck in front of Jimmy's Pool Hall with a bag in each arm, he asked Romero, Hey, did you try any of the good smoke making the rounds at the cosido? Or any other stuff? There was plenty around.

Nope, Romero answered, anxious for Sammy to get his ass off his truck so he could head north.

Oh, I forgot, Sammy said. You don't drink, smoke, or do drugs; you the all-American boy who happens to work for a drug dealer. And Sammy Q. got off the truck gingerly and headed to Jimmy's, praying that was the last of Romero.

Oh, Sammy, Sammy, Romero said to himself, you'll get your day in court one day soon, and drove off.

CHAPTER EIGHTEEN

ike, after hanging up the phone with Pa Hanks, grabbed a piece of pan dulce from the kitchen table and headed out the house to his car. He didn't see his parents around, but it was late, almost noon, and his parents were always doing something while he slept. It was best he didn't see them anyway, because after last night's conversation, it was best to let it rest. He told his parents about breaking up with his girlfriend, Linda Barela. He could tell his mother was upset, although she didn't make a big deal about it. He wanted to tell them before they got the news from some comadre who didn't know all the specifics. His father seemed to be OK with it, but his father was cool with most things he did, except losing a job or ending up in the slammer. He got a little uptight when that happened, but he got over it, soon enough. His mother was a little more delicate, and he had to be careful with his choice of words. But he did promise her that perhaps after graduation from college, if Linda was still interested, they could be a couple again. His mother gave him a hug and dried her eyes; she was big on optimism. His father gave him a "yeah, right" look and continued sipping his coffee.

He had parked his car behind the garage and could not be seen from the street. He looked around the back and front of the house, still nervous about the burden he had taken on. He stayed home last night, and that was rare for him. He didn't sleep all that well and kept hearing noises outside the house, all through the long night. He was sorry now he had kept the poison, but it was too late; what could he do, run it over to the cops? Or take it to Sammy Q. and ask for a piece of the action? They'd laugh at him and give him nothing, maybe a kick in the ass, for his troubles. Dump it, which was the best option, but not yet, he thought, greed being the major player. Shit, he was plenty scared, and it wasn't fun. This wasn't the typical kind of bogie-man shit you played with friends when kids. This was the real, evil killers who put the hurt on you and yours until they got what belonged to them.

Mike took a peek down and up Chavez Street, the street in front of his house, looking for any strangers in vehicles he wasn't familiar with. Seeing none, he walked back to his car thinking that maybe if they did catch him, they'd only slap him around and warn him not to take other people's property. He laughed out loud, saying, Wishful thinking, buddy. He knew if they didn't kill him outright, they'd carve up his face with a sharp instrument and amend his equipment downstairs to guarantee he didn't have to concern himself with the opposite sex for the rest of his life. And finally, just to make sure he stayed honest, in case he contemplated any type of revenge, they'd damage his kneecaps so thoroughly with a sledgehammer that hobbling with a cane was the best it would ever get. But that was pure speculation on his part, jittery nerves, he thought, that was all. He had to think like a criminal and stay ahead of the game. Sure, he realized the game was dangerous like no other, but so far, he had everything covered—almost everything. Besides, the winnings could be big time, for him, anyway. As long as Ramon kept his mouth shut—and he knew Ramon could be as stubborn as a mule. When he didn't want to talk, nothing or nobody could make him. So Mike said, Hell yes, got in his tin can of a car, and rolled out of the driveway and made a left on Chavez Street. He had to drive downtown and visit Pa Hanks.

Mike drove west on Chavez and noticed the old Salazar place, a couple of blocks from his house, had been refurbished. A new family had moved in, as had others in the last few years. Many of the old adobes had been abandoned when the owners relocated to other states to find work. They stopped paying taxes on the properties, and the assessor's office sold the properties cheap. But now, it wasn't like before when abandoned houses stayed abandoned and were vandalized and eventually, in some cases, utilized for illegal activities. Now there was an influx of people looking for cheap housing, staying in the Eastside barrio, and changing the dynamic— for better or worse, Mike couldn't say at this point. But he remembered not too long ago when the few people who moved in and rented were treated like outcasts by some of the natives. People like Delfina Madrid and her ilk, who believed it was their right to run the show. They controlled all church events, including fiestas and bingo, because their influence over the priest was always well established. They handpicked the councilman for the Eastside and any other flunkies they wanted to represent them at city hall. They had to be from the founding families of Las Flores, true bluebloods with impeccable credentials; newcomers need not apply. They looked down on poor, honest people who wanted to contribute but made it clear they could contribute cash, if they had it, as long as they maintained their distance. Even the weddings for the bluebloods were large and ostentatious. If you weren't invited, you were out of the loop. Of course all that arrogance went to shit as that generation died off, and the new one couldn't pull off the same crap anymore.

The Eastside barrio was growing left and right. Mike knew his parents accepted the change. They went out of their way to welcome the newcomers. They'd take them food, show them the church if they were believers, and tell them about the services offered at the community center. Francisco, Mike's father, helped them fix up their homes, if they asked. Mike's parents talked to him about the importance of helping out the newcomers and not badger them like in the old times. They talked to him of new schools that could be built and teachers hired to teach, of other jobs that would open up in construction and other areas. They saw this as vital so that the young people wouldn't have to leave to look for jobs in other places. Mike listened, but he didn't care; all he cared about was the kids he had to beat up and the pretty girls he had to impress. The new influx of teens had to be put in line to show them who the boss was. Most of them were easy: a few words here, a slap on the face there, and they were convinced. But of course there was always a knucklehead or two who had to find out the hard way. They had to find out the blazing speed of his hands and power behind that speed. They had to taste the humiliation of being put down, knocked down, and hurt enough to not get up and go another round. They had to experience the letdown of being beat up among strangers in a new place, with not a friendly face to give them a hand. But the worst part was the stream of urine, the sticky, smelly piss, that rained down from the victor to make sure the hierarchy was never questioned again. So you made an enemy or a friend for life; that depended on how much pride and anger the defeated boy had. But Mike was beyond that silly shit now, and it gave him the shivers to even think about it. Besides, he had bigger fish to fry.

Mike kept driving west on Chavez toward Mora. He'd turn right on Mora and go north all the way to Church Street. Mora ran parallel to the railroad tracks. The tracks separated the Eastside barrio from downtown and the Westside. As he drove, he came to the conclusion that he had matured a lot in the last year. His interest in fighting and acting bad had dissipated, like a bad dream. Spending a little time in the slammer opened his eyes and scared him. That was a sad way to live, he thought; if you were going to be a pinto and risk your freedom, go for something big. He wanted to go to college and be an educated man. He loved learning and books. He didn't want to go to college just to get a good job and lord it over people; no, he wanted knowledge about stuff. He wanted to know things about the world and what made people tick, to visit many countries and check out the sights. But it was so difficult to get in and start the process. Already people in the barrio were laughing at them behind their backs, knowing they were fuck-ups and calling the project Hector's Folly. Some of his teachers had told him he could do it, but he had to stop being a smartass. And for him that was the most difficult thing to do; shit, being a smartass was his security blanket. Yeah, he could work construction with his dad, maybe even start his own company one day, but he didn't want to do that. He could join the military and take orders day and night from ignorant A holes, but that wasn't him. He wanted good memories, not of being locked up like an animal, but of something beautiful, like when his father, Francisco, met his mother, Alma, in the Mimbres Valley, of all places. It was a love story, a true, old-fashioned love story, and he never tired of hearing it. His mother always told it, although his father also contributed, in his shy way.

The story began in Silver City, a town in western New Mexico. His grandfather, Arturo Sr., and his crew had completed some work there and had started another project outside the small town of Mimbres in the Mimbres Valley, a short distance west of Silver City. Arturo Sr. had secured a contract to build a couple of modest homes in the area. He relocated his small crew there and had them pitch tents on the worksite, which saved money on hotel bills. Francisco, Mike's dad, who was usually left behind on out-of-town projects, was brought along to help with the cooking and gain some valuable experience. Around three or four in the afternoon, Francisco took his break before helping the cook prepare dinner for the men. He walked around the verdant area, impressed with the trees, meadows, and wildflowers of late spring. One day he saw the local school bus drop off what was, to him, an extraordinary, beautiful girl. He was in the middle of a meadow, picking wildflowers, when he started walking toward her. When he got to the road, he stopped. As she passed, their eyes met, and she said hi. He stared at her without saying anything because he couldn't utter a word. When he finally came to his senses, he said hi, but it was too late. She was already down the road, heading home. Francisco was frustrated for the first time in his young life. He was known as Mr. Cool and had a reputation for his maturity and common sense, but this threw him for a loop.

Francisco wanted to go after the girl but decided against it. The crew had been warned by his father to stay away from the local women, except in a bar. But this was only a girl, he thought, but still, he didn't want to create any problems for his father. The farmers and ranchers in the area were people you didn't want to mess with. He started walking back to the construction site, his mind going every which way. Before he realized it, he was at the camp, not knowing how he got there so fast, with the wildflowers still in his hand. He usually put them in a safe place after he picked them, pretending he had given them to his mother. If the men saw him with the flowers, they'd never let him forget it. This time he had the flowers in his hand, walking on air, not hearing the laughter of the men or the cook asking for help. He cleaned out an empty coffee can, filled it with water, placed the flowers in the can, and put the can in the middle of the table. He sat down and studied the flowers, seeing in the petals the face of the beautiful girl he had encountered. His father wasn't around, so he didn't care about the jokes or about the cook ordering him to do this and do that. When dinner was on the table, he got up and walked to his little tent he had set up away from the men, who played cards and drank half the night, laughing at their dirty jokes. He didn't have an appetite for food. He sat on the grass under a tree a short distance from his tent. He asked himself, What the hell is going on? He was so happy that he wanted to yell out, he wanted to laugh; could it be love? No way—what did he know about love? He lay on his back with a blade of grass between his teeth as the light of the sun disappeared, and he looked at a million stars while the image of the girl refused to go away.

The next morning, after a sleepless night, Francisco was still in the clouds. He kept looking at his watch every five minutes; time was dragging for him. He had to see that girl again, if only from a distance. Close to twelve noon, he went to the camp to peel potatoes for lunch and dinner. Francisco's father didn't return to camp, which was nothing new but also a big break for Francisco. Arturo Sr. didn't like slackers, and he'd sent him home pronto if he noticed Francisco stargazing. He also didn't like for his men to go into town after work during the work week. Men with money in their pockets and a taste for pussy always created problems, especially in a small town, unless there was a brothel close by; that was his reasoning for not allowing them going into town every night. He didn't want any problems with the locals; that's why he always brought his best workers on the road. He could come and go as he pleased, but he was the boss, and his crew respected him because they knew he was always looking for new jobs for them, and he never bragged about his doings. He returned ready to work and inspect the work done, and it better be done right and a little ahead of schedule, no ifs or buts about it.

Gonzalo Prieto, the crew's foreman, gave Francisco a list of materials they needed from town. Gonzalo liked Francisco for his intelligence and all-around good behavior. He never made fun of him and was glad Arturo Sr. had brought him along. Francisco was the gofer, and Gonzalo didn't have to spare one of the men for a couple of hours on errands. Francisco was all smiles; he knew he could kill a couple of hours and not be sweaty and smelly for later. The cook came running from the construction site with a list for food. Francisco grabbed the list and ran to the truck, and then slowed down, conscious of his actions, and looked back as Gonzalo Prieto smiled and waved.

By 2:30 p.m., the truck had been unloaded and the potatoes peeled. He washed as well as he could in the stream a short distance from his tent. He brushed his teeth again and again and then left for the meadow to await his destiny. He was in the meadow by three, nervous, checking the time, selecting the most beautiful of the flowers, but this time he was closer to the road. At ten after three, he couldn't stand it anymore. He decided to go back to camp and forget about it; it was driving him crazy, the waiting, the thoughts in his mind, the butterflies in his heart. Forget it, he said. Then he saw the yellow bus stop, and he froze. He couldn't stop trembling; the door opened, and she stepped out. But as soon as her feet hit the ground, a boy also jumped out and engaged her in conversation. Francisco freaked and dropped the flowers, and tears swelled up in his eyes. He was in pain and a lot of hurt but an unknown pain he had never experienced before. He didn't know what to do; he wanted to die and begged for the ground to swallow him up. He was going to walk to the far end of the meadow and hide, when the boy walked off to the opposite direction, and she kept advancing toward him. He had accidentally stepped on the flowers when he made an effort to move on down the meadow. She was approaching with her eyes on him. Francisco made a clumsy movement with his hand to clear away any evidence of the tears that might still be hanging onto his cheeks. He walked toward her, before she got too far ahead, like yesterday. But this time she stopped and waited for him.

Hi. My name is Alma, she said.

Hi. And he waved his hand, as cool as he could do it. I'm Francisco Montes. How corny was that? he thought.

Tell me, she asked, in a voice that made his heart ache, you ditch school again today?

And they both laughed. Can I carry your book bag? he asked, a lot more confident.

OK, she replied. I just live down the road.

They walked leisurely on that country road, laughing and talking with a familiarity as if they had been friends for years.

When they approached Alma's house, they both stopped. He handed her the book bag, knowing it wouldn't be cool to meet her parents at this point.

Can I walk you home tomorrow? he asked.

OK, she answered, with that voice that made him want to press her against himself and never let go.

They walked backward, facing each other, until she waved and had to turn around, almost at the front door of her house. He waved back and finally turned around, happy and excited as he had never been before in his life. As soon as he was a distance from her house, he skipped, he ran, he jumped with his arms extended and plucked something only he could see from the air. The birds were singing, the flowers were in bloom, and he was in love; life is good, he kept repeating, again and again.

Francisco met Alma every day after school for two weeks. He walked her home, offering her a handful of wildflowers each time. He eventually met her parents. The father was a corpulent, taciturn rancher who always had on his head a sweaty, beat-up straw cowboy hat and constantly scratched the salt and pepper stubble on his sunburned face. The mother was also a woman of few words. They both listened and studied Francisco, accepting the fact that their daughter's destiny was in the hands of the young man. They loved their daughter, Alma, so much and valued her good judgment that they accepted her love for the boy without question.

The only thing that troubled Francisco was that he couldn't break the ice with Alma's father. Francisco, was used to talkative people. And although Francisco wasn't like his father or brothers, who never shut up, Alma's father was too quiet. One early evening, he drove to Alma's house in the truck to take her out for a spin. He saw Alma's father with the hood open of an old pickup that he seemed to be working on. The man had a frustrated look on his face as he scratched the bristles on his face with his thick fingers. Francisco approached slowly, as not to upset the man even more. Francisco asked if he could be of assistance, as polite as ever. The farmer looked at Francisco with an "OK, kid, you asked for it" look and said yes, with a slight smile on his thick face. Francisco brought his toolbox from the truck and had that old pickup roaring in about thirty minutes. He also helped Alma's father repair a couple of decrepit tractors that had been idle for a while. From then on, Francisco could do no wrong in the eyes of Alma's father. Alma's father realized that Francisco could work with his hands, fix things, and that his daughter, Alma, the song of his heart, would never go hungry. He even offered Francisco a nip of his special homemade wine, called pisado by the locals. Francisco at first was shy, hesitant, but after he tasted it, he liked it. It was a lot better than the cheap store-bought wine some of the men drank.

The last couple of days on the job were hell for Francisco and Alma. The homes were almost completed, and the crew had to move on. He spent those last days sulking and in tears. When he returned from Alma's house, he went up to his tent without saying a word to anyone. Gonzalo Prieto was the only one who tried to console him. They talked late into the night about his situation. He didn't want to leave Alma, but he knew he couldn't stay. Gonzalo Prieto advised him to perk up, that it wasn't the end of the world; easy for him to say, thought Francisco. That he could write Alma and call her, even drive up to see her, until they were ready to get married. That the distance only made their love stronger, and in no time, his parents would come and ask for Alma's hand. But his father was difficult, Francisco argued, and he might refuse to talk to Alma's parents. Gonzalo Prieto agreed that his father was difficult, but he would see how unhappy he was without Alma and cave; most parents did. You really think so? asked Francisco, a little more optimistic because Gonzalo Prieto was convincing and seemed to know what he was talking about. Gonzalo Prieto had kept Francisco away from his father, sending him on errands as soon as his father arrived at the construction site. Gonzalo Prieto knew Francisco's father was a man with little patience and not big on sentimentality. If he noticed Francisco acting like a lost boy in love, he'd send him home and remind him that there were plenty of girls in Las Flores to screw around with until he decided on the one he wanted to hitch up with.

It happened as Gonzalo Prieto had predicted. Alma graduated from high school in June, and in early September, they were married. Francisco's father finally gave in and asked Alma's parents for her hand; of course, the wedding would take place in Las Flores. But Alma and Francisco didn't care, as long as they were together. It was a long, difficult battle for Francisco to convince his father that Alma was the girl he was going to marry; the girl he loved and wanted to spend the rest of his life with. His mother was all for it, from day one, but his father was hardheaded and not one to give in easy. He finally went along with it because Francisco was spending too much time driving to Mimbres and back to see Alma. He didn't want Francisco to elope and make his home in the Mimbres Valley. So they went as a family to Mimbres and asked for Alma's hand, on the conditions the wedding was to be held in Las Flores and that the young couple lived in Las Flores. Arturo Sr. was civil to the farmer and noticed right away, by the condition of the house and the rancho, that the man was barely above water financially, and that if he hadn't lost everything by now, for sure he'd lose it in the near future. But that wasn't his concern; his only concern was to get his boy married to the farmer's daughter and get them settled in Las Flores. Arturo Sr. was his amiable self, made everybody laugh with his jokes, and was even rewarded with a couple of bottles of pisado, the homemade wine everyone seemed to like.

What a story, Mike thought, as he drove to downtown. He wished something like that would happen in his life. Meet a sweet girl and love her, plain and simple. Leave out all the crazy shit, all the twisted sex that screwed up his mind and turned him into a flesh-eating predator. He wondered if it was only him, or was every guy like that? He couldn't ask his father—he could, but his father seemed to be above that needy craving. He couldn't ask his grandfather, because his grandfather probably say, Go for it, Mikey; the more, the happier. And his friends—his friends couldn't be trusted to be honest about sex, no way. They exaggerated every detail and lied with a straight face in order to be the top dog, the know-it-all, the champ with the biggest equipment. So he couldn't discuss it seriously with anyone. Maybe with time, the answers to his questions, his anxieties, all the crap involved in being a man, would be a little bit more simple; but maybe not. He said hell with it and decided to get some gas.

Mike pulled into Bailey's Garage located on Mora before Alameda Street, opposite the railroad tracks, the oldest gas station in Las Flores. He drove up to an ancient pump. Old Mr. Bailey was sitting on a split log outside, next to the opened garage door. He was whittling away on a small piece of wood, carving up what resembled a dog, spitting tobacco juice into a rusted coffee can. Mike got out of his car, removed the gas cap, cranked up the ancient gas pump, and begin filling up.

Hey ya, Mike, how's yo pappy and mama? asked Mr. Bailey, in his hillbilly way of talking.

Oh, dey's fine, Mr. B., as fine as fine can be, answered Mike, mimicking the old goat, but not in a mean way; he liked old Mr. Bailey. Put this here gas on my tab, will ya, Mr. Bailey? 'Preciate it, sir.

Sure will, son; not to worry.

Mike had a tab with Mr. Bailey. He worked for him on and off to pay if off; not for long though—a week here, a couple of days there. He didn't rip him off much—a candy bar or two, a quart of oil for his car, small things the old man would never miss. He did take a carton of Camels and gave it to his padrino, his godfather, as a

Christmas present, but that was a long time back. Mike didn't smoke, although he had tried it, along with Ike, his white friend, who lived in Las Flores, but that was when they were in the fourth grade. He got dizzy, threw up, and never tried it again. He had talked to his friends on more than one occasion, not to break into Mr. Bailey's residence in back of the gas station and extract any cash. He warned them that Mr. Bailey was an old hillbilly who slept with a loaded double-barrel shotgun and several dogs and that he'd shoot to kill anyone attempting to break in. Besides, he told them, old Mr. Bailey didn't have much cash around. His business had been slow for years because the newer, more modern gas stations had been depleting his profits on a daily basis. Not that Mr. Bailey cared; he did his thing in order to stay busy and not vegetate, as others his age were doing. Besides, he relied on friends and old customers he had serviced over the years to keep him from going under.

Mike filled up and opened the hood of his old Chevy and checked the oil. He replaced the dipstick and shut the hood with a bang. He opened the passenger door of the car and took out a washed ten-pound flour bag and walked over to Mr. Bailey with the sack in his right hand.

Mr. Bailey, sir, can I leave this sack in my locker for a bit? It's a surprise birthday present for my girlfriend and one for my mom.

Go 'head, son, hep yoself, answered Mr. Bailey, his eyes on the carving.

Mike walked into the garage of the gas station, which was full of used, greasy car parts. A dog followed him in, thinking Mike had a treat for him. Hey, Brownie, Mike said to the dog and scratched it on top of the head and around the ears. He found his old locker, which was empty except for some girly magazines that had lost their allure some time ago. He pitched the flour sack, which contained nothing more than flour mixed with sugar, in the locker. He shut the locker door and walked out of the garage with the dog following him. Let any punk try to get by Mr. Bailey, see what he gets, thought Mike. Nothing for you, my friend, you little flea bag, he said to the dog. Maybe next time, OK?

Mike got in his car and, before he drove off, stuck his head out the window and said, Adios, Mr. Bailey. You have a good one.

Mr. Bailey waved with the knife in his hand, getting up to document the amount of gas Mike had pumped on a little scratchpad he kept in the pocket of his soiled work shirt.

Mike stayed on Mora and continued north, knowing the traffic was lighter, avoiding Alameda and Santa Teresa, before he crossed the tracks into the Westside. Mora was an older street with older buildings next to the tracks and some homes on the opposite side. It was not an attractive area. Too many junkyards, welding shops, and other operations that needed space, and the coming and going of trucks was never an issue. He caught the green light on Alameda but had to stop on Santa Teresa. He was going to make a left on Church after crossing Esperanza, drive west, cross the tracks, and hit downtown. Pa Hanks had his office on Church and Armijo, close to the courthouse, not too far from Main Street.

Mike parked his car on a Safeway parking lot on Armijo and walked to Pa Hank's office, which was behind the courthouse, out of the way but close to the action. Pa Hanks had worked as a public defender out of the DA's office until he opened his law office. He knew the ins and outs of criminal law and the hypocrisy of small- town politics. He'd fight a good fight and had kept a good many out of the can including Mike. He believed in plea bargaining, but only as the last resort, and fought until the end for the best possible deal. His passion for making money was behind him, along with his youth, so that freed a lot of his time for more important things. He enjoyed the challenge of working with the primos and keeping them out of situations they'd regret later. He was a good friend of the Montes family, especially Mike's grandfather, Arturo Sr. Not only did he do legal work for Arturo Sr.'s construction business, but he also, on several occasions, kept young Turi and his wild friends from a stay at Santa Fe State.

Mike walked up to a cluster of small offices situated around a small courtyard surrounded by Alamo trees. There were metal benches in the shaded courtyard and nothing else. He stopped in front of the second door with peeling black-and-white lettering that read Patrick P. Hanks: Attorney at Law. He took a deep breath, a sigh of relief; this was the first time he hadn't come to ask Pa Hanks to get him out of trouble. It felt good; he even smiled as he opened the door and walked in the office. Ofelia, Pa Hank's secretary, was not behind her desk. She was probably out to lunch, Mike thought. He closed the door; no waiting customers as usual. He went behind Ofelia's desk to another door. That was the entrance to Pa Hank's main office. The door was open, and Pa Hanks was standing in front of a metal filing cabinet with a stack of papers in his hand.

Pa Hanks was not a large man—not as large as his reputation, that is. But with his buzzed crewcut and clean-shaven face, he looked younger than his years. The gray in his hair was more pronounced, Mike thought, but his slim build gave him the look of a man who took care of his appearance and health.

Pa Hanks turned and caught a glimpse of Mike. Mike! he said as he placed the papers on top of the metal cabinet. They greeted each other like old friends: a handshake, a hug, smiles all around. Sit, my friend, and he pulled a chair close to his desk and closed the door. I'm so glad to see you, Mike. And how's your father and mother?

They're good.

And your grandfather?

Oh, he's the same; saw him the other day. They were on their way to Juarez to buy some liquor, they said.

Yeah, right, said Pa Hanks, with a twinkle in his gray eyes. He had taken several trips to Juarez with Arturo Sr. He still smiled at the memory.

Anyway, I want to thank you for the letter of recommendation you wrote to UNM on my behalf. That really helped.

Hey, congratulations, you got into that program Hector wrote up for you guys. Pa Hanks removed his wire-frame glasses and placed them in the pocket of his crisp, white shirt and rubbed the bridge of his nose. Mike glanced at the numerous law books that lined the shelves of Pa Hank's office library, impressed as always. Words were written in those books, he thought, millions of words that had, in many cases, deprived his people and native people of their property, backed by force and violence. Gringo law that defined land and water rights and left the early Hispanos confused and defeated. They could work the land they no longer owned for little or no pay or move their asses across the river, back to old Mejico. Elegant words on paper had made a tyrant back in Spain king of the world, with the right to send his subjects across the ocean with a cross and a flag, backed by gunpowder and horses, to take whatever there was to take—and take they did, including the native women, because they had the law and God on their side. The law was a funny business, thought Mike, written by the powerful to benefit the powerful but left with enough hooks to help your ass out, if you knew how to work it.

Pa Hanks, you still the man, said Mike, as he addressed Patrick James Hanks, the elderly, wiry attorney with the ready smile who could turn a jury around to his side and bury a witness for the prosecution with his quick thinking and acid tongue. He liked to be called Pa Hanks, especially by the younger kids like Mike, who were full of life and energy, too good to be wasted behind prison walls. Your letter got me in the door, Pa Hanks. I won't let you down.

Don't worry about it, Mike. It was my pleasure. I know some of those old farts, and I know their agenda. But more important, I had your record sealed. You are clean to go. The last incident happened a couple of days before you turned eighteen, so that helped. And the new DA dropped all charges, finally. That dickhead chief of police wanted to send you up, and the judge at the preliminary hearing was his cousin. Even though there weren't any witnesses, and the man you beat up refused to testify against you. It was a sham. And also a shame.

You know, said Mike, looking at Pa Hanks in the eyes, I had to kick that animal's ass. I had to. You shoulda seen what that animal did to his kids. I was with the oldest girl in first grade. She seemed as if she was shell shocked, and all the kids treated her like shit, including me. I ain't lying, Pa Hanks. I pinched her on the arm when we did the circle dance. I wanted to see some reaction and a change of expression on her tormented face. She never talked or smiled. She was abused by the bullies at school and abused by her father at home, but of a different sort. It was physical, sexual, and brutal, and no one moved a finger to help her. I wasn't aware, going through that stupid age and all, but later I recognized the violence because I grew up seeing what that asshole did. I made a promise in my early teens that the bastard was gonna be punished, some way or another.

Mike still got emotional talking about it and sad. He thought he was doing the right thing, but others didn't, and it cost him, cost him a lot. Anyway, he continued, I saw him one night leaving my friend's car in a place where there are usually not many witnesses. I went crazy, and I beat him with my fists, and then I kicked him on the face and head. He was bloody and crying like a baby, but the last kick to the ribs silenced him, and I thought he was dead. I left him there, but he survived. His relatives put pressure on him to tell, and he did. You know the rest, Pa Hanks. You saved my ass.

Well, Mike, said Pa Hanks, scratching the side of his nose, you're a smart young man. I believe your intelligence will provide the insight you need to avoid dumb things in life; makes things more easy. And how's your friend Ramon? asked Pa Hanks, ready to move on.

Ramon is still Ramon, answered Mike.

Is he still painting?

No, he stopped; he's in love.

Oh, boy! That can happen. I really liked that painting he did. Remember the one with the raven crucified on that silver cross. I offered to take it to Taos and show it around, but he said no. The colors in the painting were electrifying. I mean, I'm not an art critic, but wow.

He burned it, said Mike, not wanting to be a comadre. Said his mother was afraid of it.

Too bad, said Pa Hanks, but it was his property; what can you do?

I liked the one he did in art class, added Mike, in a better mood. It was a white stallion galloping down a mountain with a raven on its back. The mountain is ablaze, and you can see the same color of the fire in the horse's eyes. On top of the mountain can be seen a face of a demon, a demon so scary that only Ramon could paint it. The art teacher offered to buy it from him, but Ramon refused. Said it was a gift for me. When the other students asked him if the stallion was running away from the flame or the demon, he answered, ask Mike. I need to get it framed. There was another one; few saw that one. The principal asked Ramon to paint one for his office. Ramon, already sporting a little rep, agreed. Ramon painted a healthy black bull eating grass in a lush, green meadow. Behind the bull, lifting its tail, was an old, emaciated beggar. Gold coins fell out the bull's ass into a gold spittoon on the ground. It was thirty by thirty inches, and the colors jumped out at you. The beggar was in rags, barefooted, and had no flesh on the hand and wrist holding the bull's tail. You get the picture. I never saw that painting in the principal's office or any place else around the school, and I looked but never asked.

What a shame, said Pa Hanks, shaking his head. Ramon could be another surrealist, like Salvador Dali.

More like a Gerardo Chavez, added Mike.

Who's that? Pa Hanks asked.

A Peruvian artist—does abstract work like Dali but more intense.

Live and learn, said Pa Hanks. I'll check out his art. You must have had a good art teacher, Mike.

She was born and raised in Peru and exposed us to artists from South and Central America; combine them with Europe and Mexico, and it added to a dynamic mix, but I'm no art critic. I'm not trying to be a smartass, OK, Pa Hanks?

Pa Hanks knew Mike was not a smartass—not with him, anyway. The young man had too much respect to play silly games. So he ignored it, as he sometimes had to ignore some expressions from a young, intelligent, articulate vato whose confidence to stay focused kept him above water. And he also knew it was time to change the subject, and he asked Mike if Ramon was safe or at home, at least.

Home, yes, answered Mike, but safe, I can't guarantee, because Ramon gets into this and that. He left the hospital before he was discharged, and he told me he had to drive, or Danny would die. He drove the car to save Danny, and Danny still ended up dead. The cops want to pin him to Danny's death. They want to nail him with a DUI and vehicular manslaughter. If they can't nail him with a DUI, they will cite him for driving without a license—and the fact that he shouldn't be driving anyway because of his seizures—and stick him with Danny's death. You know how they do, Pa Hanks. You're around it all the time; you can smell it from both sides and choose the side of the brothers. I really respect you for that.

OK, Mike, this is what we can say in Ramon's defense. We can say that Ramon had been seizure-free for one year, and he was going to apply for a driver's license or had applied. That he could drive because he had been seizure-free for a year, plus he was driving with a licensed driver; maybe that will give us something to play with. The motor vehicle division will not give out any information on licensing; it's confidential, and it may not be used as evidence in any trial. So Ramon could claim he applied for permission to take the license test, and the cops are going to do what? Of course we have to get Ramon to go along with our plan; if he nixes it, that's that.

Ramon's gonna have to go along with it, because Ramon can't do time. It will kill him and kill him pronto.

I hear you, Mike, said Pa Hanks, feeling a little sad for Ramon. But like you say, we have to help him, one way or another. So I want you to ask Ramon if he was seizure-free for a year or longer, and if he did have one or more, if he recalls any witnesses around at the time. Let me know if he wants to be helped, and I'll start looking out to see what the mental giants plan to do. They have to move fast on this or forget about any charges, at least the more serious ones. And remember, Mike, continued Paw Hanks, I'll be here in case you need any assistance while you're at UNM.

Thanks, Pa Hanks. I appreciate that, and I'll talk to Ramon. Give my regards to your folks, and the best of luck.

After handshakes and hugs, Mike left Pa Hanks's office. Mike recalled the scene at his preliminary hearing when he was busted, and his grandfather, Arturo Sr., had to be restrained by his father. His grandfather, using salty language, attacked the chief of police and called him ignorant and stupid for trying to send his grandson to prison. He was almost placed under arrest but for his father and Pa Hanks. His grandfather was escorted outside the building, but before he left, he yelled at the chief that the next election, he'd be out on the streets or worse. And that's what happened. His grandfather still had some political muscle in Las Flores.

Mike was driving back to the Eastside, listening to "Strike Like Lighting," by Lonnie Mack, on the radio. His car was old, but it had a good sound system, thanks to his friend Angel, who was a wiz at installing electronic gadgets. The sizzling guitar beat, the volume full blast, sent Mike to a place far from Las Flores. He left everything behind and let the music rock him and roll him with unparalleled pleasure, which made the heat and the hot leather seats more tolerable. He was driving south on Mora Street, bobbing his head with the beat, when across from Mr. Bailey's gas station, in the middle of the street, like a mirage, stood a woman in black, with her arms in front of her, signaling for him to stop. He said Shit and stopped the car right in front of the woman, the front bumper almost touching her knees. He turned the radio off as the woman walked to the passenger side, opened the door, and climbed in. She told Mike to park in the shade of the vacant building next to the gas station, which he did.

The woman, wearing a black dress and headscarf, was Shonofa, and she didn't say a word until Mike parked the car in the shade of a vacant building next to the gas station.

We need to talk, she said and smiled. We need to talk, you and I, about something very important. I'm glad I ran into you. I wouldn't want to bother you when you're home. I wanted to talk to you before you left town, and I know your leaving, so please, don't say you're not.

OK, said Mike, not knowing what else to say. He knew who she was and the story about the flying man; everyone did. What he didn't know was why she had stopped him in the middle of the street and why she had to talk to him, unless she wanted to hustle him for cash, but she was not known for that.

Mike, she said, looking at him as if they were buddies. I saw you put the bundles in your car, in Snake Town, you and the boy Ramon. I also observed when the bundle was found by the boy who died and the boy Ramon. Now listen, my son, Shonofa assured Mike, still smiling, this is not a shakedown. I want nothing at this point. We have all we need; the Lord provides in difficult times. I just want to tell you things you don't know about your future. You will leave Las Flores and become successful, but you will return in ten years or more. You will be successful here also, when you return as an educated professional with high morals. The poison you have in your possession will open the door, but your intelligence will save you from falling into the dark pit that drowns so many. I know all this, my son, because I have made it a point to know it.

OK, Mike said, getting a little pissed but not wanting to show it yet. He should kick her ass out of the car, he thought, but he wanted to know what the crazy woman was driving at.

Shonofa, the women in black, pulled out a tiny doll from a small cloth pouch secured around her neck by a thin leather band. To Mike, it resembled a Guatemalan worry doll, sold by the Indians in Guatemala but sold in the States as well.

See, Mike. She showed him the doll. It had a small M on the body of the male doll. This is you—and she smiled some more—but didn't let him touch it. I protect you, my son, and your father and mother. I have them in the little bag also, which never leaves me. I pray night and day for almighty God to protect you, and she will. Even when you live and study in California, you will be protected as long as I live.

Mike started to get nervous. He didn't believe in that crap but didn't like the idea of anyone carrying him around in a little bag.

This isn't like voodoo or bruja, black bruja stuff, is it? Mike asked, a little worried.

Oh, no, my son. Santiago and I, we do not ever call on the forces of darkness. And she crossed herself. We rely on God and her power to do good. We have been tempted many times at night in the desert by evil spirits, but we are strong, and they cannot defeat us. Do not worry about evil demons; we will protect you against any harm that comes your way. That is a promise, a promise we will never break.

But why, asked Mike, why me? How do you know my name? And my parents—why us?

Let me tell you, my son, and you will see it is not a mystery at all. When my man, Santiago—the Flying Man, as most people call him— and I first started out wandering in the desert, we were not prepared. We refused to stop thinking about material possessions and comfort. We were punished by the Almighty, and we almost starved to death. Your father and mother found us by the road in bad shape, brought us to their home, and nourished us until we could function again. They are kind people, your parents, and they saved us from extinction while others drove by and ignored us. We learned from them many lessons in the short time spent with your wonderful parents. We learned to focus on our love and forget the past, with all its material implications. We learned that less is more, that all we needed was in front of us, that comfort was an illusion that made the mind weak, and that eating just to eat put a strain on the digestive system and other vital organs that perform so perfectly without so much junk in them.

Where was I? asked Mike, a little more relaxed. I don't remember you guys staying over at the house.

You were staying with your uncle for a week or so; that is what your mother told us. But she talked about you with much love in her heart. She shared pictures of you in various stages of your young life. In those images, I saw the potential, the strength, the resiliency that were going to help you make something of yourself—a great man, Mike.

OK, so what do you want from me, lady? I mean, I don't have anything to give you. A couple of dollars, that's it.

Shonofa—please call me Shonofa. I am aware you have nothing now, my son. I do not want anything from you now. Not a thing, nada. When you return to Las Flores—and you will—I might need something then. It could be food, a little cash; who knows. By then you will be in the position to be generous, and you will help out, and it will come from your heart, not because you owe us anything— you don't.

They both sat silently, watching the cars drive by on Mora Street, like they had nothing else to do. Mike was thinking. He still couldn't figure out what the woman wanted. She knew he had the stash but kept saying she didn't want any part of it now, but in the future she expected some help from him, if she needed it. His parents helped her once when he wasn't there, but his parents helped all kinds of people. They never mentioned the odd couple, but to his parents, they wouldn't be odd, just people in need of help. Now he was worried; maybe someone else saw him and Ramon drive out of Snake Town with the chiva.

OK, Shonofa, Mike said, let me ask you. When Ramon and Danny found the bundle in the desert, did you see anyone else around? Any cars or people on foot in the area—do you remember? You sure you didn't see anyone around when Ramon and Danny found the package?

Let me tell you again, my son, said Shonofa, patient as a mother breast feeding a hungry child. When the boy who died and the sick one found the package, we saw no one around. The only humans out there were us, but we are good at hiding and can even disappear, if we want to. No witnesses, no one around for miles and miles. Our eyes are like the eyes of the eagle; they have to be, to survive in the desert. Even at night, we can see and smell humans' miles away. When they drove to Snake Town, no one followed them, because there was no one around but us. The next day, a big truck driven by a large man, along with Sammy Q., came looking for the package but of course found nothing. Then a tall, bony boy came and searched for hours; we thought he was going to die, searching. He also left empty handed. A couple of days later, two boys came to search for the package. One was tall and beefy, the other one thin and not as tall. They were lazy; they smoked and talked for at least a couple of hours and left, not really bothering to look. I guess they knew that whatever they were supposed to find wasn't there. By then it was obvious that the package contained something of value, and someone was putting some effort in an attempt to recover it.

So, at Snake Town, when you saw Ramon and me drive away, did you see anyone in the area? Did anyone follow us at a distance?

No, no, my son, not a soul in sight. We stayed there for almost an hour after you left, and nothing moved but the gentle wind. From there we walked through Snake Town up to Santa Maria, where the loner, Juan Jose, allows us to sleep in an empty house that belongs to him. We saw no one, not even Juan Jose. Don't worry; everything is going to work out, and with that, I must be on my way. And she continued to smile at Mike. I have delivered my message and wish you god speed. I must go and find my man. I do not like to be away from him for too long. He is not in the best of health, and I must see to his every need.

Where is the Flying Man, if you don't mind me asking?

He is in the desert where he feels more at home. He doesn't like to come into town unless it is absolutely necessary. She looked at Mike and smiled as she said, My love for that man is as vast as the universe, beyond comprehension. I kid you not, my son. A love as deep as the deepest ocean, and it continues to grow and drive us to an eternity of ecstasy. One day, I am positive, you will also feel the rush of tender sentiments that knock you off your feet, and the balance you once believed made your life real becomes only a memory of a fading landscape. We fall without touching the ground, and our laughter echoes in the night like a magic orchestra only we can hear. Love, my son, true love, deep love—oh, what a blessing it is.

Mike was left speechless. He didn't have the words to say anything about anything, so instead of acting the fool and attempting to say something profound, he asked her, Do you want a ride at least halfway?

If you were to be so kind, but it might be out of your way, I'm afraid. No, it's OK, insisted Mike. I'll at least get you closer so that you won't have to walk so far.

That is very generous, my son. If you can get me to the edge of Esperanza, I can walk to El Camino de Lagrimas and meet Santiago in that area.

OK, I can do that. And this conversation never happened, right, Shonofa?

I don't remember a word. And she put her fingers on her mouth, puckered her lips, and let her fingers fly, like as if she was throwing someone a kiss.

Mike, feeling much better now, made a right on Mora and drove toward Esperanza Street. They drove without saying a word. Traffic was picking up, and he felt kind of weird with the woman in black next to him. The woman was called crazy by many but seemed lucid and on the bright side to him. He had never spoken to her before and went on what others said about the odd couple. He knew about the Flying Man; everyone did. Their story had been covered by a newspaper, somewhere. He didn't remember the details, but they made the front page.

Mike made a right on Esperanza and drove east. He glanced at Shonofa and attempted a smile, but it didn't work. He kept his eyes on the streets, thinking he'd be seen by some nut, and the word would get out that he was making out with the crazy woman. He wanted to laugh out loud, especially if Linda and her friends saw him, he thought. They'd have a baby. But he said fuck it and relaxed and even engaged the woman in conversation.

Tell me, Shonofa, he said, still having a tough time saying her name and talking to her as if they were pals. What do you and your man do? I mean, what do you actually do out there all day?

You don't mind me asking, do you?

Of course not. She turned to face him, as confident as ever. I paint scenes of the desert, the desert in all its beauty, and Santiago contemplates on the meaning of life. I make my own paintbrushes from the leaves of the yucca and also make my own paint from roots and plants.

Ah, Mike said, a little too quick. So you're an artist; you create art of the desert?

No, my son; as someone wiser than me once said, humans do not create. Only God creates. We imitate; that is all we can do. But the yucca, she continued, not acting superior, is a very useful plant, as we learned from the native people. We make yucca-root tea to clean the blood, soap and shampoo, and even sandals—see? She pulled up her black skirt a little and showed Mike her roughhewn sandal. From the mesquite bean pods, we dry them and grind it into flour and make bread. Or we can make jelly or wine if we care to. The leaves can be infused with water and used as eye drops. With nopales, we can make tacos or use tunas to make candies or jelly. So you see, my son, the resources are out there, and many others we have yet to try. As I said, God provides. When I first started painting, it was on cardboard or paper we collected. One day, Juan Jose, bless his heart, brought me canvas-covered frames from town and advised me never to stop painting. We eat little, so food is not our main concern. We eat what God provides; if she does not provide, that means she does not want us to eat. We do not consume animal products, at all. Gluttony is not what the body is about, my child, but one day you will see for yourself. We keep busy, but at the same time we do not rush. We repose and conserve our energy for more important things that life has to offer.

Wow! Mike said. You guys got it together. He didn't want to come off as too phony, but he was impressed.

As they reached the end of Esperanza Street, Shonofa said, You can drop me off here, my son, and I will walk the rest of the way.

Are you sure? I can drive up to Snake Town.

No, no, my son; you have done enough. I appreciate your kindness. I am to meet Santiago along El Camino de Lagrimas, and if he sees the car, he will hide. Then I have to find him. It is easier this way, but thank you, my son, and God bless you.

Mike stopped the car in the middle of the street, and she walked off, looking straight ahead, crossing the Old Albuquerque Road and connecting with El Camino de Lagrimas. Mike made a right on Caballo Blanco Road and drove south toward Chavez Street and home. He was hungry now, and he knew his mother had a feast waiting for him, as usual, and then maybe some repose after. He liked that word; he was a great believer in repose.

CHAPTER NINETEEN

ercedes Sosa entered the Las Flores Community Center as if she was royalty. She was tall and dark skinned, had long straight hair, and was proud. She was proud for many reasons: one was that she completed all her education at UNM and refused a full scholarship at Harvard, having been unwilling to freeze her fine ass in that polar region. She walked emanating authority but with a feminine presence that made people look at her, even if they didn't like what they saw. She had the perfect legs for high-heel shoes and the tight ass for expensive clothes. But she was too sophisticated to wear anything too tight and show off her sculptured body. Her makeup was light, except for her lips, full lips that glistened with a bright-red lip gloss. Her face was exotic, a mixture of Asian and native peoples, difficult to describe—a beauty not seen on the cover of Vogue, that was for sure.

Mercedes Sosa was a Latina attorney employed by the feds out of the US attorney's office in Albuquerque. She was the compliance officer in charge of investigating irregularities in the federal grant programs. They were matched funds or full grants given to community centers and others who were willing to fill out the cumbersome paperwork. She had an appointment with Hector to go over the books and maybe stay for a little visit. And, Concha promised her a taste of a membrio pie she had made especially for her.

As Mercedes Sosa walked into the center in her expensive heels, a vato going out said, Hola, chula.

Mercedes, without looking at him, said, Mercedes Sosa to you, turd face. Mercedes was known for a tongue like barbed wire and didn't hesitate to lacerate without mercy anyone who tried to mess with her. But she was considered the nicest person by people who liked her.

Mercedes! Mercedes! cried out Connie, Hector's secretary, as she jumped out of her chair behind her desk and almost ran to Mercedes, like a little girl who finds her first Easter egg on her first Easter egg hunt. Connie adored Mercedes Sosa. She loved her long, straight black hair and expensive clothes. She loved almost everything about Mercedes, but what she loved best was her smarts and education and the fuck-you attitude she displayed with royal gusto. She hugged Mercedes as she hugged her favorite aunt. She hung around close to her elbow, complimenting her on shoes and dress—as if she knew anything about it. She tapped Mercedes on the shoulder with little taps, unable to keep her hands away from her. She acted giddy and kind of silly, something that Connie was not known to be.

So how is Hector treating you, Connie? asked Mercedes, to see if Connie would stop with the fuss.

You should ask me how I treat him, said Connie, a twinkle in her eyes and a full smile on her face.

OK, how do you treat him?

Like the old dog he is. And they both laughed.

Finally Concha came from the kitchen and told Connie to settle down and get back to work. She walked Mercedes into the kitchen and showed her where the books were piled up on a table waiting for her. But she insisted that Mercedes must have some membrio pie and a cup of coffee with real milk and sugar or hot chocolate. Concha also loved Mercedes, as much or more than Connie. She respected and admired her resolve and the powerful role model a woman like Mercedes Sosa was to women in general and to Latina women in particular. She was proud to call Mercedes Sosa her friend.

Sit down, Mercedes. Sit over here on this chair and have some pie, said Concha, as a mother tells a daughter when she has her best interest at heart. The books are ready, hermana, and Hector is in his office, not being himself. I don't know what to think.

Mercedes, waiting for the pie to cool, said, It might be a guy thing, Concha. Don't worry about it. Hector has these down days but miraculously tumbles back into action. So don't worry about it, Concha. It's not worth it.

It's not that I'm worried about it, Mercedes; it's just that he keeps in his office more than usual, and he has to be out here more and help run the show. The pie has cooled; why don't you have a bite and give me some feedback so I can perfect my technique. I value your word as no other and promise to be open minded on whatever you say.

Mercedes Sosa kept her eyes on Concha, giving her her complete attention. She had excellent listening skills and distinctive facial expressions to draw in people with her compassion and help them want to open up to her. She was eating the pie, but her eyes never left Concha. She liked Concha because to her, Concha represented the Latina women who fought to survive, women who had been abused by a theocracy of men with little or no love in their hearts. Women who had been abandoned by careless men and shunned by the sisterhood, raised kids alone, and done all right; that was Concha to her. Concha also reminded Mercedes of her own mother but in a different way. Her mother was a woman difficult to establish any kind of relationship with, but Mercedes still loved her like a saint. She kept her eyes on Concha and kept silent. She knew her friend Concha needed to talk and wanted to talk, so she just listened.

An hour later, Mercedes Sosa knocked on the door of Hector's office. The door opened; she walked in and closed the door gently behind her.

Hey, Hector, Mercedes said. I didn't catch you at the wrong time, did I, Hector? I mean, we did have an appointment to go over the books.

No. Hey, Mercedes, Hector said, embarrassed. No, silly, I remembered. I was just going out to meet you so we could go over the books, you—you know.

The books are done, responded Mercedes, all business. Concha—and she emphasized "Concha"—Concha and I have gone through the books. Concha takes care of business, and her paperwork is in order. Yours, I'm afraid, is a little sloppy, Hector, and I find no excuse for that. I want to point out a discrepancy on one voucher that

I happened to glance at. A twenty-five-dollar voucher was put in the hands of a Brazilian couple in their late twenties. You know the rules, Hector; we do not hand out money to indigent people, regardless of where they're from. We hand out food and a referral to some other agency on the city or state level. Hector, continued Mercedes, thoroughly enjoying it, I understand twenty-five dollars is not much, but rules are rules. I do not want to write you up on this because this little blip could affect your outcome for the next federal grant you write. And I know you are famous for writing successful federal grants, Hector. So think about it. If I were in your shoes, Hector, I'd pay the twenty-five out of my pocket and chalk it up as an error. Send them the twenty-five and avoid a real audit by the GAO. But do what you want, Hector. I'm just giving you a little free advice.

OK, Iron Lady, I get it, said Hector, wanting desperately to change the subject. I was wrong. They were a young couple from Brazil, of all places. They were broke; that's what they said. I had no reason to doubt their story. I never guessed the US Treasury would go broke over twenty-five bucks.

Funny, funny, Hector—you should take a gig at a comedy club, make people laugh to forget their problems, or join the circus and be a clown. Next time you feel generous with tax dollars, open your wallet, and pitch in as much as your conscience will allow you. The girl was pretty, right, Hector? She was bronzed with braided hair and had big tits and wore a low-cut blouse. Her skin was smooth and moist; it looked juicy, and you fell for her, didn't you? Your weakness as a man always comes through, doesn't it, Hector? You couldn't say no to a pair of tits, right, Hector—because I'm sure it wasn't the guy who turned you on, was it? Am I giving you too much credit? It was the girl who got you licking your chops, wasn't it?

Not to change the subject, Hector interjected, before Mercedes made a career out of her interrogation, but what about lunch?

What about it? asked Mercedes, annoyed that Hector cut her off when she was just getting started.

Well, I mean, we can go to the Azteca and get a bite to eat and talk some more.

No, Hector, no can do. I promised Concha and Connie to have lunch with them; besides, others might see it as a conflict of interest or that I am letting you get away with something. So we better not socialize in public, but if you want, I'll meet you at your place around four or five. We can talk then without any interruptions. That OK?

OK, Hector said, not sure if he wanted her to come over at all, but he didn't have the guts to tell her. She was a hot mama, but he wasn't sure if he had the ammunition to sustain a full attack. He had been under a lot of stress lately and had lost interest in passion. He didn't want to have to explain it, so he abstained, even leaning toward celibacy, in these unforgettable times.

All right, babe. I'll be home. Stop by, and we'll talk. We'll have a few drinks, listen to some good music, you know. How's that sound? How about a kiss on the lips, sugar, before you go meet with the girls? Yes?

No, Hector. Mercedes put her long arms out to stop any advance Hector might contemplate. We can't. We're on the clock, and it's just not right, so see you later. Ta-ta.

At four thirty that same day, Hector was picking up all kinds of stuff left scattered here and there. Since Concha quit him, the house was a mess. He had to wash the dishes and plan a simple dinner in case Iron Lady wanted to eat. What the hell, he said. This is work, and it ain't even Saturday yet. The house—a large adobe house, old but well kept—had belonged to Hector's mother before she passed; Hector, on returning to Las Flores, retired and checked into the house that now was his. It still had some of his mother's mementos, like plastic on the sofa and pictures of Santos all over the house. But the house had furniture, some good, some not; it had everything he needed, and he didn't have to spend any cash on furniture. He just went straight into his old room and made himself comfortable from day one. The house was difficult to keep up without help, and Tupi still wanted to sleep in the bed with him—at the edge, of course. Tupi made a mess and a lot of noise at night, but he felt sorry for the old dog and let him have his way.

The last place Hector was tidying up was the area he created for himself after his return. He had sent to his mother's home a mahogany bar with matching bar stools before moving from Los Angeles to Chicago. The bar looked out of place in the large sala. He put it in a corner of the room and moved a smaller leather couch and easy chair from the sitting room and set them next to the bar. He also placed a coffee table in front of the leather couch, hung up some of his paintings behind the bar, and made himself at home. His music box was on top of the bar, and his LPs were scattered around the sala and throughout the house. It was almost 6:00 p.m., and Mercedes Sosa had not arrived or called to cancel. He had been picking up and cleaning for almost two hours. He decided to take a break and leave the rest. He poured a stiff one from the bottle of bourbon and then put on some music and sat on the couch, trying to figure out what he was going to do.

As Hector put his lips on the glass to take a sip, there was a knocking on the front door. He was going to put the glass down but took a good hit anyway. He knew who it was, and there was no point in running to the door like a dog. He walked the length of the long sala to a hallway that led to the front door. He knew it was Mercedes but wasn't sure if he wanted to see her. But it was too late for that now, so he opened the door and let her in. She had been there before and followed Hector to the leather couch and sat down. She had a glass of bourbon with ice in her hand before she could say please. But instead, she said, Nice music, Hector. I do not believe I am familiar with it, Hector; what is it?

Oh, that's Carlos Chavez, said Hector, with a shrug. He's a Mexican composer, and we're listening to Sinfonia India, also known as Symphony Number Two. Carlos Chavez, continued Hector, with more enthusiasm, now that Mercedes showed interest, composed this music in the thirties. This is one of his few works that uses Indian themes in a classical composition that combined modern music with what some call antiquated sounds. Some of the musical instruments utilized were musical instruments used by the pre-Colombian people.

Hector took another big hit from his bourbon and drained the glass. He felt the sweat on his forehead and did nothing about it but filled his glass and looked at Mercedes Sosa with eyes that were on fire. He wanted to rip off her clothes and ravish her on the couch as he had done on other occasions, but he knew things were different now, and the best he could do was talk. Some of the instruments used, he continued, not taking his eyes off Mercedes, seducing her with his words, his knowledge, he wanted to believe, were the Indian drum; water gourd, or tenor drum; the teponaxtles, or xylophone; grijutian, which was a string of deer hoofs; and the raspador yaqui, or rasping stick. There were other native percussion instruments, and Chavez incorporated the sounds they produced with classical music. It's a unique composition, as you can hear, its texture and sound introduces you to a fusion of melody that is powerful, beautiful and distinctive.

But if they never heard the actual music, how can they be so sure that the instruments are producing the exact sound, the sound of the ancients? asked Mercedes, still fucking with Hector and loving it.

Hector bit his lower lip and wanted to slap the bitch, but he didn't. Instead he said, as calmly as the situation called for, Chavez, Mercedes, Chavez was influenced by his connection with the Mexican Indian culture—see what I mean? He would ask the oldest members of indigenous people in the cities and in the rural areas to play any instrument they were familiar with. They did and produced some extraordinarily beautiful music utilizing those same instruments. Later, when the Spanish guitar was introduced to the Americas, it added to the music, and it became popular among some circles. Los Folkloristas, a famous Mexican group play great indigenous music, and they also studied with the elders to learn more about the music. Raiz Viva, for example is a remarkable number utilizing those instruments.

You have never played it the times I have been here; of course, I haven't been here that often. Is it something you picked up recently? Or is it one of those things you didn't want to share with me, Hector? Tell me. I'll understand.

No, no, baby. Hector, caught off guard, his fire gone, became defensive without realizing it. I had it in a box. I just found it; it was well hidden, even from me. And he tried to laugh, but that failed. I found this jewel in Cambridge, Massachusetts. Can you believe it? I couldn't find it anywhere. I was in some training in Boston, right? Took off early to go check out the bookstores in Cambridge. I found some treasures, let me tell you, but this takes the prize. I found a copy of Frank Waters's first novel, The Lizard Woman, used but in good shape. But that's another story. No, really, Mercedes, I wanted to play this music especially for you. I share everything with you, babe. You know it. He wanted to stop lying, but he couldn't, so he just kept it up.

Mercedes Sosa put the drink on the coffee table without tasting it. So, Hector, how are you getting along with Father Benji? asked Mercedes, with a huge grin on her beautiful face, changing the subject as easy as changing shoes.

Hector made a face. Another thorn in the ass, he thought. He took a small sip. The fire had fizzled, and he was left with an aching desire to go to bed, alone. But he stayed in the game. Did I tell you, he said, what the crazy bastard wants to do? He wants to use the center for high-stakes bingo—can you believe that? I mean, they rake in a good amount of cash on the regular bingo every night; now he wants to squeeze more bread out of the people by putting on a show. High-stakes bingo, my ass.

The poor man might need some cash, said Mercedes, still grinning but with less emphasis.

I'm sure he does; we all need some cash, baby, and that's a fact. He's up to his ears in debt. You think he made those trips to Vegas to visit the archbishop? He sends money to his lazy family in Spain and expects the people here to subsidize their lifestyle over there. Maybe he missed a couple of payments, I don't know, but he sure seems anxious to get his paws on some cash, if you ask me.

Did you discuss it with the board? asked Mercedes, loving Hector getting all busy over the nutty priest's predicaments.

Hell, no, answered Hector, frowning. I don't want to tussle with the nutty priest; don't look good to the public. I'll be the bad apple, no matter how I approach it. Besides, I got better things to do.

Like what? asked Mercedes, cool but not grinning. Doing Concha?

Hector looked straight at Mercedes and thought, Shit, here it comes. Mercedes was too gifted to show what she had on him; instead she'd carve him up piece by piece, like a stuffed turkey, and then stab him in the heart with one big thrust. That was her style. That was the way she did things.

No, hold on, Mercedes, said Hector, as convincing as he could say it. That was a misunderstanding. It started out as a joke, then it—

No, you hold on, Hector. And she stood up as if she was cross-examining a witness who had thrown dirt on her client. I wouldn't call it a joke, Hector, when another's feelings are involved. Let me put it this way, Hector. And she crossed her arms over her chest as if she wanted to protect her perfect breasts from Hector. It might have been a joke to you—in bad taste, but a joke—but to her, perhaps it was an emotional, tender experience. She gave you her body, and with it went her heart and soul. You think a mature woman like Concha is going to take her clothes off and jump in bed with anyone? Is she a puta, a prostitute? I don't think so. When a woman gives herself to a man like Concha did to you, she gives everything, everything she has. And she expects, if not love, at least some respect.

No, baby, you—I mean, please. Hector was desperately attempting to sound sincere and find the right words to defend his position, but he had slipped too far into the shit to do any good. Mercedes Sosa was quick of mind and could verbally slap anyone silly, if it was in her interest to do so.

I don't mean a joke, like a joke, that, you know. It was a joke told by—started—meant to be funny, not my idea, no way; it just caught on, and, and—well, it's there.

You're right, Hector; it could be a stupid joke, even a rumor, spread by malicious people looking to do harm. But when the truth comes from Concha—when she tells me, with a broken heart and tears in her eyes, then there is some slight truth in the rumors—don't you agree, Hector? Your motivation for doing it is beyond me. I guess I didn't satisfy your basic instincts, and you roamed; that is the simple truth, and you can't deny it. And by the way, I started seeing someone else, and he asked me to marry him, and I accepted. He's younger than you but not younger than me. He's an attorney with the state, and we are in love. You knew it was going to end, Hector; it was only a matter of time. You knew before I did, and that's what hurts. When I got the story from Concha, I realized you are a desperate man, and a desperate man can never be trusted.

No, baby, don't leave me. Don't get married; I'll marry you, if you'll have me. I love you, Mercedes. I love you very much, but I thought you didn't love me—couldn't love me—that you were waiting for the right door to open to make your exit. I'm sorry, Mercedes. Take me back; I'll change. You'll see.

No way, Hector, it's too late for that. You told me some time ago that you were in love with Paloma Picasso. I didn't believe you because I didn't know about your—how can I say it—problem.

Paloma Picasso was the love of my life, said Hector, conflicted more than ever for begging Mercedes to take him back and screwing up the episode with Concha. He closed his eyes to focus on the image of Paloma clearer. She was the woman I adored and fantasized over for a major portion of my life. A woman who gave me stars in the head and a desire not common to the majority of society. She was my beloved and the reason for my sanity being intact. I don't expect you to understand that feeling, Mercedes.

But you never met her, Hector, added Mercedes, with a devilish smile on her sexy mouth. Even if you had by accident, she's famous, and you're a desperate nobody. How can you even dream of having such a destructive fantasy? You might see her image on a calendar or something a little trendier, but it will be the same thing. You will take it to your favorite place and whack your brains out. Then Paloma Picasso would be just another calendar girl, until you had to beat your meat again. Please don't call that love; maybe a childish infatuation that we all have as children. Nothing more, nothing less.

Please don't talk so obscene when you mention my love, pleaded Hector, almost in tears. I have a picture of her in my wallet, of Paloma in all her grace. And don't call my love for her a childish agitation, Mercedes. Love to you is a fallen angel, never to fly again.

You talk about love as if you own it, responded Mercedes, resentful that Hector was lecturing her on love, a subject he obviously knew nothing about. You treat a woman like she should be eternally grateful for sharing her life with you. With that attitude, you love yourself more on a grand scale and have no need for anyone else. I'm with a man now, Hector, not with a creature of habit, needy and insecure, who cares only for number one. You're in a pickle, Hector, and I don't want to be around when the axe drops on your fuzzy head, and it will drop. I'm fully aware of what men with a particular passion are capable of doing to satisfy that passion. In the macho hierarchy, you insulted the primo close to if not at the top, and he will act and do something stupid to hurt you and hurt you bad.

No, baby, don't believe what you hear; nothing will happen to me. I promise. I got everything under control. Tito understands it was all a joke. No harm, no foul; everything is cool. Stay, Mercedes; I need you now more than ever. We can make it, Mercedes. I can make you happy. Just give me a chance—one chance, that's all I ask. Please, honey, one chance.

Don't "honey" me, Hector. It ain't gonna work. I'm out of your life, and you're out of mine. If you have it under control or not, it has nothing to do with me, Hector. One of your problems, Hector, is that you're fast on the mouth but slow on the brain. Good-bye and good luck; you'll certainly need it. Don't call.

Mercedes Sosa picked up her purse and walked out the door and out of Hector's life, as she promised she would. Hector stared at her as she walked out, undecided on what to do: cry or take a drink. He decided to take the drink. He sat on the couch and said, Man. What was that all about? he kept asking himself, a little distracted, staring at the brick wrapped in paper that had come crashing through his window during the early morning hours, when sleep was heavy and the soul was wandering in endless space. The breaking glass with the force of the brick had shattered his nerves, and a screeching echo of fear had hit the most vulnerable part of his psyche and woken him up in a panic. He hadn't known which way to run or what to do to protect himself from the violation of his space. He had finally jumped out of bed and attempted to control the fear that turned to anger when he realized it was only a brick, a warning. And the words on the paper were always a message, written with chicken blood, words misspelled by the ignorant amateurs whose aim was to intimidate. He was glad he hadn't grabbed his gun and run after them—a stupid move on his part, because playing the dangerous game was what they wanted. He had never shot anyone before in his life, and he didn't want to start now.

And then Mercedes, who had mommy issues, came knocking and delivered another blow. She was blowing steam about love and commitment, a subject he always considered an abstraction, although he fought for the concept; the idea of loving a woman appealed to him. But get real, he muttered; at his age, all he wanted was a calm relationship with the freedom to move around, not get hot and bothered and become a slave to a piece of ass, regardless of how hot it was. Besides, he had to be thinking of a way to get out of town and fast. He couldn't tussle with these assholes that had nothing better to do. So he sat on the couch with Tupi on his lap, patting the old dog on the head, his only loyal ally. Miss your old mommy, huh, Tupi? Hector asked the dog. I do too, but glad she ain't here to see the mess I'm in. The alcohol consumed his energy, and his brain called for sleep. He was aware that the cauldron of fear would return. The night would be long and lonely. He didn't feel like driving to his favorite watering hole, a jazz club in the Westside. It wasn't the kind of place Tito Brito and his friends would visit, but he didn't want to take any chances. Not that he was afraid; well, he was, but only because they would hurt him, hurt him in a bad way to embarrass him and teach him a lesson. No, they wouldn't kill him outright. That was too easy, but they would probably leave him incapacitated. To Hector that was a death in itself.

Hector studied The Desperate Man, a black-and-white etching by Albrecht Durer. He had had it enlarged and used it in his therapy sessions to get his clients thinking and talking. The central figure was a man on one knee, tearing his hair out in an agitated state as others watched; thus, The Desperate Man. He purchased it at a Berkley bookstore and learned later that it was a newly developed technique, back then, called etching, in which the design was marked on a metal plate with acid instead of cut by hand. Durer tried it, as he was always seeking new modes of expressions, and composed it at random— didn't even give it a title. Hector kept his eyes on the man and the woman, leaning on an elbow, with exposed breasts, next to him. Her eyes were closed, as if she refused to acknowledge the actions of the man. He asked the dog, Am I the Desperate Man, Tupi? He let out a chuckle but not convincing enough to satisfy even him.

He had had it framed and hung the print behind the bar. It had always been one of his favorites, but now it had a new meaning. He wanted to believe he wasn't there yet, but the night changed everything for him. During the day he could talk and act tough, bullshit people, and be in charge. Nighttime was a different story. His eyesight was bad, and he refused to wear glasses during the day, but at night, it was worse, and without his glasses, he was lost. He could see close up, but distance was a blur, and here he had to have owl eyes to navigate the streets that were more than safe during the day but could be treacherous at night. Fuck, he said out loud, why did I ever return? I could have retired anywhere. But he knew damn well why he returned but was playing the fool: a mortgage-free house and plenty of easy pussy, and if you didn't get any, it was because you didn't want it. Why else would he return?

CHAPTER TWENTY

That same night, as Hector was sitting on his couch with Tupi contemplating on his predicament, Sammy Q., Javier, and Jr. were standing in the middle of the street outside Sammy's carport discussing theirs.

It's not out there, Sammy. We looked, said Javier, puffing away at the Faro Sammy had provided. They were a short distance from the carport, having a conversation as if they were in the kitchen enjoying a cup of chanate. They didn't want the rest of the gentlemen drinking in the carport to catch any of their conversation. Javier continued coughing as he inhaled the sweet smoke of the Faro—not his favorite smoke.

Listen, Sammy, added Jr., more comfortable with the Faro, although his favorites were the Horseshit cigarettes. Listen, Sammy, the shit ain't out there. We looked everywhere; couldn't find nada. They lied to you, Sammy. Some motherfuckers playing you for a fool, and you letting them.

That's OK, guys. You did all right—did what you could, I'm sure. Anyway, it's best, in a way, 'cause Hector won't have any reason to kick you out of the college program. Zero tolerance, remember?

Fuck Hector in his fat ass, jumped in Jr. There ain't no zero tolerance on making a few bucks here and there. I mean, we was only delivering a package to you. What that package contained or didn't contain had nothing to do with us. Ain't that right, Sammy?

You know that's right, my man. I take care of you guys—always have and always will. Let's forget about it, OK, boys? Just pretend it never happened; you guys are not involved in nothing, nothing that goes against the grain. Now, let's get off this road 'fore some drunk knucklehead runs us over and don't stop for shit, continued Sammy, herding the two boys to the carport. Let's go have a drink, you guys. It's on me. Whatever you want. You guys deserve it, 'cause you spent a long time in the hot sun searching for something that, like you say, might not even be there. And if it ever was, it's gone by now.

Hey, Sammy. Javier stopped him before they reached the carport. You ain't gonna slip us some of that watered-down sotol, are you?

Sammy looked up at the much taller Javier and said, in a low voice, as if he was giving his son serious advice, You don't know the difference between watered down and the real stuff. You drink what I have and what I give you, watered down or not. The time comes when you have a gathering in your own house, and you provide the booze; then talk to me about taking shortcuts to make things easier.

Hey, Sammy, Jr. interrupted, not listening to a word Sammy was articulating to Javier. I don't want any of that cheap Tokay Jiggers drinks. That shit taste bad. You like it, Javier? Andale puto, dime.

You don't have to drink any drink Jiggers or the others drink, Sammy said, in the same calm and even voice. Everyone has a distinctive taste, and they choose what gets them quicker to their happiest place on earth. You drink what we have in the house. This is not the first time you been here. You been coming since an early age, and you never had any complaints about my modest collection. But let's go in, join the rest, and celebrate your acceptance to a great institution of learning. You are the heroes of the barrio and perfect role models. Maybe some of the kids in the barrio will follow your example of sacrifice, instead of hero worshipping bullies, junkies, and thieves.

But, Sammy, interrupted Jr. again, not sure if Sammy was taking it the wrong way. I wasn't saying I didn't want to drink the cheap wine. I'll drink it, and you know it. I was just saying that it taste—you know, you know, Sammy—that it taste bad. That's all, man, that's all.

Let's forget it, guys. Come on up. Let's fix you a good one. Sammy's place had the usual characters, older men with a choice of living that unsettled many people. Jiggers, the philosopher, the intellectual, had no equal at Sammy's. He was a tall and lanky man with the whiskers on his sunburned face, tangled like the nest of a wild bird. His teeth, the ones he had left, were blackened, and his gums were purple and swollen. He was on his back on the floor with his head resting on a rimless car tire. He had an open book on his chest with his hands on top of the book, as if preventing it from flying away. His eyes were closed, but there was no sign he was in a deep sleep.

Hot Jimmy was sitting on a plastic chair that seemed like a tight squeeze, his gut almost resting on his knees. He was wearing tight Levis, a bit too long for his short legs, but he padded them into his scuffed-up cowboy boots. His pudgy face was clean shaven, and he was so light that red veins could be seen on his nose and cheeks. A white Stetson hat covered his gray hair and made him look younger. He was talking his usual talk about all the women he had fucked. He went into descriptive images and intimate details of disproportionate lovemaking. The drunker he got, the more women were added to his tale of debauchery. He held a beer in his right hand and shot glass of sotol in his left. The only time he put down the beer was when it was empty or to scratch his crotch as if the chatos were eating on his huevos.

Then there was Beto, Beto Calendario, a short, stocky man in his middle years, strong in character as well as physically. Beto was known for his heart of gold, and he always desired the best for everyone. Some in the barrio claimed that life had been unfair to Beto. It was true that his wife of many years and mother of his children had run away with some pendejo who later abandoned her, penniless, in the city of Abilene in the great state of Tejas. A phone call from her, and Beto drove all the way to Abilene and returned her home without expressing an incriminating word. On the contrary, he apologized to her repeatedly for neglecting her most basic needs. He absolved his eldest son when the young man, in a drunken rage over the use of the truck, scorched the home, rendering the family homeless for a period of time. And then there was his youngest daughter, who joined a biker clan and returned after several months, pregnant and her body defamed with questionable tattoos. Beto allowed her back into the family with little acrimony, never inquiring about the father of the child, and when the child was born, treating the new member of the family as he did the others, with love and affection. Beto didn't mind what was said behind his back; he took everything with a grain of salt, especially when he heard people say that you have to have a splatter of the devil's shit on you to survive the squeeze of life in a tolerable manner. Beto had relatives in Chihuahua and was very proud of his relations but had never visited Chihuahua. He was under the impression—although a primo for three or four generations—that if he visited, he might be kept in Mexico against his will.

As Sammy, Javier, and Jr. walked into the carport to join the others, Beto raised his shot glass of sotol and said in a loud and proud voice, Sotol is the national drink of Chihuahua. He blushed and wanted to apologize, but he wasn't sure why.

Who gives a fuck about Chihuahua? said Javier in a loud and angry voice, almost on top of Beto. No one gives a fat fuck. No one. So don't say shit like that unless you got it on paper to back it up.

Jiggers opened his eyes, sat up, closed the book, and placed it on his lap. Still on the floor with his back on the tire, he said, looking up at Javier, You watch your filthy mouth, you young cocksucker. What the fuck you know about Chihuahua? Besides the known fact they murdered Pancho Villa there. Let me tell you about a place and event you will never find mentioned in your history books, continued Jiggers in a raspy voice, his red-shot eyes not leaving Javier. The name of the place is Janos, in the state of Chihuahua. Let me enlighten you with a little learning, son, before you go to the university and learn how to be even more ignorant.

Janos, Jiggers continued, before Javier could respond, was a little desert town between El Paso and Chihuahua. Janos is historically important because it is where the scalp hunters of Sonora State massacred the wife, mother, and three children of Goyathlay, known to you all as the Apache, Geronimo. You see, my friend, continued Jiggers, licking his dry lips with his scabby tongue, the governor of Chihuahua made peace with the Apaches and distributed supplies to them at Janos. They couldn't beat them, so they paid them off; that was the only way they could calm down those mighty warriors. Jiggers was on his knees now, like a starving mendicant pleading for a bone or a mad professor admonishing his students on their weak study habits, and he gestured with his knurly hand as if he meant business. The Apaches would come into Janos, you see, but they left their women and children with a few warriors near the hills, just in case shit happened—smart, right? The men would spend the whole day in Janos, boozing and socializing with the Mexicans; nothing wrong with that. But—and Jiggers hesitated, closed his eyes, and turned red with anger. He attempted to stand but decided against it; with his fists clenched and his head down, he continued. But at the end of the second day, on their way back to camp with their provisions, the Apaches were met by some women from camp. They were in tears; they had escaped to warn the men about the massacre back at the camp. Now, listen to this, Jiggers said, with visible tears in his reddish eyes as he lifted his shaggy face to look at his audience. A detachment of murdering Mexican soldiers had force marched all the way from the State of Sonora, which had not made peace with the Apaches, and massacred the women and children left behind in camp. Geronimo had brought along his wife, mother, and three children, as I told you already. Man, they were all slaughtered, along with more than a hundred Apaches, and almost an equal number were taken captive. The Apaches realized it was fruitless to engage the Mexicans; they didn't want to lose any more people, so they retreated to an area set up for emergencies. Geronimo, who had lost his entire family, couldn't even go back and claim their bodies. Now that's cold, said Jiggers, scratching his neck, attempting to control his rage.

Beto looked like a cat lover who had just crumpled a kitten that dashed out in front of his car. He looked at Jiggers and wanted to say something, but it was best not to say anything. He hated to see his friend Jiggers so distressed. And the young man Javier reminded him of his son, the arsonist, whom he loved with all his heart. Both were young and vigorous but unhappy because they wanted everything now and were never satisfied with the little they had. Instead he asked

Tomasito in a shy voice, Tomasito, my good boy, can you add a little Kool Aid to my sotol? I'm feeling it strong tonight.

Not a sound was heard except the crickets, singing their never-ending song. They looked at Jiggers as he composed himself, not wanting to impose their thoughts on a subject both interesting and sad, a subject they had no knowledge of, although Geronimo was their favorite hero. Sammy was taking advantage of the pause and taking notes like a college student in a porn class. Sammy knew Jiggers was the man, and his knowledge always helped him outtalk and outflank any asshole who thought he had the smarts cornered. Javier, pissed as he was, also refused to jump in at this point; it wouldn't look good, and looking good was his main thing. Besides, he was sure Jiggers still had something to say, and say it he would, even if he was battered and his teeth were flying out his bloody mouth.

Jiggers lifted his head and wiped away imaginary tears from his bloodshot eyes and faced the young man, who had become a blur in his vision. He recalled he was at Sammy's, and Sammy was cool. Sammy would protect him against any unnecessary roughhouse, because Sammy Q. loved the information that came his way, especially if that info was attached to historical events.

Jiggers rubbed his mouth with his hand, wanting a drink but deciding to wait, not wanting to lose his captive audience over a drink. So he said in a calm voice, the anger splintered, maybe disrupted, by the pause—it was difficult to put a finger on it with Jiggers: Geronimo would have a burning hatred for the Mexicans that lasted most of his adult life, and who in their right mind could blame him? Who? he repeated. Knowing he was not going to get an answer, he continued. When the brave warrior Geronimo returned to the United States, he didn't go the headwaters of the Gila; he didn't want any memories of his dead family. No, instead he decided to get revenge for the massacre at Janos by organizing a war party. A war party—you know what that means? asked Jiggers, playing with his audience, flashing his eyes, proud of his knowledge, and daring anyone to contradict him. With the permission of chief Mangas Coloradas; Cochise, chief of the Chiricahua Apaches; and Juh, his cousin, chief of the Nedis Apaches from the Sierra Madre in Mejico; the war party, under the leadership of the three chiefs, headed to the State of Sonora to kick some ass. You have to know, explained Jiggers, Geronimo was never a chief, as some ignorant people claim. He was a war leader, and a damn good one. It was a large war party, and they did all their traveling at night and on foot, taking enough food and water for three days and three nights. Upon arriving in Sonora—and Jiggers paused to blow his nose on a soiled handkerchief—the Apaches chose the town of Arzipe, in which many of the Mexican soldiers were stationed who had participated in the Janos massacre.

Jiggers paused again, seeming as if lost in thought, fighting to retain what was familiar but not sure of the footing. He needed a drink; his glass was empty and his throat dry, but he had to prove to himself, if not to anyone else, that he could wing it.

Go on, Jiggers, called out Sammy Q. Don't leaves us hanging, brother. We all listening; we all ears; go on with the story. I'll get you a drink in a minute.

Jiggers, hearing Sammy mention a drink, jumped back into it. Well, anyway, he said, with a sly grin on his thick lips. Almost lost it, he thought. Saved by the bell; can't put a good man down—hell, no. He continued, Arzipe was a beautiful little town, built like a natural fortress between two mountains, but there was only one way out, and the Apaches—you got it—were behind the rocks and trees, blocking the only exit in or out of that beautiful town. The Mexicans sent eight men out with a white flag to try and deal, perhaps pay off the angry Apaches. Excuse me, boys and girls, continued Jiggers in a better mood, the Apaches didn't come all that distance to chat over biscuits and coffee. They killed the eight sent out and pissed on the white flag. The Mexicans realized the Apaches were serious and didn't want to fuck around; they marched out to engage them. Geronimo, who hated the Mexicans more than anyone, asked the three chiefs for permission to lead the attack. The chiefs agreed, and Geronimo charged in front of the warriors again and again—had the devil in him, I tell you. The fighting was close hand-to hand-combat, with Geronimo doing the job of two men, killing Mexicans left and right. He was so enraged that the Mexicans started to call him Jeronimo. Jeronimo, Jeronimo, called out Jiggers, with a little laugh. That was what the Mexicans were yelling. They were crying for Saint Jerome, their saint, for help, after feeling the wrath of the crazed Apache. After killing many Mexicans and losing a few of their own, the Apaches decided to break up and go across the border before Mexican troops would come to the aid of Arzipe. From that day on, Goyathlay had become Jeronimo to the Mexicans and Geronimo to the whites.

Bravo, Jiggers, bravo, cried Sammy. Well done, my friend. And he offered him a plastic cup full of Tokay wine. You the man, Jiggers, insisted Sammy, before Jiggers wandered off on an opposite direction and bored them with the story of when he got his ass kicked in Nuevo Laredo.

Jiggers took a huge gulp of the wine and gazed at the young man Javier, confident he would never get a history lesson from the numb nuts at the university such as the one he just got. Jiggers still disdained the professors at the U for rejecting his tenure bid—and all because he supported and joined the Tiger of the North, Reyes Tijerina, in his struggle to confiscate land grants that belonged to his people. And the little shit of him sleeping with some of the female students and boozing a little too much; everyone did it, he thought. Shit on them; he had left it all behind and traveled the world, free of worries and responsibilities, searching for an answer to a question he never bothered asking. He always returned to Las Flores, to the Eastside barrio, the place he loved to hate. He was born and raised here and was always welcomed at Sammy's, and people like Sammy existed all over the world, and he always found them and had a good time with these folks. Of course he had a little money— his Social and the laughable pension he received from the university, which couldn't buy him a sack of beans—but what the hey, he thought. He wouldn't change a thing if he could.

Javier couldn't stay quiet any longer and blurted out at Jiggers, What does all that have to do with sotol? You old bag of decaying shit.

Jiggers, shocked out of his ancient battles with nameless professors and deans, responded in a perfect intonation, That's what your mother screamed when I fucked her in the ass, son.

Javier jumped up fast and furious, knocking his plastic chair down, as Jr., buzzed out of his mind with the mota Sammy had given him, jumped up also, taking a cue from his friend, Javier. Jr. didn't know what was happening; his mind had been on pussy all this time, but if Javier was going to let some blood flow, he was in his corner, ready to back him up regardless of the outcome. Everyone else backed away from Jiggers and Javier, except Sammy Q.

Sammy walked up to the taller Javier and said, in a calm voice, as if telling the children that recess was over, Now, now, Javy. He was the only one that could call him Javy. Calm down, OK? It's only Jiggers. You know Jiggers, man; Jiggers is Jiggers. Whatcha gonna get by beating on him, huh? You gonna feel good tomorrow when the word gets out you beat up on old Jiggers? C'mon, Javy. It ain't worth it, brother; what the fuck you gonna tell the vatos, you bad 'cause you can slug out poor Jiggers after that history lesson he gave us? No, man, that's not you, bro. You're better than that, and you know it. And you better sit your ass down, Jr. Ain't gonna be no rock and rolling here tonight, hear me?

He better watch his mouth, said Javier, almost to himself, picking up the plastic chair and putting his ass back in it. Jr. did the same, not sure whether to laugh or talk to Javier. These two young wolves listened to and respected Sammy Q. They were hard, strong, explosive youths, who in an instant could release their pent-up energy in a physical way and inflict a hell of a lot of hurt on the old, defenseless men. They could destroy Sammy's carport full of junk and turn it into a permanent junk pile. But they'd never do that to Sammy, unless it was something beyond their control. To them, Sammy Q. had always been the best vato in the barrio. When they were in their early teens, and the older assholes treated them like shit, Sammy let them hang around and never made a big deal about their age. Sammy had always looked beyond their nervous years and accepted them as young people with feelings, able to say no or yes to anything that contradicted their upbringing. They knew if they got too drunk, Sammy would take good care of them, at least until the vomiting stopped. Then he took them by the hand and left them on the front door of their homes. The next day, sick from the booze, they would return to Sammy's to get a fix or brag about the experience. Sammy was always delighted they had survived their ordeal, but he knew that was the only way to learn and become more responsible. Sammy always gave them what they needed to get through those times of uncertainties, when the departure of childhood and the lonesome road to adulthood could become a train wreck. To Javier and Jr., Sammy Q. had been their savior, giving them the opportunity to brave a lot of the vices they were going to realize anyway but at a later date, a time when they'd have more important things to do.

Jr. and Javier respected Sammy Q. and loved him like a useful uncle, even though he was only about ten years their senior. Sammy had been in the trenches from an early age, fighting a war he was sure to lose but never hanging up the gloves, so they listened to him like to no one else. They would never destroy his property because this was the place that influenced a large part of their adolescent development. Sammy's was the place that attracted them like no other. No sports or community activity had the intoxicating pull that Sammy's had. They tasted and experience things when taste and experience were at a premium. Being around those crazy adults with booze, drugs, gambling, and profanity-laced conversations was an elixir during that formative age. When they brought girls to Sammy's, he always let them use his bedroom, as long as they kept the door shut so Granny couldn't hear anything.

Jiggers closed his eyes, waiting for the beating to start. He had been pounded so many times that it wasn't even funny. He had been done under by the best racist cops in Los Angeles, bitten by K-9s, and even set on fire by thugs in Dallas. He took the bad with the good. He knew he couldn't put up a fight with these hooligans, so he just curled up and let them beat on him all they wanted. With luck, someone might stop them before they did any real damage, and then again, in some cases, no one lifted a hand until he was bloodied, broken, and left for dead. But he didn't care; he didn't fear anyone or anything. Fear didn't stop the violence, he always said. Some people needed violence like they needed air to breathe.

At this time, Hot Jimmy interrupted, not giving a gig about what Jiggers had said. So I fucked this heifer, he said, in a loud and almost desperate voice. After we finished, I asked the pig, did I hurt you, sweetheart? She looked at me as if I was crazy and said, No way, Tarzan; why you ask? 'Cause you moved, I told her. And Hot Jimmy started laughing like a man gone berserk. His huge gut giggled like a tub of gelatin as he pulled down his tight T-shirt with both hands to keep his belly covered.

And Beto, with a huge smile, said to Jiggers, ignoring Hot Jimmy, You tell them, compa. You educate these fine boys and send them away with a little bit of wisdom; never hurts. I tell you, compa, these boys will appreciate what you do for them, someday. On that, I can put money on, hard cash, if you ask me.

Jiggers, not hearing a word, opened his eyes and, not feeling any chingazos coming his way, said to Sammy, Hey, Sammy, fix me up a Larry Fanary. I like those little puppies.

Javier and Jr. looked at Sammy and asked at the same time, What the hell is a Larry Fanary?

Oh! It's an invention Tomasito came up with, answered Sammy, scratching his balls with his hand inside his pants pocket, pocket- pool style. You place a flour tortilla on the flame or grill, if you have one; turn it over until it gets a little crispy; scatter some small pieces of yellow cheese on top. As the cheese melts, you turn off the heat, put the torta on a plate, and add some Karo syrup on top of the cheese. But it has to be the dark corn syrup, not the white. Very good. You should try one.

Hey, Tomasito, fix Jiggers a Larry Fanary, OK, mijo?

I ain't gonna fix Jiggers shit, answered Tomasito, not bothering to look at Sammy, but he continued pouring drinks and collecting cash. Last time he didn't pay, Sammy. Said you were cool with it.

I did so pay, cried out Jiggers. Here, you little sissy. He pulled out a crumpled five from his filthy sock and flung it at Tomasito.

I ain't gonna touch anything that comes from him, said Javier, pointing to Tomasito.

Hay si, culitos, cried out Tomasito, with his right hand on his hip and gesturing with his left at Javier and Jr., making all kinds of funny faces. Jus' 'cause you going to college don't make you special; you still a couple of pendejos.

Jr. and Javier stood up again, ready to put the fear of God on Tomasito.

Sammy again asked them to chill. C'mon, guys, take her easy; it's only Tomasito. He don't mean nothing. Let him make you a Larry Fanary; it's on the house. Jesus, you guys are ready for action. Why doncha go to Chiva Town and play hide-and-seek with the Snipers?

No, don't go; I'm only kidding. Stay. It's OK; only kidding. Ha-ha, you know me, guys.

Jiggers sat up as Sammy calmed the attack dogs and, with the book in his hands, said to Sammy, Hey, Sammy, you should read better. I won't say shit, because I respect the written word too much for that, but Louis L'Amour? C'mon on. You wanna read something good, read People of the Valley, by Frank Waters, or The Yogi of Cockroach Court, also by Waters. Man, at least The Bounty Hunters, by Elmore Leonard. But I know why you like L'Amour, Sammy Boy, continued Jiggers, an unrestrained grin on his puffy mouth. You like the tall, strong, man-of-few-words protagonist who always gets the good-looking chick at the end, donchu? You wanna be like that fucker, donchu, Sammy? You wanna run away with that white piece of ass, am I right, Sammy Boy? Be the man with the plan and get it right all the time—that you, Sammy Boy?

Sammy looked at Jiggers and smiled. Let me write the titles down, Jiggers, said Sammy, and searched for his pen and scratchpad among the junk, happy as a bee in a poppy field.

What do you care what Sammy reads? Javier asked Jiggers, still pissed off because he couldn't put a boot up his ass.

Jiggers looked at Javier, stuck his index finger in his mouth, and flicked it out toward him, without saying a word.

Javier and Jr. stood up, gulped their drinks, and said, We're out of here, Sammy, and left.

Sammy turned to face them, still smiling, and said, See you guys later. He knew they'd return later, when the old guys were passed out or gone home; they always did. OK, folks, let's put on some music, he said, as he addressed his compadres. The youngsters are gone. He put on Jose Alfredo Jimenez—love and drinking music, everyone's favorite. They were sad and macho songs that tore into the heart, brought forward forgotten emotions, and made you want to hug a friend, if you had a friend. As more of his friends arrived, Sammy turned up the volume and joined in singing the lyrics of the king of Mexican composers. Even Jiggers forgot his bitterness and sang out loud, in not a bad voice, about women gone bad, cantinas, Tequila, horses, and pain, heartfelt pain. They wept like children and touched their hearts when they heard the golden voice belt out, "El amor es como el mar, cristalino y profundo." They sang and drank, forgetting their tedious existence, enveloped in a cocoon of a rich ancestral cultural determination that could never be erased, although attempted in many fronts. Sammy forgot to collect money for the booze, but he didn't care. He cared only for the happiness he brought his friends. Tomorrow, he would worry about it, no doubt; tonight was party night. He saw the sad Tomasito singing with a glass of Kool Aid in his hand. He walked over and put his arm around him, and they sang along with the others about a faithful dog who never left his master, even sleeping on top of his grave at the cemetery where he was interred— killed over a woman.

CHAPTER TWENTY-ONE

Sammy Q. and Tomasito were driving in the bright but not early morning after a night of serious partying. They were not miserable because Sammy smoked weed and drank little, and Tomasito drank only Kool Aid. The mota helped Sammy from getting too dependent on booze; besides, he had to stay on top of the game, ready to intervene, in case of disputes that could lead to turmoil, as evidenced last night. He never underestimated his cultured friends. So after a hearty breakfast of chorizo with fried eggs and potatoes and seeing to the needs of his Granny, he invited Tomasito to take a ride with him.

Sammy drove east on Martinez Street for about half a mile and then cut a left on Caballo Blanco Road, heading north. The late morning was clear and bright, and the sky was pure blue, with no clouds in sight. The Turquoise Mountains could be seen in the distance, calm and supreme.

Where we going, Sammy? asked Tomasito; no one ever called him Tomas anymore. I thought you said you didn't have a license to drive or a car.

Don't worry, Tomasito, said Sammy, smiling, as he always did when asked a stupid question. As you know, this ain't my ride. It belongs to Hot Jimmy. He left it last night, late last night, 'cause he was too polluted to drive and decided to walk home—a smart move on his part, don't you agree? We're returning this carrucha, because in the first place, it don't belong to me, and second, I wouldn't own it if given to me free of charge, along with a case of beer. That's the reason I'm returning it. Besides I don't want it parked around my pad 'cause it might have a dead body in the trunk, and you know what sort of problems that can bring. But before we return the car to Hot Jimmy, who I'm sure is doing something more creative than worrying about his car, we're going on a little visit.

Like what? asked Tomasito, picking his nose with his index finger and studying the contents. Not knowing where to put them, he made them disappear under the car seat.

Well, said Sammy, pretending he didn't see what Tomasito did. For one, eating menudo to ease the hangover, then getting on top of his vieja to cure the second half of the hangover. You get a little raunchy with a hangover, Tomasito, and your chicote sometimes gets out of control and behaves in an uninhibited manner; what can I tell you? It wants to whip some ass—know what I mean, my friend? So by the time we return the car to Hot Jimmy, he will be done with his chores and might be ready to move on to his next adventure. Maybe by then, he'll start thinking about his car.

Why do you call me Tomasito, Sammy? My name is Tomas, and some people talk about me as if I'm bad news.

Fuck what people think or say, said Sammy, really meaning it. People will always talk, my friend. So not to worry; people will talk, as long as talking is cheap, pretending or ignoring the fact that what usually comes out of their mouths is nothing but mierda. I call you Tomasito because Tomasito was one of the revolutionary leaders who killed and scalped Governor Bent in the Taos uprising of January 19, 1847. A bad mother, Tomasito, a bad mother—a real Indio with balls of steel, you bet. See, General Kearny appointed Charles Bent acting governor of New Mexico, while the sonofabitch rushed to help out in the conquest of California—but that's a long story, my friend. He was a brave man; this Tomasito we're talking about. He risked his life to rid New Mexico of the hated gringo. Just like you are, brave and honest, and that's the truth, sir. Nothing but the truth.

Sammy paused and looked at Tomasito and then back at the street. He decided to change the subject because Tomasito showed no interest in history of any kind. He had gained weight, and his acne was clearing up. He looked a lot better than when he first moved into Sammy's house. He had lived a hard life at his aunt's house in Chiva Town. Sammy liked Tomasito, liked his charm, which was not recognized by people who were invigorated by their own ignorance, and that was sad, he thought. Sammy was hard on Tomasito many a time, but he believed that was part of the education he was attempting to instill in the young man. And that's why he was taking him to visit his friend, La Conga, a woman who specialized in cheese wrappers.

So that's why I call you Tomasito, continued Sammy, keeping his eyes open for coppers. Hey, the name Tomasito is no joke, my friend; you are courageous to put up with all the shit people throw at you. They bite like vultures and make you bleed, yet you hold on and keep going, and the stains of anger haven't penetrated your soul. Now that's courage, believe you me, little bro. Tomasito is a name solidified in honor, the honor that goes to men who will die to be free. With a name like that, you have every reason to be proud of something. If all else fails, think about it.

Yeah! Yeah! Sammy, whatever you say. And Tomasito raised his hand to touch Sammy on the shoulder but changed his mind. Where we going, Sammy? You not taking me back to Chiva, are you?

Hell, no, said Sammy, smiling. I never do that, unless you ask me to. I'm gonna tell you, OK, but don't get too excited. I'm getting tired of people saying you're a lefty. I'm gonna prove to 'em you a macho goat, like the rest of us—shut them up, no more talking shit behind your back, enough of that. We'll put a stop to that garbage today, yes sir, today.

Why you wanna do that? Who cares what they say? Wasn't that what you were talking about?

Oh, good, you were listening; I like that. Let's show those billy goats you also got the—the billy in you, si o no? So I'm taking you to the house of a friend of mine who happens to be called La Conga. She's a good woman, and she's gonna talk to you in a language that might be confusing at first, but it gets simple quick, believe me. You about to become a man, my friend, and the pleasure and pain that come along with it depend on your imagination. If you ride the bull now, maybe you'll find out on which side of the arena you belong and enjoy it longer. You haven't slept with a girl, have you? It's OK—you can tell me.

I don't get what you mean, Sammy, said Tomasito, turning red. I've slept with a girl—my cousin Monchy—but nothing happened, just sleep. I say hi to some girls, and they turn their faces. I don't get it, continued Tomasito, almost in tears. I ain't gonna ask them for nothing, Sammy. Just a hi don't cost nothing; what do it cost?

Could be nothing to you, my friend, said Sammy, trying his best not to show his anger, because he could relate to what Tomasito was saying. But a whole enchilada to a conceited, selfish bitch. But let me tell you, Tomasito, I ain't taking you to no girl. I'm taking you to be with a woman, a woman who can change your life, as she had done for many others. Mike Montes—you know Mike? Sure you do. He's been to see La Conga; many in the barrio and beyond have, and the reviews have always been positive. That's unless you have a malfunction, and your equipment needs adjusting. Of course you'll blame La Conga; who else you gonna blame? Not yourself, for God's sakes. Denial is in your best interest. Anyway, Tomasito, you'll have your first sexual gratification, and you'll be a better person because of it, that I can promise you. You don't have to thank me now, my friend; you will when you're ready. Of that I'm more than sure.

But, Sammy, said Tomasito, with a concerned look on his face, I'm only sixteen, and wanted to wait till I was at least twenty-one or two to try anything like that. That's what they teach us in church—to wait.

I'm sure they teach you a lot of things in church, Tomasito, but sometimes you look the other way, like when you get carried away and eat meat on a meatless Friday. Things that people tell you not to do—guess what? They've already done them, but they believe they are saving you from going to hell. So don't worry, my friend, but let me ask you this: have you done a girl? I mean sex, like fucking, back or front, it don't hardly matter. Have you? Reason I ask is that I can tell La Conga your situation, and she can decide what the occasion calls for and service you at your own tempo. So don't worry, my friend. It's not like getting into a stinky girl. This is gonna be just lips and mouth, and nothing in between.

I don't know, Sammy. I've never been with a girl, but being with one is nothing to brag about.

Well, my friend, let's put it this way. When I was your age, there was nothing worthwhile to brag about except getting some pussy. I don't want to compare our situations, OK? You've lived, in many ways, a sheltered life. I don't mean privileged—far from it—but controlled more, until now, that is. I was an orphan, still am, and had, let's say, the opportunity out of necessity to explore life's secrets at an early age—the bad ones along with the good ones; the pretty along with the ugly. Now, don't get me wrong, Tomasito; I'm not a saint. Nor am I a sinner. It's just that I've done a lot of stuff that although I'm not proud of it, I ain't gonna kick myself in the ass over it.

Sammy glanced at Tomasito and then back at the road. They were still on Caballo Blanco Road going north. They had left Mariposa and Calle de las Golondrinas behind, and they were almost at Esperanza Street, and after that was Piñon Street, where La Conga had her house. He sensed that Tomasito was nervous, worried about the encounter, but Sammy still believed he was doing the right thing for Tomasito. Kids his age came to La Conga's with their chests up, walking on three legs, proud as stallions, believing there wasn't a mare in the corral who could resist their sword. But Tomasito was quiet, in a reflective mood, like going to a funeral he had no business going to. He kept his eyes straight ahead, not looking at Sammy or asking questions. He wanted this to happen, but his religious indoctrination and other unexplainable things were placing all these obstacles in his thinking, making everything more confusing; that's what Sammy thought. Sammy also believed Tomasito wanted to please him because Sammy had helped him out in a big way, but he wasn't sure if the price was too high. They stopped on Piñon Street and made a left; a couple of blocks, and they would be at La Conga's.

The road to La Conga's house was a road well-traveled, a road taken by many if not all of the real vatos from the Eastside barrio of Las Flores. It was a journey filled with expectations, especially for the youthful first timers. But also an equal amount of worry, in some, that their performance would be less vigorous than that of their amigos. They didn't yet comprehend what La Conga had to offer them. This wasn't a test run in the cat houses of Ciudad Juarez, where anything could happen; no sir. In the first place, La Conga never took her clothes off or went to bed with anyone; she was firm about that and refused to compromise for anything or anybody. Maybe in her younger days she might have done the around-the- world stuff, but nowadays, she remained fully dressed and utilized all her energy on her specialty. She explained to every client she treated, so there wouldn't be any misunderstandings, that she only sucked out all the juice from the sweet potato, if there was any juice to begin with—nothing more, nothing less, and all for a small donation. Take it or leave it. Of course she never mentioned that at the moment of their explosion or a little before, she gently pushed her thumb into the house of cards, and the floodgates opened, and the milk and honey poured out in buckets. The majority of the young folks—and even the men, as sophisticated as they believed they were, having squeezed the lizard's head many a time—had never felt any action on that side of the hill. The double dose of pleasure from the brain, the likes of nothing they had ever felt before, could in some crumble their foundations and create a challenge to their definition of what a man was all about. That was her specialty, and some never returned, while others couldn't get enough. But one thing she could bet money on: most never talked about that exceptional, delirious impression that made them shed tears in the middle of a sleepless night. But she was gentle until the end, wiping the moistened gland with tissues and placing them in a paper bag shaped like a basket that she kept under the bed, out of sight. She never rushed anyone but always asked, in a low voice filled with motherly kindness, if you could wiggle your toes for her.

Sammy made a left on Piñon Street and parked in front of La Conga's house. He looked around to see if La Conga had any customers, but he didn't see any cars parked close to the house. He breathed a sigh of relief, it was early, and it seemed to him like they were the first visitors. He didn't want to wait in the sitting room with

Tomasito because at times the groans and screams in the moment of pure pleasure could be heard through the closed door and intimidate the uninitiated. It was a small house, with no close neighbors, maybe a little more shabby than the others, but La Conga loved it as much or more as she could love anything or anybody. There was a sitting room with a worn cloth couch with no legs, resting flat on the discolored linoleum-covered floor that had supported the weight of many boots and shoes throughout the years. A milk crate decorated with Christmas wrappings, with a small lamp set in the middle, was the only source of light for the night visitors. On the opposite side of the room were a couple of wicker lawn chairs, the paint long gone and with sizeable holes, but still serviceable. A coffee table of the same material was between the two chairs, with dated magazines of Popular Mechanics and other nondescript titles for the interested. A small kitchen could be seen to the far left of the sitting room as one entered the house. There was a closed door in the middle of the sitting room, presumably La Conga's private bedroom, and another door on the far right, a room with a bed where she performed her magic, where she exorcised the demons from the soul or multiplied them to excess; that depended on the maturity of the client.

Sammy, with the hesitant Tomasito following him like a timid puppy, walked into the house like it was his second home. La Conga came in from the kitchen, drying her hands with a paper towel. She smiled, as she always did, but also had a surprised look on her face —not to see Sammy, because Sammy Q. was a steady customer, but to see him with such a young boy.

She had been known as La Conga as far as memory could register. Her Christian name had been swallowed up in the dust of changing events, and no one ever appeared with the resolve to resurrect it. She was a woman who perhaps in her youth had some visible traces of attractiveness, but the decades of a harsh existence had eroded all if not most of those questionable attributes. Her lips were soft, like rose petals, and her eyes, lagoons of obsidian with specks of gold, glistened, as if transmitting signals to unseen phantoms. Her ageless face was wrinkle-free, but the years had imposed pale blotches on her dark skin, leaving the imprints of a distorted ashiness, as if bleach had been sprinkled on her face throughout the years. Her smile seemed friendly enough but left an impression that she was laughing inwardly at a joke everyone else was too naïve to comprehend, even if broken down to the simple truth. Her hands were bony and masculine but not disproportionally large, like the inactive hands of a mediocre, retired pianist, whose image of a keyboard conveyed reflections of pain and defeat. But her hands could be as gentle as a newborn lamb or as vigorous as an attacking bull. Her emaciated figure in her scarecrow attire could project a perception of vulnerability to an undisciplined man, but her abstract smile could promptly transform into a snarling rendition of a wounded badger's and snake out a blade so swift as to make a man's blood turn to ice in his veins. And that distinction kept many men honest in their lust and discouraged them from taking advantage of an otherwise carnal business transaction.

Hi, Sammy, she said, still smiling and looking at Sammy to make sure he knew this was the correct address he wanted to be at. And before Sammy could answer, she said, And who is this fine- looking young man you have with you?

Oh, this is Tomasito, my friend, answered Sammy, relieved that La Conga wasn't busy. He wants to feel like a man, and we were hoping maybe you could help him out, if that's not asking too much.

Well, we'll see about that. She was still looking at Sammy, waiting for an explanation.

It's OK, my friend; he stays with me, so I guess I'm his guardian. No one else has stepped up to claim him.

Tomasito attempted to hide behind Sammy, but Sammy was too short to be of any help. His hands, now fists, were positioned in front of his privates, and his feet were turned inward, with his knees almost touching. His head down, eyes looking at the floor, he slouched behind Sammy, wanting to disappear, but the eyes of La Conga were not to be denied. He couldn't grasp what his role was with this thing, this Creature from the Black Lagoon. He was scared, anxious, and ready to run out the door. If this was a joke, he thought, on Sammy's part, it was beyond funny. It was sick, and he was supposed to do what to her? Or maybe he was asking the wrong question—what was she going to do to him? Oh, Lord, he almost said out loud, get me out of this place, please—I beg you.

That's all right, baby boy, said La Conga, still smiling, exposing her purple gums. Come along with Mommy. And she grabbed Tomasito by the wrist with a tight grip and led him to the pleasure room. Tomasito was taking tiny steps, almost dragging his feet, behind La Conga, almost in tears. He kept turning to look at Sammy, pleading with his eyes for Sammy to rescue him from the odious bag of bones. La Conga opened the door with her free hand and pulled Tomasito into the pleasure room and closed the door.

Sammy sat on the low couch after picking up a magazine, not bothering to see if it held his interest. His eyes were on the door where Tomasito had disappeared with La Conga. He was thinking whether this was the right move for Tomasito or the right time. Oh, he'll do fine, he thought and opened a page of the magazine, when suddenly he heard a loud scream from Tomasito, followed by a hard slap. Oh, shit! What now? said Sammy, standing up and throwing the magazine on the couch.

The door flew open, and Tomasito almost ran out, zipping up his zipper and adjusting his belt, tears flowing down his cheeks, looking at Sammy and asking, You happy now, Sammy Boy?

La Conga was right behind Tomasito and said, in a rage, This boy ain't ready, Sammy. Take him home, get him an ice cream cone, something—he ain't ready.

Sammy looked at La Conga, threw a few crumpled bills on the table, and said to Tomasito, No mas, Tomas, le's go.

They drove in silence to Hot Jimmy's house to drop off the car. Sammy felt bad, but saying sorry wasn't going to fix the harm done. He fucked up, fucked up bad, and he knew it. Well, he thought, Tomasito was young. He'll get over it; maybe it'll teach him a lesson: never get into anything you can't handle. He turned on the radio and found Freddy Fender singing "Before the Last Teardrop Falls." he loved Tex Mex country music. And he sang along with Freddy, in a decent voice, exaggerating the twang: "I'll be there anytime you need me by your side."

CHAPTER TWENTY-TWO

omero came barreling south down Highway 25 in his big Dodge V8, hitting a hundred easy. He slowed down close to Belen to fill up and lit out again toward Las Flores. He was angry and in no mood to mess around with anyone. His trip north had not gone as planned. He never reached Denver; he was debriefed in Albuquerque, not by the main capo but by his minions. He didn't get the chance to see his babe, Alicia Juarez, and that burned him up. He found out she was visiting campuses at Berkley and UCLA. How was he ever going to find her? he kept thinking. The sugar, the clever minions had calculated, had to be in Las Flores, and some jerk off was hiding it and keeping it out of circulation—for the time being, anyway. There was no new action anywhere, and the word had been put out to report any peculiar happenings, like too many dead junkies in a particular place. The capo and his main people were getting impatient, not hearing any positive feedback from Romero, a reliable enforcer, a man who had an interest in finding it and returning it as soon as possible. Perhaps they had to lean on him a little more, remind him of the lost opportunity to see himself in the driver's seat—a reality check, one could call it. All this and more raced through Romero's mind as he drove to Las Flores like a madman.

Romero, on the other hand, didn't appreciate it at all—none of it. They were thinking, he was sure—but not saying it out loud— that it could be an inside job. That he cut a deal with Sammy Q. and decided to keep the sugar, cut it, and deal it out on their own. It was so idiotic, so stupid, for them to question his integrity and think that he would ever take up with an imbecile like Sammy. He wasn't even aware of the operation this far south, and he had never heard of Sammy Q. and his doings. But he had to give them credit, he thought; they had a good thing going. The bird dumped special loads not far from the border, had Sammy pick it up, sent a flunky to collect it from

Sammy, threw Sammy some peanuts, and that was that: in and out, no sweat, and few knew about it. But eventually, a shipment disappeared, and his luck that it was a shipment he has a vested interest in, and there was speculation on this and that—well, ace them deep in the ass, he thought, angry as hell. He didn't like to come out to this hot, forbidden hellhole of a place. He had to find another fleabag of a hotel because he liked to move around and never stayed in one place more than a couple of nights. He didn't want to blow all of his travel money on lodging; he had other expenses he had to cover and no way to squeeze any extra cash from the brothers here. This wasn't his turf, and didn't want to get bogged down in logistics. He had to see Sammy Q. and go over the same ground until something came up.

Later that day, after Romero had found himself a new place, he drove over to Sammy's and parked his truck next to Sammy's carport and saw Sammy Q. sitting in his usual place, finishing his lunch—or early dinner; it was difficult to say with Sammy—as he waited for customers.

Hey, Sammy. Let's go for a ride. Come on.

Sammy looked at Romero like he couldn't believe the killer was back and then said, with food in his mouth, I gotta look at my calendar, Romero. Don't know what I got.

Get in the fucking truck, Sammy. You cain't even spell "calendar." Get in, 'fore I put a boot up your ass.

Sammy joined Romero in the truck, and they drove off like a young couple going to the flea market to look for bargains.

So, where we heading, Romero? I wasn't expecting you. I was waiting for some people; they were interested in buying some rims. And he continued removing food from his yellow teeth with half a toothpick.

This won't take long, Sammy Boy, said Romero. You'll be back before you know it.

Well, yeah, but where we heading? insisted Sammy. Or is it a surprise?

No, man, it's no surprise. What are you, my girlfriend or what?

They both laughed, and Sammy relaxed. He really didn't mind going for a ride as long as someone else did the driving. They drove on Martinez Street, which was next to Sammy's house, heading west to Highway 47 off Martinez. Sammy noticed that Romero decided on this route instead of going through the Westside. This route was faster with less traffic. When they got to the railroad tracks before reaching Highway 47, a couple of miles from Sammy's house, Sammy asked Romero to pull up next to a trailer loaded with cantaloupes. The cantaloupes were ready to be loaded on the railroad cars and moved out to the markets. The freight station was bustling with activity as the men busied themselves loading the juicy melons on the conveyor belts, some boxing and others driving in more trailers while others drove the empties away. Some of the trailers were parked a short distance from the railroad cars, and anyone could stop next to them and pull out melons—not many, but a few.

C'mon, Romero, pleaded Sammy, just pull up by that last trailer, and I'll grab a couple of juicy melons. Granny really loves them melons; it will make her so happy. Smell those melons, brother; you'll never get them fresher, and that's a promise.

I believe you, Sammy, but we'll get them on the way back, OK? Trust me. I saw a place in the Swamps where a stash could be hidden. Just bear with me, Sammy. We'll be in and out of that place in no time. You'll see.

They left the tracks behind and kept driving west until Martinez ended and became Highway 47. Highway 47 angled northwest toward the river. As they got closer to the river, Sammy observed, not for the first time, the fields of green, extending far out into the horizon, shimmering in the glow of the sun like a mirage on a lunar landscape. But at a closer scrutiny, they were real and flushed with produce, ready to be harvested. He saw the large red and smaller yellow pear tomatoes hanging on the vines like precious gems, their fecundity attracting wasps and filling the warm air with that distinctive odor of a rich and fruitful soil. He smelled the pungent odor of a massive creation, a visible germination, and an explosion of color without parallel that nurtures the artist and excites the gourmet. The long rows of melons, in their gold and verdant skins, like exotic orbs resting on a magic carpet, waited to be transported and admired at tables near and far, delighting the taste buds of rich and poor alike. Sammy witnessed this and more and never ceased to wonder at this land of plenty. He saw the tall stalks of green corn, with ears of healthy corn wrapped like gifts in green papyrus, with yellowish whiskers drooping out but standing tall like an army of sentinels waiting for orders that would never come to march on an enemy that didn't exist. He saw the onions, with their piquant scent, in the onion fields, resting on the swelling, fertile earth, welcoming the torrid sun as their protector from sweaty men on a mission to extract them from their warm and pleasant paradise. And he saw the milk cows getting fatter and the giant barns full of farming apparatuses and bright heliotropes around the kitchen windows, like lonely women in spring bonnets, with heads dangling, looking in before entering for a morning cup of tea. And he felt small. He felt small and insignificant, with nothing to show and no one to show it to, except a decrepit old crow he called Granny. Who chooses, he wanted to know, where one is born? In the big house or in the barn with the animals? Why did he feel like manure smells when he saw where the wealth was? He who was short, dark, and ugly in his own eyes, poor and rejected by many, abandoned by father and mother at a young age, and lacked the courage to get over it. But maybe, he pondered, it could have been worse: born not even in a barn but in a feculent, musty cave, with half his brain caved in, bats screeching in and out—now that was too dramatic, even for him, and a sly smile appeared on his thin lips.

Sammy, Sammy, Romero called him, as if they were on different ships sailing side by side but drifting to opposite destinations. Hey, where you at, man? You're not thinking of the money you gonna make when you sell the chiva, are you? Just kidding, man; I know you don't have the chiva, OK?

No, Romero, said Sammy, ignoring the rub. I was admiring the richness of the land and the food it produces.

Well, that's all fine and dandy, Sammy Boy, but don't forget the exploitation of the wetbacks and Tejanos whose blood and sweat made these swine rich on all this land they stole from the natives. Your words, brother. And put emphasis on "brother." But listen, Sammy, let me know where to turn. I know we cross the bridge off the 47; if not, we reach Belen, right?

No, man, you get on the river levee after you get off 47. You go north till you hit the bridge that connects to 25, and get off on the opposite levee, or you'll go to Belen on the 25. Where the fuck you gonna find a bridge round here?

OK, Sammy, sorry I interrupted your wet dream, dude. You don't have to get so grumpy; you too young for that.

Look who's talking, answered Sammy, still bothered by the implication he had the chiva. Why go to the Swamps? There's nothing going on that I know of, unless you heard something.

No, man, it's OK. I just have a gut feeling about this place. You'll see what I mean when we get there.

Romero crossed the bridge and cut a left. He recalled now—he was good, he thought. He drove south on the levee for a while and then eased off on the dirt road that ended up in the Swamps. The area was deserted; even the swimmers were absent from the swimming spots across the river. He drove slow as Sammy had caution, looking out for soft sand. He saw the giant Alamo where the fire pit was located and eased up close but not too close. He stopped and got off, leaving Sammy behind in the truck so that Sammy could reflect all he wanted. He noticed that the Alamo had carved into its silver trunk initials and hearts with the names of stupid shitheads cut in so deep it would take a thousand years for new bark to cover the damage done by careless assholes, he thought, and he spat in disgust. He walked to the open hole and checked it out and searched the area with his eyes, just in case someone was hanging around. No one had bothered to place the metal disk on top of the cooking pit, but that didn't alarm Romero.

Sammy, Sammy, get over here, Romeo cried, as if calling children to a snack. You gonna stay in the truck all day? C'mon, look at this.

Sammy climbed down from the truck, slow and easy, thinking, What's this lunatic up to?

See, Sammy, said Romero, a little too excited, as if seeing a cheerleader's panties for the first time. See that brick? And he pointed to the bottom of the pit at a loose brick. I'd bet money there's something hidden behind that brick. What you think?

The only thing behind that brick is dirt. I can't see anything else, said Sammy, apprehensive because the Swamps gave him the creeps, even in the day, especially all alone with a nutcase like Romero. Besides, he added, looking around in hopes of seeing one of his compadres lurking around—even a stranger, what the hell, he said to himself. There's nothing here; why be so picky? C'mon, man, most people have more smarts than that, even stupid fuckers.

That's exactly why, said Romero, acting as if he were on speed. Doncha see? And he gestured with his hands, attempting to draw a picture in case Sammy wasn't clear on his reasoning. No one looks at the obvious; we look for the complicated and are bamboozled, and that's why fools get away with murder. The geniuses put the chiva in an obvious place, right under our noses, and we didn't smell it 'cause it was too easy. We looked elsewhere, get it? And Romero gave a little chuckle, rubbing his hand together, as if at last he had discovered the mother lode.

Sammy looked at Romero, worried. He knew Romero didn't do speed. Psychos like Romero didn't need any stimulants, he figured. They were wired from birth with an active brain and a frightening imagination.

Hold on—let me find a stick and poke at it, continued Romero, happy as a raccoon in a trashcan. He turned to his right, as if he was going to go look for a stick, and pushed Sammy into the pit with his left hand.

Sammy was standing next to Romero and turned to see where Romero was going. He was off balance when Romero pushed him into the pit; he spun like a top and landed on his back in the middle of the greasy pit. Romero ran to the truck, put some gloves on, and pulled the tarp on the cab back.

At first, when Sammy landed on his back inside the stinking pit, he thought it was a joke—not a funny joke but a joke nevertheless. He believed that at any minute Romero would pull him out of the pit, and they would have a good laugh. The smell of soot and ash was troubling, making it difficult for him to breathe. Then he heard Romero at the truck messing with something that sounded like dry wood, and he went into shock. He attempted to stand up in a desperate hope to exit the smelly pit, but he slipped on the greasy floor every time he tried.

Don't do this, Romero, please, Sammy pleaded from the bottom of the pit. I'll give you what money I have—please, I beg you, not this way. Shoot me, cut my throat, stab me in the heart, but not this way —any other way, but not this, please. And his voice choked with emotion, tears running into his mouth.

Romero walked back to the pit and said, Oh, Sammy, come on now, boy. Be a man now. You the only one who knows what I did to that junky. Let's say they find his carcass one fine day, which I don't believe they ever will, but if they do, we all know you'll turn cheese eater; you'll rat; you'll take a plea and sell me down the river. And I'm to goddamn good looking to spend any time in prison for doing society a favor. Think about it, Sammy. This way two losers hit the road, never to find their way back. Try to see it in that light, will ya, brother? Besides, you don't have the shit, don't have any idea who might have it; what the hell I need you for?

But Romero, listen, continued Sammy, suffocating with the mixture of crap in the pit and the tears rolling into his mouth like acid rain. Listen, stop this sick joke before it gets out of hand. I take care of Granny; she needs me. I'm the only one that can take care of her, her medications, she—

Oh, stop it, Sammy, you little sissy. Your granny will do fine. You're not indispensable, although you might think you are. Nobody is.

Romero walked back to his truck to finish the unloading of an uprooted tree trunk, dry as a pretzel, with long roots sticking out of the bottom like thin, sapless, bony legs with no feet, resembling some kind of prehistoric subterranean critter whose nomenclature had never been classified. The roots and trunk were infested with spiders, and the spiderwebs held little white, soft eggs of fine-spun silky cotton. Other insects were embedded in the webs like mummified tourists twisted up in hammocks in a tropical paradise. He picked up the uprooted trunk from the bed of the truck as if it was a special package to be delivered to someone's front porch. He walked to the edge of the pit with it, raised it over his head, and hurled it on Sammy's head. He walked back to the truck and grabbed some more dead branches and small miscellaneous pieces of dry wood and also dumped them unceremoniously into the pit. He picked up a red military-type can of gasoline sold in army surplus stores and, humming his favorite tune, poured the gasoline into the pit, walking around the hole to make sure the gas was equally distributed all over the wood and Sammy, who was still on his back, pinned down by all the wood, still moaning but unable to move.

Romero stopped humming and pitched the empty gas can into the hole and kneeled at the edge, making sure there was no way Sammy Q. could escape, dead or alive.

Listen, Sammy, my friend—are you listening? You're gonna experience the fires of hell here on earth, man, so when you go to the real hell downstairs, you gonna be primed, my man; no surprises for you, none whatsoever. Just tell them down there that you made it a little early, just in case they weren't expecting you so soon. And remember, Sammy, your days of fiestas and siestas are over, my friend, at least here on earth.

Romero opened his Zippo lighter, flicked it once, and placed the flame under a dry branch with drier pine needles he held in his left hand, dry pine needles dropping off like flaking dandruff. The branch caught fire instantly, and he dropped it in the hole, smiling like a little boy on his first scorching of a dry tumbleweed. He jumped back in delight as the fire spread fast and furious, burning the dry wood, and he heard Sammy shrieking as he roasted inside the pit like a side of human flesh for hungry cannibals. The screaming ceased as death conquered the human struggle to survive against such odds, and all that was heard coming from the blazing pit was the popping noise of wood and sparks, and all that could be seen was the billows of acrid, swirling black smoke that escaped upward as if a tar pit had been set ablaze.

Sammy felt the crash of dry wood on his head as he attempted to push his body up with his hands. When the tree trunk smacked him on the head, he went back down, and the stump slid down to his neck and chest. Hundreds of spiders and insects crawled out of the broken cracks and nested on his face and head. His right shoulder was dislocated or worse because he couldn't move his arm to fight off the vermin that were advancing all over him. And his left arm was under the weight of the shapeless tree trunk. He struggled to push it off but failed. Other material fell on top of him, and he smelled the gasoline as it soaked his hair and eyes and trickled into his ears and mouth. He wanted to pray but couldn't remember any vital words, so he started screaming the name of Jesus, thinking it might soften Romero's heart. But the gas fumes, spiders, and dirt in his mouth made it difficult. He was choking and attempted to move, but that was impossible. The weight of the wood and fumes were suffocating him. He decided to let go, to give up, to die without a struggle. But then a ball of fire engulfed the pit, and Sammy burned in agony. The flames pirouetted around his face, and even though his eyes were shut tight, he could see and feel the flames attack his flesh. He screamed because the pain was unendurable. A primordial, inhuman howl, like one made by the first ape man when terrorized by the night and its unknown dangers, escaped from the pit, but it was ignored by Romero just the same.

Romero grabbed the metal disk, blackened and dented like a burnt tortilla after covering hundreds of fires, and placed it as carefully as he could over the mouth of the pit. He was going to throw some dirt over the metal lid but realized he forgot to bring a shovel.

He wanted to prevent the smoke from escaping and to contain the stench from spreading and perhaps alerting someone to investigate the unholy site. He looked around to see if by chance someone had happened to wander in and stopped to see who was cooking what. But he didn't see anyone, and the chirping of the birds suddenly stopped. The only sound was that of the river, like a whisper of bad omens. The silence and isolation of the inhospitable place began to creep up on him, and he wanted to get out before darkness made it more difficult for him to exit out of the complicated maze of trees and shrubs that seemed to have no end. He had praised the place as the perfect location to execute his heinous crime. But now that the evil deed had been accomplished, he was cursing it and wanted no part of it; he was anxious to flee and wash his hands of the place, as the stench of burning human flesh filtered into his nostrils.

The sun was sinking and turning the eastern horizon into a bloody ceremony of unquestionable beauty, but to Romero, it had the opposite effect. The crimson and golden rods of slanted sunlight that penetrated through the trees and mangroves seemed to Romero like the fragmented bars of a dungeon utilized by diabolical forces to confuse and confine him in this cavity of evil.

Romero was getting nervous. He jumped in his truck, pulled off his gloves, and shucked them away from him as if they were burning his hands. He fumbled with the keys and couldn't get the right key in the ignition, and as the sun kept sinking, the light kept dancing and changing to a darker red orange.

He finally got the right key in and turned it quickly as beads of perspiration tumbled into his eyes and stung enough for him to blink forcefully to clear them out, but it didn't work. He pulled on his back pocket for a handkerchief and blotted his teary, burning eyes and tried the key again. The motor made a whirring sound of defeat. He pumped the gas pedal, cursing out loud—but not too loudly, because he didn't want the dead to know that he was scared. He was only nervous, he told himself again and again. He rolled up the windows and locked the doors as the sun disappeared, and he was left in total darkness. He checked the doors to make sure they were locked, as if locked doors and closed windows could keep out the evil that lurked in the cursed swamp. He was trembling and couldn't stop. He thought he heard the screams of the dead Sammy, but that was impossible—or was it? he asked. The engine started; he turned on the lights and looked at the gas gauge. He was sure he had enough gas to clear the Swamps and reach the main highway. I'm outta of here; damn right, he kept repeating and got careless in his driving. Instead of taking it slow in his excitement to exit the place in a hurry, he swerved a little off the dirt road and the rear tire of the passenger side sank into the sand. Shit, no, he screamed. Oh God, no—not this. He pushed the pedal on first gear, and the tire sank deeper, going round and round, piling up sand behind it but getting no traction. He geared it in reverse; the same thing happened. No traction. Shovel, he thought. What! He didn't bring one. He took his foot off the gas pedal, geared to neutral, and with both hands gripping the steering wheel and his forehead almost on it, he bit his lower lip and almost cried.

What the fuck am I doing? he yelled out in frustration. He was thinking that he might have to spend the night out here in his truck, all alone. He kept the headlights on and the engine running, afraid that if he turned it off, it might not start. He raised his head and turned to peek behind his shoulder at the pit. He couldn't see a thing in the darkness, but it was still close enough to smell the foul odor that saturated the place. He imagined Sammy Q. resurrected from the ashes of hell with a posse of demons, approaching to take his revenge. He turned quickly and faced straight ahead, his hands clutching the steering wheel, because he had to hold onto something that was real.

Focus, pendejo, he kept saying out loud. You're a practical vato, a man of science, not a superstitious coward who kneels on the altar of fear. He was attempting to fight off the fear the mind creates at times just to see how much you believe in what you say. Then out of nowhere, he remembered a vato telling him what to do in case he happened to encounter certain situations. Having lived in the border states, the lands of heat and sand, this vato advised him that if he was ever stuck in the sand, to place a floor mat behind or in front of the tire in the hole the tire was creating and then drive out slow and easy. He remembered laughing at the silly fuck, thinking it was a dumb idea. But now he didn't think it was so stupid. It was better than anything he had, and it couldn't get any worse, he thought.

He unlocked the door and slowly got out of the truck. He pulled out the floor mat from the driver's side and rapidly slid it in front of the tire and pushed it as deep as he could to make sure it covered all or most of the tire. He glanced once more toward the pit, but couldn't see a thing; the whole area was pitch black—as black as the soul of Judas, as his grandmother used to say. He thought he heard something coming from the pit, something moving slowly. He jumped in the truck and locked the door. His mind was playing games with him again. He settled down; he didn't want to fuck up again. He geared the truck and pulled out the clutch carefully and unforced, giving it little gas. The tire settled on top of the floor mat and caught. He pulled out slowly, looking straight ahead, concentrating on the dirt road, sweating bullets. He finally reached the levee, forgetting about the floor mat. He just wanted out of the Swamps and never, ever to set foot in that place again, especially at night.

CHAPTER TWENTY-THREE

As Romero was resolving his problems in the Swamps, Hector was entertaining his best friend, Oscar Rubio. Oscar Rubio was Las Flores's most famous son. He was a published writer of science fiction and had actually made a little money, enough to leave his night job. He had stopped in Las Flores to visit friends and relatives on his way to Santa Fe to receive some kind of writing award. The two men were conversing in Hector's sala, Hector sitting on the couch and Oscar on a bar stool, with his back to the bar.

Hector was three or four years older than Oscar. They had grown up together in Las Flores and had been tight friends until Hector moved to Los Angeles in his late teens to complete his education and see a little bit of the world. Once he was settled in with a job and a place of his own, he encouraged Oscar to join him and pursue his writing. Forget work, he told him. Work only on your writing, and I'll help you out as much as I can. Oscar accepted his invitation and moved to Los Angeles and stayed with Hector. In Los Angeles, Oscar continued to write and rewrite some drafts he had started in Las Flores, took classes, and sometimes worked part time. Hector by now was in his first year of teaching and pursuing graduate degrees. He knew early on that he was never going to get rich working, so he got into teaching for the short hours, plenty of women, and long vacations. The money was not great, but he had good medical insurance and time off to travel, which he did.

I brought you the John Coltrane LP—or was it Eddie Harris you wanted? asked Oscar, nursing his drink.

It was Coltrane, Blue Train. Thanks, man, said Hector, in a somber mood.

Wait a minute, Guero. Oscar called everyone Guero. Did you lend your Coltrane to some bitch, believing she was into Coltrane?

A woman, Oscar, a woman.

Same difference, said Oscar. Hey, not to change the subject, but I saw your pal Ventura not too long ago. It's funny how some clowns change their dress habits when they come into some cash pedaling dope. He wasn't wearing that huge gold chain with a cross around his neck. He was sporting some J&M's on his big feet and a Rolex on his wrist, but that could have been a T. J. knockoff. But what the fuck do I know. I couldn't tell if it was the real thing if—

Please, Oscar, you probably own one but left it behind, as not to seem pretentious. You probably got a bundle of money for your first novel—what was it called?

The First Aztec on Mars, answered Oscar, smiling, happy to talk about his work. You got into it, right?

Yeah—no, to be honest, said Hector, turning red. I didn't finish it. I don't read much science fiction. I don't get it; it's just me, not the writing. You're an excellent writer, Oscar, but I don't have to tell you that. You got published and got a contract in a very competitive field; not many can claim that. I read Asimov's The Foundation Trilogy, but everyone reads that. I don't recall, but I think it was mandatory reading for one of my classes years ago. In your story, I didn't get the space critter falling in love with an orchid. I just couldn't grasp it; I know, I know. It's just me. Maybe I'm just dumb; who knows?

No, Hector, don't play that dumb act with me. C'mon. You have to read the complete story, Guero. The critters, as you called them, were evolved beyond us, but this particular one had a smidgen of feeling. His duty was exploring and collecting data; programmers had selected his career, and contentious examinations and greedy nepotism for favorable careers were dinosaurs of antiquity. His daily exploration ventures were filled with pleasure unknown to him in that other harsh environment, in which most of his time was deployed searching for moisture rocks. His greatest fear was walking into a slimy puddle of water because he would disintegrate. Remember, Oscar, the environment of their new home displayed the existing conditions not altogether different than the Mesozoic era of the late planet Earth. Anyway, one day he saw a beautiful specimen encrusted in the trunk of a primitive tree. The tree trunk was anchored in the middle of a swampy puddle. He couldn't get close to the tree trunk without sloshing through the amoeba-tainted slop. He was fearful of being inundated with water, and that fear grounded him on shore, away from the prodigy that beckoned in the most suggestive light. He felt something but couldn't figure out what it was. See, for unknown eons, their leaders had labored to root out feelings, and one in particular was the unmentionable, unfathomable impression called love by the ancients.

OK, stop, stop, Oscar, Hector interrupted. Don't tell me anymore. I'll reread the story; now I understand it better. Listen, Oscar, I want to congratulate you on your new novel. I wanted to get up there for the book signing, but I couldn't get away, man. You know how it is?

Did you read it, Hector? I send you a copy and an invite to the party after—some party, dude. There's where I saw Ventura; don't know how he got in. Looking for you, I guess.

No, I got the book, Oscar. I tried to read it, but you know, it's difficult for me to get into that kind of material. The title, uh, the title—

Dimension Infinity. Oscar completed the sentence. I know it's not your cup of tea, but that's what I write about.

Hey, no, Oscar, don't mind me. I've been distracted lately. Where you staying now?

Hollywood, answered Oscar, without hesitation.

You mean West Hollywood or North Hollywood?

No, man, I moved. Found me a nice little pad up in the Hollywood Hills.

You used to tell people you stayed in Hollywood when you actually lived in North Hollywood. Remember? asked Hector, grinning. It's OK, Oscar. Don't really matter.

It was difficult to explain, you know, to people who were out of town.

Don't worry about it, Oscar. Now you don't have to tell people shit. Listen, I'm thinking of going back to Los Angeles and might need a place to stay for a short time.

I knew that job wasn't gonna work, Guero. You retired, brother. You need to be writing all the shit you went through working in all those shitty places with all the shitty people you had to put up with.

Well, you never know how it's gonna work out, Oscar. I really believed I could help out here, get things done, you know—till I sold this place, at least. My son bought me a condo in Albuquerque, which I rent out. The problem with that is that he also bought one for his mother, my ex-wife, next door. I guess he thought that if we saw enough of each other, we'd get back together. Now you know that'll never happen, not in this lifetime. Anyway, the thing here is getting out of hand. He drank the rest of his drink and kept his eyes on the empty glass.

Oscar studied his friend for a couple of minutes without saying a word. He had a feeling something was going on with Hector. He wasn't his usual sarcastic and funny don't-give-a-shit Hector. He was on the serious side but didn't want to show it. They had known each other since they were children, and he could usually read his moods, as Hector could read his. When Hector was down and out, it had to do with women, most of the time. There was a long history with Hector of broken relationships, broken hearts, and other problems that came up between men and women seeking love. He wanted to help Hector by at least talking about it, but he wanted to be subtle and discreet, as not to put him in a defensive mood, because Hector would then clam up, and nothing would be solved.

You in deep shit over a woman? Oscar blurted out, animated as a kid opening his trick-or-treat bag. I knew it; I knew it.

It's Tito, Hector said, embarrassed as hell, scratching his beard.

Tito Brito! That crazy bastard—fat Concha's hubby? No, don't tell me you speared fat Concha? You become a bottom feeder, Guero, not even a year here. Wow, que te paso, hombre? Tell me.

Hector stood up, shook his head, and said, Let me get you another drink, Oscar. You want ice on your bourbon, or you want it neat?

I want some sotol—have any sotol, Hector?

Please, Oscar. You know you can't handle sotol; never could. I don't need you to puke your guts out all over my house. You wanna beer? I have some beer, I believe.

No, man, I'll piss all night; that's what beer drinkers do—drink and piss.

Well, then it's bourbon, Oscar. You can't do tequila, so I ain't even gonna offer.

I can do tequila. A margarita with plenty of ice.

That's not tequila, Oscar; that's a pound of sugar with water.

OK, Hector, I'll take the bourbon—but straight, 'cause I know you don't have any weed. But getting back to Tito Brito, Hector. We can handle him if we have to.

What do you mean "we," paleface, answered Hector, making an effort not to laugh.

Yeah, Oscar said, we can go talk to the asshole and tell him to fuck off, and if he doesn't, we—we'll kick his ass.

This time Hector couldn't stop the laughter. He laughed until tears rolled down his cheeks into his beard.

Then he said, still laughing, Tito and his bunch of banditos will eat us up for breakfast and spit us out for lunch. Fuck you talking about, Oscar? Get serious, man. This ain't no cops-and-robbers game played when we were kids. These mercenaries will kill you or hurt you bad, unless you do it to them first. Things have changed in Las Flores, Oscar; you gotta get with the times. Remember, you have an appointment in Santa Fe and want to make it one piece. So forget about it, OK?

No, man, I was just saying we call Ventura, and he can drive over and take care of Tito and his compadres.

You still don't get it, Oscar. Ventura, if he came, which I doubt, would lose his bearings, especially at night; he'll be bushwhacked and get his ass shot, and for what?

Oscar felt good now; he knew Hector was being Hector, and the sorry look was gone. This was the way he liked to see him, full of zest and put-downs. Few could beat Hector at that.

Hector gave him another glass of bourbon, on the rocks this time. So, Oscar, tell me, amigo, you still get high when you write?

Oscar took a stiff drink, made a face, and then said, You don't get high to write, Hector; you have to write to get high. Your mind has to be lucid but interesting at the same time, because you're digging up personal adventures and fictionalizing them beyond recognition. You attempt to create life, and as you invent it, it has to be far removed from your own reality—it has to. The assumption that you can manufacture a universe, and that's all it is, and that people approve of that galaxy or galaxies because it feeds their imagination—that's what motivates me, as other illusions have. I write because my soul is on fire, and I want it to burn forever. The burn is the high, or the high is the burn, whichever way you wanna take it. It diminishes a reservoir of self-doubts, self-hate, and other pain and suffering accumulated by accounts past and present. Stay with me, OK, Hector? Oscar pleaded, as if they were about to slash off his tongue, and he had to utter his last words.

You sex up, he continued, after taking a drink, you sex up the most atrocious events in your life, infuse them with characters of the most challenging kind, and you begin to live in a world of your own. You own the mother ship like nothing you've ever owned before, and the steering might go any which way. You stumble back, on occasion, to your real world and almost vomit at the redundancies of every hour of every day. You no longer believe you could have functioned in that insane rat race, and yet I entered another, but with bloodier fangs. The fangs ripped into my throat and released the humiliating poison that strangled me when being told to write—not every word but only about the wind that impels the mother ship.

What you think, Hector? asked Oscar. That's gonna be my main speech when I speak at the award dinner in Santa.

Hector looked at Oscar for a minute, took a sip, and said, I think it's a lot of mierda, but I'm positive your audience will love it.

Oscar bent over laughing and couldn't stop but finally did, wiping his eyes with his free hand. Why don't you come with me, Hector? There'll be plenty of food, drink, and of course pussy. C'mon, Guero. You'll have a good time. Forget about the shit here, and we'll shoot over to Taos the next day.

Thanks, but no, said Hector, amused. I don't like to be around those conceited jackasses. With my luck they'll sit me next to some asshole who'll yap all night about writing, as if he's gonna be the next Bradbury, and when you ask him about his work, he'll confess he published a few lines of poetry in an obscure rag twenty-some years in the past. And remember when you were getting some kind of recognition award for Latino writers at the convention center in Los Angeles? Well, they sat me next to this professional student, and he was yapping about his writing and shit. He wouldn't shut up the whole night. I finally asked him about his published work, and he confessed he lived with his mother and still attended college. The half-wit was ready to retire, and he was still sucking on the tit, wanting to be a writer. No, man; thanks, but no thanks. I'd rather face Tito Brito here than tangle with the goofballs you have to deal with. Count me out, Oscar, but I'm sure you'll find plenty of fools here that'll be more than happy to accompany you to Santa Fe and mingle with the artistic community and kiss ass all night.

Enough said, Guero. You never liked those griffins, anyway. Hey, why don't we go out tonight? asked Oscar, elated with the idea.

You're not in Hollywood, Oscar. We have limited choices here. Remember, you're back in Las Flores. But come to think of it, there is a new club in the Westside called The Blue Moon Jazz and Blues Club—not bad jazz, if you put your mind to it.

No, man, I do that all the time back home. I wanted to see a cockfight; it's been some time, and I was thinking of doing a short story about the characters behind the fighting gallos, know what I mean?

There was a long silence between the two men. Hector seemed hesitant to commit, pondering on the wisdom of taking Oscar to a tumultuous setting where anything could happen, or worse, allow him to venture out on his own. All he knew was that Oscar had made up his mind to attend a cockfight, and knowing Oscar, that's where he would end up, with him or without him.

OK, listen up, Oscar, Hector said. I heard about a gallo fight in Chiva Town tonight. I don't know if you want to go to Chiva Town. I mean, it's Chiva Town, and the Snipers, as you know, they run it. Not the best place to go, if you ask me, but you won't—

Hey, Chiva Town's OK, Guero, interrupted Oscar, delighted. We know those dickheads, Guero. What can they do? Take us for rivals, and beat us up? C'mon, Hector, let's go. It'll be fun; haven't been there in years. Besides, you always told me Tiny Tim was a friend of yours.

All I'm saying is that it's Chiva Town, and you know Chiva Town and the Snipers; that's all I'm saying. We know some of the older generation; the younger dudes, that's a different story.

You're getting paranoid in your old age, Guero. We're not outsiders, for Christ's sake.

Hector hated it when someone talked paranoia, not to mention age. Sure, he had always calculated the risks in anything, but that wisdom had kept him out of jail and healthy. That was more that he could say for other pendejos who attacked situations thinking with their culo.

OK, Oscar. Let's go, man. At least we won't run into Tito Brito in Chiva. He might be crazy, but he ain't stupid.

The evening was perfect, thought Hector, as they drove east on Mariposa toward San Albino. The moon was full and bright, not too warm out, as couples and children strolled on leisurely walks. It was a perfect night to walk with your mate, hand in hand, or walk the dog, whichever was more compatible. He should be walking Tupi, he thought, instead of going to a gruesome, barbarous cockfight in Chiva Town, of all places. Tupi had been spoiled because his mother walked him during the day and at night during the warm summer nights. Hector also walked him when he first arrived in Las Flores, but he wasn't steady. He had to get used again to the slower pace here. He walked fast, as if in a hurry, and even talked fast. He was citified to the max and realized he had to slow down, show more patience with the locals, and learn to live a healthier life. That was one of the reasons he returned to Las Flores, to get away from the traffic and tons of people everywhere. He got tired of driving on the freeways, tight parking, crowded restaurants, crowded parks, people, too many people, and all strangers. Here, at least most were friendly and said hi. Even if they didn't mean it, they at least made an effort. He really believed that when he moved back, he could find a good woman, settle in, read all the novels he had put aside, and even do some writing—why not? But then he accepted the job at the community center and got on work mode again, a caffeine-driven, alcohol-induced work mode, a force that molded his life for more than thirty years. He ignored Tupi, ignored the beautiful sunsets, the slow pace, the friendly people, and became a workaholic again and a grouch to many. Jesus, a grouch, he thought.

And then, to put some cream in the coffee, came Concha. How could he ever explain Concha? A moment of weakness, perhaps—a likely excuse used many times before. Lonely, desperate to be with a woman, any woman; no, he had Mercedes. Concha was a woman he worked with, a married woman he shouldn't have made a play for. He knew she was vulnerable, but he wanted her nevertheless. He knew it could lead to trouble with a capital T, but that didn't matter until later. It wasn't planned; it just happened—that was his reasoning after the fact, but he knew better. Things don't just happen, especially when it came to sex. How can you tell a woman that it was a mistake, an error in judgment, and it shouldn't happen again? He knew men like that, of course, but he didn't consider himself in that category. What do you tell a woman when your seed is running down her thighs and you want to run out, but you can't because you're in your own house, in your own bed, and she's holding onto you as if you're her last hope? A woman with an unstable husband who doesn't forgive or forget, and you have given him another issue to keep the demons alive in his crazy head, that was what Hector couldn't keep out of his mind.

Hey, Hector, snapped Oscar, whatcha thinking? Still thinking about the Snipers in Chiva Town? Don't worry about it, Guero; it'll be fine. Look, there's San Albino. Don't forget to make a left; it's faster.

Got it, Oscar. Don't worry. I'll get you there.

Hector continued thinking as he drove, attempting to ignore Oscar as much as possible. What did he regret more? he asked himself. Concha, of course, was a great concern, but he regretted leaving his boys. They were so close to getting inside the door, but they still needed his demanding hand to feel secure once inside the house. But his biggest regret was losing Lencho Reyes—a shining star, in his estimation. It was sad how he seemed to disappear from the face of the earth. His family had searched; the police had searched; even he had looked for Lencho but found no trace, dead or alive, of the young man. And now, if he left, he would probably never see Lencho again, and that was a bummer all the way around, he thought, as he drove into Chiva Town.

"Mari-mari-marijuana, mari-mari-marijuana, es lo que-la gente fuma," the Chiva Town Snipers sang out of tune, but they didn't give a crap; this wasn't a try-out for the church choir. Then they would all start laughing, throwing high fives around, and body slamming like when they scored their first dime baggie. They were standing around a huge tin tub. The tub was filled with ice, some melting, and the cans and bottles of cold beer were sandwiched somewhere in between. But some of the vatos didn't give a shit about the beer, although they drank it because it was there to drink. They had become more sophisticated and depended more on a nonalcoholic high than their parents did. They preferred mota and other stimulants to create their escape. They loved mota and its free spirit, but when they had tasted enough of the beauties of nature, their choice was chiva. The most hungry for escape abused the two, and the worse ones abused everything. The vatos hanging around the tub of beer knew who those junkies were and didn't have to treat them with respect, but they did anyway, because those crazy dopers could go off without any particular reason. And then they had to kill them before they could do damage and harm innocent civilians.

The older vatos held back, close but not too close, checking the young bucks and attempting to signal out a potential leader, so they could kick his ass and put him in line. But their main concern was with the hard-core druggies, the pendejos who were too far into the chiva and other hard drugs to maintain their obligation to the gang or to the community. They would put these junkies through "the Method," their method of cleaning them up, which was rather simple. They would strip them naked, give them a severe beating, and then throw them into a hole in the ground without water or food. A lid was placed on top to cover the hole, and buckets of dried concrete were placed on top of the lid to keep the hole sealed. They would leave them inside the hole for a couple of days to a week, depending on the strength of the addiction. If they happened to expire during their rehabilitation, they buried them in the desert, and no one was worse off. The Snipers were sure that not many would join a crusade to search for and save the junkies. If they made it, they were given a second chance with conditions: in case of a relapse, they would do the hole for two weeks, and if they survived, they would be banished from Chiva Town until they paid a huge fine—big money.

They kept watch over the young troopers, wanting to spot one so they could apply "the Method" and keep the others in line; it saved a lot of time lost on warnings and useless talk. As they kept their eyes open for a weak link, they held their beers close to their bodies, as if the beer can—or bottle, whichever was cheaper—would deter the demons from piercing their reasoning and preempt a costly strike on an innocent trooper, making them have to pay the consequences for being an eager beaver. These vatos were the vets: hard-core, prison-educated, hard-ass infantry. They were the ruling court for the Chiva Town Snipers, Tiny Tim's most trusted lieutenants. When Tiny Tim gave the war cry, these vatos knew that one or two of them would end up in Santa or six feet under. One of their objectives was to keep outsiders from invading their turf. And apparently they did a hell of a job, because the Chiva Town Snipers were not provoked. Chiva Town was not entered at will. If you had no business hanging around, you best go, 'cause the girls weren't gonna show up; it wasn't that sort of place. Even the Tejanos kept their distance, and the Tejanos were bad. The Chiva Town Snipers didn't attain their reputation because some vatos had been in the military; they gained it because a bullet with no name could come from nowhere, smashing flesh and bone, and the harm done could never be calculated in dollars and cents.

San Albino and Santa Fe Streets, running north and south, were the only streets in and out of Chiva Town, unless one entered along a northeast direction from the desert on dirt roads. The residents who lived on San Miguel Street, which ran east and west next to Chiva Town, built walls on their properties facing Chiva Town. In the beginning it was a pretext to keep the roaming goats out. There was nothing there but small sand dunes and mesquite brush on a strip of land a couple of miles long and maybe one-fifth of a mile wide, fronting the Eastside barrio. The land was hilly and sandy. It was very difficult to dig wells for water, especially for people with little money. The strip of land was left vacant for that reason, and homes were built away from the walls, a short distance north and west. As Chiva Town became more congested with people and housing, the residents on San Miguel added to the height of their walls. Some were higher than ten feet, built with mismatched brick, wood, and adobe, anything to keep Chiva Town—or San Isidro, its official name—from their view. They placed barbwire and broken glass all along the top to discourage visitors from climbing over the walls. The area became a dumpsite over the years. Old cars and trucks stripped of parts, stoves, mattresses, anything of no value was left there to rust and rot.

A couple of miles to the west of Chiva Town, running north and south, was a double chain-link fence extending all the way to Loma Street to the north. The land behind the fence, about forty acres, belonged to the federal government and was off limits. To the northeast of Chiva Town was the desert, all privately owned, of low cerros, arroyos, yucca, and sotol, until you reached the Turquoise Mountains. Chiva Town was boxed in on all sides, consisting of about ten to twenty acres of congested housing, old adobe, low-cost mobile homes, and salvaged army barracks modified and used as homes. The church of San Isidro had never been completed, even though it had been worked on for years. They utilized a deteriorated army Quonset hut for a community center, which was closed half the time for lack of funds. Some people who inhabited Chiva Town moved out, but many remained, and many more moved in, looking for cheap housing, and did their best with what little they had. Most were hardworking people who left early in the morning for their jobs outside of Chiva Town and returned in the evening and continued on with their lives as best as they could.

The younger generation in Chiva Town, as the younger generation in other places, did not see the world the same as their parents. The younger kids, mostly boys at first, adopted the dump area as their home away from home and called it Meco Seco, for reasons that were obvious only to them. They placed cardboard or old tarps, aluminum siding, boards, anything, over the skeletal remains of the rusted heaps to shelter themselves from the sun and afford themselves the privacy to do their thing. They created tunnel like shelters where they spent their time sniffing glue, paint thinner, and gasoline fumes or drinking rubbing alcohol mixed with grape fruit juice—anything and everything that got them high to alleviate the boredom of their troubled existence that was not of their making. The disjointed walls became their art gallery, where they graffitied vulgar illustrations of sexual perversions between humans and animals and profanity in misspelled English and Spanish—their own language, as they saw it. Some attempted dignified murals of nature scenes or famous battles, but these were defaced as soon as they showed any promise. The only scenes never portrayed on the walls were negative caricatures of the Chiva Town Snipers. The Snipers patrolled Meco Seco to make sure the young wolves didn't start their own gang or put up graffiti insulting them, which in the future could create problems for the Snipers. A gang of young, crazy glue sniffers would never be tolerated by Tiny Tim, and the punishment was severe for any activity along those lines, even though they were no more than children. The Snipers, were also always on the lookout for future recruits; some of the youngsters would be initiated soon enough, as many had relatives in the Snipers, but some would never work out for lack of the discipline needed to function in a military-type organization. The Snipers allowed the young vatos to hang out in the shadow of the walls to remind the young vatos that they were excluded and not wanted in any other place but in Chiva Town, and the Chiva Town Snipers were their true family.

The councilman from Chiva Town, when he was first elected and Chiva Town was incorporated into Las Flores proper, promised many things, as politicians do to get elected. They promised to clean up the dump strip and remake it into a green zone of parks and playgrounds for all citizens to enjoy. They were going to talk to the property owners on San Miguel Street and ask them to lower the walls and make them more uniform for a more aesthetic look. They were going to remove all the graffiti and plant trees next to the walls to provide privacy for the homeowners. Promises are easier said than kept; they become empty words, eventually forgotten, until the next election. They did open a patch of dirt to the north of Chiva Town, close to the desert, for a baseball diamond. The kids had to construct their own backstop with plywood and chicken wire. They used rocks wrapped in flour bags for bases and set up wooden crates for benches. The councilman kept his old house in Chiva Town for voting purposes and moved to nicer digs in the Westside, where he actually lived—a classic movida, as Hector would say.

Nothing got done in Chiva Town, and Meco Seco became the hangout for the kids with no other alternatives. The younger generation was more rebellious, and even the young girls wanted to make a place for themselves under the walls. They offered hand jobs or blowjobs to the older teens to pay for protection when the boys their own age, ten or eleven, bullied them and attempted to push them out of their selected turf in the dump. This presented a new problem for the Snipers because they couldn't lean on the teeny boppers, as they did on the boys, without risking a blowout with someone in the gang who might be related to the girl who needed to be reprimanded. The older girls in their early and late teens wanted to be part of the Chiva Town Snipers and not just girlfriends, dolls, or wives. They wanted to wear the colors and kick ass along with the vatos in the trenches. Tiny Tim allowed a few girls to work with the Shadows. The Shadows were a select few gang members who kept a low profile and didn't flaunt the gang colors in public. The Shadows collected the money from drug and stolen-item sales, although they never touched the products; another unit was responsible for that. The Chiva Town Snipers were not big-time drug dealers or thieves. They only sold enough to finance the buying of arms, booze for their parties, and a little to keep their food bank supplied. Once or twice a month, the Shadows would make a trip in their van north to Albuquerque or to El Paso to the south and solicit nonperishable food items from grocery stores or wholesale warehouses. The food would be parceled out to the old, retired Snipers, ill and poor, who had served the gang with distinction. It was also given to the housebound, elderly poor—but discreetly, as not to embarrass anyone with handouts at the dilapidated community center. The Shadows made home deliveries and never asked for accolades, preferring to keep their activities private.

The Chiva Town Snipers didn't want any girls in their ranks. They could serve as auxiliaries on a limited basis and perform other services, but that was all. They had enough people already. They were picky and selected only the best-qualified candidates. They could put fifty or sixty soldiers in the trenches on any given time and had ten to twenty hard killers—prepared to die, if they had to, for the cause—plus a reserve of old timers who would come out of nowhere, unannounced, with hatchets and double-edged axes and cap opponents on the knees. They were never called, but they were always ready, just in case. The Chiva Town Snipers had no ambitions of taking over new turf. They just needed a small, disciplined army to control the young wolves from killing each other and robbing or extorting the hardworking citizens of Chiva Town. The glue sniffers could break into houses all they wanted, but not in Chiva Town. The police never patrolled Chiva Town; there was no need. The Snipers took care of business their way.

When Hector and Oscar Rubio drove close to the house where the cockfight was going to be held, Hector parked the car across the street, a short distance from the house, although there was ample parking closer to the house. He removed his glasses and placed them in the glove compartment and studied the street and cross streets in case of a fast getaway; best to be prepared, he thought. As they crossed the street and entered the front yard of the house, they could hear the singing coming from the rear of the house.

Mari-mari-marijuana, mari-mari-marijuana, es lo que-la gente fuma.
Mari-mari-marijuana, mari-mari-marijuana, es lo que-la gente fuma.
Mari-mari-marijuana, mari-mari-marijuana,
Pasa-le un toque a mari-ana,
Mari-mari-marijuana, mari-mari-marijuana
Hay te cuento-lo que paso, mañana.

Oscar turned to Hector while they waited to be escorted to the backyard. I love that song, Hector, and these dudes know how to party, man. They sound cool, and from the vapors emanating from the rear of the house, I believe it's gonna be a smoke-out—whatcha think, Guero?

Put your peace pipe away, White Feather; these young kids don't utilize pipes unless they're smoking something lethal that pounds their brain with pleasure or nightmares not yet captured on canvas. Let me put it to you this way, Oscarito, Hector said in a serious tone. These dudes can attack for no reason, turn against you, and tear you to shreds, and there ain't no one who can stop them or want to. So please, Oscar, don't space out if they offer you smoke. They might not get your trip and kick your ass, and where does that leave me? So be a good boy, Oscar, and remember, you're not with the intellectuals you left behind in Hollywierd. These vatos are a little edgy, and mota doesn't do to them what it does to you. By now, even though it's still early, they have gone through a pharmaceutical cornucopia of cocktails that keeps them on their toes, and they are smoking mota to pass the time. Their brains are swimming in an uneasy ocean and are waiting for the tap in before the sharks arrive. They smoke to socialize with the carnales and to show them they can still butt heads with the goat and come out ahead, with their trompas held high. They know the veteranos, the lieutenants, are giving them the eye, and acting like a pendejo will only provoke demerits from the cagey lieutenants. One little fuckup, and they end up chasing kites. If you can't take the weight, don't pack it on, is what they say. They're on edge, Oscar, ready to pop and release the demons that play havoc with their fuzzy minds.

No, Hector, it's cool, man. I'm from here. I grew up in the barrio and understand the ins and outs of barrio life. I get the schizoid rebellion these vatos are going through. I get it, Hector. I know where it comes from and where it's going, at all times. I know.

You don't know shit, said Hector, without raising his voice. When we were young and living here, we were pussies, Oscar, nothing but. Sure, you go around the corner, smoke a weak joint, and thought you were all bad. We have never been beaten senseless and urinated on when unconscious. In our time, a fight was clean, between two bodies and on occasion a blade, but that wasn't common. Our thing was girls, Oscar, girls and books, not duking it out with the Chiva Town Snipers—or anyone else, for that matter. We recognized our limits and didn't cross the line unless absolutely necessary. Now, in these heady days, these youngsters can turn into psychos at a moment's notice and do serious damage. The place has changed, Oscar, and so have some of the people surviving here, so don't make any waves, and you won't get your shoes wet. Oh, and one more thing, Oscar: don't call anyone Guero, especially if they're on the dark side. They might not take to it kindly.

As Hector was talking to Oscar, educating him in the etiquette required to have a healthy and successful visit, a pair of vatos, the picket crew, advanced to inspect their credentials. They were Chiva Town and didn't have to prove it to anybody.

Hey, Hector, my man, cried out one of the soldiers as he recognized Hector. C'mon in, brother; happy to see you here. He turned to his pal and said, Hey, Flaco, it's Hector from the center— you know him?

Yeah, I know him, said Flaco, with a surly face. He's the old muff told me I wasn't welcomed at the pinche center no more.

Now, Flaco, said the talkative cowboy, let bygones be bygones. Hector's cool with me, and that carries a lot of weigh, bro. Besides, Flaco, my man, he's a friend of Tiny Tim. So forget your shit about Hector; you don't want Tiny Tim on your ass, 'cause you're too fragile, Flaco. The weight'll break you like burned toast.

C'mon, Hector. Don't mind Flaco; it's his time of the month. We're in the back. Tiny Tim ain't here, but you can talk to the mayordomos, the Louis—they all here.

What about the cockfight? blurted out Oscar, after Hector had pleaded with him not to speak unless addressed.

What about it? asked the cowboy, as Flaco came up fast toward Oscar.

Who's this? asked the cowboy, pointing to Oscar, as if Oscar had been missing in action all this time.

Oh, shit, thought Hector. Here we go, and we just got here.

This is Oscar, said Hector, as clear as he could without raising his voice. Oscar was born in Las Flores; he's a primo. Born and raised here—a bro, my friend. We grew up together; then he moved—

He was going to say "to Califa" but thought better of it and said, "Out of state." He's visiting and wanted to see the gallos, you know; it's been a long time.

Don't they have any gallos in Eh-ley, becerro? asked Flaco, with a smirk on his face.

But I have to drive to East Los Angeles, said Oscar, and—

Can we go to the back? interrupted Hector, anxious for Oscar to shut up.

The gallos were cancelled for tonight, said the cowboy, in a good mood again. Tiny Tim decided to take the gallos to a farm outside Belen—more money, better gallos, you know how that goes. But the party is on in the back. C'mon, I'll take you, although there is really no need, Hector—most everybody knows you. Tiny Tim might return later tonight or stay over, depending on the action. The chulas are sure to join us soon, and you and your amigo might score a piece of snatch.

Flaco started laughing again, a cannabis-induced laugh where he couldn't stop, even if he wanted to.

Hector's nerves started acting up. His comfort level, not exactly high, disintegrated, and he wanted to kick himself in the ass for letting Oscar talk him into bringing him here. Now that he was advised that Tiny Tim was absent from the scene, he worried. Oscar could be a liability, and that alone was a cause for alarm. Tiny Tim, he was sure, could get them out of a situation, but the others it was difficult to assess. He didn't know how long their whip was because these commandos were not friends he confided in.

No gallos, complained Oscar, as they were led through the side of the house to the backyard, where the fiesta was taking place.

It was a large yard where the house in the front and a house in the back shared the sizeable backyard, where the dance for the party was to be held. The younger vatos were around the tin tub close to the rear window of the front house. They were taking hits straight from bottles of 151 Rum or sotol and then chasing it with guzzles from tallboys of Old English 800 malt. When the bottles of spirits had been passed around, they carefully placed them on the ledge of the window. The vets were standing along a good-sized open portal that extended all along the yard of the back house, from one corner to the next. There were chairs all along the wall inside the long porch, but the big boys were all standing next to the railing, sucking on their brews and mason jars full of sotol and other alcohol that would blaze in close proximity to a lighted match. The porch was dark, with the only light coming from an open door of the house. There was where Hector headed to pay his respects to the heavies who ran the show in the absence of Tiny Tim. They seemed to be waiting for an excuse to be provoked and unleash their pent-up anger in an orgy of violence. But they comprehended the violence had to be justified, or Tiny Tim would get a hair up his ass and lash out with a fist of iron that left scars not easily forgotten. They waited and watched, like cobras, ready to strike in order to justify their existence.

Hector walked up the few stairs to the porch, determined to make the best of the situation. He couldn't just leave; it was too late for that. He conversed with the generals, most of whom he had known as youngsters who were still learning to wipe their asses when he left Las Flores to see what the free world had to offer. These vatos had stayed and grew up to be felons, perhaps not by choice or desire but for whatever reason, but the main one was that the system became too complicated for them to work it, and instead they got snarled in a machine that offered security in a very fearful world. He went to each one and touched skin so as not to offend or slight anyone, carried on a brief conversation that did not probe, and everything was sweet.

Oscar, on the other hand, went straight to where the young bucks were singing, or attempting to sing, their favorite song and passing jays in a communal setting. Oscar joined the circle because it wasn't tight, shoulder-to-shoulder tight, which meant the circle was open; there existed space between the vatos, and others could join the circle. The floor was open, and anyone could try his wit or join in singing the pot song. If the circle was tight, they were having a serious conversation for their ears only and didn't tolerate intruders, unless it was Tiny Tim or some other fuck with pege.

Oscar was ignored; they knew he was with Hector and got the word from Flaco that he was a big-time meco. He wasn't offered a beer or a drink of the hard stuff; that was a sign that indicated you could stay but at your own expense.

Pass the smoke around, brother, said a vato with a baseball cap to his eyes and a full-brush mustache covering his mouth. Let Pops have a taste. He repeated it with a sarcastic smile that pushed his brush upward on the edges of his mouth.

I already hit it, son, responded Oscar, a little hurt but looking straight at the vato. I may be older than you, and at times, bad shit passes my way, but this is definitely some of the worst shit I've ever smoked. So don't flatter yourself on being all about and knowing the properties of Cannabis sativa and dismissing those who might have the same knowledge on smoke—or more of it.

The vato studied Oscar for a second or two, wondering what planet he was from. The other boy scouts were involved in their own conversations or joking around but could jump in quick, if the brother needed assistance.

I don't know whatcha talking about, Pops, said the vato with the brown baseball cap. He had the same grin on his ferret face but attempted to suppress it by biting his brush with his lower teeth. It's kind of funny, he continued, 'cause most men your age are into booze and usually don't like to hang with us because of the smoke.

You keep calling me Pops, son, when you know in your heart I'm not your old man, responded Oscar, getting a little personal but not pushing it. Did he run out on you? Is that it? I see you have this penetrating hatred for men who remind you of your old man, but you should get over it because soon you'll father a child, if you haven't already, and you'll find out firsthand the tremendous responsibility it encounters, and then, and then only, can you judge your father and men in general.

The vato with the cap pushed it up, away from his eyes, to take a better look at Oscar. Then he said, with a bite in his tone, What are you? A fucking psychologist? Or a wannabe with a mouth full of manure? What the fuck you know about my old man? You don't know shit, just talking outchyour ass, and if it wasn't for your age, I'd kick your old funky culo right now.

The other gang members immediately stopped their bantering and directed their attention to their colleague, who seemed to be having a little problem articulating his point of view to a stranger whose understanding of their ways was limited. They turned to glance at the vets, still drinking on the porch, signaling with their body language, Give us the go, and we'll plant these worms in the ground before you can say chivero.

Whoa! Woah! intervened Hector, doing a quickstep from the porch before things got out of hand. You're right, my friend. We should be with our own circle of friends. No need for violence; violence is the last resort. We were just leaving, and you're right— my friend is no psychologist to attempt to analyze your life. He's not a psychologist, for Christ's sake; he may be a psycho, but that's it. Anyway, we must be on our way, and thanks for the smoke, but please, don't listen to my friend. Sometimes the mota does funny things to his head, and he rambles. His topics vary, so one really never knows what to expect from this one. But one good thing about my friend, continued Hector, trying his best to talk their way out of a situation they had no business being in, is that he listens. When I tell him to stop, that he has gone too far, he shuts up, as you have witnessed here.

Next time, said the vato, ignoring Oscar and turning his full attention to Hector, with his right hand in the back pocket of his baggy jeans, next time he ain't gonna stop in time and is gonna be put on a stretcher, and if you open your mouth to help him, your ego is gonna have to pay a price. We lost all respect for our elders and tend to abuse them, if given license. That doesn't mean there has to be a daddy issue; it's just that we don't give a fuck anymore because the older folks, like you two, have done nothing to make us proud. Turning the other cheek never did anyone proud.

Hector saw the young thug put his hand in his back pocket and was positive it wasn't to reach for his wallet to share a picture of his siblings at the dinner table. The other clowns were hissing and cracking their knuckles, forming a circle around Hector and Oscar. Flaco, salivating at the mouth like a rabid dog, ran to the porch to ask the lieutenants for a code red. He wanted to crack Hector on the face with his brass knuckles and shatter his jaw beyond repair. The heavies, scratching their oversized guts, kept their silence but monitored the situation with their eagle eyes. They had nothing against Hector. He had always treated the chiveros with respect when they applied for assistance at the center. They knew him and Oscar as men of peace and saw no reason to spill their blood in a frenzy of fists and kicks by these pendejo blowhards, who should be saving their anger and energy for later in case outsiders tried to crash their party. Besides, they could have been invited by Tiny Tim, and in that case, they were guests, and guests of the Chiva Town Snipers were never treated badly. So Flaco sat on the top step of the porch, frustrated, sulking, and smacking the wood with his clenched fist until one of the Louis said, Cut the noise, you soiled sack of shit.

Hector started to sweat as he saw the predators forming a circle around them, closing all avenue of escape. One shove or false move, and they were dead meat. They were waiting for the word to come from the porch, giving them the green light to pounce without mercy. Hector felt a little fortified because the heavies were silent, which meant no attack unless provoked, which meant if he and Oscar were insane enough to initiate action. The Snipers, although seen in negative terms by many, were a disciplined, formidable little army that followed the chain of command, even when they were buzzed.

That's a cultural shift, my friend, said Hector, emboldened by the fact that the lieutenants were not going to release the dogs of war on Oscar and him. I don't want to discuss it here, he continued, praying that Oscar kept his jaws at ease, but perhaps when we meet again—under different circumstances, let's say—we can continue the discussion.

Hector was throwing himself under the train, but he had to keep the insect thinking that a meeting and conversation were upmost in his mind.

Don't bet on it, answered the vato, his hand out of his pocket, still coherent. But you never know; circumstances change for unknown reasons, and you do things you don't ordinarily don't do. And I'm positive you can attest to that without the slightest hesitation, but correct me if I'm wrong.

We really have to leave now; give my best to Tiny Tim. Sorry we missed him—tell him, said Hector, anxious to get away before they had to beg for an exit. And like I said, he repeated, as the Snipers moved out of the way to let them through, and he pushed Oscar ahead of him, perhaps we'll get the opportunity to converse one day.

Hector and Oscar, at a fast pace, crossed the street and got into the car, leaving the young gangsters in the backyard playing grab ass, singing their pot song, and laughing. They left them in their safe and secure, exclusive environment, a world that provided them with an authentic fraternity, a brotherhood that ensured a semblance of power in their otherwise powerless lives.

Jesus, Oscar, blurted out Hector, adjusting his glasses, as they drove out of Chiva Town. Whatcha trying to do, get us killed?

No, Hector, get a life; those little punks don't cut any ice with me, said Oscar, talking big again after almost soiling his briefs when the Snipers were cracking their knuckles. I play my heart-attack shtick, and hey, they back off.

You still performing that stunt? asked Hector, keeping both hands on the wheel and his eyes on the street, not wanting to end up on a dead-end street.

Hey, man, it works. Some shit gonna beat you up or rip you off, I grab my chest and scream, Heart attack. Now who wants to fuck with a homicide rap for a petty crime? Not many, that's who.

Listen, Oscar, said Hector, relieved Chiva Town was behind them. The boy scouts at the party back in Chiva Town couldn't care less about your ticker. You play that shit, and they put your skinny ass in that tub of ice water and hold you down till you give up the spirit.

Ha-ha, said Oscar. Don't let me get started on religion.

CHAPTER TWENTY-FOUR

he next day, late after lunch, Romero parked his truck in front of Sammy's house and chuckled because he still couldn't believe he had been rattled at the Swamps by supernatural thoughts. He wanted to go back tonight, around midnight, and without a flashlight, just to prove to himself that he could do it. But of course he wouldn't do it; all talk on his part. It even gave him the shivers to think about it. He got out of the truck and walked through the carport to the door of the house. He was going to go inside the house without knocking, confident that Sammy Q. was not anywhere around the premises. But as he got to the door, Tomasito appeared in front of the door, with his finger up his nose, digging deep. He then pulled his finger out and flicked the product toward Romero.

Romero looked down at Tomasito and made a face. You disgusting little shit, he said, what species of monkey are you? Or animal or what? Damn!

I ain't no monkey, he said, not intimidated by Romero, but you a big ape. Sammy Q. ain't home. You wanna buy something—a beer?

No, I don't want no fucking beer; I came to visit Sammy. I'm gonna go to his room, if you don't mind.

Sammy Q. is not home. I run the business when he's gone. Granny cannot see people.

I don't want to see Granny. And he opened the door, almost knocking Tomasito down. The interior of the old house was dark and had the musty smell of people who didn't bathe on a regular basis. The kitchen was cluttered with dirty dishes and spoiled food. He kept walking down a hall and saw a closed door with a poster of the zodiac tacked to it. He was sure that room belonged to Sammy. As he placed his hand on the doorknob to open it, he saw Granny in her wheelchair come out of her doorless bedroom. She had dark shades covering her eyes and her gray, greasy hair in a bun on top of her head. Que buscas, cabron, she asked, knowing there was a stranger in her house, a big man with a brutal heart. She had on a dark- colored wool something covering most of her frail body, but on her lap was a .38 Smith & Wesson revolver, and she was clutching it with her right hand, as if it was her favorite rosary.

Romero realized the woman was blind and could easily be disarmed. But he was a big target, and the space in the house was limited for him to maneuver quickly enough to grab the weapon. She might get one shot off and clip him, not seriously but seriously enough to require attention and bring in other people to see what was going on. He decided not to say a word and gamble that Sammy's door was not locked. He placed his hand on the doorknob, turned it slowly, opened it, jumped inside, closed the door behind him, and moved pronto away from the door, just in case Granny fired through the door after him. Inside Sammy's room was darker than the rest of the house. The only window was nailed shut, and an expensive Navaho blanket was secured to cover it and not allow any light to enter the moldy room. The bed, with stained, ruffled sheets, had the jumbled look of when sweaty bodies tossed and turned in them for years without ever taking them off for maintenance. There was a small lamp resting on a chair without a back next to the bed, and a myriad of books was scattered throughout the room collecting dust, hardbacks as well as paperbacks. The room was so dark he couldn't read the titles on the books, so he turned on the lamp with its dim light. He noticed a medium-sized table with several cases of beer and gallons of the fiery sotol. Next to the gallons of sotol were several plastic funnels of different sizes and other empty jugs and bottles of water, utilized by Sammy to water down the sotol and sell it as pure.

Romero didn't know where to start looking for the chiva. The smell in the room was horrible, and it was too dark to look for any hiding places, even with the lamp on. And without any gloves, he refused to move the bed or search under it for fear of touching something disagreeable and revolting. He had to get back outside; he was feeling nauseous and claustrophobic. He opened the door quickly and stepped out of the room slowly, but Granny was still in the same place, in her wheelchair with the gun on her lap, and she repeated in a raspy voice, Que buscas, cabron? He closed the door behind himself, pretending not to see her. He was hoping to see the monkey boy and try to get some information from him, but he was nowhere in sight.

Once back outside in the carport, he saw what was, in his estimation, a gate to the backyard: a couple of large, oily boards, riveted together somehow and hung on the wood fence with rusted aluminum strips and bolted with screws and nails on two by fours that held up the wood fence. The gate, crooked and about to collapse, could be pulled open with a screwdriver that had been pounded into the sagging boards. Romero was so tall that he looked over the dilapidated gate to search for dogs. Not seeing any, he pulled the gate open and walked into a garden of earthly delights.

The backyard of the property stretched out long in the back and was kept private by aging peach and apricot trees along the back and one side. Behind the trees and all around the backyard was the same disjointed fence made of oily, mismatched boards put up hazardously, without any pattern or thought given to any aesthetic reasoning. Romero stopped and observed the accumulation of junk that had not ceased for at least a hundred years. The only cleared area was a straight, well-worn path to a wooden shithouse toward the back of the property, no doubt where Sammy's pals relieved themselves. Romero saw, tacked on the door of the shithouse, a black-and-white bull's-eye firing-range replica that was apparently used for darts. He could smell the overloaded stench of that gathering place, and he was glad he had done Sammy in, because Sammy dearest was ripping off Granny's pension check, buying booze, drugs, collecting junk, and not even thinking of providing Granny with the necessities to make her life a little more comfortable.

Romero spat, disgusted, as he witnessed the patched-up fence and the yard littered with useless, antiquated objects. There were stacks of wood as high as the fence, long and short, thin and wide, all cracked or torn, some crusted heavily with peeling paint, resembling a third-world-country lumber yard. He saw an old piano under a pile of dried Christmas trees, with the top and keys missing. There was a turn-of-the-century wooden wagon with rusted metal wheels, with the axels cemented in the earth. The platform of the ancient wagon was loaded with boxes of empty, dusty bottles, nuts and bolts, obsolete mining equipment, threadless rubber tires, and dented rims, adding weight to the ungraceful skeleton of the wagon, dashing its hopes of ever being pulled by a team of muscular mules again. There was the carcass of an old Ford, stripped by collectors and left stranded, with little hope of resurrection. There was a moth- eaten army sleeping bag in the back, probably utilized by the monkey boy when not welcomed in the house, thought Romero. On the opposite side of the yard, away from the john, he saw a metal hand pump, still in use because there was a large bucket that caught the drips and served as drinking water for the dog and feral cats that lived in the multilayered abode of secured hideouts and the rich ecosystem of never-diminishing food supplies. He also saw bees and yellow jackets buzzing around the water bucket and shoots of green grass and weeds, sucking up the precious water, creating a sanctuary for insects and other critters around the water pump. He was positive there was at least one dog—probably went along with the monkey boy—and many cats, judging by the little bundles of shit half-buried in the weed-infested yard. There was a ripped, moldy mattress with springs dangling out and boxes of melted candle wax strewn on top, left there, perhaps, after an unsuccessful investment in candle making. The melting, overflowing wax trapped leaves, insects, fur, peach pits, and other unsavory objects that happened along. To Romero it resembled the undisciplined landscape painting of an acid freak, with its layers of melted, gelatinous wax sparkling in the sun and exposing a structure of unresolved chaos. But the worst revelation was a skunk submerged to its neck in a pot filled with battery acid. The face of the skunk was still whole, as Sammy must have placed the critter in the acid the day he disappeared, not wanting to kill it outright and have to deal with the odor.

Romero had enough; he wasn't going to walk in that graveyard of landmines and expose himself to any further contamination that had already overwhelmed his senses. He turned to leave and, out of the corner of his eye, to the far side of the house, almost hidden by piles of deteriorating plastic bags of an undetermined leaking substance, he saw a tiny vegetable garden. It was squared and carefully fenced with mesh wire, and the well-crafted thin boards were painted white. There was an effort made to keep it clear of weeds and segregate the red tomatoes from the healthy green peppers and control the mint in its own space. The diminutive garden was a contradiction to the disheveled yard; he wanted to take a closer look to see if it was real, maybe pluck a tomato or two. But he said Hell no and bolted the backyard, almost demolished the fragile gate, packed his large frame into his truck. and drove off.

Romero was upset and disappointed as he drove off—slowly, because he didn't want to attract attention. He was disappointed because he hadn't found anything of value during his search and upset because it seemed Sammy was still messing with his head, even from the grave. The skunk in the acid was over the top, and the perfect garden in the middle of that mayhem made him think of his mother's neat house and garden back in Denver. He was homesick, he'd admit to that, but he wasn't a momma's boy, although he had been accused of being one. It was just that he missed the Mile-High City with its crisp, clear air and green trees and grass; besides he got to see Alicia Juarez, at least from a distance. He missed her most of all and didn't even know, for sure, if she had any feelings for him; that was the ass kicker. He was driving east on Martinez and made a left on Caballo Blanco Road without thinking. He recalled that Sammy had mentioned an old prostitute who lived on Piñon Street that he had befriended. He told Romero if he ever needed relief, to check her out, knowing that Romero would never abuse his body in that way. He opened the glove box and pulled out a piece of paper where Sammy had jotted down the house number anyway. That was it, he thought: Sammy gave him the obvious place he had stashed the chiva. He knew Romero would never go there, but if he did, Sammy didn't have to lie or make excuses about it. Sammy even wrote the address on paper, not hiding anything. Jesus, he thought. Sammy again.

Romero parked his truck in front of La Conga's house as if he was a regular paying customer. It was early, and too early, he wanted to believe, for busybodies around asking stupid questions. He climbed the few steps on the open porch and knocked on the flimsy screen door gently, so as not to alarm anyone inside the house.

La Conga opened the door and studied him for a second or two. Then she asked in a dry and defensive manner, What can I do for you?

Romero looked down at the disgusting little woman and answered, as friendly as he could, I need to talk to you; may I come in?

Are you a cop?

Heavens, no; far from it. I'm a friend of Sammy Q.

Her attitude changed, and she even smiled. Sure, come right in; you new in town, right?

Yes, I am. Sammy told me about—about—you know, your business.

She opened the door wider, and Romero walked in, having to lower his head before knocking it on the door frame. He made a quick evaluation of the layout of the small house and decided that they were alone, and she didn't have many escape routes.

La Conga was all smiles now. It was early, she said, but if pressed for time, she would make an exception. She saw a big hunk of a man, young, clean, good looking as hell, no tattoos signifying pinto or banger or both, and the best part was that he was shy. She knew she would bring him to his knees and make him cry uncle with her specialty; she never failed.

But before her thoughts were completed on how to make the young Hercules forget his troubles, the brute grabbed her by the left wrist with his right hand and squeezed, saying at the same time in an angry voice, Sammy left something for me here, and I want it. Now, bitch, or I'll pull your arm outta your scrawny shoulder.

La Conga, without saying a word, dropped to the floor, almost between Romero's long legs, and before he knew what was up, she slashed him deep in his right calf with a box cutter she held in her right hand. Romero screamed and let go of her wrist, and she bolted like a large rat on her hands and knees to the bathroom and locked the door behind her. The blade had cut through Romero's jeans and sliced the calf about ten inches below the knee.

I'll kill you, bitch, he screamed over and over. He took out his handkerchief and tied it around the wound and stuffed the bottom of his blood-soaked trouser leg inside his boot. He limped to the bathroom door, knowing that he had her trapped; kicked in the door with his left size-fourteen boot; and sent the door almost off its hinges. To his surprise, the bathroom was empty, but the screen on the open window had been removed. Now he was really pissed. He limped to the screenless window, not believing any human could use it to escape. As he put his big face forward to peek out the small window, his nose was almost torn off by a monstrous dog that came inches within his face, so close that he smelled the dog's bad breath, and a shower of drool splattered his sweaty face. Goddamn! he yelled. What the hell was that? Then he saw the beast of a dog, barking and jumping, with its huge front paws banging both sides of the window. It was some kind of mastiff, the color of dirt and with the body of a large sloth but with the agility of a saber-tooth tiger. The dog would back off and then run up and attack the window with the force of an earthquake. When the giant dog backed off, Romero got close to the window, but not too close. He noticed a full-grown bulldog almost under the window, chewing on a stout piece of lumber, also growling, waiting for him to come out and play fetch the stick. The piece of lumber was thin in the center, jagged and splintered, as if someone had chiseled it with a dull hatchet. The bulldog, with some white shit all over its eyes, was also drooling what seemed to Romero to be blood, and he also took time from his chewing to look up at the window, as if anticipating someone throwing a hamburger out to him.

In the middle of the backyard was a hut or a small garage that seemed to Romero to have evolved from a chicken coop. Plywood was placed around the wire, with adobe and brick to reinforce it; a flat roof with broken glass and rusty nails sticking out discouraged roof dwellers. A tiny window on every side of the hut had metal bars interlaced with barbwire, which made it almost impossible to breech. The front door, the only door, faced the bathroom window, and it was constructed with thick, hard wood. Scraps of rusted metal sheets were nailed in at odd angles, giving it a quilt-like appearance. In the middle of the door was a round opening, and Romero saw the double barrels of a sawed-off shotgun peeking out like the eyes of a curious animal.

Romero grabbed a can of hairspray, ready to spray the monster dog in the eyes the next time it jumped on the window. But the witch seemed to anticipate what he was thinking. She made an unrecognizable guttural sound, and the dog from hell put his huge head down to the ground and backed off. Then he trotted off like a deformed pony and circled the fenced yard. Romero could see the rutted trail inside the six-foot-tall chain-link fence. There were no trees, bushes, junked cars, or doghouses, nothing but a cleared dog run around the property, all the way to the house, on both sides. There was no chance of scaling the fence through the back or sides of the property. Every angle could be seen by the dogs, and the large yard was so empty that he would be an easy treat for the big Satan or a doggy bag for the slobbering jaws of the powerful bulldog. Romero had to give La Conga credit for providing herself with such a formidable safe house. But he was still pissed at the bitch for slashing him, and he was going to smoke her out of her hole, somehow.

Romero was still bleeding. He opened the medicine cabinet and took out a bottle of rubbing alcohol and some cotton balls. He rolled up his jeans very carefully, looked at the nasty cut, applied the soaked cotton ball on the cut, and made a face, smarting from the sting.

Go ahead, use my stuff, motherfucker. He heard La Conga's voice shout out from the hole in the front door of the hut. But that ain't gonna help you any, you overgrown cow. That blade that cut into your ass was dipped in dog shit for two weeks or longer. So you better go see a doctor soon, or the poison will go up your leg, and they'll have to cut it off, and when you're a gimp, I'll send my boys to cut off the other one.

What boys? Romero was going to ask her. Sammy Q. and the monkey boy? He was about to laugh, but he didn't.

So if you're coming out, big boy, c'mon. You got the balls, then c'mon—I'll blow your dick off, and my dogs can have the rest. You gonna be a pretty sight when the police collect what's left of you. I haven't fed them for three days. See what Spider has done to that lumber? That's what your ass is gonna look like when they get going on you. So c'mon, cowboy, show me your stuff. Make your move before my clients arrive and start asking questions on why you bleeding in my bathroom. And if you're prepared to give them a blowjob, that's OK with me. It's good training for when you lose your leg; you'll be the only one-legged cocksucker in these parts.

Romero got close to the window slowly, looking out for the hound from hell. Listen, bitch, and listen good. He also yelled. I don't want any trouble. I just want what Sammy left here; it belongs to me, and I'm here to collect it. That's all. Just let me have it, and I'll leave. I promise.

The only thing Sammy left with me was his seed in my mouth, and you're too late for that, big boy. So it's best if you get the fuck outta my house, and maybe, just maybe, I won't accuse you of rape.

Romero started to think. He looked at his watch, and it was close to five. Even if he could neutralize Cerberus and his brother, Orthus, and make a run for the shack, it was a good thirty or forty yards from the back door of the house. On a zigzag run, he could maybe avoid some of the pellets, but that was a big risk; he was a big target with a cut leg, and if he went down, the bitch could reload or use another gun through the hole on the door and shoot him at will; who was to stop her? He hadn't even brought his own piece— not a clever move on his part, he thought. Then what if she filed charges and accused him of rape? That would be an embarrassment. Jesus, he said, that would be worse than eating shit. So he decided to cut his losses and leave. In his mind, the bitch was crazy, and there was nothing worse than dealing with a crazy bitch. He slowly backed out of the bathroom and gave a quick look around to see if there was a place she could have stashed the chiva. He didn't see any, so before he left, he stuffed his other jean bottom into his boot so that he wouldn't look odd. He walked out the front door as if he were a happy camper, satisfied with the services rendered and at a reasonable price. He tried not to limp but made a dash to his truck and made a quick getaway to see a doctor or get medical aid at a hospital.

CHAPTER TWENTY-FIVE

ector had promised the group one last session when the buzz of his resignation had circulated around the center. He gave the board a heads up; he gave them some lame excuse for leaving because he didn't want anyone to say he just up and left and, if the books didn't balance, accuse him of sticking his hands in the pot. But maybe, he was thinking, maybe he didn't promise his group a thing, and why would he? Oh, they'd probably say he was a nice guy, but at this point, that shit didn't matter to him anymore, and if it did, he couldn't get carried away with it. In a way he felt bad because he didn't give these guys as much time as he would have liked to analyze their phobias, as he had done with prior groups. He liked to give feedback to his clients who were closer to zoning out and suffering without knowing why their emotions had altered and why they ended up on such a torturous path. He always attempted to expound on their pitiful attempts to act rational when "irrational" was tattooed inside their skull.

Hector waited in his office his last Saturday. Monday was his last day to tie things up and exit. He was early, not being able to sleep in—better said, not being able to sleep at all. The predicament with Tito Brito had not been resolved and would probably never be. Another brick through the window in the middle of the night—or an attempt on his life—was too unsettling to pretend it never happened. He was going to leave town in a couple of days and leave Tito Brito behind. Tito had been a nightmare in his life for the last couple of weeks. He wasn't scared, but he was practical and gave fear another name. That preoccupation consumed his energy and hobbled his concentration, and he found no time to read over his notes that he jotted down from time to time so as not to make his clients nervous.

He didn't want to open the door to his office—not yet, anyway. What if they played him for a fool, he wondered, amused and at the same time pissed off. They're all getting drunk at Tito's garage and laughing at me, he kept thinking. Maybe he acted too arrogant when addressing them. No way, he said out loud, what do I care what these flakes think? But of course he cared; everyone cared, unless the mind was in the garbage disposal with the switch on. Hector was no different than the rest, with the need to be stroked—distinct, perhaps, because he acted the tough-guy act—but caressed nevertheless.

Hector, on this last occasion, had allowed a newcomer to join them at this late stage of the therapy sessions, but he figured he made the rules, so he could break them. This particular person was a woman, an older hippie he met at the off-college campus when he was doing the paperwork for the Saturday therapy sessions at the center. She introduced herself as Dawn Moon—they always used nature names back then, she had repeated on several occasions—a retiree who took classes for pleasure, not because she had any intentions of launching a new career. They became friends because Dawn had an interesting conversation and kept him on his toes on subjects he thought he had a good handle on. Dawn, who had seen many therapists in the past, she claimed, wanted Hector to invite her to the session to unwind and let go some steam that was clouding up her vision. She insisted, not in a pushy way but in a way that gave evidence she was hurting, that a session in a therapeutic atmosphere would cleanse her for a while and save her some cash at the same time. Hector finally assented; what was the point of refusing her? What harm could she cause the macho vatos he was seeing? He wasn't even sure they would show up, anyway. He could see that the meds were isolating her, and she was the type of woman who needed interaction to uplift her spirits. She needed to talk, but most importantly, she needed people who would listen or at least pretend to listen.

Hector decided to join the group, if indeed there was a group assembled. He made them promise no farewell party or gifts. He didn't care for sentimental bullshit, he said and also promised them—a promise he couldn't guarantee—that the sessions would continue, with or without him. There was no doubt in his mind that he was going to miss his clients, but he didn't want to show it. There was a certain risk of getting too close, too involved in their lives. Some were skating on thin ice and vulnerable to manipulation, while others could turn violent at the drop of a hat. Better to keep his distance, as he always did, and allow them to depend on each other to resolve their inner conflicts. Hector was surprised they were all present and all quiet and serious, probably because of the woman in the circle—a woman they never seen before, a woman who perhaps was going to replace him.

Dawn Moon studied the group of men in the circle and wanted to smile. They seemed hard on the exterior, but inside they were marshmallows, ready to melt. Her hair, long and falling on her shoulders, had lost the thickness and color of wheat; all that remained were strands of straw the color of winter clouds. Her skin was raw and white. She wore no makeup but held off the wrinkles pretty good. Her lips were thin but had kissed enough men to know the difference between the dead ones and the ones who still loved to dance. She studied the men in the group, knowing in her heart she could learn nothing from them. In her opinion, the life she had lived would scare these simple lads and maybe push them over the edge —something not very difficult to accomplish, she had no doubt. She was going to talk to these men, her brothers in the bunkers of despair, about the illusive butterfly of love. Love to her was that emotional feeling that changed the events of human history when the first caveman decided to share his rock and his cock with another human being instead of with another wild animal.

Pete Rios was very taken because of Hector's departure. The sessions had helped him tremendously, and he appreciated Hector for his patience and sound advice. As for the others, it was difficult to gauge; there were signs of relief, but more time was needed. The group had lost some members, but the main core remained, not sure if they could handle someone else coming in at this late stage and replacing Hector. Hector was their main man, and even though they loved to put him down every chance they had, they hated to see him leave. Pete Rios looked at the woman now and then, pretty sure she was going to take Hector's place. He wanted to introduce himself, but the others would see it as kissing ass. He was waiting for his friend Leo Lemon but finally had to admit that Leo was a lost cause. Jesus, he thought. Hector wouldn't even accept a gift or a little party. What a trooper, what a vato, cold as ice but warm and fuzzy when it came to helping people in need.

Hector joined the group as he always did, a cup of chanate in one hand and a pad and pen in the other. He was surprised all were present, along with Dawn. He had lost three—or four, with Leo Lemon—but Hector never counted on Leo. To Leo, the sessions were to fill a gap in his day and talk nonsense. Hector really hated to leave his group, but the deal was done. He only wished they would find someone who really cared and helped his clients. His attitude changed as soon as he joined them. He wasn't negative and really liked to be involved in their struggle to set themselves free of the demons they harbored in their souls. It was therapy for him also, although this last time, he wasn't going to share any of his own personal narrative.

Good morning, my friends, said Hector as he joined the circle. This beautiful morning gives me the pleasure to introduce a new member to the group. I know; I always said no latecomers could join. I made an exception this time because my friend Dawn asked me if she could participate, and who knows, she might even run the sessions when I leave. There are only a couple of them left, so please make her feel welcome. I introduce to you Dawn Moon, a woman who is, like everyone here, in need of warmhearted comradeship. So as the gentlemen we all are, we will allow her to go first. I'm sure none of you will mind.

Some of the men gave her a smile, while others glared at the floor, deciding whether to stay or leave. This was their show, they figured, not hers; friend or not, she would dominate the conversation with her feminine mystique, they were sure. Hector was a letdown, they conceded. First because he was going to run away because some pendejo was going to do him in, leaving them out in the cold; then he invited some stranger to disrupt their cohesiveness they worked so hard to attain when the freak Leo Lemon stopped attending the sessions. Well, what the hell; they decided to stay. They were curious to hear what she had to say. She seemed desperate to share her story, and desperation always brought out the best in people, as Hector always used to say.

Dawn Moon looked around at the group in the circle, the same circle she had visited many times but with different faces, and yet, for the first time, she felt self-conscious. She couldn't explain why, but she didn't want to slide too much into her introspective self or attempt to resolve her dilemma intuitively, as she had attempted before, which only led to stronger meds and a disastrous outcome. No, she was convinced that she had to talk it out in an intimate group, because for her, there was no other way. The pain was too intense and the alternatives futile.

Thank you, Hector, she said in a sincere manner. And thank you, all the rest of you men who decided to stay and listen. I apologize from the bottom of my heart for intruding on your session. I will be honest with you: I had no other place to turn. My cash is low to pay for a private session, and the county has a waiting list of many days. The pain, as you all know, does not wait—cannot be put off until you find a sitter. It's a twenty-four-hour chewing of the rats on your soul. And although my fixation might seem trifling to some here, it is my Golgotha. And please, if you want me to leave after my conversation, I'll understand, but I would love to stay and listen to the rest of you. I'm not new to sessions, and my insight will perhaps help, but I will do as you wish.

I ran because I was weak, and I was weak because of his hot-and-cold emotional escalations, she began, in a voice trained for the stage. Even the men who glared at the floor lifted their eyes and focused on the woman, who seemed honest and had a story to tell, not just some siren Hector had brought in to distract them from the fact he was running away like a scared rabbit. The intense heat was suffocating. She continued, holding on to the words, reluctant to let them go: But his frigidity was debilitating. I didn't mind being covered with snow, in all its soft, pure whiteness, but his was polar and bitter. And I was young—not in years but in love, and my heart was touched by his passion, or what I believed was passion, when making love. The seed of love was planted in my heart, and roses of numerous colors matured in a perfumed garden of unparalleled delight. I kissed them with the joy of discovery, neglecting the pain along with the thorns, until my lips bled, and I shed tears, because the light had finally penetrated my senses, and I saw what I didn't want to see—refused to see.

Dawn paused, took a sip of water from her water bottle, and bit her thin lips. She had transformed from a cocky, overbearing woman to a vulnerable, yielding grandmother type, irresistible to hugs. She wanted to stop and leave, feeling a little better, but she realized that this group was an educated bunch and was absorbing the little she had disclosed about love. Love was a subject they all had in common, even though some would never admit it. It was natural to fall in love and fight the battles that came with it, although in some cases they could be deadly—but that was also part of the game.

I will continue, she said, but if you want me to stop, say it, and I will stop. She knew they wouldn't stop her; being men, they couldn't stop a woman who was reaching deep into her soul to entertain them, regardless of the consequences. To him, she said, and some of you might relate to this, I was Love—his private piece of art he admired and speculated upon its meaning, until his warped reality was exposed, and he treated me worse than a slave. After all, to him, that was what I had become: a sex slave and nothing more. I left him, as one leaves a burning house, to save my life and, more importantly, the life of my unborn child. I wanted to be loved as the morning dove is, gentle and graceful. I wanted the warm feeling and emotional joyride that the spirit of love blows your way. I wanted the touch of hot lips, burning with desire to transport me, like magical music, to an Alpine meadow of heavenly passion. I wanted to feel safe and desired in the arms of a strong but gentle man. That was what I was giving and asking for in return; was that too much to ask? I realized I was in love with a spineless coward, and it hurt, but I was naïve and pretended I had found true love, tender love, with a perfect man—the wish of how many? But as you can see, I was trapped, as many women have been since the beginning of human relationships. And I dare tell that I had to return to the beast, as I had no other recourse. And I prayed—did I ever pray—that the child, his child, would soften his heart, and he would accept the responsibility and love the child like he never truly loved me.

Dawn paused again; her timing was excellent as she let the words sink into the hearts and minds of her fellow troubadours. Pete Rios's eyes were riveted to Dawn like a nail to a magnet. His heart and soul embraced this woman. His mind was shattered and scattered, like the ashes of a burning ship, by the wind of possibilities. He could love this woman like she desired, if she only let him. He was also searching for love as she so eloquent recited. He would go the extra mile for a woman who wanted to be loved like that, he thought, for a woman who wanted to give all of herself, completely. He trembled as he thought of the maybe. But how could he approach her? It was forbidden by Hector for people in the group to get intimate, but it was all guys before; now that Dawn had joined them, and Hector was leaving, who was going to stop him from making a fool of himself? he wondered. Well, he decided, it was better making a fool of himself with Dawn than with the younger chicks who always wanted to shake him down for anything they could get.

He beat me with his fists, she continued in a somber tone. He beat me black and blue, as if it was in his nature to beat women— and I was pregnant with his child. He beat me for leaving him, and he beat me for returning, bloated and expecting. The first blow broke my nose, and I went down to the floor, but I kept both hands on my belly to defend the life within me, as any mother would do. I didn't raise my hands to protect my face as he punched me, busting my lips, as tears and blood soaked my throat and breasts. Then he grabbed me by the hair and pushed me on the couch and forced himself on me like a brutal beast. After satisfying his wild passion, still furious and out of control, he screamed that the couch was where I was going to sleep from now on. That I had lost all privileges of a married woman when

I ran off to God knew where.

Pete Rios jumped out of his chair, aggravated like a jealous husband, and said, fuming, I'll kill the sonofabitch. Tell me where he lives. I'll kill him for sure—I'll kill him. He'll never lay a finger on you again, I promise.

The men in the group all looked at Pete and then at Hector. Hector said to himself, Oh shit, and then to Pete, Calm down, Pete, calm your urge to commit violence. This is not a vigilante junta, Pete; this is a gathering of peace-loving people. Inciting violence with harsh words does not do anyone any good.

Pete placed his hands on his bald head, turned red, and pleaded, I'm sorry, Hector. Ms. Moon, please forgive me. I got carried away. Please, please, I beg you to forgive me; it won't happen again, I promise. It's just that—that men who beat on women turn my stomach. I can't help it.

It's OK, Pete. We all feel that way, I'm sure, said Hector. But you know the rules; you cannot interrupt when someone else is talking, and you know why. So please, Dawn, continue. And he passed her the box of tissues.

I'm sorry if I upset anybody, said Dawn, but this is not easy, and it doesn't get any better. So if you want me to stop and leave, say the word.

Of course not. Hector cut her off. You have the floor; continue, please.

He left me there on the couch, in the living room, a bloody mess. Said he had to go because he had a date. Of course I felt like a fool. I had given so much and received so little in return. But what else could I do? I had no real family to turn to, and the few friends I had were in no position to provide me with the assistance I was going to need. So I returned home; after all my name was still on the mortgage, even though I had not contributed with house payments for some time. But I believed, as every woman believes, that the birth of a child would soften a man's heart. I was wrong but had few options. I was economically dependent on a man—my husband, in this case—as many women have been throughout our history, and that's the simple truth.

Anyway, Dawn continued, keeping her eyes on her audience, I cleared out the extra bedroom as best as I could, dumping all the junk he had collected in the backyard. I moved in there so as not to see the women he brought to the house and bed in the same bedroom that was once sacred to me. The night my water broke, my neighbor had to rush me to the hospital, and I gave birth to a healthy baby boy, an angel from heaven that made my life complete as a woman. I had never, even in the most horrific days of my pregnancy and abuse, contemplated giving up my baby for adoption, as had been suggested many times by that brute that called himself a man. Now I could clearly see why I held onto my dear boy; it was a miracle in the making, and I did all the heavy lifting. To suckle that innocent wonder with food that my body produced was a joy beyond all others that a human can experience. Too bad men cannot realize such a transformational delight; maybe their natures would change for the better—no offense meant.

Dawn paused, pain on her face as she reached deep into her heart to finish her narration. I took the love of my life home. The savage glanced at the perfect baby, and even though he had the same characteristics as him, he cleared out of the room, still in denial, still hateful. I nursed my beautiful child and promised him unconditional love as long as there was life in me to give. I needed a little time to get back on my feet, get my baby stronger, and then leave the hate-filled, brutal man. I didn't want my only child, the love of my life, to be influenced by a brute who had no respect for women, even if he was the father. When I breastfed him and held him close to me, he smiled, and at that glorious moment, I knew he loved me like no one ever had. In his heavenly smile, I saw a bright future for the both of us. I conversed with my darling son and told him all the good things we were going to accomplish together. I was so happy that I ignored all the ugliness that was occurring in the house: the drinking, the drug abuse, the women in the bedroom I had to put up with at all hours of the night and day. One evening, early, I was alone in the living room holding my baby in my arms, listening to the music of Bach. I had just fed him, and I was rocking him, content that all in his innocent world was good. Then a bullet crashed through the window, and I panicked. I jumped off the rocking chair and ran to my room for cover. I ducked next to the bed, protecting my baby with my body. I was crying, praying, trembling, scared to death. I didn't know what to do. I didn't hear any other shots, but I felt the blood on my hands as I held my love. I begged God for it to be my blood, not his. Oh God in heaven, not his blood, I cried. Then I ran out the door to my neighbor's house, screaming for somebody to call an ambulance, but it was too late.

Dawn's tears rolled down her cheeks in buckets. She bit her thin lips and dabbed her eyes in an attempt to control her emotions, but she couldn't. She cried and cried, deep sobs that made her frail body quiver with spasms, a pain that touched every fiber of her heart. A pain only a parent can feel when a viable part of her or him is erased for good, never to see the light of day again, a void never to be filled, even in the best of times. Hers was the grief and sorrow of a woman who wanted to be loved but was jilted and found true love in motherhood, and that was also taken away from her. Her tears were as real as her pain was real; it was in that reality that she struggled and suffered a slow journey to the grave, where her unendurable existence would come to an end.

Hector was touched. He knew Dawn had a history, but not one this tragic. He also knew she was on meds for something, but wow, he thought, this cut deep. Pete Rios was wringing his hands. He didn't know what to do; he felt helpless. He wanted to cry but didn't dare; that wouldn't solve anything, he thought. The other men in the group sat tight, hesitant to move. One wrong body motion, they thought, could be interpreted as insensitive. Dawn's sad story hit close to home. They knew men like her husband and what they did to women and usually took sides with the man, unless it was their sister or a blood relative who was the victim. But now after hearing

Dawn recite her unhappy tale, they felt bad, guilty, something—but hopefully tomorrow, they thought, away from the group, they might have a more objective conclusion.

Dawn controlled her emotional eruption somewhat, dried her eyes, and sipped some water. Her words were now spoken in anger, anger at herself and at the world she had to live in, that same world that had taken so much away from her. I died a thousand deaths, she said, biting her lips, which by now were blood red, managing her words for them not to come out too belligerent. But I was a coward—still am, in a way—and I couldn't take my life, do away with myself. I wanted to—and maybe deserved—to join my baby in heaven, for that's where I was positive he was. But I also wanted vengeance with a capital V. I wanted my husband dead—not the shooter, my husband—because he had been warned to stay away from that young girl because her boyfriend was a twisted, cowardly banger with the intelligence of a carrot. I even paid a hitman, but he took my money and laughed at me. And what could I do? Run to the police and tell them I had been ripped off by the man I paid to kill my husband? No, I left the town behind. I ran for safety—story of my life

—so I could attempt to put together in my head and heart a healthy transition and avoid any more downfalls. I had to learn to keep away from men who come in sweet but go out bitter. I travelled from city to town to village and back again. And I ended up here, of all places— no offense. I like it here. I tried religion, East and West and in between. They helped for a time, until the pain returned with all its ramifications. I did drugs, you all know; everybody does drugs. Like that was the answer, right? Yep, I tried the drugs—"meds" as they are called in polite society. They damaged my internal organs and frazzled my mind with visions of prehistoric landscapes until they crashed into molten lava, and I ended up strapped to a gurney or in a padded cell of a state asylum. I stopped the drugs when I began to resemble a skeleton—the chemical drugs, that is. The natural, not yet.

Dawn stopped talking; she sipped her water and waited for questions. Her tears were dry, and her voice was back to normal. She felt much better, and she was ready to take on the world again. The men in the group, including Hector, were silent. They looked at Hector and then at their shoes. They didn't want to venture forth and ask a stupid question and get Dawn all emotional again. It was a tragic story, and their drama was lightweight compared to her never- ending pain. Even Pete Rios, the big comadre in the group, would sound superficial if he took the floor at this point.

Hector waited in silence, waiting for Pete to make a fool of himself, but Pete didn't bite. OK, guys, he finally said, if there are no questions for Dawn or discussion, someone else can take the floor. No one volunteered, and the silence continued. Well, then, said Hector, glad he could end the session early. If no one wants to talk, let's end it. It was my pleasure working with you all, and don't worry —I'm positive someone will take my place, and you can continue your therapy. Say your thanks to Dawn for sharing some of her private life. Dawn smiled as best as she could, waiting for them to come up to her, but they just sat like dummies, avoiding eye contact. Hector stood up and walked back into his office, shutting the door behind him.

Pete Rios had plans to ask her out for a coffee after the session, but he changed his mind. The woman was plutonium, he decided, and he couldn't carry any more weight than he was already carrying. The woman was bad news all around, and another meltdown like today, and there was no guarantee he wouldn't go under along with her. He just wanted to go home and hit the sack and forget about her.

The other men felt the same way as Pete. They felt Hector played it smart, allowing the woman to go first and blowing their game out of the water. Who would have any interest in their say, after listening to her novela? Hector set them up, they thought. Even on the last session, he went away laughing. He wanted the session to end pronto, and he brought in a pro. They knew Hector had been exposed to this kind of trauma or worse. He had groups in the rougher areas of the different cities he had worked in. They, on the other hand, were like virgins to this sort of heavy sorrow. And now the woman was sitting there, expecting thanks for a trip into an emotional hell. They were pissed off because they were more conflicted now, thinking their concerns were minor, even petty, compared to what was going on in the real world.

Dawn, after waiting and no one saying a word to her, said, Ok. She walked up to Hector's office and raised her hand to knock, changed her mind, headed for the front door of the center, and left the premises.

CHAPTER TWENTY-SIX

ike Montes was in bed contemplating his future. He had Lola on his chest and was still nervous because of the ten pounds of pure heroin he had stashed away that Ramon knew he had. He had decided to dump it in the river but had to have Ramon along as a witness. He was sad because Hector had given them a pep talk and told them he had resigned as director of the center and was leaving Las Flores. All of them had their admission papers to UNM except Jr. But that was a clerical error, he assured Jr. Hector told them that they were in, that it was up to them to buck up and follow through. To be sure to attend the special orientation for incoming freshmen and not miss any financial aid deadlines, and he promised them to check up on their status and to call and see if they needed any assistance. The boys didn't believe him; they were silent for most part, feeling that their pillar of wisdom, Hector el Viejo, was leaving them to fend for themselves.

Mike was also sad because it was on this day, two years ago, that his friend Marco Rodrigues had blown his brains out with a .22. They were the same age. Before Marcos took his life, he shot his dog dead, so as to take him along on that mysterious trip. Mike was devastated because he considered Marcos a true friend and had dined with the family at their humble home on several occasions. That was the time he had gone with his grandfather and uncle camping and fishing. He was gone only a week, but when they returned, Marcos had been cremated because the church would not consent to have him buried in the cemetery. His mother and father attempted a compromise, but the priest would not bend. Only his grandfather, Mike thought, could have made a difference, but they were up in the Sangre de Christo Mountains, and when they returned, it was over. His father was not as aggressive as his grandfather and had more respect for church authority. His grandfather, on the other hand, always had to have his way or no way, regardless of whether it was a secular or a reverential predicament.

Mike put Lola away, took a shower, and got dressed, but couldn't forget Marcos. If he had only been here, he thought, Marcos might be alive today. Mike remembered Marcos leaving for Albuquerque for five or six months. He was going to work in some construction job, already having dropped out of school. He saw him once or twice during that time, and Marcos had seemed OK. He was a little sad, but he missed his family, and he admitted he missed the barrio. They talked, but the only thing Mike recalled was that Marcos mentioned a girl he had met in the Duke City. He didn't make a big deal about it; said she was just a girl. Mike felt bad because he should have asked more questions of his friend and gotten him to talk more about the girl or other things that could have been troubling him. And when Marcos returned from Albuquerque, probably already planning to take his life, Mike wasn't around to talk him out of it. That's what made him feel so bad. Marcos probably went to his house looking for him. Not finding Mike, the only real friend he had, Marcos decided to end it, once and for all. This was all conjecture on Mike's part; he really didn't know what Marcos had to put up with, but that's all he had. The feelings of grief, resentment, and anger— emotions he had never felt before, not this intensely—flooded his mind, day and night, after the tragedy. And the worse thing about it was that he couldn't talk about his feelings to anyone. His mother fell apart crying because Marcos had a special place in her heart. His father looked at him with sad eyes, wanting to know if he had any preconceived notions to copy Marcos. His friends didn't care about Marcos that much to go into an in-depth discussion about his death. And even Ramon, his best friend, clammed up when Mike talked about the death of Marcos. Ramon acted more jealous than concerned when the conversation about Marcos came up. Lola was the only one he could talk to, but the feedback was limited.

"The arrows of pride, prejudice, and greed, released from the gods of dissension, landed in the barrio and made a mockery of benevolence": that line always stayed with him from Oscar Rubio's epic narrative, The Seeds of Self-Hatred, introduced to a small group of seniors in his last year of high school. And this added to his anger at many people in the barrio who had ignored and treated Marcos and his family as second-class citizens for years. Just because they resided a short distance outside the barrio in an isolated area surrounded by mesquite bushes, not too far from the cemetery, and they were dark, they were called Indios, as if anyone from the barrio was excluded from that mixture of Spanish and Indio blood. The father was in and out of prison for signing checks on money he didn't possess. The family was on county assistance, and the stiff shirts condemned this relief as nothing but abetting laziness, unless it was one of their relatives receiving the aid. They tended to confuse laziness with poverty when convenient and denounced the mother raising five children on her own, with a husband in prison doing time, for attempting to put food on the table. Mike hated these assholes, bigoted sons of bitches, narrow-minded hypocrites, worshiping a Christ every Sunday who never abandoned the poor. That was the reason he was not going to church on this Sunday after his mother had pleaded with him to go; he couldn't stomach the deceitful assholes on their knees pretending to abide by the words of Jesus Christ or the benevolence of the Virgin Maria. That was another reason Mike wanted out, to get far away from this place, and not to see close up the bullshit people did to other people of lesser means. He was proud of his parents; they at least had treated Marcos like his other friends and helped out his family with food and clothes, and his father always made repairs to their house when needed. Now he was not only sad but pissed off also.

Mike got dressed, grabbed an apple, and decided to take a walk to Hector's house. He was going to ask Hector for a ride to California. If Hector said no, then he was going to find Ramon and dump the chiva in the river. Hell with it all, he said. He couldn't take the pressure of holding onto it. He thought it was going to be easy at first, but the more he thought of ways to make a profit with it, the more complicated and dangerous all avenues seemed. Manny mentioned a collector in town, and that made him nervous. As he bit into the apple, an idea crossed his mind. What if he told Hector about the chiva and offered to share the cash if Hector would take it to Los Angeles and sell it? Hector could only say no. He couldn't kick him out of the program because he wasn't in charge anymore—he could, but that would consume time and lengthy explanations. Hector didn't have that kind of time anymore. He was packed and anxious to leave. So there was nothing to lose, he thought. He was screwed anyway, so might as well try, and Hector might bite. After all, he reasoned, Hector had worked in the inner city counseling drug addicts and pintos, and Mike was sure Hector had connections— more than he had.

Mike started walking west on Chavez street. It was Sunday, and the traffic was light. The morning was clear and bright, not toasty yet, although it was close to noon. But what else is new, he thought. This is Las Flores. The weather people must be bored to death. Same weather, day after day for the whole summer—sweet ass job, he said, laughing, in a better mood but still thinking about his friend Marcos Rodriguez. Marcos was tall, taller than Mike, tall and skinny with a dark complexion and straight black hair. He wanted to learn how to fight. Mike taught him how to hit the speed bag and punching bag. He was hitting well and improving on his left hook on the heavy bag. Mike kept reminding him that with those long arms, he could put people down, but he had to learn how to use his power effectively. He emphasized that a powerful hook to the head or kidneys with a right cross to the ear, followed by a kick to the balls, could put most guys down and some out. But he had to utilize his speed and power, attack relentlessly, and never hesitate to go in for the kill. An experienced ass kicker, Mike told Marco many times, could sense his hesitation, go under his long arms, and hook him low before he released his kick, and he would find himself on his ass. Marcos was improving with the fundamentals, Mike recalled, but lacked the anger that could turn him into a killer. And Mike could never understand why Marcos didn't have the anger, the rage needed to hurt or cripple an opponent bad enough that other suckers would think twice about starting anything with him. Here was a guy, he would tell himself, who had been shitted on all of his life and still couldn't get into the zone. On the contrary, Mike had it good compared to Marcos, and he would go berserk in a fight. He got so carried away that he beat on anyone that was close; they would have to hold him down to calm him and get him out of the zone. That's crazy, he thought. He was afraid of the zone now; didn't like it; wanted nothing to do with it anymore.

Mike crossed Calle de los Angeles from Chavez, reached Baca Street, and turned right on Baca, going north. Hector's house was located on Baca, or Cow Street, as some called it. He kept thinking of Marcos. It must be scary to put a bullet in your head, he thought. It takes a lot of balls to take your own life. And what if you don't die— then what? You would be a veggie for sure, with people laughing at you for doing a poor job. He recalled that not too long ago, Marcos wanted to play Russian roulette, but he never took him seriously. Maybe that was his mistake, but they had both been drinking. That was when he carried a gun, which was stupid, but they all did, and that was like playing Russian roulette in itself, because some dumb shit was going to pull his piece, and someone was going to die, quick and easy. He sold his gun to Sammy Q., but Marcos kept his. But he still wondered how it would feel to place that cold steel barrel on your temple or inside your mouth and squeeze the trigger. The decision to pull or not to pull the tiny, deadly lever and the explosion in your brain if you did end it all, forever. Wow, what a way to go, he thought. Can't change your mind once you squeeze. Hell, man, it's too late. Forget all the bullshit here, and go join Marcos on the other side. Naw, he said out loud, I'm too much of a coward, and I love life too much. Maybe one day, when I'm cornered without an exit, but not now. Damn he said, I hope Hector's home.

Mike approached Hector's house on Baca Street, about three blocks from the church, on Calle de Las Golondrinas. He could see some of the cars leaving the late Sunday Mass and others arriving for the activities the church put on after the late Mass. He was changing his mind about telling Hector about the sugar. He knew Hector could be unpredictable and even mean, at times. His grand idea didn't seem as grand now as it had when he thought of it. Shit, he thought, I better turn back before he spots me. Too late—Hector was loading boxes from his garage into the trunk of his car. He waved to Mike, and Mike had no choice but to stop and offer a helping hand. Mike dropped the apple core into some shrubs and said, Hey Hector, packing up?

You got it, Mike—packing up and leaving town. Story of my life, Hector said, wiping the sweat from his face. Whatcha doing up here, Mike, casing my house so you can be the first one to loot my stuff? Just kidding, Mike, just kidding. C'mon in, Mike; that was the last one for the trunk. Travel light; that's the trick. And he slammed the trunk shut. I've got some iced tea. C'mon, join me. And they walked inside the house and parked in the kitchen.

As they sipped the iced tea, Mike could see Hector was in a good mood, but that could change, fast. So he decided to go ahead with his idea. All Hector could do at this point was to say no and throw him out. But again, he could say yes, and Mike could get a ride to Los Angeles with someone who was familiar with the City of Angels. And maybe he didn't even have to tell him about the chiva; maybe he could sell it himself and keep all the cash. Why the hell not, he thought.

Hey, Hector, Mike said, after taking a sip of iced tea. This is good tea, man. I need a ride to Los Angeles. Can I ride with you? I'll help with the gas.

Hector took a sip of tea himself, grabbed a cube of ice with his teeth, and left it in his mouth. He looked at Mike and smiled. Talking with the ice cube in his mouth, he asked, Fuck you gonna do in Los Angeles, Mike?

No, man, I got relatives out there, Mike responded, a little too defensive. I wanna go to college out there, you know. I got primos, tios, out there. Can't hang here no more.

No can do, said Hector, chewing on the ice. I travel alone— always have. Habit of mine.

Look, Hector, said Mike, getting serious. He decided to shoot the whole wad and placed his glass on the table. I've got ten pounds of pure heroin I need to move out of Las Flores to a more favorable market.

Hector spit the rest of the crunched ice back into the glass before he choked. He was attempting to clear his throat and tell Mike to stop joking. But then he saw on Mike's face and especially his eyes that the boy was serious, a la brava. Hector placed his left hand on his mouth, rubbing his cold lips with his fingers.

Hector finally said, after pacing around in the kitchen and looking out the kitchen window to make sure no one was about, I don't need to know that Mike. You know what kind of shit you can get into by telling people that story. Anyway, where could a nice, clean- cut guy, like you without any money pick up a load like that? How do you know it's pure? asked Hector, showing a little interest.

Well, let me tell you, said Mike, moving his chair closer, looking around in case there was somebody else in the house. We alone? Mike asked.

Not really. Tupi is in the living room taking a nap.

You remember Danny Madrid and the car crash? continued Mike, ignoring the last remark. As you know, Ramon survived. Ramon told me about how he and Danny had stumbled onto a package out in the desert while they were shooting rabbits. Mike told Hector the whole sad story, everything, except where he had the chiva stashed.

So how do you know it's pure? Just because Ramon told you it was?

No, look, Hector. Danny did chiva, OK? But he never had any good chiva. He bought off Sammy Q. and the chiveros. It was cut and cut—weak shit. When he had the real stuff, not black tar, he couldn't handle it; he took too much. He didn't know.

Was Lencho Reyes involved in any of this? asked Hector, concerned.

No, man, Lencho's gone. I even looked for him. I wanted to apologize to him, help him out. My parents said he could stay with us, if he wanted to. No, Lencho has nothing to do with this, I promise —only Ramon and me. Ramon wants no part of it. He said I could do whatever I wanted with it.

Yeah, right. That's what they all say. So you were gonna make me your mule, is that right, Mike? I give you a ride to Los Angeles, and you take the shit without telling me, we get busted, and I take the rap? My car, and you just a passenger. Clever boy, Mike.

No, Hector. I was gonna tell you, man, if you gave me a ride. I was gonna tell you all about it, Hector. I know you know people, and I don't; simple as that.

OK, Mike, so what do you want? What do you expect out of this treasure chest you claim to have?

Oh, I have it, I sure do. I was thinking sixty-forty.

Sixty-forty my way, Mike?

No, Hector, my way. I got the shit.

You may have the product, my friend, but it is me who's gonna take all the risk. I got to take it across state lines. I got to connect with criminals to sell it. You really think you can step out of Las Flores for the first time, go to Los Angeles or any other big city, and sell four and a half keys of heroin? They'll kill you and take the product, or you'll sell to an undercover dick. And what do you think you'll get in prison, Mike? With no gang backup? A good-looking, young, clean-cut guy like you?

OK, Hector, take fifty, and split it up the middle, said Mike, trying hard not to smile.

You were gonna settle for fifty all along, weren't you, Mike? You a clever little fucker, my friend, said Hector, shaking his head and pouring Mike some more iced tea.

Thanks, Hector, love your tea. How much you think we can get for it?

I have no idea, Mike. I usually don't finagle in those types of transactions; last I heard, before I arrived here, it was around a hundred and seventy-two dollars per gram, take or add some. It's like the stock market; it fluctuates. Supply and demand—you know how that goes. So if like you say, you have four and a half keys, change that into grams, multiply the grams by a hundred and seventy-two, and we—Hector looked at Mike—we might make a little money, but you do the math.

So you'll take it and sell it, Hector? Mike was biting his nails, trying not to make it too obvious, not wanting to chew on any more ice. He already knew the answer; he was only asking to be polite. He knew that the old dog had converted pounds to kilos and kilos to grams before Mike took his second sip of iced tea. Hector knew the price per gram, while Mike was still trying to calculate in pounds.

Hector gave a big sigh and said, Esta cabron, amigo. I'll take it and sell it, but there are certain conditions you have to meet before I agree.

Conditions, always conditions with old folks, Mike thought. He knew it was too good to be true; man, why make it complicated? he wanted to say, but he didn't; best to listen to the boss.

OK, Hector, hit me with your conditions.

Before we continue with this conversation, I want to make sure we are both on the same ticket. Once we put this thing on the road and give it wheels, it's a done deal, bro. You can't change your mind every other week; that's number one. Number two, I won't take you with me, and the reasons are obvious. Now, are you really serious about leaving Las Flores? Do you really want to leave behind the financial aid packet from UNM? If the answer is yes, and you are absolutely sure, well, then, let's do it. But you have to be patient and wait here until I make arrangements over there. I will send you a letter with the final instructions. Do exactly as I say, no ifs or buts. And as for not taking you with me, I'm taking a big risk, as it is. And if anything happens, your parents will never forgive me. Your parents were always here for my mother when I was away. Your father fixed up anything that needed fixing on the house, and your mother always assisted my mother when she was ill; they were church partners. It's very simple, Mike: I'm looking out for your interests. If you don't agree, you and your pal Ramon can try and peddle the smack in downtown Las Flores or flush it down the toilet. Take your pick. But make it quick 'cause I leave tomorrow, around five or six in the evening. I'll drive through the desert at night and arrive in Los Angeles early morning, in time for the early commute.

And I know I can trust you, right, Hector? Mike said, with an easy grin.

Like I told you, Mike, you have few choices. If you had more options, you wouldn't be here.

I read you, Hector. No, it's a good plan; let's do it, said Mike, unsure, but not having the experience to negotiate at this level.

I'll write and give you more instructions, more info. Give me a couple of weeks—a month at the most. Wait here. Don't leave to Califa. I need a little time to get the best price for the poison and a little time to cover my tracks. There can be no connection between you and me. I'll send a letter with no return address for your eyes only—burn it after you read it. Deliver the product to me no later than five o'clock tomorrow evening. Neighbors, if any, saying their farewells will see the sack as a bag of chilies or something I'm taking to your relatives in California. And remember, Mike, you take care of business with your pal Ramon. I don't care how you do it, but be sure he knows nothing. One fuck-up, and we're dead.

Don't worry, Hector. I got that covered.

You best have, Mike. Now let's shake on the deal—a sealed, verbal contract between caballeros sin caballos.

You got it, Hector. You the man, said Mike, and they touched skin, the reference going over his head. Mike felt stupid. He had a feeling he had given up the store to the wiseass Hector. In three weeks' time, Hector could cash in the chiva and leave the country, if he wanted to. And there was nothing he could do about it, Mike thought. He still had the sugar, and that made him feel a little better. He could change his mind, but he wouldn't. As far as he was concerned, it was settled, a done deal; let the cards fall where they may. And he breathed a sigh of relief.

So, Hector, you're saddled up and ready to ride out west? asked Mike, spirited now that the negotiations were over.

Yeah, Mike. It's not easy, but you do what you have to do.

Let me ask you before I leave, Hector. What's the story on Juan Jose? How's he tied up with Delfina Madrid?

Hector, relieved that Mike didn't ask for any particulars on the reason he was leaving Las Flores, said, That's a hell of a story, and some people around here pretend it never happened. I remember some of the history, but then I left to California. My mother, whenever I received a letter or we talked on the phone, kept me current on the happenings out here. Juan Jose was from Santa Maria, as you know. Santa Maria is a short distance east of Snake Town, a small village emptied by mining interests. Juan Jose and his family were the last to depart, fighting the mining conglomerates to the end.

Hector rubbed his lips with his fingers, gazing out the kitchen window, his mind taking him back to a time that seemed like a dream, a dream linking him to the despair of his youth. Juan Jose, he continued, turning to address Mike, Juan Jose was not very tall, but was big, well built, solid, with the kind of muscles you get when you push heavy weight. And he had attitude—plenty of it—written all over him. He was the kind of person you didn't fuck with, unless you're stupid. He didn't visit Las Flores much, until he became friends with Danny's father. Danny's father had a band, played the guitar, and sang. He was a good guitar player and had a decent voice, the kind some women take their panties off for. Juan Jose played base and at times vocal backup. But more than anything, he was the muscle; mess with Danny's father, and you better be buying flowers for your approaching funeral. He never said anything, the silent kind—you know them, Mike—around others, but when he did find some words, and they were directed at you and no one else, you better have your medical insurance card in your wallet, if you were lucky enough to have coverage.

Hector took a sip of iced tea and continued. Danny's father was already married to Delfina, a beauty in her own time. Danny Jr. was a couple of years old, and there were rumors she was pregnant again. Delfina never accompanied her husband and his band to any of the colorful events where they performed. Their music was not unlike the music of Little Julian Herrera, famous in El Monte, California, a fusion of swing, boogie-woogie, mambo rhythms, and lots of Mexican influences. I guess you're too young to know much of that music,

Mike. They played and sang slow songs in Spanish and English, the type makes you cling to your babe and never want to let go. I tell you, they had huge crowds at the Knights of Columbus Hall, the one on Alameda Street. The gossip was that their marriage was not made in heaven, and the presence of Juan Jose didn't help matters much. Those two were always together. When Danny's father had a liaison with a woman or girl, Juan Jose was his cover and alibi. If Danny's father was ever threatened by a jealous husband or boyfriend, Juan Jose would take matters into his own hands and settle the problem—discreetly, if he could, but it didn't matter, as long as he got it done.

Am I boring you, Mike? Hector asked, amused, scratching his chest as if he had ticks without even realizing it. I understand young people become bored and distracted listening to older folks talk. I was that way myself at a young age, and I don't expect you to be any different. I'll continue with the story, but only if you're interested. I'm sure we both have other things to do.

No, man, keep going, Hector, Mike said. I asked you about him, not the other way around. Who doesn't want to learn more about the story of the Mystery Man, Juan Jose? I always wanted to know the story, but you're right, people around here either forgot or don't want to be bothered with it. I even asked my parents, and they changed the subject but in a clever way. And you know that Danny, when he was alive, would never talk about his father, and you couldn't get a peep out of Vivian, even if you begged her. So by all means, Hector, please go on.

Danny's father, Mike, Hector continued, with the patience of a true storyteller, and I don't have to draw you a picture—he liked the ladies. You could say he was a player. They appeared in public with their long black hair braided in ponytails that reached their waists. They had full mustaches and trimmed beards. Juan Jose, in summer, wore a sleeveless black T-shirt with a white cross stitched in front, and in winter a black leather jacket with a skull and bones on the back, done with luminous paint that glowed in the dark. Sure, it's common enough now, but back then, Mike, it was revolutionary, a big deal.

They made a lot of noise with their Fender electrics and drums, and on special occasions they brought in an accordion player and horns to add picante to the corridos and polkas that the older folks loved. They played all the local joints and in towns and villages on either side of the highway. Danny's father was writing original music for the band and was thinking of expanding to larger dance halls in bigger towns. Remember, Mike, that was the time I left Las Flores. I missed a lot of the story, but my mother and others gave me detailed accounts on the happenings. My mother knew I had a crush on Delfina when I was younger, and maybe she believed that if Delfina divorced, I would return to Las Flores and pursue her.

Well, Mike, let me wind this story down, said Hector, enjoying every minute and adding more ice to the pitcher of iced tea. I could write it as a soap opera, a tragic one, and still couldn't do it justice. Anyway, the mining conglomerate succeeded in emptying Santa Maria. Juan Jose's family was the last one to be pushed out, but pushed out they were. There were rumors of a large settlement, but that was disputed. They gave them what they gave everyone else, which was nothing—peanuts. The family relocated, refusing public assistance, and Juan Jose joined the military. We later found out he was with the Army Special Forces, doing dirty work in Central America and the Middle East, but again that was just people talking.

Hector stopped, poured the last of the watered-down iced tea in his glass, and, seeing Mike's glass half-full, didn't offer any. He placed the pitcher back on the table and said, Listen, Mike, don't get me wrong. I'm not attempting to imply that Juan Jose was a bad person. He was a badass, not a bad person. He didn't want to leave Danny's father and the band, but he knew he was the cause for a lot of the friction between Danny's father and Delfina. He returned on leave and baptized Vivian. Delfina adamantly refused to allow Juan Jose to baptize Danny, but Danny's father promised him the second child, regardless of the protest from Delfina. There was a huge baptismal party, as you can imagine. The two friends reminisced for days, and during that time was when Juan Jose promised Danny's father that he would look after his family, if there was ever a need to. Everyone knew by this time that Danny's father was seeing a woman with an unforgiving partner, the kind of woman not easy to forget or leave alone, even though you're married. Juan Jose, after days of partying and hanging out with Danny's father and the band, didn't want to return to his post. He wanted to continue to protect Danny's father, especially now that he had added new skills to his repertoire. But Danny's father convinced him not to screw up his career, to complete his enlistment, and when he was discharged, there would always be a place in the band for him.

Hector paused and took a sip of what was mostly ice water by now; a pained expression was apparent on his face. He was going back in time. It was a messy situation, still in his memory as if it happened only yesterday and still applicable, to this day, and him not learning anything from it. Christ, he thought, what's the use of reasoning, when we allow our swords to determine our destiny? Sorry, Mike, he said, as if awakening slowly from a deep slumber. Juan Jose, he continued, returned to the military, and Danny's father continued seeing that woman. One night, the husband or boyfriend caught them in bed, in his house. He shot Danny's father in the lower torso, beat the woman unconscious, and cut her face severely enough to disfigure her. He threw Danny's father out in the street to die like a dog. Danny's father survived, but the bullet went out his back and damaged his spinal cord. He was left to spend the rest of his days in a wheelchair and dependent on others for his basic needs. The woman left town, and of course Danny's father didn't press charges; it was a matter of pride, you know—maybe you don't, yet. He realized that sending the man to prison was not going to restore his manhood; that the culprit would eventually pay a heavy penalty, and prison would only protect him more than punish him. See, Mike, Danny's father played with fire and only felt the heat, on occasions, but eventually, the flame consumed him, as it does all who play dangerous games. And he wanted to add, That's why I'm leaving town, but he didn't. Instead he said, A mighty lesson to digest, my young friend. Anyway, he lost everything, which to him was his manhood, because not even his children brought him any joy after the shooting. He felt he was useless and depended more and more on booze and painkillers to get him through the days and long nights, thinking about what he had lost, never thinking about what he had gained.

It is very difficult to put yourself in his shoes, Mike, Hector continued, putting the cold glass on his cheeks, trying not to think of his situation with the nutcase Tito Brito.

So what happened next? asked Mike, seeing that Hector was sweating, and it wasn't even that hot inside the house.

Oh, let me tell you, said Hector, as he shook himself out of his discouraging thoughts. Juan Jose was informed about the shooting soon after. The young man who shot Danny's father didn't leave town. He was a small-time hoodlum from Las Vegas. He didn't know about Juan Jose, or if he did, didn't seem to care—a huge mistake on his part. They found the thug a couple of weeks later out in the desert, in a hole, with half of his body exposed to the elements. His ears and nose had been surgically removed, he had been scalped, and his tongue was missing. The coroner's autopsy assumed the poor fool had been alive when the unpleasantness was performed on him. They didn't even bother going into further detail to explain what atrocities they discovered in the lower extremities of the damaged body. Naturally the cadaver was in pretty bad shape when found—I mean, naked in the hot sun all day, chewed on by wild animals at night; not a pretty sight, Mike. Juan Jose sneaked into town and executed his duty, without a word being said or a gun fired. The police didn't expend any real resources on the investigation. To them it was just another drug deal gone south. The death, although gruesome, of a petty drug dealer, thief, and wife beater didn't deserve the merits of a full, all-out investigation; case closed. But the sad part, Mike, was that Danny's father wasn't into vengeance anymore. He knew about the shooter found naked out in the desert; he knew it was going to happen, sooner or later. It was news for weeks in the barrio, not in the newspaper. Danny's father knew nothing would gain him the use of his legs, and the depression was destabilizing his mind, like termites destabilize a piece of wood. So he did what any honorable man in my opinion would do: put a bullet in his head and ended it all.

Wow, Mike said, really touched. Jesus. What a sad ending; no wonder Danny and Vivian refused to talk about their father. At the same time, he was thinking and worrying about what could happen to him for keeping the chiva. He kept looking out the kitchen window to see if any strangers were lurking around. And people called Ramon crazy, he thought. Yeah, crazy like a fox—passed on the chiva to him, washed his hands clean, gave him all the worry and responsibility, and asked for a little cash in return. Slam dunk for Ramon, he figured. But wasn't he doing the same? Passing it on to Hector and asking for more than a little cash? Shit, what a mess, he thought. And he kept thinking about the poor slob Juan Jose had butchered out in the desert.

Listen, Mike. Hector interrupted Mike's disturbed thoughts. I'll repeat: I don't want you to get the impression that Juan Jose and Danny's father were bad folks. They did what they had to do, under the difficult circumstances. Juan Jose became a hero to many of the young people in the barrio. Danny's father, he had his followers, mainly because of his music. That's why I think the people who were around during that time—and still are—refuse to talk about them out of respect. And you have to remember that Juan Jose is still around and still dangerous, so why disturb a wasp's nest by asking stupid questions?

No, Hector. I understand, especially now that you shared the story. I would never ask anyone anything about Danny's dad. But let me ask you this, Hector; I don't want to be nosy, and don't get offended— are you, uh, Danny's biological father? I heard that once, some time ago, but you don't have to tell me if you don't want to. I also heard you left town because Juan Jose promised to fix your wagon—not my words, whatever that means.

That's not true, Mike; never happened. I'm not denying that Delfina was a prize, a beauty, and I did have a thing for her, but that's as far as it went. Sure, I contemplated it at times, as others did, but it never got off the ground. Just like I'm sure you have a hard-on for her daughter, Vivian, but you'll never get a piece of her.

How do you know I haven't scored with Vivian, Hector? asked Mike with a smile on his face.

You're not so different than I was at your age, Mike. To pursue a beautiful woman takes a lot of time and effort. The great sacrifice might not be worth the trouble if the sex is flat, the emotions one sided, and the mystique becomes routine; what's the point? Delfina fell in love with Danny's father, and probably the main reason was that he serenaded her with love songs that brought tears to her eyes and touched her heart as never before. And even though her parents were against the marriage—the young man already had a reputation as a heartbreaker—she went ahead and married him. But he continued playing with his band and never stopped looking for pussy. So being with a beautiful woman never guarantees you'll stay close to home all the time, especially if she's into herself so much that she seldom extends a helping hand. I know you're too smart to ride that train, Mike, but perhaps I'm wrong. I wouldn't want to put any ideas in your head and spoil your fantasies.

Mike looked at Hector, scratching with the tips of his fingers at the patch of hair on his chin. Lots to think about, Hector, he finally said. I'll leave you to your packing. I have to go find Ramon.

Oh, Mike, before you leave. One more favor I have to ask of you. Tomorrow, when you drop off the cookies, I want you to take Tupi and keep him at your house. He gets along with your mom. He's too old for the trip, and the city is no place for an old dog. The poor thing doesn't have that long to live, and there's no reason to put him through any discomforts. And by the way, my son is picking up the rest of my stuff and putting it in storage. He'll also put up the old place for rent or sell it; that's up to him. So until it's rented or sold, check around once in a while, just to see that everything is OK.

Sure thing, Hector. We'll take care of Tupi, and I'll do my rounds or ask my dad to.

Mike left Hector's house with a sense of relief. Now he had to settle with Ramon. Shit, he thought. Ramon could mess everything up.

CHAPTER TWENTY-SEVEN

omero was in a Circle K market in the Westside, close to his motel, purchasing the necessities to make his life a little more comfortable: toothpaste, shaving items, bandages for his cut, snacks, and other items. When he paid for the things, he stopped with bags in hand in front of the magazine rack to check out the photos of the babes, when he heard "Gerald" in a loud voice. He was startled; nobody called him by his first name, especially here. He turned his head to his right and saw Bryan Hercules, a huge ear-to-ear smile on his face, with arms extended, ready for a hug.

Romero turned around and looked at Bryan with a puzzled and not-too-happy look on his face. He starred straight at him and around him wondering who this little shit was.

It's me, Gerald—Bryan, Bryan Hercules, your cousin. Remember that family reunion in Denver a couple of years ago? Bryan insisted, happy as a monkey eating lice. We were introduced —you didn't even know you had family out here, remember? My mother is half-sister to your uncle Rafael; that makes us third or fourth primos.

OK, Romero said, not recalling who this shit was. Let's step outside, why don't we? It's kind of crowded in here.

Bryan followed Romero to his truck, where he put the bags in the front seat. Now tell me, he asked Bryan, are you sure you got the right primo?

Oh, yeah, cousin, Bryan answered, elated, I'd never forget you. All the other cousins, nada, no hint, but you—like a snapshot in my brain. Isn't that funny?

Very funny, jackass, Romero wanted to say, but he didn't. Maybe this little cunt could be useful, he thought; no point in hurting his feelings at this early stage.

So what brings you out here? continued Bryan, still grinning, doing a poor job of concealing his joy.

I—I'm doing a friend a favor, you could say, Romero answered, not sure if he wanted to talk about his business.

What kind of favor? I can help; just ask.

Romero hesitated and then said, It's a little complicated. And he looked to his right and left to check if anyone was close enough to listen. I'm sure I can trust you, right? Bryan, is it?

Yeah, you can trust me with your life, primo.

We'll see, bro. A friend of a friend asked me to—as a favor, by the way—to locate something of interest that belongs to him. Now you're a big boy, Bryan, but if you think this is going to put you in a place you don't wanna go, fine—I understand. This particular item was dropped in the area and never recovered. What I mean by that is that it disappeared. My friend believes that one of the locals found the package and kept it, not really comprehending what was found or comprehending well enough to attempt to profit from it. Now I'm here to mediate with the folks who have it before someone else is sent, someone more unreasonable and impatient with a volatile disposition. So that's why I'm here, Bryan. If you know anything about this or anybody who's foolish enough to hold onto the product in hopes of cashing in, you best help them and tell me who they are.

Bryan studied Romero, in awe of his cousin. He had liked him since the first day they were introduced some years ago in Denver. He was impressed with his size, his build, and his all-American good looks. Romero had ignored him since day one, but Bryan didn't care. He had followed him around at the gathering like a lost puppy, and he wasn't the only one. Romero was like a rock star; Bryan remembered all the girls, cousins and not, catering to his every need. And now here he was. Bryan had the opportunity to help him; how cool was that? he thought. He wanted to take Romero home and show him off to all the neighbors like the priceless stud stallion that he was. Perhaps Romero would consent to an invitation to church. They could arrive late and go all the way to the front pews, making everyone notice them. After Mass, once outside the church, Bryan would politely ask the parishioners to wait in line as he introduced him, the girls first. Wow, he thought, maybe Linda Barela would notice him for bringing his cousin to church.

Let me think, Bryan said, scratching the few hairs on his chin. There is Sammy Q. who deals in substance—small time, though. He might have it; then again, he might not, and the reason I say that is because Sammy Q. has a big mouth—for a little guy, that is. It would be all over town by now. Then there is Lencho Reyes—a user, but he's no longer around. He disappeared; no sign of him anywhere, as if the earth swallowed him whole. He was my friend, and I really miss him. No, definitely not Lencho; he would have told me. We were tight, even though I don't do drugs. I can't think of anyone else who might have the balls to pull a trick like that and not brag about it.

Romero, ready to dismiss the little shit, said instead, Listen, Bryan, think of a smartass who thinks he's bad and clever, just to prove a point. Someone who might do it for adventure, to kill the boredom, or maybe even for profit—who knows. Anybody in this category that you can recall?

Bryan was scratching under his left armpit with his right hand; he always got a heat rash on the same spot. He was anxious to help Romero, but he couldn't think of anyone because he didn't live in Las Flores. He lived a short distance from town, but he told people who didn't know him that well that he lived in Las Flores. Then an idea came to him, and he said, Wait a minute, Gerald. He liked calling Romero Gerald instead of Geraldo, his legal name. I think I might have something. And he stopped scratching, not wanting to gross out his favorite cousin.

There are these two pendejos, Jr. and Javier, who I know do drugs, but they're on the stupid side—not the sharpest knives in the drawer. And he laughed with gusto, thinking Romero would laugh also, but he didn't. There is a third fucker, Bryan continued in a serious tone—he didn't want to give Romero the impression he was dealing with a flake. Mike Montes. Now there is a smartass as any I can think of. He hangs with Sammy Q., but I'm not sure he does drugs. We're all in the same program, except Sammy Q., and he acts like a badass all the time—Mike, that is. Not Sammy.

Program? asked Romero, showing a little interest.

Yeah, said Bryan, proud that he could at least claim that. We're in a program called College Bound and have been accepted to UNM on full scholarships. We start this fall, everyone except Lencho Reyes. He got dropped because of drug use. Then he disappeared.

Any girls in the program?

Not this year, but Hector—he's the director of the center—he wrote the grant, and he said that next year he was going to include girls.

That's nice of him.

Nice is his middle name, said Bryan, attempting to sound cute. Of course it is, as is mine. Tell me, Bryan, why do you think this Montes character might be connected with this business?

I can't say for sure, Gerald, but I just have a gut feeling he might be—nothing really concrete, just a gut feeling. Bryan wanted to take back what he said about Mike, but it was too late. He wanted Romero to lean on Mike a little, scare him some, maybe slap him around—not to hurt him but just enough to knock him off his high horse. Bryan was angry because he knew Mike was still with Linda Barela, and he had a thing for Linda. And Linda Barela wouldn't even give him the time of day; that's why he wanted someone to teach Mike a lesson. He couldn't do it, so why not let someone else do it for him, he thought.

Romero was sitting in his truck with the door open and his legs out on the asphalt, while Bryan was standing in front of him. Romero looked at Bryan, trying to decide if this little pendejo was on the level or just wanted attention. It was getting hot, and he wanted to get back to the motel, soak in the tub, and change the bandage on his leg. Bryan seemed to have a thing against this Montes vato, and he had no time to waste and get involved in personal vendettas.

Finally, he said, impatient, Look, Bryan, this is serious stuff. Now think—any connections to this character Montes? If you have a dislike or something against this vato, I understand, and if I have time, I'll help you out. If no connections, I'll see you—maybe at the next family gathering, who knows.

Wait, Gerald, please, Bryan said, a little too desperate. Ramon—that's Mike's friend—he survived the car crash, and Danny Madrid was killed.

And that means what to me?

Danny Madrid was a stoned junky. Him and Ramon maybe found the stuff, and—

Did they find any product around the crash site? asked Romero with a bite in his words.

I don't think so; it was never in the paper. Just broken booze bottles.

Is the other boy a junky also?

No, no. Ramon, he's a—he has seizures. He just hangs around with Danny because he likes Danny's sister, Vivian.

Was this boy Ramon seriously injured? Is he still in the hospital?

No, he wasn't injured that bad. He left the hospital. But—but Ramon asked to see Mike while he was in the hospital after the car crash.

And how do you know this?

Because he asked me to tell Mike to come and see him. I happened to be at the hospital checking on my grandma.

Romero was silent; the heat inside the truck was bothering his cut. He wanted to leave and go soak in the tub, even though it was a bit small for him; he had no other choice. He wanted to scratch the itch around the bandage, but didn't want to have to explain to the curious Bryan any more than he had to.

OK, Bryan. He ended the silence with a sigh, fighting not to lose his patience. You gave me a dead junky, a boy with seizures, and a smartass; what's the connection?

I—I think that Danny and Ramon found the package and put it somewhere safe. Then after the crash, Ramon wanted to tell his friend Mike what happened. Like confess, you know?

No, I don't know, Bryan. I don't get it. The product is still missing after the accident. A junky would never trust anyone with a stash, especially someone who has seizures. The only possibility is that somebody arrived at the crash scene, pulled out the package, and left without giving any assistance. And it couldn't have been Montes, because his friend was hurt, and I don't believe he would leave him behind, you know, seizures and all.

That's all I have, Gerald. But I can do this for you. I can go and check out Mike's pad, look around, just in case. With Ramon, I wouldn't even bother.

That's up to you, Bryan. Just don't get me involved. I wouldn't want your mother to think I put you up to it if things don't work out right.

No, Gerald, not a problem. The Montes are never home. I see them all the time in the community or at church. And Mike, he's never home. Always riding around with Linda, he was going to add but thought better of it. So you see, there's only three of them; I can keep tabs on them easy. It's not like there's a whole flock of them.

Like I said, that's your thing. And Romero handed him a card with the name and number of the motel he was staying at. If you find anything, he said, call me at this number, and leave your name and phone at the front desk, and I'll get back to you. And Bryan—no surprise visits; they are very strict when it comes to visitors.

Cool, man, not a problem. Are you still going to college?

Romero didn't want to start another conversation but wanted to be polite in case he needed him for something.

I got my degree in business, he said, a little stiff as he put his long legs into the truck.

So what do you do now, Gerald?

I'm in loss control.

What's that? asked Bryan, not wanting to let go.

I work for a large insurance company, replied Romero, closing the door but still talking to Bryan through the open window. I check out building sites to see if they're up to code, fire, safety issues. If they are, we insure them; if not, we write up some recommendations they have to follow if they want our coverage.

How cool is that. Bryan beamed. Are you working on a graduate degree?

I'm working on a teaching credential and a master's in education. I want to coach football or basketball, maybe go into administration, who knows. If he says "cool" one more time, I'll slap the little shit, thought Romero.

Hey, listen, Gerald, you wanna go home for lunch with me? My mom will be more than happy to see you, and she'll fix us a great lunch. C'mon, man.

I would love to, Bryan. But I have urgent business to attend to. Next time, maybe. See you. And he drove off.

Romero was driving to his new motel on Sierra Street off Alameda, and he was thinking of the hassle of finding a motel with a large tub. He moved from the last one after the incident at La Conga's. This one cost a little more money, but the tub was larger, and it was closer to town. He had planned to go back to La Conga's and teach the bitch a lesson but decided against it. It wouldn't look too professional if got locked up for beating up on an old prostitute. She probably had cop clients up the ass and people hanging around at all hours. No, he said out loud, I lost that one, as he listened to Vivaldi's Four Seasons on tape. Then he started thinking about Bryan's last name as the music relaxed him. What a last name— Hercules, he thought. If they were really related, he must ask his mother to see which side of the family it came from. He wouldn't mind changing his last name to Hercules. Gerald Hercules, he repeated several times. It fit him perfectly, he thought, with his strength and good looks—watch out, world. He'd grow his hair long—wait, he said, that was the other guy. Fuck, he said. Must be the meds. He had asked the doctor for painkillers and something for the cut, in case of infection. He told the doctor he gashed it on barbwire attempting to release a cow caught up in it. Looking for strays—that was his job, he told the doctor, as if the doctor gave a fuck. He didn't want to take any chances because of what La Conga had said about her knife and dog shit. He finally drove into the motel, parking in front of his room. He was dying to get in the tub and soak for a couple of hours. After the soak, he was going to take a long nap and study his next move. He would give this trip another day, two max, and then head back north, probably empty handed. He didn't even want to think about it. He only wanted to think about his babe, Alicia Juarez.

CHAPTER TWENTY-EIGHT

hen Mike was visiting Hector and his parents were gone from the house, Bryan Hercules walked up to the Montes residence on the pretext he wanted to ask Mike a question about the UNM financial aid packet. He parked his car on Calle de los Angeles and walked to Chavez Street, where Mike lived. It was a short walk of a couple of blocks. He didn't want to park too close to the house in case the neighbors were about. He had an official envelope with official papers to cover his ass if Mike or his parents were home or caught him by surprise.

He entered the yard of the large house. He was a little nervous but confident that no one was home. A small gate that led to the front door was ajar, and halfway to the screen door, he stopped and called out, Mike, yo, Mike, and waited. No answer; he called again, a little louder. Then he tried, Mr. Montes, Mrs. Montes—Bryan Hercules here, Mike's friend. He walked closer to the screen door and noticed the door to the house was not closed. He called again just to make sure; nothing. Instead of going into the house, he went straight to the four-car garage to take a look-see. He entered the garage through the front; the front double door was halfway up. He didn't see anything of interest: a couple of trucks used for construction, work tools, and material to repair homes. He was getting nervous because the garage was large, with many cabinets and lockers of metal and wood. He'd never be able to search or go through each of them, he thought; it would take him all day. He went out a side door to the back of the garage and was surprised to see Mike's car between the garage and a toolshed. The car couldn't be seen from the street. Not only was it behind the garage, but there were fruit trees and shrubs on the perimeter inside the fence of the property, and that kept the backyard pretty private. Now Bryan was worried—more scared than worried. If Mike was home, and he saw him poking around his backyard, no telling what his reaction would be. Bryan had seen Mike fight, and although Bryan talked big in front of the guys, he wouldn't want to face him alone in his own backyard.

Mike, he called out again. You here? It's me, Bryan. He waited. His hands were sweaty as he shifted the envelope from one hand to the next. He called again, just to make sure, and when he didn't see Mike or anyone else come out of the house, he relaxed some. He's not home, he thought, and if he is, he's in a deep sleep or doing some chick, oblivious to the rest of the world. What if it's Linda Barela? he wondered. He blushed and got angry and jealous. Shit, he said, and went into the toolshed and saw the same work material and tools as in the garage.

Bryan walked slowly to the front door of the house and knocked several times on the screen door, repeating his name and stating he was looking for Mike so they could go over some info from UNM. He opened the screen door and let himself in. The door, beveled glass on an oak frame, was wide open, and it seemed to Bryan too heavy to bother closing. People still didn't lock their doors in some areas of the Eastside barrio; that would come in the future. Bryan entered the house, his heart thumping. If Mike caught him inside the house, he could beat him to death, and no court in the land would convict him, of that he was sure. He stopped and called out again, louder. His voice was breaking up, and he was breathing heavy, with sweat on his skin. This was new to him, going into someone's home uninvited. He was going to turn around and leave while he still could. But he recalled Gerald, his cousin, and how bad he wanted to please him. He convinced himself that he was no thief and that he hadn't broken in. The door was unlocked and open. His courage went up a notch, and before he knew it, he was in the kitchen and then the den, surprised not to see any dogs. He folded the envelope and secured it in his back pocket, confident the house was empty. He entered the main hall and peeked into open doors, searching for Mike's bedroom. He found it at the end of the hall. He was going to knock, but the door was open. He stood at the open door and hesitated. If Mike found him inside his room, looking through his things, he would execute him, without any qualms whatsoever.

Bryan was so nervous now that he was insides Mike's room that he couldn't concentrate. He kept looking at the door. Jesus, he wondered, how can anybody do this for a living? It's stressful work. He saw a couple of large bookshelves filled with fiction and nonfiction books. So the man reads—or is that just for show? he thought as he opened a closet door and saw boxes of shoes stacked on the closet floor. He removed the box top from one box and saw a pair of new shoes. He felt like trying them on, just for the hell of it, but decided against it. This is insane, he whispered, and his stomach continued acting up because of his jittery nerves. He turned his attention to Mike's bed after closing the closet door. The bed was unmade and the sheets disheveled. He wanted to smell the sheets to see if he could get a whiff of Linda Barela, positive that Mike had done her good, perhaps as early as this morning. But he didn't follow through; he decided it was too low, too sick, for him to even think about it.

Bryan looked around the room and saw nothing worth looking into. He was going to check under the bed, and then he was out of there, he decided. He went down on his knees and pulled the sheet up on the bed. He saw a plastic container and said, bingo. He pulled it out recklessly, thinking he had hit the jackpot, and his primo Gerald was going to be proud of him. But his impulsiveness did him in again, as always. He brought the plastic container close to his face to take a better look, and he came in eye contact with the critter Lola. He shrieked and pushed the container back under the bed. He had a fear of spiders that bordered on the insane. He attempted to stand up but lost his balance and landed on the floor. Breathing heavily and sweating, he crawled on all fours as fast as he could out of Mike's room. He grabbed on the doorframe and struggled to get on his feet. The nausea set in, and he ended up in a room he didn't recognize. He tried to focus and find the kitchen, but the sweat was running into his eyes, and his vision was impeded.

He finally made it to the kitchen and out the door. He walked as fast as he could without running. The panic attack was still going strong when he found his car. He opened the door to the passenger side and sat on the curb. He was nauseated, shivering, hyperventilating, with hot flashes coming and going. He didn't dare vomit; he kept telling himself, If I vomit, I'm done for. Once the vomit came, he couldn't move for at least a couple of hours. Any movement would cause more dizziness and bring more vomit. Focus, he kept repeating, focus on an object. He focused on the door handle of the driver's side. He knew the panic attack wouldn't last more than ten minutes. If anyone saw him and recognized him, word would get back to his mother that he was drunk in public—another worry.

The apprehension began to subside, and Bryan began to breathe normally. The nausea was under control, and his heartbeat slowed. Then he remembered the envelope, and he almost panicked again. He searched for it desperately; what if he had dropped it inside the house? Oh my God, he thought. I can't go back there. He finally fished it out of his back pocket and flung it in the car, breathing a sigh of relief. Now he realized why he had been so nervous in Mike's room as soon as he entered. He had glanced at the large photo of the tarantula on the wall, but he had averted his eyes and pretended he hadn't seen it, never even dreaming that Mike had the real thing under his bed. He was going to wait ten minutes and then go home and take a nap. Fuck my primo, he said. This shit ain't worth it.

CHAPTER TWENTY-NINE

Vivian Madrid entered the Eastside community center a little before lunch. She walked straight to Connie, the secretary, and asked to see Hector. Connie was taken by surprise. She knew of Vivian Madrid but had never met her or seen her up close. She was struck by her beauty; the eyes of another woman, in her opinion, were the only honest judge of physical female attractiveness. She had heard comments of Vivian's perfection, but mostly from boys and men, who used different criteria to judge beauty among women —usually vulgar, concentrating on a few body areas, and ignoring the rest. Women, on the other hand, never mentioned Vivian Madrid, not to her, and now she knew why. Vivian was wearing tight jeans, light-blue leather sandals, and a turquoise silk sleeveless top. Her long hair was in a ponytail held by a blue ribbon. She had no makeup or lipstick on, no jewelry, and her flawless, milk-colored skin made her green eyes transparent like high-quality Burmese jade. To Connie, it was as if she had tried her best not to look pretty. Lucky bitch, thought Connie.

May I help you? asked Connie, attempting to appear indifferent.

I need to see Hector, said Vivian, her eyes on Connie.

Do you have an appointment?

No, I don't have an appointment. Why would I need an appointment? What is he? Governor, state senator? Emperor of China? What?

Hector is very busy, said Connie, not amused.

My mother happens to be on the board of directors of this— she was going to say shithole, but instead she said, center. And she wants me to give Hector some vital info, she lied.

Well, in that case, knock on the door; that's his office. And Connie pointed to Hector's office. Connie didn't want to get in a tiff with Vivian Madrid and then get a talking-to by Concha or some members of the board. Anyway, Hector was leaving; today was his last day. Why should she be screening his visitors? she thought.

Vivian turned without saying another word and walked straight to Hector's office. Connie couldn't keep her eyes from looking at the gorgeous Vivian. She had the look people would pay money to see all glammed up on the cover of a magazine, and even from behind, she looked stunning. Jesus, thought Connie. Even her elbows are beautiful. I gotta lose some weight, she kept thinking, and stop eating Concha's food.

Vivian Madrid walked into Hector's office without knocking. Hector, with both feet on top of his desk, was leaning back on his office chair and talking to Oscar Rubio, discussing his departure and when to expect him in Los Angeles. When he saw Vivian enter his office, he sat up, said quickly to Oscar, Gotta go, call you back, and hung up the phone. He jumped off his chair as if his house was on fire and walked rapidly to meet her at the door.

Come on in, Vivian. Take a chair, he said, as if he had been expecting her, not knowing why he was getting all excited. No, thanks. I rather stand, she said, all business. As you wish, said Hector, offering a weak smile. Is your mother OK?

I need a ride to California, and since you're going, I want to go with you, said Vivian, ignoring the question about her mother. She was not here to discuss her mother; she wanted to make that perfectly clear. I will pay my way—gas, food, whatever—you name it.

This little girl doesn't mince words, thought Hector. Like mother, like daughter. He had not seen Vivian since she made her first communion years ago. She had worn the most elegant white dress, and her hair had been done by pros, but that was expected. She was more attractive than he had imagined, but why shouldn't she be? She was born with the genes of beautiful parents, and she was not to be denied. And here she was, a young lady, asking him for a ride to California. Life was so full of tricks, he thought.

Are you sure you don't want to sit? asked Hector again, in an apologetic manner.

No, I'm fine. You sit, if you care to.

Don't mind if I do. And he walked back behind his desk to his chair and sat, his eyes on her.

Listen, Vivian, Hector continued in earnest. Don't take this personal, but I can't give you a ride to California for the simple reason I'm not going straight to California.

I don't mind, said Vivian, dejected.

No, it's not that simple, Vivian, said Hector, trying hard not to sound cold. I'm going to make a couple of stops in Arizona and Nevada, and I don't know for how many days. The people I'm going to stay with are not the kind a young lady like yourself would feel comfortable with—or safe with, for that matter. I'm not saying it's a criminal element, but there will be a lot of heavy drinking and mostly men. You know—anything can happen. And I do not want to have to explain, if something was to happen, to your mother or godfather, Juan Jose.

Hector told Vivian this made-up itinerant travel plan to discourage her from wanting to tag along. He was going straight to Los Angeles. And he was going to do all the driving at night and alone. He was transporting an illegal cargo across state lines, and didn't want to attract attention. If Vivian came along for the ride, and Delfina did not approve, she could send Juan Jose after them. He didn't even want to think of the consequences. Even without Juan Jose, Delfina knew some of the older cops from Las Flores. She could make up a lie, they would go after him, and there was a bust in the making. Other than that, he would love to take Vivian to California; who wouldn't? He'd be alone with her for eight hundred miles and even show her the sights along the way and once there. But he couldn't do it; he would not compromise Vivian's future—or anyone else's, for that matter—because he wanted to cash in on some illicit gain.

Why don't you ask your godfather, Juan Jose, to take you to California? asked Hector in an appeasing tone.

Vivian was ready to leave. She knew the old gruff was not going to bend, and she wasn't used to asking more than once for anything.

My mother, said Vivian, in her frosty demeanor, would never permit Juan Jose to take me. And Juan Jose would never leave my mother, unless he had to. Besides, there are other ways of getting to California.

Well, again, I'm sorry, Vivian, that I couldn't help you, but if there is anything else I can do for you, just say the word. Hector stood up to give her a hug or a handshake, but Vivian turned and walked out without saying a word.

While Vivian was inside the community center talking to Hector, Juan Jose, her godfather, was wiping dust off his new Buick. He had parked as close as he could to the front door of the center so Vivian wouldn't have to walk too far. After he finished dusting the car, he sat on the hood with arms crossed, exposing his muscular biceps. He was wearing a white cotton shirt with the sleeves cut off, and a large tattoo of a skull with a dagger shaped like a cross embedded in the skull could be seen on his right shoulder. The skull had beads of red dropping from the holes that were once eyes, with some letters that were faded under the skull. He wore tapered khakis and Mezlan dress sandals from Spain and a large watch with turquoise mounted on the silver band clasped to his wrist. It was a hot day, and the hood of the car was hot, but he didn't mind. He was hatless as always, and with his aviator sunglasses and buzzed haircut, he resembled a bronze statue of a contemporary gunslinger. He didn't say a word to anyone leaving or entering the center. He turned his head only when another car parked next to his. He gave a look, warning them to be careful when they opened the doors of their cars. He hated it when people dinged his car. He was especially cognizant of impulsive teenagers and children who were always in a hurry and slammed doors open and shut.

Juan Jose was a quiet but intimidating presence. He said few words, but he usually didn't have to say anything. His body language and facial expression were enough. When rowdy teens or young adults approached the center to enter and saw him perched on the hood of the Buick, they shut up or lowered their voices. When adult men or women, came close to him, in most cases, they averted their eyes, not knowing what the man was capable of. Juan Jose took it all in stride, knowing the power he held over these simple folks. He never asked for it; it was just the way it had to be. People knew who to mess with and who was off limits. They made up their own minds about what was for real and what was not.

Juan Jose was concerned about Vivian leaving to California. He was unhappy with the fact he couldn't take her and look after her, as he had done even before she was born. His main goal in life had been to protect Vivian and her mother, Delfina Madrid. That was the promise he had made to his best friend, their father and her husband, before his premature death. Now he was torn because he couldn't leave Delfina alone, especially after the death of Danny, her beloved son. He took some responsibility for Danny's death, but Delfina never allowed him to discipline the boy. He was aware the allowance he was giving Danny was used to buy drugs. But if he didn't give Danny any money, Danny would have turned to stealing, and that would have only added insult to injury. He tried, but Delfina, the mother, was the one who had to lay down the law, but she was in denial. There was little he could do but do his best to keep the poison away from Vivian.

Juan Jose was thinking about Vivian going with Hector to California. He didn't trust Hector. He remembered Hector and his pal Oscar Rubio; a pair of mama's boys. Oscar had become a writer, and Juan Jose had read his books, but Hector—Hector never changed; that was his opinion. He always remembered Hector as a lightweight. Hector could never shake and bake in the world of men like he could. He was always hiding behind words, using words like a sword to cut through reality and avoid the truth of being a man, a real man. Some called him clever, but Juan Jose called him a coward: a man who could only take the good and not the ugly, a man who loved the summer but not the heat—something that was integral to its essence—was a question mark and not to be trusted, he thought. Maybe he shouldn't be so hard on Hector, he reasoned. After all, he seemed to be doing good work running the center. It was just that he couldn't see Vivian going to California with him, and he couldn't put a finger on why, or if he did, he didn't like to think about it. So he waited in the hot sun for Vivian to come out of the center and tell him where she wanted to go next.

When Juan Jose saw Vivian walk out of the community center, he gave a sigh of relief. He knew right away she had been turned down by Hector. No go, he thought. He knew his little girl very well: the way she carried herself, the look on her face, and her habit of never asking for anything from anyone more than once. He jumped off the hood of the Buick as if he suddenly felt the heat and opened the door for her. She always sat in front, along with him. By her looks and body language, no questions were to be asked; that meant no conversation of any kind. When she was in this kind of mood, she would listen to her favorite rock station. When she was in a talkative mood, she would listen to her favorite Shubert tape. He loved it when they talked about books. One of his favorites was The Arabian Nights. He had purchased in London an expensive leather-bound copy, translated by Sir Richard Burton, and given it to her when she turned seventeen. It gave him a lot of pleasure to tell her about the places he had visited that were mentioned in the book—places like Bagdad and Basra in Iraq and other ancient cities. Of course he never discussed what he had been doing there, besides taking in the sights, but there was no need to. He never tired of hearing her talk of Scheherazade and how she kept the king interested with her tales of adventure and love. He was proud of her because she loved the poetry in the book and worked at its meaning.

Juan Jose was driving cast on Santa Teresa and then cut a left on San Albino, heading north. All she said when she got in the car was "home" and played with the radio. Juan Jose was in a happy mood. He didn't want to show it, but he was glad Hector had refused her request; not many people would say no to his little princess. And that was a problem and had always been a problem. She could get what she wanted from almost anyone. Fortunately, she wasn't aware of the power she had over people yet, or she didn't care, content to stay in her own world and not bother with others. But that was changing, and that was what worried Juan Jose. She was a woman now, and Delfina nor anyone else could stop her from seeking her true purpose in life. Her obsession with being a model and an actress troubled him. He knew she would be exploited by those assholes in Los Angeles and have nothing to show for it but grief, but there was little he could do about it except enjoy the time they had together. Anyway, he thought, he had a surprise for her. He wanted to smile but didn't dare. Once home and her mood changed, he was going to give her Kahlil Gibran's The Prophet. That book would keep her occupied for a while, and he was hoping they could go into a deep discussion about Al Mustafa, the Chosen One.

CHAPTER THIRTY

Romero drove north on the Old Albuquerque Road. He was in a bad mood. He hadn't slept all that great, and the cut on his calf was still bothering him. Today was his last in this shithole of a town, he had decided last night. He was going to take a loss, and that didn't help his mood any. But maybe, he thought, he could squeeze some cash from the street vendors in Denver when he returned. His reception from the big boys was going to be less than cordial, but that couldn't be helped. With Sammy Q. gone, he didn't have many leads to work on. He didn't believe for one minute that Bryan was going to be any help, of any kind. He was exhausted by the heat, eating crappy food, and sleeping in smelly beds. The cut on his calf was also a concern. It didn't seem to be healing, although the doctor had assured him it was OK.

It was late morning, close to noon, as he drove slowly, checking out the expanse of the desert floor east of the Old Albuquerque Road. If he kept driving north, he would eventually hit Albuquerque, but that seemed like an endless journey, although it really wasn't. He was tired of the dry landscape, of the dry soil that spread out like patches of old, tattered carpet on the thirsty earth, under a clear sky and a flaming sun, relentless in its passing. Romero lacked the imagination and patience to see and treasure what the area had in abundance. There was, for instance, for all to see, the desert paintbrush with its flowers of brilliant color, bright orange or red tips. The sagebrush, a shrub with small white or yellow flowers, smiling in the sun, which together created a bouquet of natural beauty. There was the lovely sotol, or the desert spoon, as some called it, with its full clusters of white flowers and a long silver stalk in the middle, reaching for the sky. The ocotillo, or flaming sword, with its crown root that could grow thirty feet high, with crimson blooms clustered together like the gathering of nobility at the crown. And of course there was the cholla cane cactus, with its spiny, cylindrical, fleshy stems growing on rocky flats or slopes as ground creepers, shrubs, or even trees, with their white, purple, or yellow flowers on fleshy stems like precious gems pleasant to the naked eye. Plus, there were countless other beauties of nature that unfolded during this time of the year, and one didn't have to be a botanist to relish the panorama of a sophisticated and diverse universe. But to Romero, a man confounded with an environment he couldn't come to grips with, angry and confused because his quest had become an unpredictable challenge, his eyes only saw a hot, dry, inhospitable country, inhabited by people he sometimes believed were from another planet.

Romero drove slowly on the crumbling asphalt of the Old Albuquerque Road. He'd scan the area for the last time, and that was it. He was going to drive on the old road north, hopeful he might see something. His destination was an old barn he had seen when he was last with Sammy Q. not too far from Snake Town. They hadn't checked it out because they were in the search for Lencho Reyes, and after finding Lencho, they were in no mood to rummage around in an old barn. That was the last place he was going to search. The chiva was no place to be found, and he was low on cash. It was time for him to return to Denver and report his position to his brokers. In a way, he was relieved; he needed to go back home among his own people. He wanted to find out about his babe, Alicia Juarez, and his standing with the main capo. For all he knew, he might find himself out in the street, selling chiva to junkies. Shit, he thought, that was the pits. He couldn't do that. He had a reputation to uphold; besides he had made some enemies in the mean streets, and reprisals were always a way of life in his line of work. And yet he couldn't help but smile. He was going home to the Mile-High City where he could breathe clear, clean air and see green again. But he missed his mother's cooking more— spaghetti with giant meatballs in a sauce fit for kings and green-chili pork enchiladas. He was tired of eating hotdogs and chips and other garbage he was forced to eat to save money. He missed the perks that came along with the job as the capo's main driver. He got a bundle of cash, hundred dollar bills, when he drove the big boss to the East or West Coast on business in the Lincoln Town car, a smooth ride, like sailing on a calm lake. His boss was leery of leaving any paper trail with his name on it, so he allowed Romero to handle all the transactions in cash. They stayed in the high-end hotels and motels of his choosing. He ordered the wine and other spirits in the high-priced restaurants they frequented; even though he didn't drink any, he had a taste for expensive alcohol. He tipped generously; it wasn't his money after all, and they were always seated in discreet areas of the clubs and casinos they visited along the way. He was known to be clever, especially in the financial arena, and even though the capo had attorneys and accountants at his calling, the capo sometimes asked him money-related questions. Romero had never completed his degree in business, like he told everyone he had. He was a few credits short, but he still felt he was a gem in the topsy-turvy world of unpolished stones, although he might have been alone in that assumption.

OK, Romero kept on thinking, what if he did lose his executive position, and they kicked him out of the organization after all the good work he had done for them? What the hell; he still had a future. He wasn't going to lie down and play dead; hell, no. Maybe the Denver PD could utilize a man of his talents. Be a cop—why not, carry a gun in public. Mess with people, and get paid for it, but the paperwork was a hassle, he figured. If he executed a lowlife as a cop, he'd have to fill out a mountain of paperwork and write all kinds of reports. If he put down a scumbag now, that was his business, and he didn't have to write a report to nobody because in his line of work, usually nobody gave a shit. But he would look good in uniform and pick up the babes, he thought—maybe even a rich bitch to secure his future. But he would only go to a certain age. The ripe fruit he left to the desperate ones, those fellows who would screw a dog just to screw. He happened to be on the privileged list where scoring pussy had never been an obstacle, the fortunate ones who turned away pussy because their plates were always full. But the discipline would be a bitch, he considered. He would slap the first asshole who would bark orders at him. That was why he could never be a cop. Maybe a professional hitman; he was that good, he assured himself. But what if he was approached and offered cash by an undercover cop to execute another undercover cop? An attempted hit on a cop promised big time in the slammer, and everyone hated you, from the judge to the bailiff. You were branded the worst of the worst, close to a child molester. But behind prison walls, among the criminal element, you would have some respect— maybe enough to help survive the early brutal years. Romero finally said Fuck, out loud. He never realized jobs had so many contradictions and scratched his head, feeling for the imaginary bald spot. He came to the conclusion that he was not a nine-to-five guy; it was a long nightmare the eight-hour slave. He might as well stay where he was and forget about changing occupations; it could be a health hazard and was not necessary to survive.

Romero had packed all his belongings in his truck, checked out of the sleazy motel, and was on his way out and away. From the Old Albuquerque Road, he would take Piñon Street or Esperanza west all the way to Highway 25 and push north all the way to Denver, stopping only for gas—that was his plan after checking out the barn. Goodbye Las Flores, he mumbled under his breath, not wanting to get too excited because he still had a long drive ahead of him.

Romero was not too far from Snake Town, still driving north. The vast area east of the Old Albuquerque Road was uninhabited desert, but unknown to Romero and many others, the land was being bought and sold for future development. He made an effort to stay focused on the task before him, but it was difficult because the anxiety was getting the better of him. He stopped the truck suddenly. He had almost run over a dead rattlesnake in the middle of the road. He geared in reverse, stopped, got off, and approached the dead snake cautiously, with a plan to cut off the tail with the rattles and take it back to Denver and show it off as a conversation piece. Of course he would never tell the truth and say he cut it off a dead rattler; that would make him look like a pussy. As he advanced on the dead rattlesnake with pocketknife in hand, he realized it had been hit by a car or truck as the poor thing attempted to cross the road. He also noticed numerous wasps all over the snake in a feeding frenzy. The yellow jackets were feeding on the roadkill, and there was no way they were going to allow Romero to get close to their meal and cut off his prize. Romero said, No way. He didn't plan to fight the wasps for the rattle. He figured the wasps had rattlesnake poison on their stingers, and he wanted no part of that. He couldn't take his eyes off the miniature bloodsucking vultures making a snack out of the once-proud snake. The wasps were going crazy in the hot sun, flying around the big rattler, tearing into the meat without a care in the world and defying Romero, who was standing close to cut into their dish and find out if he too would be added to their menu. Romero looked at the condition of the snake, shook his head, and thought, What a way to go; I'm a two-legged rattler and will never go like that, never. He turned and headed for the truck. Once on the road again, he passed what appeared to be a couple of scarecrows in black. He looked again, realized they were people, and geared in reverse. They were sitting on the dirt a short distance from the road, facing east. He stopped the truck, rolled down the window, and stared at them, not knowing what to say. He parked right in front of them but didn't get out of the truck. The woman, dressed in a black smock, was painting on a square, framed canvas placed on a small easel. She was using crude paintbrushes and had tiny metal containers filled with assorted colors of paint scattered around her. The man, also in black, with a scraggy salt-and-pepper beard—more salt than pepper—and unbrushed hair to his shoulders was placing pebbles and miniature sticks on top of each other, building a lopsided pyramid. Then he grabbed dirt with his hands and slowly released it on top of the uneven little structure. He repeated the same function in a hypnotic fashion, spreading his legs further apart when he methodically started a new pile.

The man and the woman continued to enjoy their diversion, oblivious of Romero and his truck. Romero was not used to the idea of being ignored, especially by desert ragamuffins.

Finally, he said, in a loud voice, Hello, is anybody home?

Shonofa and the Flying Man, Santiago, continued to ignore him.

Why are you so rude? he asked, losing his temper, not used to being ignored.

Shonofa, the woman in black, raised her eyes from her canvas and said in a moderate tone, You are the one who is rude, my child. You are blocking my view of that crest overgrown with blue yucca that I am attempting to capture.

Oh, so you do talk? asked Romero, wanting to laugh at the crazy bitch who was playing artist in the hot sun in the middle of nowhere. Listen, I just need some information, and I'll be out of your way in a flash. Have you by any chance seen a package lying around hereabouts, unattended? Or someone finding a package and carrying it off? I'll pay you some money for any information that will help me recover my—my package. You two seem to spend a lot of time out here, am I right?

Shonofa, in the same tempo, looking beyond him, said, We do not want or need your money. If you want information, it will not cost you a penny. We have not seen or heard any human movement in Elysium. And she gestured with the paintbrush in her hand to include the area around them. The only movement and sound is the whisper of the wind and the sweet music of the desert birds, but I am aware you have no interest in any of that.

Romero was losing his patience. He was hot, and the exhaust from the truck was bothering him. He turned off the motor, tired of being nice and polite. He wondered from what nuthouse these two had escaped from.

What about Granddaddy? And he made a motion with is head toward Santiago, the Flying Man. Santiago was still sitting on the dirt constructing miniature pyramids. Has he seen anything, or does he spend his days building heaps of dirt close to his crotch and pretending he's growing a bigger cock?

Shonofa stood up without using her hands, the paintbrush still in her right hand, holding onto it as if it was a magic wand. She looked straight at Romero for the first time. Mind your indecent mouth, she said in a dignified voice. What Santiago, my man, is designing you have not yet evolved enough to comprehend. So go back to your den of apes, and scratch for lice, as your kind tends to do.

Romero was not amused. "Ape" was one word he didn't appreciate being called. The bitch was not as crazy as he thought her to be, and now that she was standing, she didn't look as fragile as she had when he first approached her. The man resembled a pile of dry bones in black clothing, but the woman appeared solid and even healthy looking. He stayed in the truck with no plans to get out and talk to them. He couldn't afford another mishap like at La Conga's. He didn't know what the woman had hidden up her sleeve, and he didn't want to find out either. He was too close to going home, too close to eating his mother's food, sitting around the dining room table, and having a civilized conversation with friends and relatives to allow this freaky woman and her oddball mongrel boyfriend to impede his plans.

I tried to be nice, he said, incensed and offended. I offered you money to help you out for any information you could provide. That's all I asked; nothing more.

And I told you we don't need or want your bloody money, she answered in a restrained but unwavering voice.

When he heard "bloody money," Romero was outraged and almost got out of the truck but thought better of it. His forehead furrowed, and his lips twisted as he said, I—I—have a mind to—to—

To what? Shonofa completed his sentence. To hurt us, to beat us up, or maybe to murder us in a violent spree and leave us out here for the animals to devour? And she placed the paintbrush gently on the easel. A small, greasy bag appeared in her hand from somewhere. She shook the bag, and the bones inside rattled as if awakened from a deep slumber. She looked at Romero and said, Los Huesos de la Muerte: the Bones of Death.

Romero laughed out loud and said, Think I'm gonna fall for that? You fucking witch.

Shonofa looked at Santiago, still sitting on the dirt, and said, He doesn't believe. Santiago gave her a nod with his chin, not saying a word.

Shonofa opened the bag and held it with her left hand up to her nose. With her other hand, she pressed her index finger to her nostril and blew with her open nostril into the bag. She did the same with the opposite nostril. She held the bag, still open, with her two hands and blew into it with her mouth. She talked to the bones inside the bag, words that Romero couldn't hear, and even if he could, he wouldn't know what she was saying.

You think you're gonna scare me with those chicken bones? I told you I don't believe in that crap.

Whether you believe or not is irrelevant, my son. When the Bones of Death touch you or something that belongs to you, you forfeit your life. You will die a miserable death for the pain you have caused others, and there's nothing you can do about it.

I'm not your son, you old hag, responded Romero, talking tough but a little unsure.

You will be nobody's son except Satan's. She took the bones out of the bag and flung them at Romero, hitting the door of the truck below the windshield. The bones splattered on the door and then slid down slowly to the dirt, leaving a brownish stain of a misshapen likeness of a ghastly corpse with arms elongated toward the ground, as if reaching for something invisible to the naked eye.

Romero looked down at the stain on the door of the truck and the pieces of bones on the ground, which seemed to be squirming like worms on the dirt. But he attributed that to the glare of the sun. The sun was playing a ruse on his eyes—that was all, he thought.

Next time you play that trick, I'm gonna make you wash my truck, he said, because he had nothing else to say.

There won't be a next time for you, Mister, Shonofa replied, calm as ever. Your days are numbered, and you can bet money on that.

Romero geared the truck and pulled out fast, spinning the tires and leaving the erratic couple in the dust. He drove at high speed for a short distance and then slowed down, thinking of going back and teaching those two clowns a lesson. But then he said, Fuck them; it's not worth the trouble. He was nervous about the encounter but would never admit it. He was still a product of his culture, and although his mother never deliberated about the throwing of the Bones of Death, his grandmother blamed that deed for the death of his grandfather. She would detail the grisly incident to anyone who would listen. The first time he heard her talk about it, he was six or seven, even younger, and it was over some property that he had been cursed with the Bones of Death. Years later when his grandmother was older and the images in her mind were a lot more convoluted, she claimed her husband had been damned over a woman, leaving her a widow at a young age. She went into explicit details concerning brujas and the black arts after dinner on cold winter nights as the family huddled around the wood stove. The young Romero held tight to his mother's arm as his grandmother filled his head with stories of the headless man on horseback searching for his head and his assassins, at midnight, and people taking the forms of animals in the night to create mischief. The abduction of infants by Satan and his army of witches unsettled him the most. His grandmother went on about how the Master of Darkness marked the infants with his claw on the eyebrow and how that mark would rescind the one of holy baptism the child received through the church. Even though Romero was not a baby, he feared being taken by witches and rebaptized by the devil. That was the source of the many nightmares and the consistent bedwetting that didn't stop until he was almost ten years old or older. The nightmares and the bedwetting stopped when his maternal grandmother passed. The terrifying tales ended and with time were forgotten. And that was a good thing for Romero because at ten years, he was a big boy, too big to be reeking of urine. Some of those stories were still embedded in his subconscious, and fragments could surface and alter his perception, as happened in the Swamps when he did away with Sammy Q.

Romero continued driving, attempting not to think of anything but the task at hand. He didn't want to think of things he didn't want to deal with at this point. He was biting his lower lip almost to the point of bleeding, a habit left behind from his teenage years, or so he had come to believe. Why was he doing that again? he asked himself. Why was he doing shit he used to do back then? Like scratching his head when he really didn't need to? Or pulling on his lips as if they were made out of rubber? These were habits of his youth he had worked so hard to overcome. The awkwardness and clumsiness that he had to go through when growing up, he recalled, did a number on his head. He was so tall and big, always running into kids or bumping into furniture. "Ape, ape, dig a hole and fall in dead," hounded him until he learned to fight back and hurt kids. Then when he was in the sixth and seventh grade, he began to transform into a tall, good-looking teen who could use his size to his advantage. He was no longer the ape but the guy to be with, popular with both boys and girls. But he never forgot or forgave the name callers, and he punished them one by one and never stopped until he was feared by one and all and secured a huge reputation as a bully. All through high school, he had his way with girls and beat on guys that gave him even a wrong look. He wasn't popular anymore, although he believed he was. His only friends were thugs and putas, the outcasts who couldn't be relied on as true friends. By the time he was in college, he was beyond making friends and became a loner, making small change as the muscle for a small-time mafia group that sold drugs to college students and needed an enforcer to collect money owed. After college he graduated to the ranks of big dope, big money, and a brutal criminal element. He joined a lawless professional enterprise and worked up the ranks until he was sipping coffee with the main capo—but as an employee, not as a member of the family. So he was always an outsider, and he never felt it more than now, driving alone on a lonely desert road. He even missed Sammy Q. At least with Sammy he could converse, bullshit, or something. But now, he thought—and he hated to think about all this shit—one mishap after another, and this desert road and this desert town never seemed to end. Tears almost came to his eyes as he looked left and then right and saw nothing but stretches of never- ending dry landscape that looked all the same to him. The loneliness seeped into his blood and traveled like a plague through his veins until it exhausted every particle of his being and dragged him down to a dark place of little hope. The fact of being alone in this world of brown dirt and brown scrub, a world with few green trees, darkened his outlook and saddened him to a point of wanting to scream out the truck window that he was a man, a man with a heart and feelings, like any other man, for the entire world to hear. But he didn't cry out; What was the point? he thought. There was no one out there to hear anything. He kept it all in and sucked on his lips as he saw the barn in the distance standing like a decaying battleship in the middle of a lunar crater.

The barn, he repeated, the barn—like a child when he spots an ice cream truck. The barn was located on an abandoned farm site and was the only thing standing. The house had been demolished as were all other sheds and buildings. Any farm equipment had been removed years ago, and nothing was left but the old broken-down fencing and dried-up fruit trees. The barn was ravished by time and neglect. The roof on half of the barn had rotted and collapsed, leaving a huge hole on the side facing west. The huge front doors were missing, resembling a toothless mouth facing the road as he drove up, welcoming all strangers to enter and visit the bats as well as the ghosts within.

Oh, shit, what is this? Romero wondered as he drove off the Old Albuquerque Road as the road curved to the northwest. He cut a right and headed straight to the barn on a rutted, weed-choked road that had retired years ago. The only reason he was going to stop was that he needed to take a piss, and the old barn was as good a place as any. He wasn't even going to look around and waste more of his precious time. He stopped the truck, looked around, got out of the truck, and walked slowly and deliberately, keeping his eyes on the withering, door less barn, worried that the walls or ceiling might collapse on him and mess up his plans of going home.

CHAPTER THIRTY-ONE

ike, getting up late as usual, left his house and drove straight to Mr. Bailey's. He picked up the fake chiva from his locker in Mr. Baily's garage to show Ramon he still had it. He didn't stay and talk to Mr. Bailey, as was usually the case, because he was in a hurry, but he did offer him a couple of dollars to pare down his tab. Mr. Baily was all smiles when he set his eyes on Mike. In return Mr. Bailey offered Mike the little dog he had been whittling on for some time and said to forget the money and just come in a couple of hours and work it off. Mike didn't get if it was a compliment or a put-down with Mr. Bailey; it was sometimes difficult to follow his stride. But Mike said he'd think about it, whereas before he would have jumped at the suggestion of a couple of hours of labor—paid labor.

Mike put his raggedy car in gear and left Mr. Bailey behind, raising his hands, showing a small piece of wood in one hand and his carving knife in the other, with a smile on his face as wide as the Rio Bravo. Mike opened the glove and pitched the dog carving in, which resembled a tiny pony more than any dog he had ever seen. The carved dog, or pony, fell on top of four or five others that had also been pitched in the same way at different times, also donated by Mr. Bailey. Damn, Mike said, I need new wheels. I'm gonna get me a good car soon; it better be soon, or I'm screwed. And he drove to Ramon's in search of his friend and the only one who could muck up his plans.

Mike left Mr. Bailey's garage and drove on Mora north to Esperanza. On Esperanza he would cut a right and drive east. He felt this was the quickest way to reach Ramon's house and catch him before Ramon started on his daily adventures. Mike still had to convince him, if he was home, to take a ride to the river to dump the chiva. Ramon had to be assured that Mike had no bad intentions in mind, like drowning him in the muddy waters so he could keep all the cash from the chiva. Of course Ramon had no reason to fear any foul play from

Mike, but Ramon had a huge imagination, as Mike knew so well. Mike was aware that Ramon's world was changing and changing fast, and as the differences in his observations confused him more and more, many of his images had a double meaning. Ramon might be on that voyage, and he would be the first and last to admit it. Mike still believed Ramon's imagination might save him from the nuthouse—not a good place for anyone. He just didn't want to be around when it happened; that it was going to happen, he had no doubt. The odds were against Ramon. The only thing that could save him was his art, but Ramon was too conceited or immature to understand that artists can do and say whatever they want. Mike had attempted to convince Ramon that as an artist, he could live in different worlds, live an unusual life and get away with it. Society leaves artists alone, he told him on many occasions. That's how you can live, vato, Mike had insisted. You can live in a community that's more sensitive to the needs of its people or stay in the environment you are now and live among people who give a shit if you are dead or alive.

Mike cut a right on Esperanza and drove east to Ramon's house. The traffic wasn't too bad, with a car or truck here and there. Ramon's a hard nut to crack, he said out loud, listening to loud rock music. He has turned into a Brazil nut and will never crack, unless it's by his own hand. You hear that, Ramon? Mike was almost yelling as he drove, his nerves bunching up on him, even though he would never admit it. Mike was talking to Ramon in a loud voice because he believed Ramon could tune in and hear him. Ramon could be a hundred miles away, and Mike was positive Ramon could pick up on his voice and recognize the anger or lack of anger in every phrase he uttered. Ramon, at times, to play with Mike's head, would repeat words Mike had said in his absence without missing a beat. Mike thought it was creepy, and he warned him not to pull that shit with other people because they might be more insensitive, panic, and accuse him of having a relationship with the devil. Mike advised him to avoid getting a reputation that would single him out; the dark force in his corner would make his life a little more difficult, especially in the Eastside barrio.

Mike saw the cluster of rust-colored government-subsidized housing on the right side of Esperanza, a block from Santos Street, which ran north and south. He slowed down and drove into the small driveway of the first house, the house where Ramon and his mother lived. The house, like all others, was small, constructed with wood, plastered, and then painted. Like rusty nails in a glass of clean water, came to his mind as he parked the car and turned off the radio. Ramon used to say that at times, and in some of his artwork, he would paint a glass of clear water with rusty nails in the bottom of the glass. Ramon would never explain to anyone the meaning behind the rusty nails and clean water. Mike asked him once, and Ramon only said it was his house and no more. Mike waited in the car for Ramon to come out, as he always did. If he didn't come out in around five minutes, Mike would lean on the horn, but not aggressively. If that didn't work, he would have to get out of the car and knock on the front door, and that was the most difficult one because he was going to see Ramon's mother whether he liked it or not. Ramon's mother, and Mike concurred with others, was a saintly woman, a woman who could do no wrong but whose emotional makeup was at times upsetting.

Ramon and his mother were extraordinary, thought Mike, as he waited for Ramon. Everyone loved them, but no one helped them. Ramon's mother never got over the setback when her husband, Ramon's father, gave her a beating and left her with Ramon in her belly. She was left alone with relatives on old black-and-white photographs scattered throughout the house. Their faces were pale, and the men sported heavy, dark mustaches that covered their upper lips and almost went into their mouths, while some of the women had their hair behind their heads in a tight bun. Their clothes were funeral dark and ill fitting, too tight on some and loose fitting on others, and Mike guessed they were borrowed, but he couldn't be sure. To Mike they were animus who came alive at midnight and engaged in conversation about the good old days. He did not particularly care about visiting with Ramon's mom. The house was always too dark and gloomy, and the men and women in the photos seemed to glare in the dim light, as if angered with the intrusion.

OK, said Mike. Here goes the horn. And he placed his hand on the horn tab, and the horn pulled out a weak tweet. He hesitated to use the car horn because of the tweet it put out. He had attempted to fix it but gave up on it; couldn't find the part in the junkyard. It wasn't a very masculine sound coming from a masculine car, he thought. Besides, he didn't want any jokes coming from the guys over it. The jokes could get downright nasty, as well as personal; it was a no-win situation. He was ready to go knock on the door with a feeling in his gut Ramon wasn't home, and he'd have to chase him all over town, a job he didn't want to take on. Please be home, Ramon, please, just this one time. I need you, brother, Mike whispered as he approached the door and knocked.

Mike waited for Ramon or someone to open the door and tell him what he already knew but wasn't positive about. He practiced in his mind what he was going to say if Ramon's mother answered the door. Jesus, what could he really say? he thought. Once she laid those big, sad brown eyes on him and started telling her story, dripping with despair, it was not easy to run away, as much as he wanted to. To her, Mike imagined it was like a psych session, but without the bullshit. And of course he wanted to hear about what other people had on their plates and what devils or angels planned their itinerary.

Ramon's mother opened the door abruptly, and Mike saw she was already dabbing her eyes with a washcloth—not good, he thought. She was in the same house robe she had been wearing the last time he visited. Her long hair was graying but still thick, hanging loose over her shoulders with that brush-you-later look. She seemed older than she actually was, smaller and fragile in her cloth slippers, but Mike figured that the wear and tear of raising Ramon had taken its toll. Her skin was pale, the color of wax. She had few wrinkles, but her face was puffy and reddish around the eyes. Her eyes were large and almond brown, set deep in her face. She had the sad eyes of a woman who had suffered and shed many tears. She projected in her eyes defeat and misery, but they were like magnets for Mike, and he could never avoid those pools of tepid water.

Miguel, hijo, pasa, she said in a voice full of desperation. She closed the door behind them and led Mike to a modest sitting room, small but comfortable. The drapes were drawn, and the whole house was dark in order to keep it cool against the sun that was already kicking ass. Sit, por favor. And she pointed to a puffed-up couch.

Thanks, but no thanks—I have to go. I'm looking for Ramon, Mike said, as he looked into her eyes. Even in the dim light, Mike could still see her large brown eyes on him, pleading for him to sit and listen to her tell what was going through her mind. Mike felt so bad seeing her in the condition she was in that he almost sat on the overstuffed couch, but he knew the reason he was here and why he needed to find Ramon.

Is Ramon home? he asked, attempting not to sound too rushed or demanding. I need to talk to him.

No, Ramon is not home, Miguel. and she dabbed the tears with the washcloth. He has not been home for a couple of nights now. I was just going to call you. I'm beside myself with worry, Miguel. I called the hospital and the police station, but no word from Ramon. That boy is pushing me, Miguel. Ever since the accident, all he talks about is California; California is all I hear. He didn't lose nothing in California and will find nothing there, nothing but trouble. He has it in his mind his good-for-nothing father will help him, give him a hand, ha—he will be disappointed, very disappointed. He is angry because he wants money, Miguel. I tell him I have no money to give him, nada. And he leaves without saying where or with who, not calling or nothing. Look at me, Miguel. I'm a bundle of nerves, and my medication is running low, but does he care? I don't think so. Don't get me wrong, Miguel—I love my son only as a mother can. And I would sell the house, if only it was mine to sell, and give him all the money, all of it, to spend as he wished. But sadly we rent, and I haven't worked in years, so I can't even borrow money. And I cannot make him understand that or anything reasonable, for that matter. She dabbed her eyes again but kept them on Mike the whole time.

Mike felt uncomfortable, as he knew he would. Her eyes had been on him the minute he entered the house like the tragic, unhappy eyes of a woman in mourning. He wanted to promise her money, but he couldn't. He didn't even know if money was the answer. He turned his anger and frustration to Ramon instead. Little shit, he thought, didn't even realize what he was doing to his mother. Maybe he knew but didn't care, which was worse.

I will find Ramon and talk to him, said Mike, wanting to leave before he compromised himself. Don't worry, Estela. That was her name, but Mike didn't like to call her by her first name. Now it didn't matter.

Please do, Miguel, she said, holding on to the dish rag in one hand and her emotions in the other, but not doing a good job at it. Ramon listens to you more than anyone, she continued, tears rolling down her pale cheeks and her voice barely audible. You are his only true friend. Please find him, Miguel, and bring him home where he belongs. He belongs here with me. I am the only one who can take care of his needs, as you well know.

Mike left Ramon's house pissed off, not only at the way Ramon treated his own mother, Estela, but the way Ramon was treating him. Ramon knew where he lived, Mike thought. Why the fuck didn't he come over to his house and talk about his problems like he used to before, instead of taking off and making the situation more difficult than it had to be? He was glad that the chiva was by now in California. He had taken it out of the hiding place and delivered it to Hector at the time planned without a hitch. The only thing Hector said as he put Tupi in Mike's car was, Don't call me; I'll call you, as if Mike had a number to call him; for all he knew, the chiva was going east instead of west, but there was shit he could do about it. All he could do, which was nothing, was to wait for a letter or a call, wish and wait, wait and wish. But for now he had to find Ramon and take him to the river and dump the fake chiva. He had to show Ramon the actual dumping of the fake chiva in the river, bag and all. So if Ramon wanted to play any games—Mike was sure he didn't, but if he did—the game was on him.

Mike reversed out of Ramon's driveway, made a U-turn, and headed west on Esperanza, thinking that maybe Ramon was downtown at Jimmy's pool hall. No. He reconsidered. Too early, and those punks at the pool hall would give him too much grief. Perhaps he's at Sammy's, he wagered, but the action at Sammy's was relatively quiet since Sammy Q. had disappeared. Tomasito was attempting to keep up the business, but only the most loyal customers stayed on, waiting for Sammy's return. Besides, Tomasito was a minor and he didn't have the connections Sammy had to buy what he needed to keep customers interested. Tomasito had mentioned to Mike when they met by coincidence downtown that some relatives of Granny had visited and wanted to put Granny in a home and sell the house. They scurried out of the house like scared rats when Granny cocked and pointed the pistol at them. Sammy had disappeared without a trace, and he had never been gone this long before—Granny told everyone who would listen. He would never leave Granny for more than a couple of days, and that was rare. Granny had gone to the police to report him missing, but they ignored her, telling her that Sammy was a big boy and that he would show up any day. No, he thought, Ramon wouldn't go to Sammy's now, with him gone. Ramon couldn't stand Tomasito; he never gave any reason, but Ramon was like that. When Ramon was at Sammy's, which was not often, he wouldn't drink booze or do drugs. He would only listen to the conversations and observe the folks exaggerate their stories. And that's why they liked him: he kept his opinions to himself, kept his mouth shut, and listened.

No, he wouldn't go to Sammy's, Mike thought. And he would not even think of going to Vivian's house, unless he had some money to show Vivian. Except—no, he thought, it was crazy even to think about it. Ramon would never cut a deal with anyone and tell them he was holding onto the chiva. No way. Ramon wouldn't do him like that, Mike reasoned, not Ramon. Anyone else, yes, but not Ramon, never. But if he did show up at Vivian's broke, and Vivian was in a bad mood, one word to Juan Jose, and putango. Juan Jose wouldn't hurt him per se but verbally slam him around, and words hurt Ramon more than physical punishment.

Hell, where could the little shit be at? Mike wondered as he drove west on Esperanza, getting closer to downtown. Why am I even bothering with Ramon? he asked himself. Who was Ramon going to tell, and in his state, who in their right mind would believe him? Ramon never talked much; he talked to him, but not to strangers. And Ramon always isolated himself a lot of the time; he was a loner to the max. Who could find him? But then again, Mike thought, there was his connection to Danny, and even though Danny was dead, he was a known user. So that's why he had to find Ramon. He couldn't risk it; any little chance they might be discovered was too big of a chance. Motherfucker, he said out loud and made a U-turn on Esperanza, missing a car by inches. He's at the barn. He's gotta be at the old barn. He wouldn't go to Snake Town; that would be too easy. Goddamn, I'm so stupid, he kept repeating. Of course he's at the barn; there's no place else, and he's waiting for me to go get him as always. Esperanza, going east, would take him all the way to the Old Albuquerque Road, which ran north and south. When reaching the old road, all he had to do was cut a left and go north for a short distance, and he would be at the barn in no time.

Mike felt much better with the idea of looking for Ramon in the barn. He had to be in the barn, he thought. It was the perfect place for Ramon to hide: an abandoned building to call his own, isolated but conveniently close to town in case he wanted to return home. If Ramon had been away from home for two or three nights as his mother had told Mike, and if he stayed all those days and nights in the barn, he was going to be a little untidy, to say the least, and Mike smiled with the thought. He smiled because Ramon was the type of guy who hated dirt on his hands. The type of guy who had to take three or more showers a day in the summer, and his shirts had to be ironed, or he wouldn't wear them. Mike teased him that his mother, Estela, had to iron his socks for him, and the only reason he stopped painting was that he didn't want to get paint on his precious hands. But that wasn't funny anymore, if it ever was. Ramon's appearance didn't matter, and Mike promised himself not to say a word about it to him. He just wanted to take Ramon out of the filthy barn, take a quick drive to the river, dump the fake chiva, and take Ramon home for a cleanup—and maybe later, depending on his mood, invite Ramon out for a burger and Coke. Ramon liked that; he liked his burger and Coke with fries, but not at Fat Henry's. He preferred a drive-in. He liked to eat in the car because he felt others stared at him when he was eating in an inside joint.

Ramon liked to check people out as they came in and out of the burger joint and remarked on their behavior, people who were not aware of him observing them, and he discussed them with Mike in the safety of the car. He criticized girls on their dress and claimed he could tell the couples who were having sex or planning for it in the near future, just by holding hands and their body language. He pointed out the married couples because they never held hands, the guy always sneaking a peak at other women and looking for a piece of ass on the sneak. Mike just listened and said Really and Wow, not fully understanding how a guy like Ramon, who never tasted a piece of ass, could know so much about the sex game and how people reacted to animal lust. He could also tell, just by observing, he claimed, which women were beaten and forced to have sex and which women never got enough of it. He told Mike, more than once, he could tell by the facial expression that the couples put out in public and other things, but never went into details. But that was Ramon, Mike pondered. Difficult to figure out but his friend nevertheless.

Mike was still on Esperanza, a block or two before he reached Caballo Blanco Road, which ran north and south, when he had to stop. There was a backup of cars stopped on Esperanza going east and the opposite side of the street. No way, he said, this don't look good.

What's the hold up? he asked a man walking back to his truck, which was parked in front of Mike's car.

Someone hit a dog crossing the street, and when the idiot stopped to help the dog, he was rammed in the rear by a truck. The truck flipped over to our side of the street and caused the backup.

Anyone hurt? asked Mike, pissed off with the delay.

If you consider the dog anyone, the man answered, also pissed off. The dog will not bother anymore chickens. Other than that, no major harm. Cars have to be towed, but we pushed them to the side of the road. They can fight over it there. I'm in a hurry. I can't waste all day while these fucking people debate who is right and who is wrong—fuck that.

I hear you, said Mike, as the man got into his truck, ignoring what Mike said or not hearing him. But the cars started to move.

Mike crossed Caballo Blanco, which was where most or all of the traffic going east on Esperanza was heading, turning left on Caballo Blanco and moving north or turning right and going south. He got to the Old Albuquerque Road without further incident and cut a left. He drove north and passed El Camino de Lagrimas and after that Piñon Street. He drove a little faster, anxious to see Ramon and take him home. He saw the barn in the distance and slowed down. He made a right and entered as he approached the long driveway of the abandoned farm. As soon as he entered the dirt driveway, he saw a white Dodge Ram parked in front of the barn. I wonder who that is, he asked himself. Maybe Ramon has a friend now. He was debating whether he should proceed or return to town. OK, he said. It's probably one of the Apodaca boys checking on the old property. But the Colorado license plate on the truck gave him reason to be alarmed. It's nothing, he thought. Those Apodaca boys are scattered all over the place. He circled in front of the truck and parked his car facing the exit—didn't want to take any chances in case he had to make a quick getaway. He felt silly doing it, but he did it anyway. He was going to leave the car keys in the ignition but decided to take them with him. As he approached the broken double doors of the barn, he saw a light-green Ford truck with tinted windows stop outside the dirt driveway and then drive away very slowly, going north. Mike couldn't recognize the driver because of the tinted windows.

Huh, he said. That was strange. Wonder who that was? And he turned and walked into the smelly old barn.

CHAPTER THIRTY-TWO

Ramon drank the last of his water from his water bottle and pitched the empty bottle aside. He had been in the musty barn for a couple of days, maybe longer; he had lost sense of time. He was sitting on a pile of old straw he had gathered and pushed against the massive wooden beam that held up the loft. Empty bags of chips were scattered around, the only food he had eaten while in the barn. He gazed out of the double doors of the huge loft, facing east, and at the mountains beyond. He wished he could fly and get lost in those mountains. He could fly all the way to California and see his father. He had been thinking of his father lately and wasn't very pleased with him as a father. Why didn't his father ever write him a letter or called him, something? That was the question he kept asking himself over and over until he came to the conclusion he didn't have a father, that his mother invented him for the purpose of covering up an affair with a man who ditched her.

Ramon recalled how difficult it had been growing up without a father. When he was little, it hadn't mattered; at that age, he was satisfied with all the attention he got from his mother. But as he got older, and other kids talked about their fathers, it got him thinking, and he realized he didn't have one. He remembered he was in the fifth or sixth grade when the teacher told the class to make something for Father's Day; it was the same shit every year. And every year he refused or faked something. This time he was drawing or painting—he forgot what—when the teacher came to him with a silly grin on her ugly face and asked him if he was doing something for his father. He looked her in the eyes and said, No, it's something for your mother, bitch. Of course he was sent to the principal's office. The principal was going to swat him on the ass with a large paddle he kept in a closet. The principal liked to swat the Mexican boys because they took it without complaining—little macho fuckers, he used to call them, and they never complained to their parents. The Anglo kids bawled as soon as they saw him take out the paddle, so they got away most of the time with a warning. But Ramon reminded the principal that if he had a seizure while being paddled, and the nurse had to call an ambulance, his mother was sure to sue him and the school district. The principal wasn't as stupid as he looked. He understood the consequences of any mention of him swatting a boy with seizures appearing in his brag sheet, especially if the boy had a meltdown in his office. It wouldn't help his next promotion any. He gave Ramon a two-day suspension instead, and the teacher demanded an apology, Ramon refused and wanted an apology from the teacher, which never happened either.

He did miss growing up without a father. Why deny it? he thought. Some kids at least had a grandfather or uncles, older brothers, or cousins. He had no one, only his mother and old photos of ghosts collecting dust who were supposed to be his relatives, but he never recalled meeting any of them. He now believed, which was sad, that his mother was an orphan, had an affair with a traveling salesman, collected the old photos from a yard sale, and invented herself a family.

Ramon kept turning the empty bags of chips around to see if by chance not all were empty, more to do something with his hands than from the desire to eat. He remembered this older boy from the neighborhood whose father had run off and left the family as his father had. The boy was always boasting that when he grew up, he was going to find his father and kick his ass for abandoning the family. The boy eventually found his father, but the man was old, sick, and pathetic looking. The boy couldn't lay a hand on him. But this boy had an older brother, sisters, uncles, a family, while he had nobody. That was sad, he thought. For a while he could escape in his art, but even that bothered his mother. What he loved to paint was considered too dark for most people to appreciate, but painting landscapes was too boring for him. His mother even brought the priest over to the house to take a look at his paintings. The priest told his mother that a demon was working through Ramon and that it was best for her to take him to church and for Ramon to confess and pray. And after, if he still felt the need to paint, he could copy the holy images of Christ on the cross, the holy mother, and the saints. So he gave up painting; he wasn't going to go to no church, and for sure he wasn't going to copy others' work, religious or not. And what about Mike, he thought, his only friend? It seemed like Mike was ignoring him lately—Mike, always bragging about his girls and shit. Always acting so tough. He wished he could see him attempting to sell the chiva; that was going to be comical. He needed a good laugh. Staying in the stinky barn turned out to be a big mistake, he thought. But his life was an even bigger mistake, and who could he blame for that? But what the hell, he said, what does it matter, anyway? Ever since the death of Danny, he couldn't get it together, and his mother was on his case day and night, reminding him that they had no money—as if it was news to him.

Ramon placed the picture of Vivian Madrid he had cut from the yearbook in his shirt pocket after staring at it for some time. Vivian Madrid didn't give out any school pictures or sign yearbooks; that wasn't her thing. Ramon could never figure out what she did with her school pictures, if she refused to part with them or no one asked her for any. Maybe she never bought any and pretended she didn't want to give them out. Anyway, he didn't give a crap anymore, so what was the point of thinking about her? She didn't care, so why should he? At this moment the rope seemed more attractive than Vivian Madrid—or anyone else for that matter.

Ramon kept his eyes on the rope that was attached to a pulley secured to the top of the frame of the open double doors of the loft. He recalled as if it was only yesterday when Mike and he used to run and jump on the double rope, used to haul up bales of hay, swing down to the ground, and then race up the loft on the ladder inside the barn and jump off again. That was fun, he thought, but now he was thinking of wrapping the rope around his neck and jumping off. Rats; if he only had the balls. He kept staring at the rope, wondering if the rope could be the solution to his dilemma and at the same time curious about the condition of the rope and pulley—could it hold his body up until he croaked? He would have to run, jump to catch the rope, wrap it around his neck, and let go. If the pulley gave or the rope busted, he would end up on the ground with a broken back or neck, adding to his troubles in a big way. But then he remembered seeing an old rusted pitchfork around when he first arrived. He saw it to his left, almost covered with straw. He pulled it out and placed it next to him. With the pitchfork, he could force the rope into the loft, and he could grab it with his free hand and do it. He inched close to the edge of the double doors on his butt. He looked down, and the distance to the ground made him dizzy. No way, he said and scooted back to lean on the beam a safe distance from the opening. He didn't remember the loft being so high from the ground. It was a good thirty or forty feet, and he had forgotten he was afraid of heights. For good reason, Mike always advised him never to look down once he grabbed the rope, and he never had.

Ramon closed his eyes. He was weak from little food and lack of sleep and now dizzy. He wanted water but knew there was none. He had to decide what to do next. He couldn't stay in the hot barn another day—he just couldn't. He realized now he could never jump for the rope, but he didn't have to. He could use the pitchfork to swing the rope to him, grab it, make himself a necktie, and jump off, with his eyes closed, of course. The trick was to secure the double-ended rope tightly around his neck so one end wouldn't go down to the ground with him and splatter him like a rotten pumpkin. What a display, he thought, his body dangling, lifeless, from the old barn and the crows pecking on his eyeballs, just like in the movies. But he had to decide whether it was a good idea to leave Vivian Madrid's yearbook picture in his shirt pocket. If it was found on his person, when they cut his body loose, the gossip would report it as a tragic love suicide. Some would say that he couldn't take the rejection, that he couldn't live without her and took his life to prove his unending love for her. If he took the picture out of his pocket and tore it into a thousand pieces and scattered the pieces all over the loft, then his suicide would just be plain and simple about a crazy boy who couldn't cope with the stress of living in a complicated world. Then he got furious at himself; why was he so concerned? He was going to be dead, gone, what the hell did it matter what people said or who said it? Shit, he cried, and placed his hands over his eyes in an attempt to hold back the tears, but he was unsuccessful.

Ramon looked at his soiled hands and was sure his face was even a lot filthier. There was nothing he could do about it, not a thing; he was helpless, and that was the reason he ended up in the old, stinking, abandoned barn. Where else could he go? Here, at least he was away from people who couldn't or wouldn't help him. Even Mike —Mike, his friend, was silent about the money he had promised to give him. Mike was playing the hard-to-get game, a game Ramon knew so well. Ramon became annoyed and frustrated at the turn in his life after the death of Danny. Danny Madrid might have been what he was, but Ramon liked hanging around with him. And it wasn't just because of Vivian, as some speculated. Danny was funny, fun to be with, and in many ways kind. Danny never asked stupid questions and lived from day to day, enjoying every minute of it. But after Danny's death, Ramon noticed people looked at him in a puzzled way, as if to say, Come clean, boy; we know what you're about. Or confess, you little shit sucking murderer, and do some time, hard time. But the worse thing was the dream that turned into a nightmare that he kept having about Danny and the cemetery.

It was a vivid and scary but in his opinion a pointless dream. It always started out the same, and the ending was usually the same. It was late at night—a moonless, starless night—and he wandered alone in the desert. He walked and walked in a landscape of gloom and darkness, devoid of sound and light. It was as if the sounds of night critters and all the vibrant life of the desert had been sucked clean by the blackness of the night. He walked and walked until he entered a cemetery, a cemetery in a deep valley he didn't recognize, but it was always the same, in the same bleak valley. He was exhausted, but he couldn't stop; some unrecognizable force pushed him on like invisible hands, forcing him to march through the graveyard like a soldier in pursuit of a fleeing enemy. Once in the graveyard with its bone-white tombs, he stumbled over an empty coffin, but he didn't fall. As he walked on, he was blinded by a glaring light in the middle of the distressing cemetery. The light was painful but at the same time summoned him like a beacon in the middle of a vast, shadowy wasteland. As he got closer to the blazing light, he realized it was the glow of flames in the shape of a cross or a sword. The fiery, burning cross was on top of Danny's grave, and even though it was not the cemetery in Las Flores, where Danny was put to rest, he knew without a doubt it was Danny's grave. The fiery cross grew in proportion as he came closer, reaching higher, the arms of fire extending out and the yellow-orange and blue flames dancing in a devilish fashion. The relentless dancing flames encouraged him to advance to Danny's grave, which was now an open pit, breathing the fire out like the mouth of an awakening fire- breathing dragon. But even though he was trembling with fear and reluctant to approach the fierce inferno, he wanted to escape the murky ink of a world without light, and so he kept on walking. The closer he got to the burning cross, the more intense the scar on his face began to burn, and his head throbbed with pain, as the fire seemed to also reject him now that he was close to the grave. He would wake up with his heart pounding in his chest and sweat soaking his nightclothes, coughing, choking, gasping for air, and still feeling the fire close to his face. He couldn't go back to sleep after that, and the next day he was a basket case, tired and cranky. He used fire in his paintings to symbolize passion, but he was certain this blaze was not meant for passion of any kind, but the fire used to cleanse wicked—and in many cases innocent—people of their evil, but he didn't consider himself evil. And even in a dream state that he couldn't control, if the fire was intended to cleanse him of Danny's death, he would never succumb to fire as a punishment, even though he had been found guilty by a court of public assholes. And there was where his confusion about the dream played out. In the first part of the dream, he was pulled to the fire to pay for his deed of killing Danny; as he got closer to the fire, he was pushed away, proving his innocence as the fire refused to engulf him, giving him pain on the scar on his face and head instead so he could wake up and walk away.

The dream still bothered, frightened, and upset him because he sensed the flames getting more and more feverish and him walking closer to the center of the orange-yellow, unyielding, dancing flames. And in the most recent dream, the one he had early in the morning, he saw Danny's head and shoulders rising from the grave as the flames surged around him, and he seemed to be smiling at Ramon. His hair was on fire, but he didn't seem to mind. But other than that, his face was the same—almost the same, that is. There were blotches of dry blood from the cuts and scratches he suffered in the car crash, but it was Danny, mocking him with a smile that seemed to imply to go join him in the bottomless pit of fire or wherever he was. The smile indicated that everything was wonderful where he was, and even his friend could escape all of his problems and be content. Ramon at first thought it was the devil, but since he didn't believe in the devil, he couldn't figure what or who it was, but he sure looked a lot like Danny. So that added to his bewilderment and made his life more empty and meaningless. He had to make a choice and soon. He was running out of options; he never had that many to begin with, but now he had less. He had to act, act like a man—a desperate man, but a man.

CHAPTER THIRTY-THREE

omero finished taking care of business, and he struggled because of his tight jeans to arrange his essentials back into their warehouse. He was anxious to exit the urine-reeking barn, which had been utilized as a toilet for many years. He wanted to take a piss outside the old decrepit barn, but he also wanted to take a look inside, just in case he might see something of interest. Now he was sorry he had. The odor of human manure, along with old hay and other deposits left there unattended throughout the years, gave out a powerful stench. He finally secured the metal buttons on his jeans, settled in his furniture, and pushed gently with his right hand to make sure they were in a comfortable position. I better get the hell out of here, he thought, as he gave the place one more look. He saw nothing worth looking at but a ladder in the middle of the barn that led to the loft. I ain't gonna go up that old ladder—lord, no, he said, and he smiled because he liked to talk like that when he was popping heads in the rough areas of town back in Denver. Romero loved his sense of humor and gave out a little laugh at being so witty. He did have a sense of humor, he told himself. It was just that people didn't get his humor, and that wasn't his fault, was it?

Romero turned to leave the barn, not only because the smell was not pleasant but because there was nothing in the barn worth checking out. And he never intended to play hide-and-seek in the barn full of crap where every corner was stacked high with mounds of stinking shit. Before he took his first step out of the barn, he thought he heard a weak whimper, a moan, something, coming from the loft. At first he was going to ignore it as the sound of some wild animal roosting in the loft, but he heard it again, and this time it sounded more human. He turned very slowly to face the ladder and the loft, and he heard it again. A sound of pain, Romero thought, that only humans make. He had heard those painful moans many times before when he held his big knife under a junkie's throat and began to open the skin, and blood and white fat trickled on the blade, and the junky recognized that he was going to donate his blood to the gutter. He had to decide, and fast, if he really wanted to get involved. It could be some emotional creature who was thinking of taking his life for a road taken that was full of potholes. Hell no, he said if some pendejo has emotional problems, what the fuck can I do to help him or her? He turned to exit the barn, but he stopped and asked, What if there is someone up there who can give me some information on the missing chiva? I'll just run up the ladder and take a peek—if the situation looks out of control, I'll get down pronto and get out of the barn and say good-bye to Las Flores. That was a sound plan, he believed, as he headed to the ladder, sidestepping the dry turds, wondering why he had worn his new boots.

Romero climbed the ladder to the loft with caution. The ladder was old, and the wood was not in the most solid condition to hold a big man like him. He took one step at a time, and his calf began to bother him, but he ignored it as best he could. On the last step of the squeaky ladder, he grabbed the rail and pulled himself into the loft. He was only going to take a look from the ladder, but he couldn't see much, so he decided to try the loft. The loft was large, extending to his right and left the length of the barn. In front of him, he could see the double doors, which faced east and allowed light to enter the barn, although a patch of roof to his left, on the west corner of the loft, was caved in, giving the loft some air. The double doors of the loft, which were utilized to bring in the bales of hay during better days, did not resemble doors anymore. The side boards and most or all of the molding had been hacked off to remove the wood. The doors looked more like the mouth of an uneven cave. Romero noticed that the stink wasn't as bad in the loft, and for that he was thankful, as he scanned the loft from left to right. He saw nothing that invited his attention until he heard the sob coming from behind the beam that supported the loft. He made his way to the beam, not knowing what to expect, already exceeding his plan to take a peek and leave. He approached the beam with as much care as he did all his unusual circumstances. He came around the beam and stopped, looking down at a skinny young man sitting on a pile of straw with his back resting on the huge wooden beam and gazing out the hole in front of him, with tears on his pale face. He was wearing a soiled shirt that was once white, the long sleeves buttoned, with only his stained, filthy hands showing. His hair was short, bone short, and his smudged, unwashed, ashen face was spotted with dry tears and dirt. Only a couple of feet separated the man-child from Romero. He noticed the weak chin and black circles around his sunken eyes.

Ramon raised his eyes to look at Romero and asked, in a calm but hoarse voice, a voice coming from a throat with rusty vocal cords because of misuse, Fuck you want?

Romero, looking down at Ramon, the man-child, keeper of the old barn, said, Well, well. You must be the Raymond I have heard so much about. You look like you might need some help, brother. Let me help you; name it, and it's yours.

Ramon, resembling a raccoon, fixed his light-green eyes encircled in black on Romero, confused because Romero knew his name, even though he wasn't saying it right. He was queasy from hunger, dehydrated, and could hardly speak, but he held his own. He was not intimidated by the intruder, but it took a lot of effort.

Fuck you want, you big ape? he asked again, began coughing, and placed a hand over his mouth. My name is Ramon, he continued after the coughing spasm, which lasted at least half a minute, not Raymond. I don't know you, don't wanna know you, so fuck off, and leave me alone. I don't need or want your fucking help, and I sure ain't your brother. The coughing started again as the phlegm raced up his throat.

There's that word again, thought Romero, attempting to control his temper. Why is "ape" the first word they reach for? he wanted to know. Forget it, he said to himself, this is the little shit Bryan Hercules had mentioned—Ramon, the boy in the car accident when the junky was killed, the boy with the seizures. Maybe Bryan was onto something. Maybe this little dog turd did know where the chiva was or at least who was holding onto it. He didn't seem like the kind of vato holding on to something valuable or the kind of vato negotiating with criminals about the price of chiva—or anything, for that matter, Romero presumed. He was going to try diplomacy; that was always his first approach—not always, but most of the time.

Sorry for calling you Raymond. I didn't know, Romero said, a phony smile on his big face. I really want to help you, and you can help me as well. What do you say, Ramon? And he rolled the R as much as he could get away with, but just enough as not to make it sound ridiculous and upset Ramon even more.

Ramon glared at Romero, with his blood shot green eyes, as if he could make Romero disappear with his eyes. He attempted to stand but gave up on the idea because he felt lightheaded and too weak to do any good standing. He was confounded now even more with the presence of the stranger, and there was nothing he could do about it but talk tough, as he always did, to convince himself that he was tough—another game he played, among the many. He couldn't come up with any logical explanation for how this asshole knew his name and what he wanted—or maybe he could, but he just didn't want to admit that he could. He felt the vomit pushing up his throat, and he forced it back down, leaving a bad taste in his mouth.

Romero, with his best used-car-salesmen's smile on his big face, offered Ramon his huge hand and said, in a friendly voice, Here, let me help you up, Ramon. Bryan Hercules told me all about your unfortunate accident and about your friend not making it. Shit like that happens; it wasn't your fault. It happens all the time. So don't feel bad, my friend. Here, take my hand, and let me help you up and get you away from this smelly place. I'll take you anywhere you want to go, and that I promise you.

Ramon didn't look up to face Romero anymore; it was too much of a struggle. He talked to his large boots instead because Romero didn't seem as if he was going to bend down to look him in the eye.

You got the wrong guy, he said in a calm but throaty effort. I don't know what the fuck you talking about. I don't know any Bryan whatever, and as I told you already, I don't need or want your help. So shove your hand up your ass, and let me be.

Romero lowered his hand and bit his lower lip as his forehead furrowed, obviously displeased. I could put my boot on his skull and crush him like an insect, he thought, but not yet, little Ramon, as you like to be called. I need you alive to see what you know, if anything; then I will decide your future, you little puke. All this went through Romero's mind as he noticed the old, rusty pitchfork next to Ramon. He was going to try one more time before changing tactics. He couldn't get any information out of a corpse, and for that reason, and that reason alone, he was going to play Mr. Nice Guy and give the skinny boy another chance to come clean.

Look, Ramon, Romero said, a little more firmly, still standing tall to keep his advantage over the defenseless Ramon. I know who you are. You're the boy who survived the car crash. You're the boy who has seizures, and you're the boy who hung out with Danny the junky. Am I right? And he answered his own question. Of course I am. So let's stop the games, OK? All I want is information on something that belongs to me; it's that simple. Tell me what I want to know, and I'll leave. If you decide to stay, that's up to you. Just tell me what you and the junky did with my chiva. You heard right—my chiva. I want it back, now. If you don't have it but know someone else who does, that's OK. Give me the name or names, and everything is cool. C'mon, Ramon, you're a bright boy. Don't play stupid with me, 'cause you ain't gonna get nothing but pain out of it. You think your partners are gonna give you anything for your troubles? No, nothing, and you know it. They are already spending the loot in the cat houses of Juarez, laughing at you, drinking and partying, fucking girls—and what are you doing? I'll tell you what you're doing, if you don't already know. You're rotting away in this smelly barn waiting for them to bring you some cash. Wake up, my friend. You can wait all you want—they ain't never gonna show up, never, and if they do, they won't have a penny left between them. Bet your boots on that, brother. Tell me who they are, and I'll collect whatever money they have left and give you some, that I promise. And Romero placed his hand over his heart and made some signs with his fingers to seal the pact, believing that would convince or impress Ramon.

Ramon attempted to laugh, but his throat was full of phlegm. He cleared his throat, swallowing the mucus, making sounds like a man gasping for air. He let out a feeble chuckle. So this was the dreaded collector all the buzz was about, and a liar to boot, presumed Ramon. What people do for money, for love and money—what a screwed-up world he lived in. And he attempted to laugh again.

Talking to the boots in a faint but persistent voice, Ramon asserted, I still don't know what the fuck you saying. I know nothing of no chiva, nada. You wasting your time here. I ain't your guy. Look at me, shit eater. Look at the shape I'm in. You think I'm interested in moving dope or have friends that are? I'm dying of cancer—which was a lie, but that was the best he had for now. I came here to die with a little dignity and spare my family the misery of taking care of me. Are you happy now? You are barking up the wrong tree, and if you can't figure that out on your own, you're as dumb as you look. All the talking brought the crap up to his mouth, and he couldn't force it back down, so he inched forward and dumped on Romero's vintage black ostrich-leather cowboy boots. It was mostly yellow bile and phlegm because his stomach was empty for lack of food, but it still spattered both of his expensive extra-large boots.

God damn you—watch out, you little fuck face. Romero almost screamed, but he was too late to move back as the yellow vomit splattered his boots. I'm sick and tired of playing games with you, you little scrawny sack of shit. I'm gonna teach you not to disrespect your betters. He took a stepped forward, bent his knees, and picked up the rusty pitchfork from the straw with an extended right arm with one lunge. He got almost on top of Ramon with the menacing pitchfork in his right hand, raised some but not too high, ready to strike a bargain or a blow, and it made no difference to the furious Romero. Now tell me who has the chiva, motherfucker. Give me the names, or feel the pain grip you like an iron claw until you beg me for death. One last chance, amigo, and you can live to retell your adventures to your grandchildren. Don't make me do this. I'm not a violent, sadistic kind of guy; only when I have to be.

When Ramon heard "grandchildren," tears came to his eyes. He knew that was something he would never see or experience. Sad but true, he thought, and it made him mad, not at Romero but at everyone and no one at the same time. He didn't know anymore, and he judged it was too late to give a shit, so he said, Fuck you, cowboy. I know nothing. And he closed his eyes, as if closing his eyes was going to turn back the raging tornado that was on top of him, ready to inflict major damage on his sorry life.

Romero came down hard with the rusty pitchfork on Ramon's calf, a little above the ankle of his left leg. Ramon's legs were so bony that only one prong of the pitchfork entered the flesh below the bone, but it went deep, busting up anything in its way. Ramon screamed without wanting to scream. The pain sent electric shocks to his brain, and he couldn't shut his mouth or clench his teeth. It was like being lashed with a bullwhip on flames, all over his naked body. He soiled himself front and back several times before he zoned out, and the pain disappeared. His body started jerking until he was on his back; his eyes rolled toward his forehead, and white spittle rolled out of his mouth, but Romero never removed the pitchfork from Ramon's bleeding calf.

Oh, no, Romero said, I killed the little shit. But when he saw Ramon convulsing, he realized it was a seizure, but he didn't know what to do, so he waited to see if Ramon would come out of it, holding onto the pitchfork still jammed in Ramon's calf.

CHAPTER THIRTY-FOUR

As soon as Mike walked into the old barn, he heard a scream coming from the loft. Shit, he said. That's Ramon. And he flew up the ladder to the loft. Once in the loft, Mike slowed down when he saw a stranger over Ramon holding a pitchfork stuck to Ramon's lower leg. Ramon was on his side; his body had jerked to his right side, except for his left leg that was pinned to the floor by the pitchfork. Mike could see that Ramon was coming out of a seizure; the white spittle all over his mouth and chin and his glazed eyes, attempting to focus, proved he was right. The big man kept his eyes on Ramon, his hand on the pitchfork, but was aware that Mike had joined the conversation.

Hey, hey! Mike yelled out, outraged at what the big ape was doing to Ramon. What the hell you think you doing to my friend? Then he went down on one knee and attempted to talk to Ramon. Ramon, Ramon, you OK, man? What's going on here? Mike moved his hand to remove the pitchfork and free Ramon from the pain.

You touch that, baby, and you're gonna get it up your ass, Romero said in a not-too-friendly voice.

Mike stood to confront the towering Romero. He didn't need any introduction; this was the collector crazy Manny had tried to warn him about. He was a big turkey, and for sure a brutal killer to boot, Mike told himself. This was what kept him up at night. He was convinced that Ramon and him were in deep shit. Why hadn't he listened to Manny and followed up on his lead and at least asked around about strangers in town? If anybody knew about collectors, it was Manny. But it was too late to worry about that now. Now he had to come up with something quick to get them out of the fix they were in, and it wasn't going to be an easy thing to accomplish, with the maniac holding the cards.

What do you want with Ramon? Mike asked Romero, attempting to make eye contact with him and mask his fear as much as he could.

You must be Mike, Romero said with a grin. We've been waiting for you, Ramon and me.

Lie, uttered Ramon, still on his back.

He was ignored by both Mike and Romero, Mike because he was thinking on how to save his ass and, if he could, Ramon's, and Romero because he was certain he had the main character in his trap.

So what is it you want from…from us?

You know what I want. Do I have to spell it out? I want my chiva, ass hole, and I want it now, Romero growled, incensed. I know you have it; your friend confessed everything. We go easy on this, or we go hard: your choice. But make it fast before your amigo bleeds to death.

Liar, he's a shit eating liar, Mike. I said nothing to this big ape. Ramon cried out and went into a coughing spasm as the tears flowed into his hollow cheeks.

You shut it—your time for talking is over. And Romero pushed down on the pitchfork.

Ramon winced in pain, but he didn't scream, just bit his lower lip and closed his eyes.

OK, OK, pleaded Mike, ease up; you gonna kill him, and for what? Mike knew Romero was going to kill both of them, and this time he couldn't do much for Ramon or for himself either. Might as well tell the big ape what he wanted to hear. And he took a quick look at the rope just outside the double doors of the loft.

All right, all right, I have the chiva, Mike confessed. Let us go, and I'll give it to you. I'll take Ramon to the hospital, and after I'll drop the chiva off any place you name.

Yeah, right. And I believe in the tooth fairy, Romero said, grinding his teeth to control his temper. We'll all go. Give me the chiva, and you can drop off the monkey at the hospital or do what you want with him. But if there is some chiva missing, you owe me, big.

Before Romero said "big," Mike sidestepped him and ran to the double doors of the loft and jumped on the ropes on the pulley and flew down like a man on fire. Before he hit the ground, he grabbed the second rope and slowed down his plunge, landing on the ground hard on his feet and then tumbling on his back with his head low to break the fall. He was sure Romero wouldn't attempt the rope because of his size and weight, and if this was the cowboy La Conga was telling everyone that she cut on the leg because he tried to rape her, his injured leg could present a problem.

When Romero saw Mike flash by him to the double doors of the loft, he pulled out the pitchfork from Ramon's calf and was going to go after him and spear him like a fish treading water. But before he turned with the pitchfork in his hand, Ramon somehow pushed himself up, sitting on his butt, and wrapped his arms around Romero's pricey boot as he made a move to go after Mike. Ramon pulled with both arms on the boot, using all the energy he could muster, bringing his face close to Romero's leg where La Conga had slashed him, and bit hard through the denim.

Romero cursed and tried to push Ramon off his boot, but Ramon wouldn't let go of the boot. Romero finally slugged him with a hard left hook to the side of the face, and Ramon went down with the boot held tightly in his arms. No, yelled Romero as he limped to the double doors of the loft with the pitchfork still in his right hand. He spotted Mike running to turn the corner of the barn. Romero hurled the pitchfork like a spear at Mike. The pitchfork was way off, went down spinning, and missed Mike by a mile, as he had already turned the corner of the barn and was out of sight. Romero limped back to Ramon for his boot, which was still held tightly in Ramon's arms. Romero grabbed the boot, but Ramon refused to let go. Romero pulled on the boot so hard with both hands that Ramon came off the floor like a puppet. Romero used one hand to undo Ramon's grip on his boot, holding the boot with the other and yelling at Ramon to let go, rushing to get his boot and go after the other little shit before he got too far away. Romero couldn't understand why Ramon was strong now and so frail before. He undid Ramon's tight claws and freed the boot. He used the boot to slam Ramon on the head and knock him down on his back again but not out. I'll have to come back and finish off this fool, he muttered as he attempted to put on his boot. He was jumping around on his good leg, but he couldn't slip on the boot. Finally, he sat on his ass and slipped his big foot in the boot, knowing that was the only sure way to do it but trying to save time doing it the other way.

Mike saw the pitchfork come down as he turned the corner of the barn, but it was way off and spinning too much to do any harm. He ran around the corner of the barn to find his car, as fast as his legs could carry him. He had his hand in his pocket and fished out his keys on the run. He felt bad for Ramon, but he realized there was no way to help him except to force the monster to follow him, and maybe he would spare Ramon. He jumped in his car, slammed the door shut, and fumbled to place the right key in the ignition. His hands couldn't stop shaking, and his heart was thumping loudly, as if it was going to explode. He finally placed the right key in the ignition. He turned the key, and the engine sputtered and died. No, No! Please don't, he yelled, desperate to leave before the killer came after him. He tried again; nothing but a humming sound, and he was ready to ditch the car and make a run for it, but the engine turned. Then he pulled out the clutch too fast and killed it. Stupid, he cried, clenching his teeth, looking behind him to the cavernous gap that was the door of the barn. He tried again; this time he was successful. He geared to first and pulled out fast, spinning the rear tires, cut a left on the old Albuquerque Road, and headed for the Eastside barrio.

Romero put on his boot as fast as he could and came down the loft ladder one step at a time, quickly but carefully. Ramon had clenched his teeth on the cut La Conga had surprised him with, but he couldn't tell if the skin was breached, and he didn't want to stop to find out. Once off the ladder, he ran, hobbling to his truck, not caring if he stepped on the turds. He geared the truck and made a U, burning rubber as the V8 headed out of the driveway, almost losing control and going into a narrow ditch on the shoulder. He straightened out the truck and cut a left on the old Albuquerque Road going south, certain that Mike was driving to Las Flores. He wanted to catch him before he reached town. He was sure he had the right sonofabitch, and he wasn't going to lose him, even if he had to ram him from behind and shake him up a little. And after he got the goods from the little pussy, he would take care of him in a proper way. As for Ramon, he would burn the barn down, and if Ramon, that sick fool, was still up in the loft, that was his problem. Romero saw an older car speeding along ahead of him heading to Las Flores, and would bet his boots it was Mike, just as he suspected. He chuckled as he jacked down on the gas pedal, and the V8 roared as it lunged forward at a high rate of speed. Think you can outrun me? You little piece of shit, he yelled out, his mouth twisted in anger. Had to be that little cock sucker; he was sure it was him. There was no one else on the road, and he was going too fast not to be running away, shitting all over himself with fear, Romero assumed. The truck hit one hundred easy, and the gap between them was narrowed down significantly. His heart was racing with rage and excitement. He was close to payday, and he had done it on his own. He was proud of himself now—all the bullshit he had to put up with, and finally the payoff was within reach. Fucking A, he yelled out at Mike. Got you by the balls now, brother.

Mike saw the big truck in the rearview mirror; it was catching up to him, and the killer was sneering behind the wheel. El Camino de Lagrimas was ahead of him, and it led east to Snake Town. If the killer followed him to the Eastside barrio, at the speed they were going, someone was going to get seriously hurt. Besides, where could he hide once in the barrio? It would only lead to people getting hurt or killed. He made a quick left on El Camino de Lagrimas, his car spinning out of control, but he turned the steering wheel toward the spin, and the car straightened out—a trick he had learned from Danny Madrid. He drove as fast as he dared on the bumpy road, hoping he could make a run for it once he reached Snake Town and hide until dark or sneak into Santa Maria and ask Juan Jose for help. He really didn't know what he was doing. He was so scared that hiding in Snake Town just popped into his frightened mind.

Romero was coming on too fast and furious to make the turn on Camino de Lagrimas as Mike did. He flew by and cursed out loud. He slowed down, turned around, and made a right on Camino de Lagrimas. Thought you were going to get away, didn't you? You're mine, little doggie, he mumbled as he gripped the steering wheel so hard his knuckles were turning white from the pressure.

Mike drove as fast as he could on the rutted road; Snake Town was just in front of him and Santa Maria a short distance behind Snake Town. He saw the white truck behind him again, rapidly catching up. He reached Snake Town, jumped out of the car, and started to run, but he made a quick stop, returned to the car, and grabbed the fake bag of chiva from the backseat as the white truck stopped behind his car in a cloud of dust. Romero jumped out, almost falling, but he regained his balance and yelled out, Stop, you little shit, and give me the bag—that's all I want. Mike walked fast up the elevated ground that led into Snake Town, sure that there was no place to hide. He said, Fuck it, turned, faced Romero, and, without saying a word, thrust one hand in the bag while holding the bag with the other. He pulled out a white hand from the bag, his fist full of fake chiva, and raised it above his head so Romero could see what he intended to do.

Romero, his face contorted with anger, slowed his pace as he saw the fake chiva in Mike's hand. Hold on, Mike, he said, struggling to control his temper. You do what you're thinking of doing, and I'll break your arms and legs. Put it back in the bag, and hand over the bag like a good boy, Mike. Listen to me, and I won't hurt you. Mike said nothing, thinking he could throw the flour mixed with sugar in the killer's eyes as he got close and make a run for it.

Juan Jose appeared from nowhere. He was just standing there looking at them, as if he materialized from thin air. He was wearing curl-toed Apache moccasins, leather breeches above the knees, and no shirt. He had a black leather strap wrapped around his left arm and covering his left hand like a glove, a doubled hemp cord around his waist with a leather sheath holding a huge bowie knife on his left side, and a quiver of arrows on his right. In his left hand, he was holding his Turkish bow, and he had his right hand close to an arrow in the quiver. His eyes were behind aviator shades. He looked down at Romero from his higher position and said in a calm voice, Game's up, Mister. Pack it up, and get the hell out. Juan Jose had seen through his binoculars what Romero had done to Lencho Reyes— not inside the shed, but when he dragged him out tied to a chair and dumped him into the mine shaft. He knew Romero was a killer, but in his opinion, Romero was an amateur. He had put down professionals; to him this scumbag was a nuisance, not even a threat. He was not going to allow this mad dog to hurt Mike. Mike had played with Danny and Vivian when kids, and Mike's mother was Delfina's best and only friend, always there for her when Delfina was in need of something.

Romero stopped and glared at Juan Jose; he couldn't believe what he saw. Who is this clown? he wondered. He didn't see any cameras or crew around to be filming a movie or commercial, something. Then it came to him: Charles Bronson, one of his favorite actors in Chato's Land, from a Leonard Elmore novel.

Romero chuckled as he said, Look, Tonto. I ain't got no beef with you. Go on and play pretend; act as if I'm not here. I'm gonna take this shit with me, and nobody's gonna stop me, sabe, White Feather? OK, Mike. Romero returned his attention to Mike. It's over; don't make me chase you all over the goddamn place, 'cause I will. Put the sugar back in the bag. C'mon, make it easy on us all, and Chief White Feather can continue with his role playing.

Mike was still shaking with fear but not as much as before, now that Juan Jose had appeared, knowing what he could do with his bow. He decided to play with Romero, and he let go the fake chiva in his hand, and it dispersed like ashes in the breeze. He pulled out another fistful of the powdered flower and sugar and raised it above his head.

Stop! Romero screamed. That chiva belongs to me, motherfucker; give it here. He thought he could rush Mike, take the bag, and use him as a human shield against the crazy with the fancy bow in case he made any unreasonable demands.

Romero took a step toward Mike; Juan Jose raised the bow in his left hand, notched an arrow with his right, pulled on the cord, almost touching his right cheek, and let it fly, all in a split second. Romero heard a swish, and the arrow with the deadly looking, flattened, razor-sharp, teaspoon head entered the soft area of flesh above his left pec, close to his shoulder, like a hot knife through cream cheese. The hit knocked Romero a little off balance. He was less than twenty-five feet from Juan Jose, a big and close target, and Juan Jose was aiming down at a slant. He was more surprised than hurt. He attempted to pull out the arrow with his right hand, like they do in the movies. The shaft broke in half, and he tossed it away as if that was the end of his troubles, not knowing or caring that the second half of the arrow was sticking out his shoulder blade. He instinctively went for his gun, but it was nowhere to be found. He had put it in his suitcase, and his suitcase was in the truck.

Romero was enraged beyond control; he cursed and screamed at Juan Jose, forgetting about Mike for the moment. I'm gonna rip your heart out, break every bone in your body, strip you naked, and drag you over every goddamn cactus I can find in this God-forsaken place and leave you for the vultures and the flies to carve you up, you son of a fucking bitch, you hear me? He regained his balance and raised his arms, ready to attack Juan Jose, his anger blinding any defensive strategy that could have perhaps saved him from further harm. He miscalculated the distance between him and Juan Jose and that Juan Jose was on top of the slope. He would have to struggle to run up, on loose gravel, tackle Juan Jose, put his weight on him, and disarm him, not an easy errand to pull off.

As Romero commenced his attack like a rabid dog, Juan Jose, calm as ever, had notched his second arrow, raised the bow, pulled, and let go, easy as sliding on ice. Romero heard another swish and felt the arrowhead and shaft penetrate his throat before he could blink an eye. This time the force of the arrow compelled him back like a drunk losing command of his legs toward his truck, where he fell on his back, splintering half the arrow that was sticking out the back of his neck. Blood gushed out of his mouth and from the wound in his throat where the arrow was lodged as he attempted to say something, but he only produced a gurgling sound. Romero's thoughts were all scrambled, and he couldn't put a sentence together if his life depended on it. His head shifted a little to his left toward the door of the truck, which he never bothered to close in his hot pursue of Mike. He was losing his vision, but he could still see the stain on the door transforming and shifting into the shape of women in black pointing a finger at him and laughing. He struggled to say something again, but he coughed as blood spluttered out his mouth and down his chin and soaked the rest of his torso.

Mike kept his eyes on Romero, trying to adjust to the fact that a life had to be taken to save his own. He was frozen on the spot, still in shock that he had witnessed a real killing, too real for any comfort. Wow, he thought, that was what he always wanted to see, but it wasn't pretty—not pretty at all.

Get lost, Mike, Juan Jose called out as he ran like a deer and disappeared in the deserted buildings of Snake Town.

Mike snapped out of his trance and turned, when he heard Juan Jose, to thank him, but he was left with his mouth open; Juan Jose was gone. Anyway, he reflected, how do you thank a man who just saved your life? What words do you put together to say thanks? Get on your knees, or offer to treat him to lunch next time he's in town? Now he felt stupid, standing there with a bag of useless flour mixed with sugar and a mortally wounded man a few feet away. Shit, I gotta get outta here, he told himself and emptied the contents of the bag and pitched the bag. He was walking to his car, almost running, when he decided to give Romero a kick to the head for Ramon's sake. But as he got close to the bleeding body, he recognized that Romero was already negotiating with the devil. His face was turning black, and his torso was soaked with blood. He looked like a gutted bull. He wondered what kind of poison Juan Jose treated the flattened, razor-sharp teaspoon arrow heads with, as if it mattered; the cow was put to pasture, and whatever he used had done the job.

Ramon! he shouted. Oh, shit, I gotta go get Ramon. He jumped in his car, and the car started without a problem. He geared and circled right because Romero had parked his truck behind his car to block him off. He started to pull away from Snake Town on Camino de Lagrimas going west to the old barn when a couple of large dried- up tumbleweed came rolling his way. The sun devils seemed determined to stop and hold him accountable for the brutal death that had occurred in Snake Town. Mike drove around them. He hated tumbleweed. They were a nuisance, especially if you ran them over and portions got stuck under the car; a real mess. Ramon loved to set them on fire. He would bunch several together and light them up, and as they burned, he laughed and jumped around like a kid pissing on his grandma's pumpkin patch. Ramon, he thought. Hope he's OK; he's gotta be OK.

Mike drove as fast as he could to the barn. He knew Ramon needed to get to the hospital and promptly. As he approached the barn, he thought, What if there was another killer waiting for me in the barn, torturing Ramon? He didn't see any cars or trucks outside the barn, and he sighed with relief. He flew up the ladder to the loft, calling Ramon as not to startle him, but Ramon was nowhere to be seen. Mike walked over to the edge of the double doors and looked down to the ground, thinking that Romero might have chucked Ramon off the loft to the ground like a sack of potatoes. But Mike didn't see any crumpled body on the dirt below, so he went back to the last place he had seen Ramon alive, and it was a bloody mess. The straw was soaked with blood and other elements he couldn't describe. He followed the trail of blood down the loft ladder and outside the barn to the road, and there the drops of blood could no longer be seen. Ramon had disappeared, and Mike had no idea how he did it or where he could be. Then a thought—and along with it, panic—flashed through his mind, like falling off a tree and breaking a leg. What if another killer had stumbled on Ramon, crawling and bleeding along the Old Albuquerque Road, and had taken him to Mike's house to wait for Mike to show? His parents might be in danger, he imagined, and made a run to his car. He calmed down once he reached the car and presumed that the cowboy Juan Jose put down was a lone wolf. The people from Denver, and he believed it was the Denver crowd, would not send two or more men this far south for a package of chiva that small and so close to the Juarez rivals. But he decided to go straight home, just in case. He could call the hospital and pray that some good Samaritan had picked Ramon up and taken him in to be treated.

CHAPTER THIRTY-FIVE

Mike sulked around the house for over a week after the skirmish at Snake Town. He held Lola for hours and stayed in his room thinking. He was struggling to decide if what he witnessed at Snake Town was real or a bad dream that wouldn't go away. The blood drenching the corpse stayed with him and intruded in every dream he was having, upsetting his sleep and giving him the shivers. He had gone searching for Ramon after the madness at Snake Town. He was not in the barn, and there were signs he left the barn, but if he left alone, only Ramon knew the answer to that. He called the hospital and Ramon's mother, Estela, but Ramon was nowhere to be found. Mike didn't feel bad about Ramon; he did a little, but at least he tried, and the nightmares, he strongly believed, had less to do with Ramon and more with the killing he witnessed than anything else. Three days after Ramon disappeared, his mother, Estela, called Mike and in a sad and painful voice told Mike that Ramon was housed in a psychiatric hospital in Albuquerque, driven there by a stranger in a green Ford pickup with tinted windows. His left foot above the ankle had been amputated. Estela didn't know the reason because she had been in a state of shock when the doctor attempted to explain the reason for her son's misfortune. She doubted what the doctor said; what was not said concerned her more.

Her son, Estela clarified to Mike, was in a delicate condition, and as his mother, she was aware of that condition; she had been dealing with it since Ramon was born. She needed no doctor to tell her about her son's precarious circumstance. She comprehended the cutting off of his foot was not going to improve his overall health, but she was also aware of the implications of leaving it to rot. Mike got all this from Estela, who was calling collect from Albuquerque to tell him about Ramon so that he wouldn't worry. She also said Ramon talked to her at first and told her about the stranger in a green Ford pickup with tinted windows who gave him a ride to Albuquerque on the old road. The stranger also put on some rags to stop the bleeding on his foot. He dropped him off at the hospital and took off so as not to pay the bill. After that, she stressed, Ramon didn't say a word to anybody. He became a self-mute; he refused to talk, and no one could make him, not even her, his own mother. Mike asked her several times if there was anything he could do to help out, but she seemed not to listen, as she complained about moving to Albuquerque to be close to Ramon. It wasn't the move itself, she emphasized, it was the inconvenience of leaving her home to find a new one in a strange city she never liked. But for Ramon, she conceded, she would sacrifice all that was needed in order to be close to him and see to all his needs. She said good-bye and hung up the phone before Mike could ask for her new address and the name of the hospital where Ramon was interned. He told his mother about the call but didn't go into the gory details to spare her the grief. He only told her Ramon was in Albuquerque seeking treatment for an unidentified illness and that Estela was with him.

Mike's mother and father did their best to get him out of his mood but failed. They attributed his temperament to the fact he was leaving his friends behind and moving to Albuquerque, so they left him alone to his packing, which he never seemed to conclude. One morning, his father, reading the local newspaper as they drank their coffee after breakfast, remarked that the burned bones found in the Swamps belonged to a Sammy Quintana, age twenty-six, from Las Flores's Eastside. He was finally identified through dental records, and no motive for the gruesome murder was yet known. The investigation continued, and anyone with any information was encouraged to call the sheriff's department or the Las Flores Police Department. That's a laugh, said Mike's father; those clowns will never find the killer or killers.

Por dios, said Mike's mother, and she crossed herself. Pobre Granny; we should take her some food or something. Sammy Q. was good to her.

Oh, here's another one, his father said to Mike, who was sipping his coffee with a sad look on his face. The scavenged corpse of the man found in Snake Town has been identified as Geraldo Romero, age twenty-five, of Denver, Colorado. All personal belongings were looted from the decaying body, and his truck was also stripped to the ground. No motive or suspects at this reporting, but the investigation continues. And again, call the sheriff's office with any vital information, Francisco said, a little cynical that anyone would call the cops and offer any assistance. A drug deal gone bad, declared his father. What do you think, Mike?

Don't know, said Mike, finished his coffee, placed the cup on the table, and went to his room.

He's upset, Alma, Mike's mother insisted. Sammy Q. was his friend. Maybe not a close friend, but a friend nevertheless.

I know, Alma, but he has been in his room forever. He should be out and about, having fun, seeing his friends, que no?

Well, maybe, but he might be sad at…leaving us, you know. And tears came to her eyes.

Mike was still sullen and—though he refused to admit it—also depressed. And that conversation with his father about Sammy Q. didn't help either. His domain had been violated, and he was helpless when it happened. He took pride in being in control, of keeping the intruders out, and of him running the show. But all that crumbled like stale crackers when he felt the assault of the real world on his head, a violent and desperate world populated by brutal men. He thought he was bad, a badass; busted lips, blackened eyes, and blood running out the nose came with the perks, but what that killer did to Sammy Q. and Ramon and what Juan Jose did to the killer put fear in his heart. Romero bleeding to death with an arrow embedded in his throat and one in his shoulder—and what Romero did to Sammy at the Swamps was something he expected to see in movies or read about in violent novels, not witness in that ruthless fashion. He was sorry he kept the chiva because he could have brought the violence to his parents, and that was what kept him thinking about the dreadful mess and kept him from sleeping at night. How could his parents defend themselves from that kind of vicious violence, from killers who tortured and killed for profit? He wanted to talk to Juan Jose about it, but Juan Jose might deny that he took part in anything like that and advise him to see a shrink instead. He couldn't tell his friends about it either because the big mouths would change what really happened and make a mockery of the whole matter. So he stayed in his room, stayed silent, and prepared to make the move to Albuquerque and hit the books.

The following day Mike was helping his mother, Alma, put the grocery bags in his car. They were in the parking lot of the Safeway on Armijo Avenue in downtown Las Flores. While he was placing the grocery bags in the trunk of his car, his mother was talking to some people in a green Ford truck with tinted windows, parked a few spaces from his car. Mike put all the bags in the trunk, closed it, and returned the empty basket to the front of the store. When he returned to the car, his mother was inside waiting, and the green truck with tinted windows was gone. Mike was positive that was the green truck he had seen at the barn when he found Ramon in the loft in the hands of the killer.

Oh, Miguel, exclaimed his mother, as soon as he started the car, that was Delfina and Juan Jose. She is worried sick because Vivian has left her. She's gone, Miguel; took the bus to California. Left her a note warning her not to try and find her, that she might stay with her tia in Los Angeles, or she might not. Delfina called her tia in Los Angeles, but they haven't seen her yet. That girl is going to send Delfina to an early grave, Miguel. Danny almost did; Vivian will definitely do it. She wanted to know if Vivian told you of her plans, Miguel. If you know where she might be.

Mike wanted to laugh but decided not to; his mother might take it the wrong way. He said instead, Everyone who knew Vivian knew she wanted to go to California. Delfina, Juan Jose, Danny, Ramon, me, everyone. If Delfina is surprised or concerned, it's a little late. She was aware Vivian was unhappy here, and if she wasn't, she should have been.

Hay, Miguel, said Alma, don't be so hard on Delfina. Vivian is her only daughter, and of course she is going to be concerned; as a mother, I would certainly be. Mike had nothing to say to that. His mother would defend Delfina Madrid, no matter what. So he asked her, Does that green truck belong to Juan Jose?

Yes, Juan Jose has owned that truck for years. I asked her if Vivian had taken the Buick, but she said Vivian only took a small suitcase and nothing else.

I see, Mike said, scratching his chin.

You need a new car, mijo, Alma, said smiling. Your father will buy you one, if you ask him; you know he will. I'll convince him if need be.

Thanks, Mom, but no thanks. No need for you to get in debt. I'm the one that should be buying you a new car and other things.

Oh, don't be silly; one day you will. We can wait. No hurry.

Mike was in his room packing after the grocery shopping. He was thinking about the speed with which Juan Jose got to the barn, found Ramon on the old road, and delivered him to the hospital in Albuquerque. He must have driven around Santa Maria, going over the hills, using abandoned mining roads to get to the barn that fast. But he saved Ramon's life, and that was all that mattered now. But why did he stop and then leave the old barn when he saw Mike there? That was something he would never have the answer to. Mike would put an item in his bag and then change his mind and take it out. He was also deciding what to do about Lola. He had planned to leave Lola with Sammy Q. because Sammy knew about tarantulas more than anyone else in his circle of friends. But Sammy was gone forever, and he knew who did him in. He was pleased that the mad dog was put down by Juan Jose; he got what he deserved, Mike believed, after what he did to Ramon and Sammy. Once he got to Albuquerque, he was going to locate the hospital and visit Ramon. Ramon's mother, Estela, seemed to blame him for Ramon's misfortune, not directly but indirectly. He could not fault her for it; he accepted most of the blame. He was thinking about all this and more when his mother handed him a letter.

Another letter, he thought. UNM had been sending him tons of forms to fill out. He was the last one to report to campus. The rest of the group was already over there starting college life and whatnot. He was going to pitch it in a box with the other correspondence from UNM when he noticed the return address was from Long Beach, California.

Mike shut the door to his room and locked it. His heart was racing as he studied the envelope, with excitement or fear, he couldn't tell. It came from Sotol America, in Long Beach. He hesitated before opening it. He didn't know anyone from Long Beach. He felt stressed, more now than before. If it was Hector, making fun of him for trusting him with the chiva, he would flip out at the cruel joke. He had already paid a heavy price and was still paying for Hector to play with his mind further, with a letter he had lost hope of ever getting. He opened the envelope slowly, with his hands shaking and his heart pounding.

Hey, Mike, the letter began. This letter is for your eyes only; burn it after you read it. I have some good news. The transactions went well, and you will understand the delay after you read the letter. Mike relaxed, and even a half smile came to his lips. He continued reading the letter, making sure the door to his bedroom was locked.

I have some instructions you must follow as they are written, he read on. You can make your move to California now, if you still have your mind on going. You will enroll at LACC. I know it's only a junior college, but the out-of-state fees are lower; pay them. You can transfer to USC or UCLA later or any four-year institution that will accept you. I rented a room for you in a house walking distance from the college. The owner is a woman called Elena. She is very nice and will cook for you if you wish. I paid her for six months' rent. After that time, you can stay or find another place. Take your time exploring the city, buy a modest car when you are ready, don't flash any cash around, and take it easy with the ladies. You have a safety deposit box in your name at the California Bank close by; the key is taped to the back of the letter. Open up an account, show your ID, and you can get into the box. I left you some cash—

not much, so use it wisely. Now this is the important part, Mike. The rest of the cash, your part, which is substantial—we hit the market at the right time—is in safe investments. Low yield but safe. The trick here is you cannot touch it until you reach the age of five and twenty, a mature age in my opinion. The paperwork is with the legal firm of Gutierrez, Sanchez, and Sanchez. Before you can claim your moolah, you have to show them proof of a four-year college degree along with transcripts and any other paper showing you are indeed a college graduate; by then you should have a master's degree. And Mike, don't try to bullshit these people; they have the resources to double-check all paperwork you submit to them, so don't mess it up.

Mike was getting all sweaty reading the letter from Hector. He doubled-checked the door again just to make sure there were no interruptions. Mike continued reading the startling letter from a man he believed had screwed him over. We started a company, Sotol America, to front some of the money. It's an import-export company, and for now we import Talavera tile from Mexico. We purchased— well, you did, although I put in some of my own bread—a small warehouse in an industrial area of Long Beach. A man, Nacho, keeps his eye on the place and moves the tile around. A management company runs the operation at 6 percent of anything that comes in, until you take it over and decide to keep it or sell it. It will be under your name when you reach that magic number, if you ever do. I have relocated to Rio, Brazil; thanks to you and Ramon, I plan to live well. You take care of Ramon; I don't know what arrangements you made with your friend. That's your problem. You cannot call me or try to find me. Our business transactions never happened, and no one, and I mean no one, must ever connect us, and you know the reason why. If you screw up and find that Los Angeles is too much for you to handle, you will get shit, and your part will go to my son in Albuquerque. I'm providing you with a great opportunity to do something with your life. Don't throw it away. And in the postscript, he added, Included is Oscar Rubio's phone number; call him when you get homesick. But don't depend on Oscar too much. He loves his girlfriend, Mary Jane, a great deal and acts goofy around her. Included also is the business card of the law firm and the address of the bank. Pat Tupi on the head for me, if he's still alive.

He ended the letter with an H.

Mike was stunned. He couldn't put down the letter. He would sit on the bed, stand up, and pace around his bedroom with the letter in his hand. Is this a sick joke? he asked himself over and over. No, he thought. Hector wouldn't make all this up; why bother? If he hadn't made any money off the chiva, he wouldn't waste his time writing letters to Mike. It was for real, and he smiled—better than he had ever dreamed, he thought, and he felt like dancing a little jig but didn't. The only thing he didn't approve of was the fact he had to wait until he was twenty-five to cash in, but there was absolutely nothing he could do about it, not a thing. But at least he had a place to stay and a little cash to get him through the dry seasons. He put the letter back in the envelope, folded the envelope, and put it in his pocket. Hell, no, he told himself, he was not going to burn the letter. Not right away. Maybe later when he had digested all the information and was satisfied it wasn't a dream or a mix-up or misunderstanding; so, why was he still nervous? And even though he had the key—the letter gave it legitimacy—that didn't make any sense either, but he was flustered.

Mike was repacking, leaving his heavy jacket and sweaters behind now that he was going to live in a less severe climate. Then he suddenly stopped and said, in a whisper, My parents. How was he going to break it to his parents he was going to Los Angeles instead of Albuquerque? How was he going to explain to them he was going to throw away a full scholarship for a fool's errand in a big city he had only visited once or twice in his life? His mother would be devastated and his father silent but resentful with his decision. He sat on the bed thinking. He had been so thrilled with the letter from Hector that his parents hadn't entered the picture until now. Then he came up with the idea of going ahead with the Albuquerque plan. Then once in the Duke City, he would sell his car and take a bus to Los Angeles. He would write them or call from Los Angeles, breaking the news from a distance—a coward's way out for sure, but that was the best he could do. He couldn't handle any more pain or sorrow right now. He promised himself to make it up to them later. He had no idea how, but he was confident he would come up with something. It was sad, and he was selfish, but one day he would make his parents proud and stop kicking himself in the ass. And Ramon—Ramon would have to wait; he would settle with Ramon at a later date. For now, he had to think of his own life, his own future. He had risked so much for this chance, for this dream of leaving Las Flores and tasting a little bit of the world, and he couldn't put it off any longer.

CHAPTER THIRTY-SIX

$\mathfrak{T}$upi was stretched out on the huge couch on top of a soft blanket. He was waiting for the lady of the house, his second nana, Alma, to return and give him some lap time. Her lap was soft but not as cushy as his first nana's, but it was better than her husband's, Francisco. Tupi had adjusted to his new home after the boy Mike had brought him here. He never knew the reason why he was brought to this house, but it was nice and cozy, with plenty of lap time. At the other house, Hector was gone most of the time, and when he was home, he entertained women and ignored him. His old nana, a very kind lady, spent the whole day and night with him. She fed him good food and walked him around the block several times a day, sometimes more. Hector hardly ever walked him, and when he did, he was always in a hurry and didn't wait for him to smell the bushes or take a piss. He had to move to Hector's bed because he didn't want to sleep alone in Nana's large bed and dark room. In Hector's bed, he had to sleep at the foot, and when Hector had a sleepover, he had to sleep on the floor, which was very uncomfortable. Here with Nana Alma, he had his own little bed with blankets and pillows placed next to the side where Nana Alma slept.

Tupi kept his old eyes on the kitchen door, waiting for Nana Alma to walk in. He had ventured outside the house the first few days of his arrival. The yard was large and clean. He was attracted to some chickens in the back of the garage. He was going to say hello and introduce himself when out of nowhere, a huge red rooster came running toward him in attack mode. He scampered back to the house through the little dog door that had been built especially for him. He was very scared and trembling. In his younger days, a rooster would never disrespect him that way, never. But now, when Alma took him for a walk around the neighborhood, even the children upset him. There was a time, he still remembered, when he would run with them, bark, and wag his tail—when he still had a tail to wag. Now they were loud and wanted to touch him, but they weren't very gentle, not gentle at all. But the worst was the other dogs. Some were aggressive and wanted to sniff and bite. They would growl and snap their jaws at him. The mutts and alley dogs, uneducated thugs, sniffed his butthole, showing no respect for his maturity and education. That was really scary, especially when Nana Alma stopped to converse with someone. She got distracted with the conversation and didn't notice that he was under siege. He had to get between her legs, shaking like a little sissy. It was embarrassing, but he had no choice. He was too old to fight off those mean bullies. In his time, sure, he had been game; a little tussle was not a bad idea. Now his teeth were soft, and his bark was a joke. But the worst thing was his speed; his speed was flat, like a desert tortoise, without the shell for protection. He wasn't even going to say anything about cats.

The dining at his new residence was excellent, five-star quality all the way around. Nana Alma shredded his beef, real beef, with mashed beans, and mashed potatoes with a smidgen of delicious gravy were always served on a clean plate. Hector, on the other hand, opened a can of smelly dog food and dumped it on the same disgusting dish. Or he threw in some dry, tasteless chips from a fifty- pound bag he purchased once a month and believed he had done his duty; that was not fun. Here, after dinner, having completed his business, they all retired to the living room, and it was lap time for him, his favorite pastime. Nana Alma would scratch him on the head and behind the ears while she read, while her husband Francisco put on some soothing music. Sometimes he would try out Francisco's lap, but his lap was not as soft as Nana Alma's, and he was a bit grouchy—not as bad as Hector, but a bit. After lots of lap time and snoozing on and off, they would all go to bed, and sometimes he slept at the foot of their bed. He had on occasion even snuggled in between them, but not often, as not to abuse their kindness. And at least here, no brick ever came flying through the window, scaring the poo out of him, sending him running under the bed for cover with Hector screaming like a crazy man.

He was content with his situation. At first he didn't comprehend the move here, but now it didn't matter; he was as happy as a dog had the right to be. He spent most of his day inside the house. He had lost interest in exploring outside, except to go out to perform his business in a special designated area; instead he would be on the couch waiting for Nana Alma. Once he was exploring inside the house, and he entered the boy's room because the door was open. He was sniffing under the bed, an old habit more than curiosity, when he came eye to eye with a huge, black, hairy critter. He raced out of the room, slipping and sliding, as fast as his rheumy legs could carry him. He never again ventured into that room, ever. The boy Mike was nice and patted him on the head once in a while, but he mostly kept to himself with the monster he had in the box. He waited on the couch for Nana Alma to return and give him lap time. He decided to take a nap before lunch. A dog's life was never easy, he thought, as he closed his eyes.

The End

AUTHOR BIOGRAPHY

Writer and therapist Sal Mirabal has dedicated his life help at-risk youth. He studied at California State University, the University of Southern California, and Loyola Marymount. He received his master's degrees in education, counseling, and educational psychology.

Mirabal has lived in Los Angeles most of his adult life. He is the author of Sotol, The Dance of the Scorpions, El Cerro de la Mancha Azul, in Spanish, and Tomorrow's Goodbye, all fictional novels. He incorporates Chicano culture into his novels. His fiction earned an honorable mention at the Writer's Day Festival at Mt. San Antonio College.